Riceyman Steps

Riceyman Steps

BY

ARNOLD BENNETT

CASSELL · LONDON

CASSELL & COMPANY LTD
35 Red Lion Square, London WC1
Melbourne, Sydney, Toronto
Johannesburg, Auckland

© Dorothy Cheston Bennett 1968
Eleventh edition, second impression October 1968

SBN 304 93152 7

Printed in Great Britain by
Lowe & Brydone (Printers) Ltd., London, N.W.10
568

CONTENTS

Part I

Part II

Part III

Contents

CHAPTER I

Riceyman Steps

ON an autumn afternoon of 1919 a hatless man with a
slight limp might have been observed ascending the
gentle, broad acclivity of Riceyman Steps, which lead from
King's Cross Road up to Riceyman Square, in the great
metropolitan industrial district of Clerkenwell. He was rather
less than stout and rather more than slim. His thin hair had
begun to turn from black to grey, but his complexion was still
fairly good, and the rich, very red lips, under a small greyish
moustache and over a short, pointed beard, were quite remarkable in their suggestion of vitality. The brown eyes seemed a
little small; they peered at near objects. As to his age, an
experienced and cautious observer of mankind, without previous knowledge of this man, would have said no more than
that he must be past forty. The man himself was certainly
entitled to say that he was in the prime of life. He wore a
neat dark-grey suit, which must have been carefully folded at
nights, a low, white, starched collar, and a "made" black tie
that completely hid the shirt-front; the shirt-cuffs could not
be seen. He was shod in old, black leather slippers, well
polished. He gave an appearance of quiet, intelligent, refined
and kindly prosperity; and in his little eyes shone the varying
lights of emotional sensitiveness.

Riceyman Steps, twenty in number, are divided by a
half-landing into two series of ten. The man stopped
on the half-landing and swung round with a casual air of
purposelessness which, however, concealed, imperfectly, a
definite design. The suspicious and cynical, slyly watching
his movements, would have thought: "What's that fellow
after?"

A man interested in a strange woman acquires one equine

attribute—he can look in two directions at once. This man could, and did, look in two directions at once.

Below him and straight in front he saw a cobbled section of King's Cross Road—a hell of noise and dust and dirt, with the County of London tram-cars, and motor-lorries and heavy horse-drawn vans sweeping north and south in a vast clangour of iron thudding and grating on iron and granite, beneath the bedroom windows of a defenceless populace. On the far side of the road were, conspicuous to the right, the huge, red Nell Gwynn Tavern, set on the site of Nell's still huger palace, and displaying printed exhortations to buy fruity Portuguese wines and to attend meetings of workers; and, conspicuous to the left, red Rowton House, surpassing in immensity even Nell's vanished palace, divided into hundreds and hundreds of clean cubicles for the accommodation of the defeated and the futile at a shilling a night, and displaying on its iron façade a news-paper promise to divulge the names of the winners of horse-races. Nearer to the man who could look two ways lay the tiny open space (not open to vehicular traffic) which was officially included in the title "Riceyman Steps." At the south corner of this was a second-hand bookseller's shop, and at the north an abandoned and decaying mission-hall; both these abutted on King's Cross Road. Then, on either hand, farther from the thoroughfare and nearer the steps, came a few private houses with carefully curtained windows, and one other shop—a confectioner's. And next, also on either hand, two business "yards" full of lorries, goods, gear, and the hum of hidden machinery. And the earth itself faintly throbbed; for, to the vibrations of traffic and manufacture, the Under-ground Railway, running beneath Riceyman Steps, added the muffled uproar of its subterranean electric trains.

While gazing full at the spectacle of King's Cross Road the man on the steps peered downwards on his right at the con-fectioner's shop, which held the woman who had begun to inflame him. He failed to descry her, but his thoughts pleasantly held her image, and she held his thoughts. He dreamed that one day he would share with her sympathetic soul his own vision of this wonderful Clerkenwell in which he lived and she now lived. He would explain to her eager ear that once Clerkenwell was a murmuring green land of medicinal springs, wells, streams with mills on their banks, nunneries, aristocrats, and holy clerks who presented mystery-plays. Yes, he would tell her about the drama of Adam and Eve being performed in the costume of Adam and Eve to a simple and unshocked people. (Why not? She was a widow and no longer young.) And he would point out to her how the brown backs of the houses which fronted on King's Cross Road resembled the buttressed walls of a mighty fortress, and how the grim, ochreish, unwindowed backs of the houses of Riceyman Square (behind him) looked just like lofty, medieval keeps. And he would relate to her the story of the palace of Nell Gwynn, contemporary of Louise de la Vallière, and dividing with Louise the honour of being the first and most ingenuous of modern vampires. Never before had he had the idea of unfolding his mind on these enthralling subjects to a woman.

Rain began to fall. It fell on the bargain-books exposed in a stand outside the bookseller's shop. The man did not move. Then a swift gentlemanly person stepped suddenly out of King's Cross Road into the approach to the steps, and after a moment's hesitation entered the shop. The man on the steps quietly limped down and followed the potential customer into the shop, which was his own.

CHAPTER II

The Customer

THE shop had one window in King's Cross Road, but the entrance, with another window, was in Riceyman Steps. The King's Cross Road window held only cheap editions, in their paper jackets, of popular modern novels, such as those of Ethel M. Dell, Charles Garvice, Zane Grey, Florence Barclay, Nat Gould, and Gene Stratton Porter. The side window was set out with old books, first editions, illustrated editions, and complete library editions in calf or morocco of renowned and serious writers, whose works, indispensable to the collections of self-respecting book-gentlemen (as distinguished from bookmen), have passed through decades of criticism into the impregnable paradise of eternal esteem. The side window was bound to attract the attention of collectors and bibliomaniacs. It seemed strangely, even fatally, out of place in that dingy and sordid neighbourhood where existence was a dangerous and difficult adventure in almost frantic quest of food, drink and shelter, where the familiar and beloved landmarks were public-houses, and where the immense majority of the population read nothing but sporting prognostications and results, and, on Sunday mornings, accounts of bloody crimes and juicy sexual irregularities.

Nevertheless, the shop was, in fact, well placed in Riceyman Steps. It had a picturesque air, and Riceyman Steps also had a picturesque air, with all its outworn shabbiness, grime and decay. The steps leading up to Riceyman Square, the glimpse of the Square at the top, with its church bearing a massive cross on the west front, the curious perpendicular effects of the tall, blind, ochreish houses—all these touched the imagination of every man who had in his composition any unusually strong admixture of the universal human passion—love of the past.

The shop reinforced the appeal of its environment. The shop was in its right appropriate place. To the secret race of collectors always ravenously desiring to get something for much less than its real value, the window in Riceyman Steps was irresistible. And all manner of people, including book-collectors, passed along King's Cross Road in the course of a day. And all the collectors upon catching sight of the shop exclaimed in their hearts: "What a queer spot for a bookshop! Bargains! . . ." Moreover, the business was of old date, and therefore had firmly established connexions quite extra-local. Scores of knowing persons knew about it, and were proud of their knowledge. "What!" they would say with affected surprise to acquaintances of their own tastes. "You don't know Riceyman Steps, King's Cross Road? Best hunting-ground in London!" The name "Riceyman" on a sign-board, whose paint had been flaking off for twenty years, also enhanced the prestige of the shop, for it proved ancient local associations. Riceyman must be of the true ancient blood of Clerkenwell.

The customer, with his hands behind him and his legs somewhat apart, was staring at a case of calf-bindings. A short, carefully dressed man, dapper and alert, he had the air neither of a bookman nor of a member of the upper-middle class.

"Sorry to keep you waiting. I just had to slip out, and I've nobody else here," said the bookseller quietly and courteously, but with no trace of obsequiousness.

"Not at all!" replied the customer. "I was very interested in the books here."

The bookseller, like many shopkeepers a fairly sure judge of people, perceived instantly that the customer must have acquired deportment from somewhere after adolescence, together with the art of dressing. There was abruptness in his voice, and the fact was that he had learnt manners above his original station in a strange place—Palestine, under Allenby.

"I suppose you haven't got such a thing as a Shakspere in stock; I mean a pretty good one?"

"What sort of a Shakspere? I've got a number of Shak-speres."

"Well, I don't quite know. . . . I've been thinking for a long time I ought to have a Shakspere."

"Illustrated?" asked the bookseller, who had now accurately summed up his client as one who might know something of the world, but who was a simpleton in regard to books.

"I really haven't thought." The customer gave a slight good-humoured snigger. "I suppose it would be nice to have pictures to look at."

"I have a good clean Boydell, and a Dalziel. But perhaps they'd be rather big."

"Um!"

"You can't hold them, except on a desk or on your knee."

"Ah! That wouldn't do! Oh, not at all!" The cus-tomer, who was nonplussed by the names mentioned, snatched at the opportunity given to decline them.

"I've got a nice little edition in eight volumes, very handy, with outline drawings by Flaxman, and nicely printed. You don't often see it. Not like any other Shakspere I know of. Quite cheap too."

"Um!"

"I'll see if I can put my hand on it."

The shop was full of bays formed by bookshelves protruding at right-angles from the walls. The first bay was well lighted and tidy; but the others, as they receded into the gloomy backward of the shop, were darker and darker and untidier and untidier. The effect was of mysterious and vast popula-tions of books imprisoned for ever in everlasting shade, chained, deprived of air and sun and movement, hopeless, resigned, martyrized. The bookseller stepped over piles of cast books into the farthest bay, which was carpeted a foot thick with a disorder of volumes, and lighted a candle.

"You don't use the electric light in that corner," said the client, briskly following. He pointed to a dust-covered lamp in the grimy ceiling.

"Fuse gone. They do go," the bookseller answered blandly; and the blandness was not in the least impaired by his private thought that the customer's remark came near to impudence. Searching, he went on: "We're not quite straight here yet. The truth is, we haven't been straight since 1914."

"Dear me! Five years!"

Another piece of good-humoured cheek.

"I suppose you couldn't step in to-morrow?" the bookseller suggested, after considerable groping and spilling of tallow.

"Afraid not," said the customer with polite reluctance. "Very busy . . . I was just passing, and it struck me."

"The Globe edition is very good, you know . . . Standard text. Macmillans. Nothing better *of the sort*. I could sell you that for three-and-six."

"Sounds promising," said the customer brightly.

The bookseller blew out the candle and dusted one hand with the other.

"Of course it's not illustrated."

"Oh, well, after all, a Shakspere's for *reading*, isn't it?" said the customer, for whom Shakspere was a volume, not a man.

While the bookseller was wrapping up the green Globe Shakspere in a creased bit of brown paper with an addressed label on it—he put the label inside—the customer cleared his throat and said with a nervous laugh:

"I think you employ here a young charwoman, don't you?"

The bookseller looked up in mild surprise, peering. He was startled and alarmed, but his feelings seldom appeared on his face.

"I do." He thought: "What is this inquisitive fellow getting at? It's not what I call manners, anyhow."

"Her name's Elsie, I think. I don't know her surname."

The bookseller went on with his packing and said naught.

"As I'm here I thought I might as well ask you," the customer continued with a fresh nervous laugh. "I ought to explain that my name's Raste, Dr. Raste, of Myddelton Square. Dare say you've heard of me. From *your* name your family belongs to the district?"

"Yes," agreed the bookseller. "I do."

He was very proud of the name Riceyman, and he did not explain that it was the name only of his deceased uncle, and that his own name was Earlforward.

"I've got a lad in my service," the doctor continued. "Shell-shock case. He's improving, but I find he's running after this girl Elsie. Quite O.K., of course. Most respectable. Only it's putting him off his work, and I just thought as I happened to be in here you wouldn't mind me asking you about her. Is she a good girl? I'd like him to marry—if it's the right sort. Might do him a lot of good."

"She's right enough," answered the bookseller calmly and indifferently. "I've nothing against her."

"Had her long?"

"Oh, some time."

The bookseller said no more. Beneath his impassive and courteous exterior he hid a sudden spasm of profound agitation. The next minute Dr. Raste departed, but immediately returned.

"Afraid your books outside are getting a bit wet," he cried from the doorway.

"Thank you. Thank you," said the bookseller mildly and unperturbed, thinking: "He must be a managing and interfering kind of man. Can't I run my own business?"

Some booksellers kept waterproof covers for their outside display, but this one did not. He had found in practice that a few drops of rain did no harm to low-priced volumes.

CHAPTER III

The Bookseller at Home

AT the back of the rather spacious and sombre shop (which by reason of the bays of bookshelves seemed larger than it really was) came a small room, with a doorway, but no door, into the shop. This was the proprietor's den. Seated at his desk therein he could see through a sort of irregular lane of books to the bright oblong of the main entrance, which was seldom closed. There were more books to the cubic foot in the private room even than in the shop. They rose in tiers to the ceiling and they lay in mounds on the floor; they also covered most of the flat desk and all the window-sill; some were perched on the silent grandfather's clock, the sole piece of furniture except the desk, a safe, and two chairs, and a step-ladder for reaching the higher shelves.

The bookseller retired to this room, as to a retreat, upon the departure of Dr. Raste, and looked about, fingering one thing or another in a mild, amicable manner, and disclosing not the least annoyance, ill-humour, worry, or pressure of work. He sat down to a cumbrous old typewriter on the desk, and after looking at some correspondence, inserted a sheet of cheap letter-paper into the machine. The printed letter-head on the sheet was "T. T. Riceyman," but in fulfilment of the new law the name of the actual proprietor, "Henry Earl-forward," had been added (in violet, with an indiarubber stamp, and crookedly).

Mr. Earlforward began to tap, placidly and very deliberately, as one who had the whole of eternity before him for the accomplishment of his task. A little bell rang; the machine dated from the age when typewriters had this contrivance for informing the operator that the end of a line would be reached in two or three more taps. Then a great clatter occurred at

the window, and the room became dark. The blue-black
blind had slipped down, discharging thick clouds of dust.

"Dear, dear!" murmured Mr. Earlforward, groping towards the window. He failed to raise the blind again; the
cord was broken. As he coughed gently in the dust, he could
not recall that the blind had been once drawn since the end of
the war.

"I must have that seen to," he murmured, and turned on
the electric light over the desk.

The porcelain shade of the lamp wore a heavy layer of dust,
which, however, had not arrived from the direction of the
blind, being the product of slow, secular accumulation. Mr.
Earlforward regretted to be compelled to use electric current
—and rightly, considering the price!—but the occasion was
quite special. He could not see to tap by a candle. Many a
time on winter evenings he had gently told an unimportant
customer in that room that a fuse had gone—and lighted a
candle.

He was a solitary man, and content in his solitude; at any
rate, he had been content until the sight of the newly-come
lady across the way began to disturb the calm deep of his
mind. He was a man of routine, and happy in routine. Dr.
Raste's remarks about his charwoman were seriously upsetting
him. He foresaw the possibility, if the charwoman should
respond to the alleged passion of her suitor, of a complete
derangement of his existence. But he was not a man to go
out to meet trouble. He had faith in time, which for him
was endless and inexhaustible, and even in this grave matter
of his domesticity he could calmly reflect that if the lady across
the way (whom he had not yet spoken to) should favour him,
he might be in a position to ignore the vagaries of all charwomen. He was, in fact, a very great practical philosopher,
tenacious—it is true—in his ideas, but, nevertheless, profoundly
aware of the wisdom of compromising with destiny.

Twenty-one years earlier he had been a placid and happy
clerk in an insurance office, anticipating an existence devoted
wholly to fire-risks. Destiny had sent him one evening to
his uncle, T. T. Riceyman, in Riceyman Steps, and into the

very room where he was now tapping. Riceyman took to him, seeing in the young man a resemblance to himself. Riceyman began to talk about his well-loved Clerkenwell, and especially about what was for him the marvellous outstanding event in the Clerkenwell history—namely, the construction of the Underground Railway from Clerkenwell to Euston Square. Henry had never forgotten the old man's almost melodramatic recital, so full of astonishing and quaint incidents.

The old man swore that exactly one thousand lawyers had signed a petition in favour of the line, and exactly one thousand butchers had signed another similar petition. All Clerkenwell was mad for the line. But when the construction began all Clerkenwell trembled. The earth opened in the most unexpected and undesirable places. Streets had to be barred to horse traffic; pavements resembled switchbacks. Hundreds of houses had to be propped, and along the line of the tunnel itself scores of houses were suddenly vacated lest they should bury their occupants. The sacred workhouse came near to dissolution, and was only saved by inconceivable timberings. The still more sacred Cobham's Head public-house was first shaken and torn with cracks and then inundated by the bursting of the New River main, and the landlady died of shock. The thousand lawyers and the thousand butchers wished they had never humbly prayed for the accursed line. And all this was as naught compared to the culminating catastrophe. There was a vast excavation at the mouth of the tunnel near Clerkenwell Green. It was supported by enormous brick piers and by scaffoldings erected upon the most prodigious beams that the wood trade could produce. One night—a spring Sunday in 1862, the year of the Second Great Exhibition—the adjacent earth was observed to be gently sinking, and then some cellars filled with foul water. Alarm was raised. Railway officials and metropolitan officers rushed together, and for three days and three nights laboured to avert a supreme calamity. Huge dams were built to strengthen the subterranean masonry; nothing was left undone. Vain effort! On the Wednesday the pavements sank definitely.

The earth quaked. The entire populace fled to survey the scene of horror from safety. The terrific scaffolding and beams were flung like firewood into the air and fell with awful crashes. The populace screamed at the thought of workmen entombed and massacred. A silence! Then the great brick piers, fifty feet in height, moved bodily. The whole bottom of the excavation moved in one mass. A dark and fetid liquid appeared, oozing, rolling, surging, smashing everything in its resistless track, and rushed into the mouth of the new tunnel. The crown of the arch of the mighty Fleet sewer had broken. Men wept at the enormity and completeness of the disaster. . . . But the Underground Railway was begun afresh and finished and grandly inaugurated, and at first the public fought for seats in its trains, and then could not be persuaded to enter its trains because they were uninhabitable, and so on and so on. . . .

Old fat Riceyman told his tale with such force and fire that he had a stroke. In foolishly trying to lift the man Henry had slipped and hurt his knee. The next morning Riceyman was dead. Henry inherited. A strange episode, but not stranger than thousands of episodes in the lives of plain people. Henry knew nothing of bookselling. He learnt. His philosophic placidity helped him. He had assistants, one after another, but liked none of them. When the last one went to the Great War, Henry gave him no successor. He "managed"—and in addition did earnest, sleep-denying work as a limping special constable. And now, in 1919, here he was, an institution.

He heard a footstep, and in the gloom of his shop made out the surprising apparition of his charwoman. And he was afraid, and lost his philosophy. He felt that she had arrived specially—as she would, being a quaint and conscientious young woman—to warn him with proper solemnity that she would soon belong to another. Undoubtedly the breezy and interfering Dr. Raste had come in, not to buy a Shakspere, but to inquire about Elsie. Shakspere was merely the excuse for Elsie. . . . By the way, that mislaid Flaxman illustrated edition ought to be hunted up soon—to-morrow if possible.

CHAPTER IV

Elsie

"NOW, now, Elsie, my girl. What's this? What is it?" Mr. Earlforward spoke benevolently but, for him, rather quickly and abruptly. And Elsie was intimidated. She worked for Mr. Earlforward only in the mornings, and to be in the shop in the darkening afternoon made her feel quite queer and apologetic. It was almost as if she had never been in the shop before and had no right there.

As the two approached each other the habitual heavenly kindness in the girl's gaze seemed to tranquillize Mr. Earlforward, who knew intimately her expression and her disposition. And though he was still disturbed by apprehension he found, as usual, a mysterious comfort in her presence; and this influence of hers exercised itself even upon his fear of losing her for ever. A strange, exciting emotional equilibrium became established in the twilight of the shop.

Elsie was a strongly-built wench, plump, fairly tall, with the striking free, powerful carriage of one bred to various and hard manual labour. Her arms and bust were superb. She had blue-black hair and dark blue eyes, and a pretty curve of the lips. The face was square but soft. From the constant drawing together of the eyebrows into a pucker of the forehead, and the dropping of the corners of the large mouth, it could be deduced that she was, if anything, over-conscientious, with a tendency to worry about the right performance of her duty; but this warping of her features was too slight to be unpleasant; it was, indeed, a reassurance. She was twenty-three years of age; solitude, adversity and deprivation made her look older. For four years she had been a widow, childless, after two nights of marriage and romance with a youth who went to the East in 1915 to die of dysentery. Her clothes were cheap, dirty, slatternly and dilapidated. Over a soiled white apron she wore a terribly coarse apron of sacking. This apron was an offence; it was an outrage. But not to her; she regarded it as part of a uniform, and such an apron was, in fact, part of the regular uniform of thousands of women in Clerkenwell. If Elsie was slatternly, dirty, and without any grace of adornment, the reason was that she had absolutely no inducement or example to be otherwise. It was her natural, respectable state to be so.

"It's for Mrs. Arb, sir," Elsie began.

"Mrs. Arb?" questioned Mr. Earlforward, puzzled for an instant by the unfamiliar name. "Yes, yes, I know. Well? What have *you* got to do with Mrs. Arb?"

"I work for her in my afternoons, sir."

"But I never knew this!"

"I only began to-day, sir. She sent me across, seeing as I'm engaged here, to see if you'd got a good, cheap, second-hand cookery-book."

Mr. Earlforward's demeanour reflected no change in his mood, but Elsie had raised him into heaven. It was not to give him notice that she had come! She would stay with him! She would stay for ever, or until he had no need of her. And she would make a link with Mrs. Arb, the new proprietress of the confectioner's shop across the way. Of course the name of the new proprietress was Arb. He had not thought of her name. He had thought only of herself. Even now he had no notion of her Christian name.

"Oh! So she wants a cookery-book, does she? What sort of a cookery-book?"

"She said she's thinking of going in for sandwiches, sir, and things, she said, and having a sign put up for it. Snacks, like."

The word "snacks" gave Mr. Earlforward an idea. He walked across to what he called the "modern side" of the shop. In the course of the war, when food-rationed stay-at-homes really had to stay at home, and, having nothing else to do while waiting for air-raids, took to literature in desperation, he had done a very large trade in cheap editions of novels, and quite a good trade in cheap cookery-books that professed to teach rationed housewives how to make substance out of shadow. Gently rubbing his little beard, he stood and gazed rather absently at a shelf of small paper-protected volumes, while Elsie waited with submission.

Silence within, but the dulled and still hard rumble of ceaseless motion beyond the book-screened windows! A spell! An enchantment upon these two human beings, both commonplace and both marvellous, bound together and yet incurious each of the other and incurious of the mysteries in which they and all their fellows lived! Mr. Earlforward never asked the meaning of life, for he had a lifelong ruling passion. Elsie never asked the meaning of life, for she was dominated and obsessed by a tremendous instinct to serve. Mr. Earlforward, though a kindly man, had persuaded himself that Elsie would go on charing until she died, without any romantic recompense from fate for her early tragedy, and he was well satisfied that this should be so. Because the result would inconvenience him, he desired that she should not fall in love again and marry; he preferred that she should spend her strength and youth and should grow old for him in sterile celibacy. He had absolutely no eye for the exciting effect of the white and the brown apron-strings crossing and recrossing round her magnificent waist. And Elsie knew only that Mr. Earlforward had material wants, which she satisfied as well as she could. She did not guess, nor come within a hundred miles of guessing, that he was subject to dreams and ideals and longings. That the universe was enigmatic had not even occurred to her, nor to him; they were too busy with their share in working it out.

"Now here's a book that ought to suit Mrs. Arb," said Mr. Earlforward, picking a volume from the shelf and moving towards the entrance, where the clear daylight was. "'Snacks and Titbits.' Let me see. Sandwiches." He turned over leaves. "Sandwiches. There's nearly seven pages about sandwiches."

"How much would it be, sir?"

"One shilling."

"Oh! She said she couldn't pay more than sixpence, sir, she said."

Mr. Earlforward looked up with a fresh interest. He was exhilarated, even inspired, by the conception of a woman who, wishing to brighten her business with a new line of goods, was not prepared to spend more than sixpence on the indispensable basis of the enterprise. The conception powerfully appealed to him, and his regard for Mrs. Arb increased.

"See here, Elsie. Take this over for Mrs. Arb to look at. And tell her, with my compliments, that you can't get cookery-books—not any that are any good—for sixpence in these days."

"Yes, sir."

Elsie put the book under her aprons and hurried off.

"She sends you *her* compliments, and she says she can't pay more than sixpence, sir. I'm that sorry, sir," Elsie announced, returning.

Mr. Earlforward blandly replaced the book on its shelf, and Elsie waited in vain for any comment, then left.

"I say, Elsie," he recalled her. "It's not raining much, but it might soon. As you're here, you'd better help me in with the stand. That'll save me taking the books out before it's moved, and it'll save you trouble in the morning."

"Yes, sir," Elsie eagerly agreed.

One at either end of it, they lugged within the heavy book-stand that stretched along the length of the window on the flagstones outside the shop. The books showed scarcely a trace of the drizzle.

"Thank you, Elsie."

"Don't mention it, sir."

Mr. Earlforward switched on one electric light in the middle of the shop, switched off the light in his den, and lit a candle there. Then he took a thermos flask, a cup, and two slices of bread on a plate from the interior of the grandfather's clock, poured steaming tea into the cup, and enjoyed his evening meal. When the bell of St. Andrew's jangled six, he shut and darkened the shop. The war habit of closing

early suited him very well for several reasons. Then, blowing
out the candle, he began again to burn electricity in the den,
and tapped slowly and moved to and fro with deliberation,
examining book-titles, tapping out lists, tapping out addresses
on envelopes, licking stamps, and performing other pleasant
little tasks of routine. And all the time he dwelt with exquisite pleasure on the bodily appearance and astonishing
moral characteristics of Mrs. Arb. What a woman! He
had been right about that woman from the first glance. She
was a woman in a million.

At a quarter to seven he put his boots on and collected his
letters for the post. But before leaving to go to the post he
suddenly thought of a ten-shilling Treasury note received
from Dr. Raste, and took it from his waistcoat pocket. It
was a beautiful new note, a delicate object, carefully folded
by someone who understood that new notes deserve good
treatment. He put it, with other less brilliant cash, into the
safe. As he departed from the shop for the post office at
Mount Pleasant, he picked out "Snacks and Titbits" from
its shelf again, and slipped it into his side-pocket.

The rain had ceased. He inhaled the fresh, damp air with
an innocent and genuine delight. Mrs. Arb's shop was the
sole building illuminated in Riceyman Steps; it looked warm
and feminine; it attracted. The church rose darkly, a formidable mass, in the opening at the top of the steps. The little
group of dwelling-houses next to his own establishment
showed not a sign of life; they seldom did; he knew nothing
of their tenants, and felt absolutely no curiosity concerning
them. His little yard abutted on the yard of the nearest house,
but the wall between them was seven feet high; no sound
ever came over it.

He turned into the main road. Although he might have
dropped his correspondence into the pillar-box close by, he
preferred to go to the mighty Mount Pleasant organism, with
its terrific night-movement of vans and flung mailbags,
because it seemed surer, safer, for his letters.

Like many people who live alone, he had a habit of talking
to himself in the street. His thoughts would from time to

time suddenly burst almost with violence into a phrase. Then
he would smile to himself. "Me at my age!" . . . "Yes,
and of course there's *that*! . . . "Want some getting used
to!" . . . He would laugh rather sheepishly.

The vanquished were already beginning to creep into the
mazes of Rowton House. They clicked through a turnstile
—that was all he knew about existence in Rowton House,
except that there were plants with large green leaves in the
windows of the common-room. Some of the vanquished
entered with boldness, but the majority walked furtively.
Just opposite Rowton House the wisdom and enterprise of
two railway companies had filled a blank wall with a large
poster exhibiting the question: "Why not take a winter
holiday where sunshine reigns?" etc. Beneath this blank
wall a newsman displayed the posters of the evening papers,
together with stocks of the papers. Mr. Earlforward always
read the placards for news. There was nothing much to-
night. "Death of a well-known statesman." Mr. Earlforward, as an expert in interpretation, was aware that "well-
known" on a newspaper placard meant exactly the opposite
of what it meant in any other place; it meant not well-known.
The placards always divided dead celebrities, genuine and false,
into three categories. If Blank was a supreme personage
the placards said: "Blank dead." Two most impressive
words. If Blank was a real personage, but not quite supreme,
the placards said: "Death of Blank." Three words, not so
impressive. All others, nameless, were in the third category
of "well-knowns." Nevertheless, Mr. Earlforward walked
briskly back as far as the Free Library to glance at a paper—
perhaps not because he was disturbed about the identity of a
well-known statesman, but because he hesitated to carry out
his resolution to enter Mrs. Arb's shop.

CHAPTER V

The Gift

MRS. ARB was listening to a customer and giving change.

"'And when you've got children of your own,' she said, 'and when you've got children of your own,' that was her remark," the customer, an insecurely fat woman was saying.

"Just so," Mrs. Arb agreed, handing the change and pushing a little parcel across the counter. She ignored Mr. Earlforward completely. He stood near the door, while the fat customer repeated once more what some third person had remarked upon a certain occasion. The customer's accent was noticeably vulgar in contrast with Mrs. Arb's. Mrs. Arb was indeed very "well spoken." And she contrasted not merely with the customer but with the shop.

There were dozens of such little shops in and near King's Cross Road. The stock, and also the ornamentation, of the shop came chiefly from the wholesalers of advertised goods made up into universally recognizable packets. Several kinds of tea in large quantities, and picturesque, bright tea-signs all around the shop. Several kinds of chocolate, in several kinds of fancy polished-wood glazed stands. (But the chocolate of one maker was in the stand of another.) All manner of patent foods, liquid and solid, each guaranteed to give strength. Two competitors in margarine. Scores of paper bags of flour. Some loaves; two hams, cut into. A milk-churn in the middle of the shop. Tinned fruits. Tinned fish. Tinned meats. And in the linoleum-lined window the cakes and bon-bons which entitled the shop to style itself "confectioner's." Dirty ceiling; uneven darkwood floor; frowsy, mysterious corners; a shabby counter covered with linoleum in black-and-white check, like the bottom of the

window. One chair; one small, round, iron table. No
cash-desk. No writing apparatus of any sort. A smell of
bread, ham and biscuits. A poor little shop, showing no
individuality, no enterprise, no imagination, no potentiality
of reasonable profits. A shop which saved the shopkeeper
from the trouble of thinking for himself. The inevitable
result of big advertising, and kept up to the average mark
by the constant visitation of hurried commercial travellers
and collectors who had the magic to extract money out of
empty tills.

And Mrs. Arb, thin, bright, cheerful, with scintillating
eyes; in a neat check dress and a fairly clean white apron!
Yes, she was bright, she was cheerful, she had a keen face.
Perhaps that was what had attracted Mr. Earlforward, who
was used to neither cheerfulness nor brightness. Yet he
thought: "It would have been just about the same if she'd
been a gloomy woman." Perhaps he had been attracted
because she had life, energy, downrightness, masterfulness.

"Good evening, Mr. Earlforward. And what can I do
for you?" She greeted him suddenly, vivaciously, as the fat
customer departed.

She knew him, then! She knew his real name. She
knew that his name did not accord with the sign over his shop.
Her welcoming smile inspired him, as alcohol would have
inspired him had he ever tasted it. He was uplifted to a higher
plane of existence. And also, secretly, he was a little bit
flurried; but his demeanour did not betray this. A clock
struck rapidly in some room behind the shop, and at the
sound Mrs. Arb sprang from behind the counter, shut and
locked the shop door, and drew down its blind for a sign to
the world that business was over for the day. She had a fine
movement with her. In getting out of her way Mr. Earlforward strove to conceal his limp as much as possible.

"I thought I'd just look in about that cookery-book you
wanted," said he.

"It's very kind of you I'm sure," said she. "But I really
don't think I shall need it."

"Oh!"

"No! I think I shall get rid of this business. There's no doing anything with it."

"I'm sorry to hear that," said Mr. Earlforward. And he was.

"It isn't as if I didn't enjoy it—at first. Quite a pleasant change for me to take something in hand. My husband died two years ago and left me nicely off, and I've been withering up ever since, till this came along. It's no life, being a widow at my age. But I couldn't stand this either, for long. There's no *bounce* to this business, if you understand what I mean. It's like hitting a cushion."

"You've soon decided."

"I haven't decided. But I'm thinking about it. . . . You see, it's a *queer* neighbourhood."

"Queer?" He was shocked, perhaps a little hurt, but his calm tone disclosed nothing of that. He had a desire to explain to Mrs. Arb at great length that the neighbourhood was one of almost unique interest.

"Well, you know what I mean. You see, I come from Fulham—Chelsea you might call it. I'm not saying that when I lived in this shop before—eighteen years ago, is it?—I'm not saying I thought it was a queer neighbourhood then. I didn't—and I was here for over a year, too. But I do now."

"I must confess it hasn't struck me as *queer*."

"You know this King's Cross Road?" Mrs. Arb proceeded with increased ardour. "You know it? You've walked all along it?"

"Yes."

"So have I. Oh! I've looked about me. Is there a single theatre in it? Is there one music-hall? Is there one dance-hall? Is there one picture theatre? Is there one nice little restaurant? Or a tea-shop where a nice person could go if she'd a mind? . . . And yet it's a very important street; it's full of people all day. And you can walk for miles round here and see *nothing*. And the dirt and untidiness! Well, I thought Fulham was dirty. Now look at this Riceyman Square place, up behind those funny steps! I walked *through* there. And I lay there isn't one house in it—not one—

without a broken window! The fact is, the people here
don't want things nice and *kept*. . . . I'm not meaning you
—certainly not! But people in general. And they don't
want anything fresh, either. They only want all the nasty
old things they've always had, same as pigs. And yet I must
say I admire pigs, in a way. Oh, dear!" She laughed, as
if at herself, a tinkling laugh, and looked down, with her steady
agreeable hand still on the door.

Twice before she had looked down. It was more than
coyness, better than coyness, more genuinely exciting.
When she laughed her face crinkled up very pleasantly.
She had energy. All the time her body made little movements. Her glance varied, scintillating, darkling. Her tone
ceaselessly varied. And she had authority. She was a
masterful woman, but masterful in a broad-minded, genial
manner. She was experienced, and had learnt from experience.
She must be over forty. . . . And still, somehow girlish!
Best of all, she was original; she had a point of view. She
could see. Mr. Earlforward hated Clerkenwell to be damned.
Yet he liked her to damn it. . . . And how natural she was,
dignified, but not ceremonious, willing to be friends at once!
He repeated to himself that from the first sight of her he had
known her to be a highly remarkable creature.

"I brought the book along," he said, prudently avoiding
argument. She took it amiably from him, and out of politeness inspected it again.

"You shall have it for ninepence. And you might be
needing it after all, you know."

With her face still bent towards "Snacks and Titbits" she
raised her eyes to his eyes—it seemed roguishly.

"I might! I might!" She shut the book with a smart
snap. "But I won't go beyond sixpence, thank you all the
same. And not as I don't think it's very kind of you to bring
it over."

What a woman! What a woman! She was rapidly
becoming the most brilliant, attractive, competent, and comfortable woman on earth; and Mr. Earlforward was rapidly
becoming a hero, a knight, a madman capable of sublime

deeds. He felt an heroical impulse such as he had never felt. He fought it, and was beaten.

"See here," he said quietly, and with unconscious grandeur. "We're neighbours. I'll make you a present of the book."

Did she say, as a silly little creature would have said: "Oh, no! I couldn't possibly. I really couldn't?" Not a bit. She said simply:

"It's most kind of you, Mr. Earlforward. It really is. Of course I accept it with pleasure. Thank you."

And she looked down, like a girl who has received a necklace and clasped it on her neck. Yes, she looked down. The moment was marvellous to Mr. Earlforward.

"But I do think you're a little hard on Riceyman Square," he said, as she unlocked the door for his departure.

She replied gaily and firmly: "Not one house without a broken pane!" She insisted and held out her hand.

"Well, we must see one day," said he.

She nodded.

"And if there is," she said, "I shall pay you a shilling for the book. That's fair."

She shook hands. Mr. Earlforward crossed the space between her shop and his with perfect calmness, and as he approached his door he took from his pocket with the mechanical movement of regular habit a shining key.

CHAPTER VI

Mrs. Arb's Case

YOU would have thought, while Mrs. Arb was talking to Mr. Earlforward, that the enigma of the universe could not exist in her presence. Yet as soon as she was alone it was there, pervading the closed little shop. By letting Mr. Earlforward out she had let the enigma in; she had re-locked the door too late. She stood forlorn, apprehensive, and pathetically undecided in the middle of the shop, and gazed round at the miserable contents of the shop with a dismayed disillusion. Brightness had fallen from her. Impossible to see in her now the woman whose abundant attractive vitality had vitalized Mr. Earlforward into a new and exalted frame of mind!

She had married, raising herself somewhat, in her middle twenties, a clerk of works, popular not only with architects, but with contractors. Mr. Arb had been clerk of works to some of the very biggest erections of the century. His vocation carried him here and there—wherever a large building was being put up; it might be a provincial town hall, or a block of offices in London, or a huge hydro on some rural country-side, or an explosives factory in the middle of pasture land. And Mr. Arb's jobs might last any length of time, from six months to three or four years. Consequently he had had no fixed residence. As there were no children his wife would always go about with him, and they would live in furnished rooms. This arrangement was cheaper than keeping a permanent home in London, and much more cheerful and stimulating. For Mr. Arb it had the advantages (with the disadvantages) of living with a wife whose sole genuine interest, hobby, and solicitude was her husband; all Mrs. Arb's other social relations were bound to be transitory and lukewarm.

When Mr. Arb died he left a sum of money surprisingly
large in view of the fact that clerks of works do not receive
high salaries. Architects, hearing of the nice comfortable
fortune, were more surprised than contractors. A clerk of
works has great power. A clerk of works may be human.

Mrs. Arb found herself with an income but no home,
no habit of home life, and no masculine guidance or protection.
She was heart-stricken, and—what was worse—she was
thoroughly disorganized. Her immense vitality had no out-
let. Time helped her, but she lived in suspense, undecided
what to do and not quite confident in her own unaided wisdom. An incredible letter from a solicitor announcing that
she had inherited the confectioner's business and premises
and some money in Riceyman Steps shook and roused her.
These pleasant and promising things had belonged to her
grandmother's much younger half-sister, whom she had
once helped by prolonged personal service in a great emergency.
The two had not met for many years, owing to Mrs. Arb's
nomadic existence; but they had come together at the funeral
of Mr. Arb, and had quarrelled magnificently, because of
Mrs. Arb's expressed opinion that the old lady's clothes
showed insufficient respect for the angelic dead. The next
event was the solicitor's letter; the old lady had made a
death-bed repentance for the funeral costume. Mrs. Arb
abandoned the furnished rooms in Fulham, where she had
been desiccating for two years, and flew to Clerkenwell
in an eager mood of adventure. She did not like Clerkenwell, nor the look of the business, and she was beginning to
be disappointed, but at worst she was far happier and more
alive than she had ever been since Mr. Arb's death.

She had, nevertheless, a cancer—not a physical one: the
secret abiding terror lest despite all her outward assurance
she might be incapable of managing her possessions. The
more she inherited, the more she feared. She had a vision
of the business going wrong, of her investments going wrong,
and of herself in poverty and solitude. This dread was
absurd, but not less real for that. It grew. She tried to
counter it by the practice of severe economy.

The demeanour of Mr. Earlforward, and his gift, had suddenly lightened her horizon. But the moment he departed she began saying to herself that she was utterly silly to indulge in such thoughts as she had been thinking, that men were not "like that," that men knew what they were about and what they wanted—and she looked gloomily in the fancy mirror provided by a firm of cocoa manufacturers and adorned with their name at the top and their address at the bottom.

She put pieces of gauze over the confectionery in the window and over the two bony remnants of ham, placed the chair seat downwards on the counter, and tilted the little table against the counter; then extinguished the oil-lamp, which alone lit the shop, and went into the back room, lighted by another similar oil-lamp. In this room, which was a parlour-kitchen, and whose principal table had just been scrubbed, Elsie, a helot withdrawn from the world and dedicated to secret toil, was untying her sack-apron preparatory to the great freedom of the night.

"Oh, Elsie—you did say your name was Elsie, didn't you?"

"Yes'm."

"I should take it very kindly if you could stay a bit longer this evening."

Elsie was dashed; she paused on the knot of the apron-string.

"It's a quarter of an hour past my time now, 'm," she said apologetically and humbly.

"It is? So it is. Well, not quite."

"I had an engagement, 'm."

"Couldn't you put it off for this once? You see, I'm very anxious to get straight after all this mess I've been in. I'm one that can't stand a mess. I'll give you your supper—I'll give you a slice of ham—and sixpence extra."

"I'm sure it's very kind of you, 'm, but——"

Mrs. Arb coaxed, and she could coax very effectively.

"Well, 'm, I always like to oblige." Elsie yielded, not grudgingly nor with the air of conferring a favour, but rather with a mild and pure kindliness. She added, coaxing in her turn: "But I must just run out a half a minute, if you'll let me."

"Oh, of course. But don't be long, will you? Look, here's your half-day and the extra sixpence. Take it now. And while you're out I'll be cutting the ham for you. It's a pity I've turned out the shop lamp, but I dare say I can see if I leave this door open." She gave the girl some silver.

"I'm sure it's very kind of you 'm."

Mrs. Arb cut an exceedingly thin slice of ham quite happily. She had two reasons for keeping Elsie; she wanted to talk to somebody, and she felt that, whether she talked or not, she could not bear to be alone in the place till bed-time. Her good spirits returned.

CHAPTER VII

Under an Umbrella

THE entrance-gates to the yard of Daphut, the builder and stonemason, which lay between Mrs. Arb's shop and the steps proper, were set back a little from the general frontage of the north side of Riceyman Steps, so that there was a corner at that point sheltered from east and north-east winds. In this corner stood a young man under an old umbrella; his clothes were such as would have entitled him to the newspaper reporter's description, "respectably dressed"— no better. His back was against the blind wall of Mrs. Arb's. It was raining again, with a squally wind, but the wind being in the north-east the young man was only getting spotted with rain. A young woman ran out of Mrs. Arb's and joined him. She placed herself close to him, touching him, breast to breast; it was the natural and rational thing to do, and also she had to receive as much protection as possible from the umbrella. The girl was wearing all Elsie's clothes. Elsie's sack-apron covered her head and shoulders like a bridal veil. But she was not Mrs. Arb's Elsie nor Mr. Earlforward's! She was not the drudge. She had suddenly become a celestial visitant. The attributes of such an unearthly being were in her shining face and in the solace of her little bodily movements; and her extraordinary mean and ugly apparel could not impair them in the least. The man, slowly, hesitatingly, put one arm round her waist—the other was occupied with the umbrella. She yielded her waist to him, and looked up at the man, and he looked down at her. Not a word. Then he said in a deep voice:

"Where's your hat—and things?"

He said this as one who apprehended calamity.

"I haven't finished yet," she answered gently. "I'm that sorry."

"How long shall you be?"

"I don't know, Joe. She's all by herself, and she begged and prayed me to stop on and help her. She's all by herself, and strange to it. And I couldn't find it in my heart to refuse. You have to do what's right, haven't you?"

The man's chin fell in a sort of sulky and despairing gloom; but he said nothing; he was not a facile talker, even on his best days. She took the umbrella from him without altering its position.

"Put both arms round me, and hold me tight," she murmured.

He obeyed, reluctantly, tardily, but in the end fiercely. After a long pause he said:

"And my birthday and all!"

"I know! I know!" she cried. "Oh, Joe! It can't be helped!"

He had many arguments, and good ones, against her decision; but he could not utter them. He never could argue. She just gazed up at him softly. Tears began to run down his cheeks.

"Now, now!" she soothed him. With her free hand she worked up the tail of her apron between them, and, while still fast in his clutch, wiped his eyes delicately. She kissed him, keeping her lips on his. She kissed him until she knew from the feel of his muscles everywhere that the warm soft contact with her had begun to dissolve his resentment. Then she withdrew her lips and kissed him again, differently. They stood motionless in the dark corner under the umbrella, and the rain pattered dully on the umbrella and dropped off the umbrella and round them, and pattered with a brighter sound on the flagstones of Riceyman Steps. A few people passed at intervals up and down the steps. But the clasped pair ignored them; and the wayfarers did not look twice, nor even smile at the lovers, who, in fact, were making love as honest love is made by lovers whose sole drawing-rooms and sofas are the street.

"Look here, Joe," Elsie whispered. "I want you to go home now. But you must call at Smithson's on yer way—they don't close till nine o'clock—and get them braces as I'm giving you for a birthday present. I see 'em still in the window this morning. I should have slipped in and bought 'em then, but I was on an errand for Mr. Earlforward, and, besides, I didn't like to, somehow, without you, and me with my apron on too. But you must buy 'em to-night so as you can wear 'em to-morrow. I want to say to myself to-morrow morning, 'He's wearing them braces.' I've brought you the money." She loosed one of his hands from her waist, got at the silver in her pocket, and inserted it into his breast pocket. "You promise me, Joe? It's a fair and square promise?"

He made no reply.

"You promise me, darling Joe?" she insisted.

He nodded; he could not speak in his desolation and in his servitude to her. She smiled her lovely thanks for his obedience.

"Now let me see ye start off," she cajoled him. "I know ye. I know what *you'll* do if I don't see you start with me own eyes."

"Then it's to-morrow night?" he said gruffly.

She nodded. They kissed again. Elsie pushed him away, and then stood watching until he had vanished round the corner of the disused Mission Hall into King's Cross Road. She stood watching, indeed, for some moments after that. She was crying.

"My word!" said Mrs. Arb vivaciously. "I was beginning to wonder if you meant to come back, after all. You've been that long your tea 'll be cold. Here's the ham, and very nice it is too."

CHAPTER VIII

The Carving-Knife

THE two women were working together in a living-room over the shop. An oil-lamp had been hung on a hook which would have held a curtain loop had there been any curtains. The lamp, tilted slightly forward, had a round sheltered reflector behind it. Thus a portion of the lower part of the room was brilliantly lighted and all the rest of the room in shadow. Elsie was scrubbing the floor in the full glare of the reflector. She scrubbed placidly and honestly, with no eagerness, but with no sign of fatigue. Mrs. Arb sat in the fireplace with her feet upraised out of the damp on the rail of a chair, and cleaned the mantelpiece. She had worked side by side with Elsie through the evening, silent sometimes, vivaciously chatty sometimes—desirous generally of collecting useful pieces of local information. Inevitably a sort of community had established itself between the two women. Mrs. Arb would talk freely and yet give nothing but comment. Elsie talked little and yet gave many interesting facts.

"Let me see," said Mrs. Arb with a casual air. "It's that Mr. Earlforward you say you work for in the mornings, isn't it?"

"But I told you I did when you sent me in about the book, 'm. And I told you before that, too," Elsie answered, surprised at such forgetfulness.

"Oh, of course you did. Well, does he live all alone?"

"Oh, yes, 'm."

"And what sort of a gentleman is he?"

Elsie, instinctively loyal, grew cautious.

"He's a very nice gentleman, 'm."

"Treats you well, does he?"

"Well, of course, 'm, he has his ways. But he's always very nice."

"Nice and polite, eh?"

"Yes, 'm. And I'll say this, too: he never tries to take any liberties. No, that he doesn't!"

"And so he has his ways. Is he eccentric?"

"Oh, *no*, 'm! At least, I don't know what you mean, 'm, I'm sure I don't. He's very particular in some things; but, then, in plenty of things he takes no notice of you, and you can do it or leave it *as* you choose." Elsie suspected and mildly resented a mere inquisitiveness on the part of Mrs. Arb, and added quickly: "I think this floor's about done."

She wrung a cloth out in the pail at her right hand. The clock below struck its quick, wiry, reverberating note. It kept on striking.

"That's never eleven o'clock!" Mrs. Arb exclaimed, completely aware that it was eleven o'clock. "How time flies when you're hard at it, doesn't it?"

Elsie silently disagreed with this proposition. In her experience of toil she had found that time lagged.

"Well, Elsie, I'm sure I'm much obliged to you. I can finish myself. Don't you stay a minute longer."

"No, 'm," said Elsie, who had exchanged three hours' overtime for sixpence and a slice of ham.

At this moment, and before Elsie had raised her damp knees from the damp floor, a very sharp and imperious tapping was heard.

"My gracious! Who's that?"

"It's the shop door," said Elsie.

"I'll go." Mrs. Arb decided the procedure quite cheerfully. She was cheerful because the living-room, with other rooms, was done, and in a condition fit to be seen by possible purchasers of her premises and business; she had no intention to live in the living-room herself. And also she was cheerful because of a wild and silly, and yet not wholly silly, idea that the rapping at the shop door came from Mr. Earlforward, who had made for himself some absurd man-like excuse for calling again that night. She had, even thus early, her notions about Mr. Earlforward. The undying girl in her ran downstairs with a candle and unlocked the shop door. As she opened it a man pushed forward roughly into the shop— not Mr. Earlforward; a young man with a dangerous look in his burning eyes, and gestures indicating dark excitement.

"What do you want?" she demanded, trying to control the situation firmly and not succeeding.

The young man glanced at her. She perceived that he carried a torn umbrella and that his clothes were very wet. She heard the heavy rain outside.

"You can't come in here at this time of night," she added. "The shop's closed."

She gave a sign for him to depart. She actually began to force him out; mere temerity on her part. She thought:

"Why am I doing this? He might attack me."

Instead of departing the young man dropped his umbrella and sprang for the big carving-knife which she had left on the counter after cutting the slice of ham for Elsie. In that instant Mrs. Arb decided absolutely and without any further vacillation that she would sell the place, sell it at once, and for what it would fetch. Already she had been a little alarmed by the sinister aspect of several of her customers. She remembered the great Clerkenwell murder. She saw how foolish she had been ever to come to Clerkenwell at all. The man waved the carving-knife over his head and hers.

"Where's Elsie?" he growled savagely, murderously.

Mrs. Arb began dimly to understand.

"This comes of taking charwomen you don't know," she said pathetically to herself. "And yet I could have sworn by that girl."

Then a strong light shone in the doorway leading to the back-room. Elsie stood there holding the wall-lamp in her hand. As soon as he caught sight of her the man, still brandishing the knife, ran desperately towards her. She hesitated and then retreated a little. The man plunged into the room and banged the door.

After that Mrs. Arb heard not a sound. She was non-plussed, helpless and panic-stricken. Ah! If the late Mr. Arb had been alive, how he would have handled the affair! Not by force, for he had never been physically strong. But by skill, by adroitness, by rapid chicane. Only she could not imagine precisely *what* the late Mr. Arb would have done in his unique and powerful sagacity. She was overwhelmed by a sudden and final sense of the folly, the tragedy, of solitary existence for a woman like her. She had wisdom, energy, initiative, moral strength, but there were things that women could do and things that women could not do; and a woman who was used to a man needed a man for all sorts of purposes, and she resolved passionately that she would not live alone another day longer than she could help.

This resolve, however, did not mitigate her loneliness in the candle-lit shop with the shut door in front of her hiding dreadful matters and the rain pelting on the flagstones of Riceyman Steps. She looked timidly forth; a policeman might by Heaven's mercy be passing. If not, she must run in the wet, as she was, to the police-station. She then noticed a faint light in Mr. Earlforward's shop, and dashed across. Through the window she could see Mr. Earlforward walking in his shop with a candle in his hand. She tattooed wildly on the window. A tramcar thundered down King's Cross Road, tremendously heedless of murders. After a brief, terrible interval the lock of Mr. Earlforward's portal grated, and Mr. Earlforward appeared blandly in the doorway holding the candle.

"Oh, Mr. Earlforward!" she cried, and stepped within, and clutched his sleeve and told him what had occurred. And as she poured out the words, and Mr. Earlforward kept apparently all his self-possession and bland calm, an exquisite and intense feeling of relief filled her whole being.

"I'll come over," said Mr. Earlforward. "Rather wet, isn't it?"

He cut a fine figure in the eyes of Mrs. Arb. He owed his prestige at that moment, however, not to any real ability to decide immediately and courageously upon the right, effective course to follow, but to the simple fact that his reactions were very slow. Mr. Earlforward was always afraid after the event. He limped vigorously into the dangers of Mrs. Arb's dwelling with his placidity undisturbed by the realization of those dangers. And he had no conception of what he should do. Mrs. Arb followed timorously.

The door into Mrs. Arb's back-room was now wide open; the lamp near the carving-knife burnt on the white table there. Also the candle was still burning in the shop, but the umbrella had vanished from the shop floor. The back-room was empty. No symptom of murder, nor even of a struggle! Only the brief, faint rumble of an Underground train could be heard and felt in the silence.

"Perhaps he's chased her upstairs."

"I'll go and see. Anyhow, he's left the knife behind him." Mr. Earlforward picked up the carving-knife, and thereby further impressed Mrs. Arb.

"Take the lamp," said Mrs. Arb.

"Nobody up here!" he called from the first floor. Mrs. Arb ascended. Together they looked into each room.

"She's taken her jacket!" exclaimed Mrs. Arb, noticing the empty peg behind the door when they came down again to the back-room.

"Ah! That's better," Mr. Earlforward commented, expelling breath.

"I've left my candle lighted," he said a moment later. "I'll go and blow it out."

"But——"

"Oh! I'm coming back. I'm coming back."

While he was gone Mrs. Arb had a momentary lapse into terror. Suppose——! She glimpsed again the savage and primeval passion half-disclosed in the gestures and the glance of the young man, hints of forces uncontrollable, terrific and fatal.

"I expect he's that young fellow that's running after her," said Mr. Earlforward when he returned. "Seems he's had shell-shock! So I heard. She'll have to leave him alone—that's clear!" He was glad to think that he had found a new argument to help him to persuade Elsie not to desert him.

"She seemed to be so *respectable*!" observed Mrs. Arb.

"Well, she is!"

"Poor girl!" sighed Mrs. Arb; she felt a genuine, perturbing compassion for Elsie. "Ought I to go and tell the police, Mr. Earlforward?"

"If I were you I shouldn't have the police meddling. It's all right."

"Well, anyhow, I can't pass the night here by myself. No, I can't. And that's flat!" She smiled almost comically.

"You go off to bed," said Mr. Earlforward, with a magnificent wave of the hand. "I'll make myself comfortable in this rocking-chair. I'll stop till daylight."

Mrs. Arb said that she couldn't think of such a thing, and that he was too kind. He mastered her. Then she said she would put a bit of coal on the fire.

"You needn't." He stopped her. "I'll go across and get my overcoat and a quilt, and lock up there. It'll be all right. It'll be all right."

He reappeared with his overcoat on and the quilt a little rain-spotted. Mrs. Arb was wearing a long thick mantle.

"What's this?" he asked. "What's the meaning of this?"

"I couldn't leave you to sit up by yourself. I couldn't, really. I'm going to sit up too."

CHAPTER IX

Sunday Morning

" SHE never came to you this morning?" questioned Mr.
Earlforward with eager and cheerful interest.

"No. Did she to you?"

Mr. Earlforward shook his head, smiling.

"You seem to be quite the philosopher about it," said Mrs.
Arb. "But it must be *most* inconvenient for a man."

"Oh, no! I can always manage, I can."

"Well, it's very wonderful of you—that's all I say."

This was Sunday morning, the third day after the episode
of the carving-knife.

"What's so funny," said Mrs. Arb, "is that she should come
yesterday and Friday, just as if nothing had happened, and yet
she doesn't come to-day! And yet it was settled plainly
enough she *was* to come—early, an hour to you and an hour
to me, wasn't it now? I do think she might have sent round
a message or something—even if she *is* ill."

"Yes, but you see it never strikes them the inconvenience
they're causing. Not that she's a bad girl. She's a very good
girl."

"They always work better for gentlemen," remarked Mrs.
Arb with an air vivacious and enigmatic.

Mr. Earlforward, strolling towards the steps, had chanced
—if in this world there is such a thing as chance—to see Mrs.
Arb, all dressed, presumably, for church—standing in her
shop and regarding the same with the owner's critical, appreci-
ative eye. Mr. Earlforward had a good view of her, as anybody else might have had, because only the blue blind of the
door was down, this being the recognized sufficient sign to
the public of a shut shop. The two small windows had
blinds, but they were seldom drawn, except to protect butter

against sunshine. The pair had exchanged smiles, Mrs. Arb had hospitably unlocked, and Mr. Earlforward had entered. To him she presented a finely satisfactory appearance, dressed in black, with vermilion flowers in her hat, good shoes on her feet, and good uncreased gloves held in her ringed hand. She was slim—Mr. Earlforward thought of her as *petite*— but she was imposing, with all her keen restlessness of slight movements and her changing glance. No matter how her glance changed it was always the glance of authority and of intelligence.

On her part, Mrs. Arb beheld Mr. Earlforward with favour. His pointed short beard, so well trimmed, seemed to give him the status of a pillar of society. She still liked his full red lips and his fresh complexion. And he was exceedingly neat. True, he wore the same black, short-hiding tie as on week-days, and his wristbands were still invisible; his hat and over-coat were not distinguished! But he had on a distinguished new blue suit; she was quite sure that he was inaugurating it that day. His slight limp pleased and touched her. His un-shakable calmness impressed her. Oh! He was a man with reserves, both of character and of goods. Secure in these reserves he could front the universe. He was self-reliant without being self-confident. He was grave, but his little eyes had occasionally a humorous gleam. She had noticed the gleam even when he picked up the carving-knife on Thursday night. His demeanour in that dreadful crisis had been perfect. In brief, Mr. Earlforward, considered as an entity, was nearly faultless.

Mr. Earlforward, on the other hand, was still secretly trembling as he realized more and more clearly the dangers which he had narrowly escaped in the Thursday night affair; and he had not begun to tremble until Friday morning!

"Rather early, isn't it, if you're going to church?" he suggested.

"I always like to be early if it's a strange church, and I've not been in there at all yet."

"St. Andrew's?"

"I don't know what its name is. The one up the steps in the middle of the Square."

"Yes. St. Andrew's, that is."

Without another word they then by a common impulse both moved out of the shop, which Mrs. Arb smartly locked up. In spite of the upset caused by Elsie's defection, and the prospect of future trouble and annoyance in this connexion, they were very happy, and they had quite overlooked the fact that their combined years amounted to ninety, or thereabouts. The sun was feebly shining on the Sabbath scene. The bells of St. Andrew's were jangling.

"I see you have some plant-pots on your top window-sill," observed Mrs. Arb. "Do you ever water them?"

An implied criticism! Mr. Earlforward enjoyed it, for it proved that they were getting intimate, as, indeed, became two people who had slept (well) opposite one another in two chairs through the better part of a coldish night.

"I do not," said Mr. Earlforward, waggishly, stoutly.

The truth was that for years he had seen the plant-pots without noticing them. They were never moved, never touched. The unconquerable force of nature was illustrated in the simple fact that one or two of the plants still sturdily lived, displaying a grimy green.

"I love plants," said Mrs. Arb.

They passed up the steps, Mr. Earlforward a foot or so behind his heroine.

"Now what I don't understand," said she, turning upon him and stopping, "is why the Square should be so much higher than the road. It means that all the carts and things, even the milk-carts have to go all the way round by Gilbert Street to get into the Square from the side. Why couldn't they have had it all on the same level?"

Exquisitely feminine, he thought! "Why couldn't they have had it all on the same level?" Absurd! Delicious! He adored the delicious, girlish absurdity.

"Well," he said. "It's like this. You see, in the old days they used to make tiles in Clerkenwell, and they scooped out the clay for the tiles in large quantities—and this is the result."

With a certain eagerness he amplified the explanation.

"I should never have thought of that," said Mrs. Arb ingenuously but archly. "What sort of church is St. Andrew's?"

"Oh! It was built in the 'thirties and cost, £4,541. Cheap! I doubt if you'd build it to-day for twenty thousand. Supposed to hold eleven hundred people."

"Really! But I mean, is it High or Low, or Broad?"

"I haven't the least idea," answered Mr. Earlforward. "I did go in one day to look at the reredos to oblige a customer, but I've never been to a service." He spoke jauntily.

"D'you know why I go to church—when I do go?" said she. "Because it makes me feel nice. It's a great comfort, especially when it's a foggy day and you can't see very well, and there's not too many people. I don't mean I like sermons. No. But what I say is, if you enjoy part of the service the least you can do is to stay it out. Don't you agree?" She looked up at him, as it were appealing for approval.

Wonderful moments for Mr. Earlforward, and for Mrs. Arb too!

He thought to himself:

"She has a vigorous mind. Not one woman in a hundred would have said that. And so *petite* and smart too. It doesn't really matter about her being only a confectioner."

CHAPTER X

Riceyman Square

ST. ANDREW'S Church, of yellow bricks with freestone
dressings, a blue slate roof, and a red coping, was designed
and erected in the brilliant reign of William IV, whose
Government, under Lord Grey, had a pious habit, since lost
by governments, of building additional churches in populous
parishes at its own expense. Unfortunately its taste in architecture was less laudable than its practical interest in the in-
culcation among the lowly of the Christian doctrine about
the wisdom and propriety of turning the other cheek. St.
Andrew's, of a considerably mixed Gothic character, had
architecturally nothing whatever to recommend it. Its
general proportions, its arched windows, its mullions, its
finials, its crosses, its spire, and its buttresses, were all and in
every detail utterly silly and offensive. The eye could not
rest anywhere upon its surface without pain. And time,
which is supposed to soften and dignify all things, had been
content in malice to cover St. Andrew's with filth and ridicule.
Out of the heights of the ignoble temple came persistent,
monotonous, loud sounds, fantastic and nerve-racking, to
match its architecture. The churchyard was a garden flanked
by iron rails and by plane trees, upon which brutal, terrifying
surgical operations had been performed. In the garden
were to be seen the withering and melancholy but still
beautiful blossoms of asters and tulips, a quantity of cultivated
vegetables, dishevelled grass, some heaps of rubble, and
patches of unproductive brown earth. Nobody might walk
in the garden, whose gates were most securely padlocked.

Riceyman Square had been built round St. Andrew's in
the hungry 'forties. It had been built all at once, according
to plan; it had form. The three-story houses (with areas and

basements) were all alike, and were grouped together in sections by triangular pediments with ornamentations thereon in a degenerate Regency style. These pediments and the window-facings and the whole walls up to the beginning of the first floor were stuccoed and painted. In many places the paint was peeling off and the stucco crumbling. The fronts of the doorsteps were green with vegetable growth. Some of the front-doors and window-frames could not have been painted for fifteen or twenty years. All the horizontal lines in the architecture had become curved. Long cracks showed in the brickwork where two dwellings met. The fanlights and some of the iron work feebly recalled the traditions of the eighteenth century. The areas, except one or two, were obscene. The Square had once been genteel; it ought now to have been picturesque, but was not. It was merely decrepit, foul and slatternly. It had no attractiveness of any sort. Evolution had swirled round it, missed it, and left it. Neither electricity nor telephones had ever invaded it, and scores of windows still had venetian blinds. All men except its inhabitants and the tax-collector, the rate-collector, and the school attendance officer had forgotten Riceyman Square.

It lay now frowsily supine in a needed Sunday indolence after the week's hard labour. All the upper windows were shut and curtained, and most of the ground-floor windows. The rare glimpses of forlorn interiors were desolating. Not a child played in the roadways. But here and there a housewife had hung her doormats and canaries on the railings to take the holy Sabbath air; and newspapers, fresh as newly gathered fruit, waited folded on doorsteps for students of crime and passion to awake from their beds in darkened and stifling rooms. Also little milk-cans with tarnished brass handles had been suspended in clusters on the railings. Cats only, in their elegance and their detached disdain, rose superior to the terrific environment. The determined church bells ceaselessly jangled.

"The church is rather nice," said Mrs. Arb. "But what did I tell you about the Square?"

"Wait a moment! Wait a moment," replied Mr. Earlforward. "Let us walk round, shall we?"

They began to walk round. Presently Mr. Earlforward stopped in front of a house which had just been painted, to remind the spectator of the original gentility of the hungry 'forties.

"No broken panes there, I think," he remarked triumphantly.

Mrs. Arb's glance searched the façade for even a cracked pane, and found none. She owed him a shilling.

"Well," she said, somewhat dashed, but still briskly. "Of course there was bound to be one house that was all right. Don't they say it's the exception proves the rule?"

He understood that he would not receive his shilling, and he admired her the more for her genial feminine unscrupulousness.

At the corner of Gilbert Street Mrs. Arb suddenly burst out laughing.

"I hadn't noticed we had any Savoys up here!" she said.

Painted over the door of the corner house were the words "Percy's Hotel."

The house differed in no other detail from the rest of the Square.

"I wonder if they have any self-contained suites?"

Mr. Earlforward was about to furnish the history of this singular historic survival, when they both, almost simultaneously, through a large interstice of the curtains, noticed Elsie sitting and rocking gently by the ground-floor window of a house near to Percy's Hotel. Her pale face was half turned within the room, and its details obscure in the twilight of the curtained interior; but there could be no mistake about her identity.

"Is it here she lives?" said Mrs. Arb.

"I suppose so. I know she lives somewhere in the Square, but I never knew the number."

The front-door of the house opened and Dr. Raste emerged, fresh, dapper, prim, correct, busy, speeding without haste, the incarnation of the professional. You felt that he would

have emerged from Buckingham Palace in just the same
manner. To mark the Sabbath, which his ceaseless duties
forbade him to honour otherwise, he wore a silk hat. This
hat he raised on perceiving Mr. Earlforward and a lady; and
he raised also, though scarcely perceptibly, his eyebrows.

"You been to see my charwoman, doctor?" Mr. Earlforward urbanely stopped him.

Dr. Raste hesitated a moment.

"Your charwoman? Ah, yes. I did happen to see her.
Yes."

"Ah! Then she *is* unwell. Nothing serious, I hope?"

"No, no!" said the doctor, his voice rather higher than
usual. "She'll be all right to-morrow. A mere nothing.
An excellent constitution, I should imagine."

A strictly formal reply, if very courteous. Probably nobody in Clerkenwell, except perhaps his man Joe, knew how
Dr. Raste talked and looked when he was not talking and
looking professionally. Dr. Raste would sometimes say with
a dry, brief laugh, "we medicoes," thereby proclaiming a
caste, an order, a clan, separated by awful, invisible, impregnable barriers from the common remainder of mankind;
and he never stepped beyond the barriers into humanity. In
his case the secret life of the brain was indeed secret, and the
mask of the face, tongue and demeanour made an everlasting
privacy. He cleared his throat.

"Yes, yes. . . . By the way, I've been reading that Shakspere. Very fine, very fine. I shall read it all one of these
days. Good morning." He raised his hat again and
departed.

"I shall go in and see her, poor thing!" said Mrs. Arb with
compassion.

"Shall you?"

"Well, I'm here. I think it would be nice if I did, don't
you?"

"Oh, yes," Mr. Earlforward admiringly agreed.

CHAPTER XI

Elsie's Home

THE house which Mrs. Arb decided to enter had a full, but not an extraordinary, share of experience of human life. There were three floors of it. On the ground floor lived a meat-salesman, his wife and three children, the eldest of whom was five years of age. Three rooms and some minute appurtenances on this floor. The meat-salesman shouted and bawled cheap bits of meat in an open-fronted shop in Exmouth Street during a sixty-hour week which ended at midnight on Saturday. He possessed enormous vocal power. All the children out of naughtiness had rickets. On the first floor lived a french-polisher, his wife and two children, the eldest of whom was three years of age. One child less than the ground-floor family, but the first floor was about to get level in numbers. Three rooms and some minute appurtenances on this floor. The french-polisher worked only forty-four hours a week. His fingers wore always the colour of rosewood, and he emitted an odour which often competed not unsuccessfully with the characteristic house odour of stale soapsuds. Out of ill-will for mankind he had an everlasting cough. On the second floor lived a middle-aged dressmaker, alone. Three rooms and some minute appurtenances on this floor. Nobody but an occasional customer was ever allowed access to the second floor.

Elsie was a friend of the french-polisher's wife, and she slept in the infinitesimal back-room of the first floor with the elder child of the family. She paid three shillings a week for this accommodation, and also helped with the charing and the laundry work of the floor—in her spare time.

Except Elsie, the adult inhabitants of the house were always unhappy save when drinking alcohol or making love. Although they had studied Holy Scripture in youth, and there were at least three Bibles in the house, they had failed to cultivate the virtue of Christian resignation. They permitted trifles to annoy them. On the previous day the wife of the meat-salesman had been upset because her "copper" leaked, and because she could never for a moment be free of her own children, and because it was rather difficult to turn her perambulator through the kitchen doorway into an entrance-hall three feet wide, and because she had to take all three children with her to market, and because the eldest child, cleanly clad, had fallen into a puddle and done as much damage to her clothes as would take a whole day to put right, and because another child, teething, would persistently cry, and because the landlord of the house was too poor to do necessary repairs, and because she could not buy a shilling's worth of goods with sixpence, and because her payments to the Provident Club were in arrear, and because the sunshine made her hat look shabby, and for many other equally inadequate reasons.

As for the french-polisher's wife, she moped and grew neurotic because only three years ago she had been a pretty girl earning an independent income, and because she was now about to bear another pledge of the french-polisher's affection, and because she felt sick and frequently was sick, and because she had no money for approaching needs, and because she hated cooking and washing, and because her husband spent his evenings and the purchase-money of his children's and his wife's food at a political club whose aim was to overthrow the structure of society, and because she hated her husband's cough and his affection, and because she could see no end to her misery, and because she had prophetic visions of herself as a hag with five hundred insatiable children everlastingly in tears for something impossible to obtain for them.

The spinster on the second floor was profoundly and bitterly dissatisfied for the mere reason that she was a spinster; whereas the other two women would have sold their souls to be spinsters.

The centre of irritation in the house was the entrance-hall, or lobby, which the first floor and ground floor had to keep clean in alternate weekly spells. On the previous day one of the first-floor children had dragged treacly fingers along the dark yellowish-brown wall. Further, the first-floor perambulator had been brought in with muddy wheels, and the marks had dried on the linoleum, which was already a palimpsest of various unclean deposits. This perambulator was the origin of most of the lobby trouble. The ground floor resented its presence there, and the second floor purposely knocked it about at every passage through the lobby; but the mistress of the first floor obstinately objected to carrying it up and down stairs once or twice a day.

A great three-corner quarrel had arisen on the Saturday morning around the first-floor perambulator and the entrance-hall, and when the french-polisher arrived home for his dinner shortly after one o'clock he had found no dinner, but a wife-helpmeet-cook-housekeeper-maidservant in hysterics. Very foolishly he had immediately gone forth again with all his wages. At eleven-thirty p.m. he had returned intoxicated and acutely dyspeptic. At a quarter to twelve he had tried to fight Elsie. At twelve-thirty the meat-salesman had come home to sleep, and had had to listen to a loud sermon on the manners of the first floor and his own wife's manners delivered from the top of the second-floor stairs. Subsequently he had had to listen to moans from the mistress of the first floor and the eternal coughing of the master of the first floor. . . . And all about nothing! Yet every one of the adults was well acquainted with the admirable text which exhorted Christians to bear one another's burdens. A strange houseful! But there were some scores of such housefuls in Riceyman Square, and a £4,500 church in the midst.

Sunday morning always saw the adults of Elsie's household in a paradisaical coma. Elsie alone was afoot. On this particular Sunday morning she kept an eye on the two elder children, who were playing quietly in the murky autumnal darkness of the walled backyard. Elsie had herself summarily dressed them. The other three children had been

doped—or, as the advertisements phrased it, "soothed"—
so that while remaining in their beds they should not disturb
the adults. The adults slept. They embraced sleep passionately, voraciously, voluptuously. Their sole desire in those
hours was to find perfect unconsciousness and rest. If they
turned over they snatched again with terrible greed at sleep.
They wanted it more than love and more than beer. They
would have committed crimes for it. Even the prospective
mother slept, in a confusion of strange dreams.

There was a loud, heavy knocking on the warped and
shabby door of the house of repose. It shook the house.
The children in the yard, thunderstruck by the outrage,
stopped playing. Elsie ran in alarm through the back passage
and the lobby and opened the front-door. Joe stood there,
the worried, mad look, which Elsie knew so well, on his
homely face. She was frightened, but held herself together,
and shook her head sadly and decisively. As a result of the
episode of the carving-knife she had banished him from her
presence for one week, which had yet by no means expired.
It seemed odd that Elsie, everybody's slave, should exercise
an autocratic dominion over Joe; but she did. She knew her
power and divined that she must use it, if Joe was ever to get
well of his mysterious mental malady. And now, though
she wished that she had sentenced him to only three days'
banishment instead of seven, she would not yield and correct
her error, for she felt that to do so would impair her authority.

Moreover, Joe had no right to molest her at home. She
had her reputation to think of, and her reputation, in her
loyal and ingenuous mind, was his reputation also. Therefore, with woe in her heart she began to close the door on
Joe. Joe, rendered savage by a misery which he could not
define, put his foot in the aperture and then forced the door
backwards and lunged his desecrating body inside the sacred
Sunday morning temple of sleep. (A repetition of his procedure of the previous Thursday night.) The two stood
close together. He could not meet her fixed gaze. His eyes
glanced restlessly and wildly round, at the foul walls, the
gritty and soiled floor.

"Get out of this, my boy."

"Let me kiss you," he demanded harshly.

"Get out of it."

Losing what little remained of his self-control, he hit Elsie a strong blow on the shoulder. She was not ready for it. In the idiom of the ring her "foot-work" was bad, and she lost her balance, falling against the french-polisher's perambulator, which crashed violently into the stairs like an engine into a stationary buffer. Elsie's head caught the wheel of the perambulator. A great shrill scream arose; the children had followed Elsie out of the yard and witnessed the fall of their beloved slave. Joe, appalled at the consequences of his passion, ran off, banging the door behind him with a concussion which shook the house afresh and still more awakeningly. Two mothers recognized the howls of their children. The spinster on the second floor saw a magnificent opportunity for preaching from a point of vantage her views on the state of modern society. Two fathers, desperate with exasperation, but drawn by the mighty attraction of a good row, jumped murderous from their warm and fetid beds. Two half-clad figures appeared in the doorways of the ground-floor rooms and three on the stairs.

Elsie sat up, dazed, and then stood up, then sank limply down again. One mother smacked her child and a child which was not hers. The other mother protested furiously from the stairs. The paradise of Sunday morning lay shattered. The meat-salesman had sense, heart, and initiative. He took charge of Elsie. The hellish din died down. A few minutes later Elsie was seated in the rocking-chair by the window in his front room. She wept apologetically. Little was said, but all understood that Elsie's fantastic sweetheart had behaved disgracefully, and all indicated their settled opinion that if she kept on with him, he would murder her one of these days. Three-quarters of an hour later Dr. Raste calmly arrived. Joe had run to the surgery and shouted at him: "I've killed her, sir." The meat-salesman, having himself lighted a bit of a fire, left the room while the doctor examined the victim. The doctor could find nothing but one bruise on the front of Elsie's left shoulder. With a splendid gesture of devotion the meat-salesman's wife gave her second child's warm milk to the reluctant Elsie. There happened to be no other stimulant in the house. Peace was re-established, and even slumber resumed.

CHAPTER XII

The Benefactress

THE front door was opened to Mrs. Arb's quiet knock by the oldest child in the house, an obstreperous boy of five, who was suddenly struck sheepish and mute by the impressive lady on the doorstep. He said nothing at all in reply to Mrs. Arb's request to see Elsie, but sidled backwards along the lobby and opened a door, looking up at her with the most crude curiosity. As soon as she had gone into the room and the inhibition was lifted, he ran off to the yard raising his heels high and laughing boisterously.

The room in which Elsie had been installed was crowded and overcrowded with the possessions of the meat-salesman and his wife. The walls were covered from cornice to near the floor with coloured supplements from Christmas numbers, either in maple-wood frames or unframed; a wonderful exhibition of kindly sentiment; the innocence of children, the purity of lovers, the cohesion of families, the benevolence of old age, immense meals served in interiors of old oak, landscapes where snow lay in eternal whiteness on church steeples, angels, monks, blacksmiths, coach-drivers, souls awakening: indeed, a vast and successful effort to convince the inhabitants of Riceyman Square that Riceyman Square was not the only place on earth. The display undoubtedly unbent, diverted, and cheered the mind. In between the chromatic prints were grey, realistic photographs of people who really existed or had existed. The mantelpiece was laden with ornaments miscalled "china," standing on bits of embroidery. The floor was covered with oddments of carpet. There were many chairs, unassorted; there was a sofa; there was a cradle; there was a sewing-machine; there was a clothes-horse, on which a man's blue apron with horizontal white stripes was spread out. There were several tables, including a small walnut octagonal table, once a lady's work-table, which stood in the window and upon which a number of cloth-bound volumes of *Once a Week* were piled carefully, corkscrew-wise. And there was a wardrobe, also a number of kitchen utensils. The place was encumbered with goods, all grimy as the walls and ceilings, many of them cracked and worn like the woodwork and paint, but proving tri-umphantly that the meat-salesman had no commerce with pawnbrokers.

"I thought I should like to come round and see how you are, Elsie," said Mrs. Arb kindly and forgivingly. "No, don't get up. I can see you aren't well. I'll sit here."

Elsie blushed deeply.

"I've had a bit of trouble, 'm," she apologetically mur-mured.

Elsie's trouble was entirely due to Mrs. Arb's demand for overtime from her on Thursday night. Mrs. Arb had not considered the convenience nor the private life of this young woman whose services made daily existence tolerable for her and for Mr. Earlforward. The young woman had con-sequently found herself in a situation of the gravest difficulty and of some danger. Hence the young woman was apolo-getic and Mrs. Arb forgiving. Elsie admitted to herself a clear failure of duty with its sequel of domestic embarrass-ment for her employers, and she dismissed as negligible the excuses which she might have offered. Nor did she dream of criticizing Mrs. Arb. She never consciously criticized any-one but Elsie. And yet somewhere in the unexplored arcana of her mind lay hidden a very just estimate of Mrs. Arb. Strange! No, not strange! A quite common phenomenon in the minds of the humble and conscientious!

"Was the trouble over that young man?" asked Mrs. Arb. "Not that I want to be inquisitive!"

Elsie began to cry. She nodded, unable for the moment to speak. The sound of a snore came through the wall from the next room. There were muffled noises overhead. Mrs.

Arb grew aware that a child had peeped in upon her and Elsie. The church bells, after a few single notes, ceased to ring.

"I suppose you couldn't have sent somebody across to tell me you weren't coming?" Mrs. Arb suggested. Elsie shook her head. "Shall you come to-morrow?"

"Oh, yes, 'm. I shall come to-morrow—*and* punctual."

"Well, Elsie, don't think I'm interfering, but don't you think you'd better give him up? Two upsets in three days, you know." (Four days Mrs. Arb ought to have said; but in these details she took the licence of an artist.) "I haven't said a word to you about Thursday night, have I? I didn't want to worry you. I knew you'd had worry enough. But I don't mind telling you now that I was very much upset and frightened, as who wouldn't be! . . . What do you want with men? They'll never be any good to you—that is, if you value a quiet life and a good name. I'm telling you for your own sake. I like you, and I'd like you to be happy and respectable." Mrs. Arb seemed to have forgotten that she was addressing a widow and not a young girl.

"Oh, 'm. I'm giving him up. I'll never have anything to do with him again. Never!" Elsie burst out, with intense tragedy in her soul.

"That's right! I'm glad to hear it," said Mrs. Arb with placidity. "And if you really mean it the people that employ you will be able to trust and rely on you again. It's the only way."

"Oh, I'm so ashamed, 'm!" said Elsie, with the puckered brow of conscientiousness. "'Specially seeing I couldn't let you know. Nor Mr. Earlforward, either! But it won't occur again, 'm, and I hope you'll forgive me."

"Please, please!" Mrs. Arb exclaimed magnanimously, protesting against this excess of remorse and penitence. "I only thought I'd call to inquire."

After Mrs. Arb had gone out to dally with a man and to reassure him with the news that everything would be all right and they had nothing to fear, the boy crept into the front-room with a piece of bread and jam in his sticky hand.

He silently offered the morsel to Elsie, who leaned forward as he held it up to her and bit off a corner to please him. She smiled at him; then broke into a sob, and choked and clutched him violently, bread and jam and all, and there was a dreadful mess.

CHAPTER XIII

The Passion

"I THINK I've put *her* straight," said Mrs. Arb very cheerfully to Mr. Earlforward, out in the Square, and gave him an account of the interview.

Mr. Earlforward's mind was much relieved. He admired Mrs. Arb greatly in that moment. He himself could never have put Elsie straight. There were things that a woman, especially a capable and forceful woman, could do which no man could possibly do. "Forceful!" Perhaps a sinister adjective to attach to a woman. Yes. But the curious point about this woman was that she was also feminine. Forceful, she could yet (speaking metaphorically) cling and look up. And also she could look down in a most enchanting and disturbing way. She had done it a number of times to Mr. Earlforward. Now Mr. Earlforward, from the plenitude of his inexperience of women, knew them deeply. He knew their characteristic defects and shortcomings. And it seemed to him that Mrs. Arb was remarkably free from such. It seemed to him, as it has seemed to millions of men, that he had had the luck to encounter a woman who miraculously combined the qualities of two sexes, and the talent to recognize the miracle on sight. He would not go so far as to assert that Mrs. Arb was unique (though he strongly suspected that she must be), but there could not be many Mrs. Arbs on earth. He was very happy in youthful dreams of a new and idyllic existence. His sole immediate fear was that he would be compelled to go to church with her. He knew them; they were queer on religious observances. Of course it was because, as she had half admitted, they liked to feel devotional. But you could do nothing with a woman in

church. And he could not leave her to go to church alone.
. . . He was unhappy.

"I'm afraid that service of yours has begun," said he. "I saw quite a number of people going in while you were talking to Elsie."

"I'm afraid it has," she replied. He saw a glint of hope.

"It's a nice fresh morning," said he daringly. "And what people like you and me need is fresh air. I suppose you wouldn't care for me to show you some bits of Clerkenwell?"

"I think I should," said she. "I could go to service to-night, couldn't I?"

Triumph! Undoubtedly she was unique.

Both quite forgetting once more that they would never again see forty, they set off with the innocent ardour of youth.

"You know," said Mrs. Arb, returning to the great subject, "I told her plainly she'd be much better off if she kept off men. And so she will!"

"They never know when they *are* well off," said Mr. Earlforward.

"No . . . I expect this Square used to belong to your family," Mrs. Arb remarked with deference.

"Oh, I shouldn't say that," answered Mr. Earlforward modestly. "But it was named after my grandfather's brother."

"It must have been very nice when it was new," said Mrs. Arb, tactfully adopting towards the Square a more respectful attitude than aforetime. Clearly she desired to please. Clearly she had a kind heart. "But when the working-class get a hold on a place, what are you to do?"

"You'd scarcely think it," said Mr. Earlforward with grim resignation, "but this district was very fashionable once. There used to be an archery ground where our steps are." (He enjoyed saying "our steps," the phrase united him to her.)

"Really!"

"Yes. And at one time the Duke of Newcastle lived just close by. Look here. I'll show you something. It's quite near."

In a few minutes they were at the corner of a vast square—you could have put four Riceymans into it—of lofty reddish houses, sombre and shabby, with a great railed garden and great trees in the middle, and a wide roadway round. With all its solidity, in that neighbourhood it seemed to have the unreal quality of a vision, a creation of some djinn, formed in an instant and destined as quickly to dissolve; it seemed to have no business where it was.

"Look at that!" said Mr. Earlforward eagerly, pointing to the sign, "Wilmington Square." "Ever heard of it before?"

Mrs. Arb shook her astonished head.

"No. And nobody has. But it's here. That's London, that is! Practically every house has been divided up into tenements. Used to be very well-to-do people here, you know!"

Mrs. Arb gazed at him sadly.

"It's tragic!" she said sympathetically, her bright face troubled.

"She understands!" he thought.

"Now I'll show you another sort of square," he went on aloud. "But it's over on the other side of Farringdon Road. Not far! Not far! No distances here!"

He limped quickly along.

Coldbath Square easily surpassed even Riceyman Square in squalor and foulness; and it was far more picturesque and deeper sunk in antiquity, save for the huge, awful block of tenements in the middle. The glimpses of interiors were appalling. At the corners stood sinister groups of young men, mysteriously well dressed, doing nothing whatever, and in certain doorways honest-faced old men with mufflers round their necks and wearing ancient pea-jackets.

"I don't like this *at all*," said Mrs. Arb, as it were sensitively shrinking.

"No! This is a bit too much, isn't it? Let's go on to the Priory Church."

"Yes. That will be better," Mrs. Arb agreed with relief at the prospect of a Priory Church.

"Oh! There's a *News of the World*!" she exclaimed. "Now I wonder——"

They were passing through a narrow, very short alley of small houses which closed the vista of one of the towering congeries of modern tenement-blocks abounding in the region. The alley, christened a hundred years earlier, "Model Cottages," was silent and deserted, in strange contrast to the gigantic though half-hidden swarming of the granite tenements. The front-doors abutted on the alley without even the transition of a raised step. The *News of the World* lay at one of the front doors. It must have been there for hours, waiting for its subscriber to awake, and secure in the marvellous integrity of the London public.

"I did want just to look at a *News of the World*," said Mrs. Arb, stopping.

They had seen various newsvendors in the streets; in fact, newspapers were apparently the only articles of commerce at that hour of the Sunday morning; but she had no desire to buy a paper. Glancing round fearfully at windows, she stooped and picked up the folded *News of the World*. Mr. Earlforward admired her, but was apprehensive.

"Yes. Here it is!" she said, having rapidly opened the paper. Over her shoulder Mr. Earlforward nervously read: "*Provisions. Confec. Busy W.C. district. £25 wkly. Six rooms. Rent £90. £200 everything. Long lease, or will sell premises. Delay dangerous. Chance lifetime. 7, Riceyman Steps, W.C.1.*"

"Then you've decided!" murmured Mr. Earlforward, suddenly gloomy.

"Oh! Quite! I told you," said Mrs. Arb, dropping back the newspaper furtively like a shameful accusing parcel, and walking on with a wonderful air of innocence.

"I wasn't altogether sure if you'd decided finally."

"You see," Mrs. Arb continued. "Supposing the business failed. Supposing I lost my money. I've got to think of my future. No risks for me, I say! I only want a little, but I want it certain. And I've got a little."

"It's a very clever advertisement."

"I didn't know *how* to put it. Of course it's called a confectioner's. But it isn't really, seeing I buy all the cakes from Snowman's. The whole stock in the shop isn't worth £25, but you see, I count the rest of the price asked as premium for the house. That's how I look at it—and it's quite fair, don't you think?"

"Perfectly."

They stood talking in front of a shut second-hand shop, where old blades of aeroplane propellers were offered at 3s. 6d. each. Mr. Earlforward said feebly "Yes" and "No" and "Hm" and "Ha." His brain was occupied with the thought: "Is she going to slip through my fingers? Suppose she went to live in the country?" His knee began to ache. His body and his mind were always reacting upon one another. "Why should my knee ache because I'm bothered?" he thought, and could give no answer. But in secret he was rather proud of these mysterious inconvenient reactions; they gave him distinction in his own eyes. In another environment he would have been known among his acquaintances as "highly strung" and "highly nervously organized." And yet outwardly so calm, so serene, so even-tempered!

They got to the quarter of the great churches.

"Would you care to go in?" he asked her in front of St. James's. For he desired beyond almost anything to sit down.

"I think it's really too late now," she replied. "It wouldn't be quite nice to go in just at the end of the sermon, would it? Too conspicuous."

There were seats in the churchyard, but all were occupied, despite the chilliness of the morning, by persons who, for private reasons, had untimely left their beds. Moreover, he felt that Mrs. Arb, whose niceties he much admired, would not like to sit in a churchyard with service proceeding in the church. He had begun to understand her. There were no seats round about St. John's. Mr. Earlforward stood on one leg while Mrs. Arb deciphered the tablet on the west front:

"'The Priory Church of the Order of St. John of Jerusalem, consecrated by Heraclius, Patriarch of Jerusalem, 10th March,

c

1185.' Fancy that, now! It doesn't look *quite* that old.
Fancy them knowing the day of the month too!"

He was too preoccupied and tortured to instruct her. He
would have led her home then; but she saw in the distance at
the other side of St. John's Square a view of St. John's Gate,
the majestic relic of the Priory. Quite properly she said that
she must see it close. Quite properly she thanked him for a
most interesting promenade, most interesting.

"And me living in London off and on all my life! They
do say you can't see the wood for the trees, don't they?"

But the journey across the huge irregular Square cut in
two by a great avenue was endless to Mr. Earlforward. Then
she must needs go under the gateway into a street that seemed
to fascinate her. For there was an enormous twilit shoeing-
forge next door to the Chancery of the Order of St. John of
Jerusalem, and though it was Sunday morning the air rang
with the hammering of a blacksmith who held a horse's hind
leg between his knees. Then she caught the hum of unseen
machinery and inquired about it. Then the signs over the
places of business attracted her; she became charmingly girlish.

"'Rouge. Wholesale only.' 'Glass matchers to the
trade.' 'I want five million moleskins and ten million rabbit-
skins. Do not desert your old friend. Cash on the nail.'
And painted too, on a board! Not just written! 'Gorgonzola cheese manufacturers.' Oh! The mere thought of it!
No, I shall never touch Gorgonzola again after this! I
couldn't! But, of course, I see there *must* be places like these
in a place like London. Only it's too funny seeing them all
together. 'Barclay's Bank.' Well, it would be! Those
banks are everywhere in these days. I do believe there are
more banks than A.B.C. shops and Lyonses. You look at
any nice corner site, and before you can say knife there's a
bank on it. I mistrust those banks. They do what they like.
When I go into my bank somehow they make me feel as if
I'd done something wrong, or at least, I'd better mind what
I was about; and they look at you superior as if you were
asking a favour. Oh, very polite! But so condescending."

A shrewd woman! A woman certainly not without ideas!

And he perceived, dimly through the veil of his physical pain, that their intimacy was developing on the right lines. He would have been joyous, but for the apprehension of her selling the business and vanishing from him, and but for the pain. The latter was now the worst affliction. Riceyman Steps seemed a thousand miles off, through a Sabbath-enchanted desert of stone and asphalt.

When they returned into St. John's Square a taxi-cab with its flag up stood terribly inviting. Paradise, surcease from agony, for one shilling and perhaps a twopenny tip! But he would not look at it. He could not. He preferred the hell in which he was. The grand passion which had rendered all his career magnificent, and every hour of all his days interesting and beautiful, demanded and received an intense, devotional loyalty; it recompensed him for every ordeal, mortification, martyrdom. He proudly passed the taxi-cab with death in his very stomach. Nowhere was there a chance of rest! Not a seat! Not a rail! Mrs. Arb had inveighed against the lack of amenities in the parish and district. No cinemas, no theatre, no music-halls, no cafés! But Mr. Earlforward realized the ruthless stony, total inhospitality of the district far more fully than Mrs. Arb could ever have done. He was like a weakening bird out of sight of land above the surface of the ocean.

He led Mrs. Arb down towards the nearest point of Farringdon Road, though this was not the shortest way home. The tramcars stopped at the corner. Every one of them would deposit him at his own door. Paradise for one penny! No, twopence; because he would have to pay for Mrs. Arb! He had thought to defeat his passion at this corner. He was mistaken. He could not. He had, after all his experience, misjudged the power of his passion. He was as helpless as the creatures who were beginning to gather at the iron-barred doors of the public-houses, soon to open for a couple of too short hours; and also he had the secret ecstasy which they had. He could scarcely talk now, and each tram that passed him in his slow and endless march gave him a spasm of mingled bitterness and triumph. His fear now was lest his grand passion should on this occasion be overcome by bodily weakness. He did not desire it to be overcome. He desired it to conquer even if it should kill him.

"I'm afraid I've walked you too far," said Mrs. Arb.

"Why?"

"I thought you were limping a bit."

"Oh no! I always limp a bit. Accident. Long time ago." And he smartened his gait.

They reached Riceyman Steps in silence. He had done it! His passion had forced him to do it! His passion had won! There were two Mr. Earlforwards: one splendidly uplifted, the other ready to faint from pain and fatigue. The friends disappeared, each into the solitude of his own establishment. In the afternoon Mr. Earlforward heard a sharp knock on his front-door; it was repeated before he could get downstairs; and when he opened the door he opened it to nobody; but Mrs. Arb was just entering her shop. He called out, and she returned.

"I was a bit anxious about your leg," she said, so brightly and kindly, "so I thought I'd step across and inquire."

"Quite all right again, now, thank you." (An exaggeration.)

How delightful of her! How feminine! He could hardly believe it! He was tremendously flattered. She could not after all slip through his fingers, whatever happened! They chatted for a few moments, and then each disappeared a second time into the recondite, inviolate solitude of his own establishment.

CHAPTER XIV

A Man's Private Life

ONE morning in November, at a little past eight o'clock, Mrs. Arb, watching from behind the door of her yet unopened shop, saw Mr. Earlforward help Elsie to carry out the empty bookstand and set it down in front of the window, and then, with overcoat, muffler and umbrella, depart from Riceyman Steps on business. Mrs. Arb immediately unlocked her door, went out just as she was—hatless, coatless, gloveless, wearing a white apron—locked her door, and walked across to Mr. Earlforward's. Elsie had already begun to fill the bookstand with books which overnight had been conveniently piled near the entrance of the shop.

"Good morning, Elsie. Dull morning, isn't it? Is master up yet?" said Mrs. Arb vivaciously, rubbing her hands in the chilly, murky dawn, and brightening the dawn.

"Oh, 'm! He's gone out. I don't expect him back till eleven. It's one of his buying mornings, ye see."

"Oh, *dear*, dear!" Mrs. Arb exclaimed, with cheerful resignation. "And I've only got ten minutes. Well, I haven't really got that. Shop ought to be open now. But I thought I'd let 'em wait a bit this morning."

She glanced anxiously at her own establishment to see whether any customer had come down the steps from the square. But, in truth, as she had now sold the business, and the premises, and was to give possession in a few weeks, she was not genuinely concerned about the possible loss of profit on an ounce or two ounces of tea. She wandered with apparent aimlessness into Mr. Earlforward's shop.

"Did you want to see him particular, 'm?"

"I won't say so particular as all that. So you look after the shop when Mr. Earlforward is out, Elsie?"

"It's like this, 'm. All the books is marked inside, and some outside. If anybody comes in that looks respectable, I ask 'em to look round for themselves, and if they take a book they pay me, and I ask 'em to write down the name of it on a bit of paper." She pointed to some small memorandum sheets prepared from old unassorted envelopes which had been cut open and laid flat, with pencil close by. "If it's some regular customer like, that *must* see Mr. Earlforward himself, I ask 'em to write their names down. And if I don't like the look of anybody, I tell 'em I don't know anything, and out they go."

"What a good arrangement!" said Mrs. Arb approvingly. "But if you have to attend to the shop, how can you do the cleaning and so on?"

Elsie's ingenuous, kind face showed distress; her dark-blue eyes softened in solicitude.

"Ah, 'm! There you've got me. I can't. I can only clean the shop these mornings and not much of that neither, because I must keep my hands dry for customers."

Mrs. Arb, vaguely smiling to herself, trotted to and fro in the gloomy shop, which had the air of a crypt, except that in these days crypts are usually lighted by electricity, and the shop was lighted by nature alone on this dark morning. She peered, bending forward, into the dark spaces between the bays, and descried the heaps of books on the floor. The dirt and the immense disorder almost frightened her. She had not examined the inside of the shop before—had, indeed, previously entered it only once, when she was in no condition to observe. Mr. Earlforward had never seized an occasion to invite her within.

"This will want some putting straight," she said, "if ever it is put straight."

"And well you may say it, 'm," Elsie replied compassionately. "He's always trying to get straight, 'specially lately, 'm. We did get one room straight upstairs, but it meant letting all the others go. Between you and me, he'll never get straight. But he has hopes, and it's no use saying anything to him."

"I suppose you can do this room, too, on his buying mornings," said Mrs. Arb, peeping into Mr. Earlforward's private back-room from which the shop and the shop-door could be kept under observation.

"Oh, 'm! He wouldn't let me. He won't have anything touched in that room."

"Then who does it?"

"He does it himself, 'm—when it is done."

"Does he!" murmured Mrs. Arb in a peculiar tone.

The bookshelves went up to the ceiling on every side. The floor was thickly strewn with books, the table also. Chairs also. The blind lay crumpled on the book-covered window-sill. The window was obscured by dirt. The ceiling was a blackish-grey. A heavy deposit of black dust covered all things. The dreadful den expressed intolerably to Mrs. Arb the pathos of the existence of a man who is determined to look after himself. It convicted a whole sex of being feckless, foolish, helpless, infantile, absurd. Mrs. Arb and Elsie exchanged glances. Elsie blushed.

"Yes. I'm that ashamed of it, 'm!" said Elsie. "But you know what they are!"

Mrs. Arb gave two short nods. She moved her hand as if to plumb the layer of dust with one feminine finger, but refrained; she dared not.

"And do you do his cooking, too?" she asked.

"Well, 'm. He gets his own breakfast, and he makes his own bed—it's always done before I come of a morning—and he cleans his own boots. I begin his dinner but, seeing as I go at twelve, he finishes it. He gets his own tea. I must say he isn't what you call a big eater."

"Seems to me it's all very cleverly organized."

"Oh, it is, 'm! There's not many gentlemen could manage as he does. But it's a dreadful pity. Makes me fair cry sometimes. And him so clean and neat himself, too."

"Yes," said Mrs. Arb, agreeing that the contrast between the master and his home was miraculous, awful, and tragic.

"I suppose I'd better not go upstairs as he isn't here, Elsie?"

The two women exchanged more glances. Elsie perfectly

comprehended the case of Mrs. Arb, and sympathized with
her. Mrs. Arb was being courted. Mrs. Arb had come to
no decision. Mrs. Arb desired as much information as possible
before coming to a decision. Women had the right to look
after themselves against no matter what man. Women were
women, and men were men. The Arb–Earlforward affair was
crucial for both parties.

"Oh! I think you might, 'm. But I can't go with you."
Sex-loyalty had triumphed over a too strict interpretation of
the duty of the employed to the employer. A conspiracy had
been set up.

Mrs. Arb had to step over hummocks of books in order to
reach the foot of the stairs. The léft-hand half of every step
of the stairs was stacked with books—cheap editions of novels
in paper jackets, under titles such as "Just a Girl," "Not Like
Other Girls," "A Girl Alone." Weak but righteous and
victorious girls crowded the stairs from top to bottom, so
that Mrs. Arb could scarcely get up. The landing also was
full of girls. The front-room on the first floor was, from the
evidence of its furniture, a dining-room, though not used as
such. The massive mahogany table was piled up with books,
as also the big sideboard, the mantelpiece, various chairs. The
floor' was carpeted with books. Less dust than in the den
below, but still a great deal. The Victorian furniture was
"good"; it was furniture meant to survive revolutions and
conflagrations and generations; it was everlasting furniture;
it would command respect through any thickness of dust.

The back-room, with quite as large a number of books
as the front-room, but even less dust, was a bedroom. The
very wide bed had been neatly made. Mrs. Arb turned down
the corner of the coverlet; a fairly clean pillow-slip, no sheets,
only blankets! She drew open drawers in a great mahogany
chest. Two of them were full of blue suits, absolutely new.
In another drawer were at least a dozen quite new grey flannel
shirts. A wardrobe was stuffed with books.

Coming out of the bedroom, she perceived between it and
the stairs a long, narrow room. Impossible to enter this
room because of books; but Mrs. Arb did the impossible,

and after some excavation with her foot disclosed a bath, which was full to the brim and overflowing with books. Now Mrs. Arb was pretty well accustomed to baths; she was not aware of the extreme rarity of baths in Clerkenwell, and hence she could not adequately appreciate the heroism of a hero who, possessing such a treasure, had subdued it to the uses of mere business. Nevertheless, her astonishment and amaze were sufficiently noticeable, and she felt, disturbingly and delightfully, the thrill of surprising clandestinely the secrets of a man's intimate personal existence.

Then she caught the sound of dropping water; it was on the second floor, in a room shaped like the bath-room, a room with two shelves, a gas-ring, and a sink. The water was dropping with a queer reverberation on to the sink from a tap above. There were a few plates, cups, saucers, jugs, saucepans, dishes; half a loaf of bread, a slice of cooked bacon; there was no milk, no butter. His kitchen and larder! One gas-ring! No fireplace! Mrs. Arb was impressed.

The other rooms on the second floor were full of books and dust. One of them had recently been cleaned and tidied, but dozens of books still lay on the floor. She picked up a book, a large, thick volume, for no other reason than that the cover bore a representation of a bird. It was a heavy book, with many coloured pictures of birds. She thought it was quite a pretty thing to look at. By accident she noticed the price pencilled inside the front cover. £40. She was not astonished nor amazed, she was staggered. Mrs. Arb had probably not read ten books since girlhood. To her, reading was a refuge from either idleness or life. She was never idle, and she loved life. Thus she condescended towards books. That any book, least of all a picture-book of birds, could be worth £40 had not occurred to her mind. (And this one lying on the floor!) Instantly, in spite of her common sense, she thought for a brief space of all the books in the establishment as worth £40 apiece! Before returning down the book-encumbered stairs, she paused on the top landing. Her throat was coated with the dust which she had displaced in her passage through the house. Her hands were very dirty and very cold—they shone with cold. No fire could have burnt in any of those rooms for years. She dared not touch the handrail of the staircase, even with her fingers all dirty. She paused because she was disconcerted and wanted to arrange the perplexing confusion of her thoughts. The more she reflected the better she realized how strange and powerful and ruthless a person was Mr. Earlforward. She admired, comprehended, sympathized, and yet was intimidated. The character of the man was displayed beyond any misunderstanding by the house with its revelations of his daily life; but there was no clue to it in his appearance and deportment. She was more than intimidated—she was frightened. Withal, the terror—for it amounted to terror—fascinated her. She went down gingerly, hesitating at every step. . . . At the bottom of the lower flight she heard, with new alarm, the bland voice of Mr. Earlforward himself. He was talking with a customer in his den.

"I'll slip out," she very faintly whispered to Elsie, who was sweeping near the stairs. Elsie nodded—like a conspirator. But at the same moment Mr. Earlforward and his customer emerged from the back room, and Mrs. Arb was trapped.

"I didn't notice you come in," said the bookseller most amiably. "What can I do for you?"

"Oh, thank you, but I only stepped across to speak to Elsie about something."

The lie, invented on the instant, succeeded perfectly. And Elsie, the honestest soul in Clerkenwell, gave it the support of her silence in the great cause of women against men.

"I'm glad to see you in here," said Mr. Earlforward gently, having dismissed the customer. "It's a bit of luck. I'd gone off for Houndsditch, but I happened to meet someone on the road, and nothing would do but I must come back with him. Come in here."

He drew her by the attraction of his small eyes into the back room. Books had been tipped off one of the chairs on to the floor. She sat down. Surely Mr. Earlforward was the most normal being in the world, the mildest, the quietest, the easiest! But the bath, the kitchen, the blankets, the filth, the food, the

£40 book, and all those new suits and new shirts! She had never even conceived such an inside of a house! She could hardly credit the evidence of her senses.

"I've wanted to see you in here, in this room," said Mr. Earlforward in a warm voice. And then no more.

She could not withstand his melting glance. She knew that their intimacy, having developed gradually through weeks, was startlingly on the point of bursting into a new phase. The sense of danger with her, as with nearly all women, was intermittent. The man was in love with her. He was in her hands. What could she not do with him? Could she not accomplish marvels? Could she not tame monsters? And she understood his instincts; she shared them. And he was a rock of defence, shelter, safety! . . . The alternative: solitude, celibacy, spinsterishness, eternal self-defence, eternal misgivings about her security; horrible!

"I must be opening my shop," she said nervously.

"And I must be getting away again, too," he said, and put on his hat and began to button his overcoat. Nothing more. But at the door he added:

"Maybe I'll come across and see you to-night, if it isn't intruding."

"You'll be very welcome, I'm sure," she answered, modestly smiling.

She was no better than a girl, then. She knew she had uttered the deciding word of her fate. She trembled with apprehension and felicity. He was a wonderful man and an enigma. He inspired love and dread. As the day passed her feeling for him became intense. At closing time her ecstatic heart was liquid with acquiescence. And she had, too, a bright, adventurous valour, but shot through with forebodings.

PART II

CHAPTER I

The Day Before

CYTHEREA reigned in Mr. Earlforward's office behind the shop—invisible, but she was there—probably reclining—ask not how!—on the full red lips (which fascinated Mrs. Arb) of Mr. Earlforward. It was just after four o'clock in the January following their first acquaintance. They sat on opposite sides of Henry's desk, with the electric light extravagantly burning above them. At the front of the shop the day was expiring in faint gleams of grey twilight. Dirt was nothing; disorder was nothing; Mr. Earlforward loved. For weeks he had been steadfastly intending to put the place to rights for his bride, and he had not put it to rights. Dirt and disorder were repugnant to Mrs. Arb, but she had said not a word. She would not interfere or even suggest, before the time. She knew her place; she was a bit prim. The time was approaching, and she could wait.

"I suppose we can use that ring," said Henry, pointing to the wedding-ring on Mrs. Arb's hand, which lay on the desk like the defenceless treasure of an invaded city.

Despite a recent experience, Mrs. Arb was startled by this remark delivered in a tone so easy, benevolent and matter-of-fact. The recent experience had consisted in Mr. Earlforward's bland ultimatum, after a discussion in which Mrs. Arb had womanishly and prettily favoured a religious ceremony, that they would be married at a Registry because it was on the whole cheaper. Upon that point she had taken pleasure in yielding to him. So long as you were genuinely married, the method had only a secondary importance. She admitted—to herself—that in desiring the church she might have been conventional, superstitious. She was eager to yield as some women are eager to be beaten. Morbidity, of course! But not wholly. Self-preservation was in it, as well as voluptuousness. Mr. Earlforward's individuality frightened while enchanting her. She found she could cure the fright by intense acquiescence. And why not acquiesce? He was her fate. She would grasp her fate with both hands.

And there was this point: if he was her fate, she was his; she had already been married once, whereas he was an innocent; he had to learn. She saw an advantage there. Her day was coming—at least, she persuaded herself that it was.

Thus the question of the wedding ceremony had been quite satisfactorily dissolved; and so well that Mrs. Arb now scorned the notion of marriage in a church. But the incident of the ring touched her closer; it touched the aboriginal cave-woman in the very heart of her. Do you know, she had faintly suspected that to purchase a wedding-ring formed no part of his programme! An absurd, an impossible suspicion! How could he espouse without a ring? But there the suspicion had lain! She ought to have been revolted by the idea of a second husband marrying her with the ring of the first. However, she was not. Mr. Earlforward's natural, casual tone precluded that. And she answered quietly, as it were hypnotized, with a smile:

"We can't use this. It won't come off."

She displayed the finger. Obviously the ring would not pass the joint. Mrs. Arb was slim, but she had been slimmer. He said:

"But you can't be married with that *on*. You can't wear two." (Something of the cave-creature in him also!)

"I know. But I was going to have it filed off to-morrow morning. There wouldn't be time to have it made larger."

He took the supine hand and thrilled it.

"I tell you what," said he. "What carat is it?"

"Eighteen."

"Soft!" he murmured. "I've got a little file. I'll file it off now. I'm rather good at odd jobs. Oh no, I shan't hurt you! I wouldn't hurt you for anything."

He found the file, after some search, in a drawer of his desk.

"It must feel like this to be manicured," she said, with a

slight, nervous giggle, when again he held her hand in his, and began to operate with the file.

He had not boasted; he was indeed rather good at odd jobs. Such delicate, small movements! Such patience! He was standing over her. She was his prisoner, and the ray of the bulb blazed down on the timorous yielded hand. At the finish the skin was scarcely perceptibly abraded. He pulled apart the ends of the severed band and removed it.

"Soft as butter!" he smiled. "Now lend me that other ring of yours, will you? For size, you know. And I'll just slip across to Joas's in Farringdon Road. Shan't be long. Will you look after the shop while I'm gone? If anyone comes in and there's any difficulty, ask 'em to wait. But all the prices are marked. I'll leave the light on in the shop. You won't feel lonely."

"Oh, but——!" she protested. Leave her by herself in his house—and without the protection of the ring! And before marriage! What would people think?

"Well, Elsie'll be here in a minute. So there's nothing to worry over." He spoke most soothingly, as to an irrational child. "I'd better see to it to-night. And they close at six, same as me—except the pawnbroking. No time to lose!" He was gone.

She was saved from too much reflection by the entry of Elsie. At the sight of Elsie Mrs. Arb's demeanour immediately became normal—that is to say, the strange enchantment which had held her was dissipated, blown away. She was no longer morbid; she was not supine. Her body resumed all its active little movements, her glance its authority, cheerfulness, liveliness and variety. She rose from the chair, smoothed her dress, and was ready to deal with the universe.

"Oh, Elsie! So you've come! Mr. Earlforward was expecting you. He's just slipped out on urgent business for a minute or two, and he said you'd be in to attend to customers, and I must say I didn't much fancy being left here alone, because you see—— But, of course, business must be attended to. We all know that, don't we?"

She gave a poke to the dull embers of the stove which

warmed the shop in winter; Mr. Earlforward rarely replenished it after four o'clock; he liked it to be just out at
closing time.

"Yes'm."

Elsie, although wearing her best jacket and hat, and looking
rather Sundayish, had carried—not easily—into the shop a
sizeable tin trunk with thin handles that cut uncomfortably
into the hands. This box contained her late husband's medals,
and all that was hers, including some very strange things.
The french-polisher's wife, by now quite accustomed to
having three infants instead of two, had procured for herself
a pleasant little change from the monotony of home-life by
helping Elsie to transport the trunk from Riceyman Square
to Mr. Earlforward's shop-door. The depositing of the
dented trunk on the uneven floor of the shop constituted
Elsie's "moving-in".

"I'll take this upstairs now, shall I, m'm?" Elsie suggested,
somewhat timidly, because she was beginning a new life
and didn't quite know how she stood.

"Well, it certainly mustn't be here when Mr. Earlforward
returns," said Mrs. Arb gravely.

Elsie fully concurred. Masters of households ought not
to be offended by the quasi-obscene sight of the private
belongings of servants.

"No! You can't carry it up by yourself. You might hurt
yourself. You never know. Come, come, Elsie!" as Elsie
protested. "Do you suppose I've never helped to carry a
box upstairs before? Now take the other handle, do!
Where's your umbrella? I know you've got one."

"It's coming to-morrow, 'm. I've lent it."

Mrs. Arb was extremely cheerful, kindly and energetic
over the affair of the trunk, and Elsie extremely apologetic.

"Now nip your apron on and come down as quick as you
can—there might be a customer. You must remember I'm
not mistress here until to-morrow. I'm only a visitor."
Thus spoke Mrs. Arb gaily and a little breathless at the door
of the small bedroom which Elsie was to share with a vast
collection of various sermons in eighty volumes, some State

Trials in twenty volumes, and a lot of other piled sensation-
alism.

When Elsie, still impressed by the fact of having a new home
and by Mrs. Arb's benevolent demeanour, came rather self-
consciously downstairs in a perfectly new apron (bought for
this great occasion), Mrs. Arb went to the foot of the stairs to
meet her, and employing a confidential and mysterious tone,
said:

"Now don't forget all I told you about that cleaning business
to-morrow, will you?"

"Oh, no, 'm. I suppose it will be all right?" Elsie's brow
puckered with conscientiousness.

Mrs. Arb laughed amiably.

"What do you mean, my girl—'it'll be all right'? You
must remember that when I come back to-morrow I come
back Mrs. Earlforward. And you'll call me 'Mrs. Earlforward' too."

"I'd sooner call you mum, 'm, if it's all the same to
you."

"Of course. But when you're speaking *about* me."

"I shall have to get into it, 'm."

"Now I expect Mr. Earlforward's settled your wages with
you?"

"No, 'm."

"Not said anything at all?"

"No, 'm. But it'll be all right."

Mrs. Arb was once again amazed at Henry's marvellous
faculty for letting things go.

"Oh, well, perhaps he was leaving it to me, though I've
nothing to do with this house till to-morrow. Now, what
wages do you want, Elsie?"

"I prefer to leave it to you, 'm," said Elsie diffidently.

"Well, of course, Elsie, being a 'general' is a very different
thing from being a char. You have a good home and all
your food. And a regular situation. No going about from
one place to another and being told you aren't wanted to-day,
or aren't wanted to-morrow, and only half a day the next day
and so on and so on! A regular place. No worries about

shall I or shan't I earn my day's wage to-day. . . . You see, don't you?"

"Oh yes, 'm."

"I'll just show you what I cut out of the *West London Observer* yesterday." She drew her purse from her pocket, and from the purse an advertisement of a Domestic Servants' Agency, offering innumerable places. "'Generals £20 to £25 a year,'" she read. "Suppose you start with £20? Of course it's very high, but wages are high in these days. I don't know why. But they are. And we have to put up with it."

"Very well, 'm," Elsie agreed gratefully.

Twenty pounds seemed a big lump of money to her, and she could not divide by fifty-two. Besides, there it was, printed in the paper! No arguing against that. The two talked about washing and the kitchen and the household utensils which Mrs. Arb had abstracted from the schedule of possessions sold to the purchaser of the business opposite. Elsie sold a couple of books. During this transaction Mrs. Arb retired to the office, and after it she refused to take charge of the money which Elsie dutifully offered to her.

"Elsie, haven't I just told you I'm not mistress here? You must give the money to your master."

Then Mr. Earlforward returned; and Mrs. Arb gave Elsie a sign to withdraw upstairs; and Elsie, having placed the money on the paper containing the titles of the sold books, went discreetly upstairs.

"I've taken on myself to settle that woman's wages," said Mrs. Arb, while Henry was removing his overcoat in the back-room. "She told me you hadn't said anything."

"No, I hadn't."

"Well. I've settled twenty pounds a year."

"Eight shillings a week. Rather less. Anyhow, it's better than half a crown every morning of your life for half a day's work."

"Did you give her half a crown? I only used to give her two shillings. Did you give her any food?"

"Certainly not."

"Neither did I. Unless she stayed late."

Mrs. Arb felt upon her Mr. Earlforward's glance of passionate admiration, and slipped into the enchantment again. She was very content; she was absurdly content. The fact was that Mr. Earlforward had been under the delusion of having driven a unique bargain with Elsie in the matter of wages. For he knew that the recognized monstrous rate was five shillings a day *and* food. And here this miraculous creature, so gentle, submissive and girlish, had beaten him by sixpence a half-day. What a woman! What a wife! She had every quality. He gloated over her. . . . He sat on the desk by her chair, boyishly to watch her girlishness. Then he interrupted the tête-à-tête to go and turn off the light in the shop—because the light in the office gave sufficient illumination to show that the shop was open. And he called out to Elsie:

"Elsie, come down and bring the bookstand inside. It ought to have been brought in before. It's quite dark—long since. . . . Oh! She won't look *thi*s way," he murmured, with a shrug in answer to Mrs. Arb's girlish alarm as he sat down on the desk by her once more.

"Now here's the ring I've got." He pulled from his waistcoat pocket a hoop of glittering gold. "And here's your finger-ring—keeper, do you call it? See! They're exactly the same size. It's a very good ring, and it'll last much longer than the old one. Harder. Nine carat. Looks better too, *I* think."

Mrs. Arb, examining the ring, kept a smiling, constrained silence. The nine carat was a blow to her. But, of course, he was right; he was quite right. He put the new ring back in his pocket.

"But where's my old wedding-ring?"

"Oh, I sold that to Joas. Flinty fellow, but I don't mind telling you I sold it to him for six and sixpence more than what I paid for this one." He spoke, very low—because of Elsie, with a contented and proud calm, his little eyes fixed on her. "I suppose that six and six is by right yours. Here it is." And he handed her the six and sixpence.

"Oh, that's all right," said Mrs. Arb weakly, as if to indicate that he could keep the money.

"Oh, no!" said he. "Right's right."

She put the coins in her purse. Then she said it was time for her to be "going across." (Part of the bargain with the purchaser of her business was that he should provide her with a room and food until the day of the wedding.)

"I hope you'll slip in again to-night," he urged.

"Not to-night, Henry. *It's the night before.* It wouldn't be quite nice."

He yielded. They discussed all the arrangements for the morrow. As they were leaving the back-room side by side, Henry switched off the light. Elsie had completed her task and gone upstairs. Total darkness—for a few moments! Mrs. Arb felt Henry's rich lips on hers. She was sensible of the mystery of the overcrowded shop stretching from bay to bay in front of her to the gradually appearing yellow twilight from the gas-lamp of Riceyman Steps. She abandoned herself, in an ecstasy that was perhaps less, perhaps more, than what is called happiness, to the agitating uncertainties of their joint future. Useless for her to recall to herself her mature years, her experience, her force, her sagacity. She was no better than a raw girl under his kiss. Well, it was a loving kiss. He worshipped the ground she trod on, as the saying was. A point in her favour!

He switched on the light.

CHAPTER II

Elsie's Retreat

ELSIE'S bedroom was a servant's bedroom, and always had been, though not used as such for many years. Its furniture comprised one narrow iron bedstead, one small yellow washstand, one small yellow chest of drawers with a small mirror, one windsor chair, and nothing else in the way of furniture—unless three hooks behind the door could be called furniture. No carpet. No apparatus of illumination except a candle. The flowery wallpaper was slowly divorcing itself from the walls in several places. The sash-cord of the window having been broken many years ago and never repaired, the window could only be made to stay open by means of a trick. It had, in fact, been closed for many years. When, early, she had finished her work, Elsie retired with an inch and a half of candle to this bedroom and shut the door, and could scarcely believe her good luck. Happy she was not, for she had a great grief, the intensity of which few people suspected and still fewer attempted to realize and none troubled about; but she was very grateful to the fate which had provided the bedroom. The room was extremely cold, but Elsie had never known of, or even conceived, a warm bedroom in winter. It was bare, but not to Elsie's sight, which saw in it the main comforts of nocturnal existence. It was small, but not according to Elsie's scale of dimensions. It was ugly, but Elsie simply could not see ugliness. (Nor could she see beauty, save in a child's face, a rich stuff, a bright colour, a pink sunset and things of that kind.)

She looked round and saw a bed in which you slept. She saw a chest of drawers—which would hold three or four times as much as her trunk, which trunk held all she possessed except an umbrella. She saw a washstand, which if it was duly

fitted out with water, soap and towel might one day be useful
in an emergency.   She saw a chair, which was strong.   She
saw hooks, which were useful.   She saw a window, which
was to look through.   She knew that many books were piled
against the wall between the window and the door, but she
didn't see them.   They were merely there, and one day would
go downstairs.   She thought of them as mysterious and valu-
able articles.   Although she herself had the magic gift to
decipher their rather arbitrary signs and so induce perplexing
ideas in her own head, she would not have dreamed of doing
so.

But do not suppose that the bedroom had no grand, exciting
quality for Elsie.   It had one.   It was solely hers.   It was the
first bedroom she had ever in all her life had entirely to herself.
More, in her personal experience, it was the first room that
was used as a bedroom and nothing else.   Elsie had never
slept alone in a room, and she had very rarely slept in a bed
alone.   She had had no privacy.   She now gazed on every
side, and what she saw and felt was privacy; a luxurious sensation, exquisite and hardly credible.   She abandoned herself
to it as Mrs. Arb had abandoned herself to the kiss of Henry
Earlforward.   It was a balm to her grief.   It was a retreat
in which undisturbed she could enjoy her grief.

Unpacking her trunk, she moved about, walked, stooped,
knelt, rose, opened drawers, shut drawers, with the magnificent
movements of a richly developed and powerful body.   The
expression on her mild face and in her dark-blue eyes, denoted
a sweet, unconscious resignation.   No egotism in those features!   No instinct to fight for her rights and to get all she
could out of the universe!   No apprehension of injustice!
No resentment against injustice!   No glimmer of realization
that she was the salt of the earth!   She thought she was in a
nice, comfortable, quiet house, and appointed to live with
kindly people of superior excellence.   She was still touched
by Mrs. Arb's insistence on helping her upstairs with her
box.

She looked at her Post Office Savings Bank book.   An
enormous sum ready to her hand in the post office!   Enough

to keep her for a month if anything should "happen" to her. She looked at her late husband's two silver medals and their ribbons. They were what she called beautiful. She laid them at the back of one of the small top-drawers. Her feeling in regard to her late husband was now purely pious. He had lost reality for her. She took a letter out of a dirty envelope and read, bending to the candle: "Darling Elsie, I feel as how I must go right away until I am better. I feel it is not easy for you to forgive me. All you say is quite true. And it is best for you not to know where I am. I know I shall get better, and then I shall write to you and ask you——" She cried. . . . "Joe." This man was real to her, far more real than her husband had ever been. She could feel him standing by her. She could feel his nervous arm on her waist, and she was as familiar with the shape and pressure of his arm as a blind man with his accustomed chair. She had an ardent longing to martyrize herself to Joe, to relax her dominion over him so that he might exult in ill-treating her in his affliction. But she knew that her dominion over him could alone be his salvation, and she had firmly exercised it. And she thought:

"How awkward it must have been for poor Dr. Raste. He's got another now, but not so good—no, and never will have!"

The letter was two months old and more. She had read it at least fifty times. It was the dearest, bitterest, most miraculous phenomenon in the world. It was not a letter at all. It was a talisman, a fetish.

There came a rap on the door, shattering the immaterial fabric of her private existence and changing Elsie back into the ex-charwoman promoted to "general." She shuddered under the shock.

"Elsie, are you going to burn that candle all night?" Mr. Earlforward's bland, gentle, authoritative voice! He must have seen light shining under the door, and crept upstairs in his slippers.

"No, sir. I'm just going to blow it out." She was conscience-stricken.

"Did you finish off *all* that loaf?"

"Yes, sir. I'm sorry, sir." She was still more conscience-stricken.

"Tut-tut. . . . Tut-tut."

Elsie put the letter under her pillow. She was undressed in a minute. She had no toilet to perform. She no more thought of washing than a Saxon queen would have thought of washing. She did not examine the bed to see if it was comfortable. She had never failed to sleep. Any bed was a bed. As she slipped in between the blankets her brow puckered with one anxiety. Could she wake at six in that silent house? She must! She must! She extinguished the candle. And as she smelt its dying fumes in the darkness and explored with her sturdy limbs the roominess of the bed, a sudden surprising sensation impaired her joy in exclusive privacy. She missed the warm, soft body of the furniture-polisher's child, with whom she had slept so long. Some people are never satisfied.

CHAPTER III

Waxworks

A S Henry and Violet approached the turnstile, Henry murmured to Violet:

"How much is it? How much is it?"

"One and three, including tax," Violet murmured in reply.

Half a crown for the two was less than he had feared, but he felt in his trouser-pocket and half a crown was more than he had there, and he slowly pulled out of his breast-pocket an old Treasury-note case. The total expenses of the wedding ceremony at the Registry had been considerable; he seemed to have been disbursing the whole time since they left Clerkenwell for the marriage and honeymoon (which, according to arrangement, was to be limited to one day).

The wedding-breakfast—two covers—at the magnificent, many-floored, music-enlivened, swarming Lyons' establishment in Oxford Street had been—he was prepared to believe —relatively cheap, and there were no tips, and everything was very good and splendid; but really the bill amounted to a lot of money in the judgment of a man who for years had never spent more than sixpence on a meal outside his own home, and whom the mere appearance of luxury frightened. Throughout the wedding-breakfast he had indeed been scared by the gilding, the carving, the seemingly careless profusion, the noise, and the vastness of the throng which flung its money about in futile extravagance; he had been unable to dismiss the disturbing notion that England was decadent, and the structure of English society threatened by a canker similar to the canker which had destroyed Gibbon's Rome. Ten shillings and sevenpence for a single repast for two persons! It was fantastic. He had resolved that this should be the last pleasure excursion into the West End. Meanwhile, he was on his honeymoon, and he must conduct himself and his purse with the chivalry which a loved woman would naturally, if foolishly, expect.

It was after the wedding-breakfast that Violet had, in true feminine capriciousness, suddenly suggested that they should go to Madame Tussaud's waxworks before the visit to the gorgeous cinema in Kingsway, which was the *pièce de résistance* of the day's programme. She had never seen Madame Tussaud's (nor had he), and she was sure it must be a very nice place; and they had plenty of time for it. All her life she had longed to see Madame Tussaud's, but somehow . . . etc. Not that he needed too much persuading. No! He liked, he adored, the girlishness in that vivacious but dignified and mature creature, so soberly dressed (save for the exciting red flowers in her dark hat). In consenting to gratify her whim he had the sensations of a young millionaire clasping emerald necklaces round the divine necks of stage-favourites. After all, it was only for one day. And she had spoken truly in saying that they had plenty of time. The programme was not to end till late. Previous to their departure from Riceyman Steps on the wedding journey he had seen Violet call aside Elsie (who was left in charge of the shop), and he doubted not that she had been enjoining the girl to retire to bed before her employers' return. A nice thoughtfulness on Violet's part.

Withal, as he extracted a pound note from his case, he suffered agony—and she was watching him with her bright eyes. It was a new pound note. The paper was white and substantial; not a crease in it. The dim watermarks whispered genuineness. The green and brown of the design were more beautiful than any picture. The majestic representation of the Houses of Parliament on the back gave assurance that the solidity of the whole realm was behind that note. The thing was as lovely and touching as a young virgin daughter. Could he abandon it for ever to the cold, harsh world?

"Here! Give it me," said Violet sympathetically, and took it out of his hand. What was she going to do with it?

"I've got change," she added, with a smile, her face crinkling pleasantly.

He was relieved. His agony was soothed. At any rate the note was saved for the present; it was staying in the shelter of the family. He felt very grateful. But why should she have taken the note from him?

"Thank, you, ma'am," said the uniformed turnstileman, with almost eager politeness as Violet put down half a crown. The character of the place had been established at once by the well-trained attendant.

"I'm sure it's a very nice place," Violet observed. She was a judge too. Henry agreed with her.

There was a spacious Victorianism about the interior, and especially about the ornate, branching staircase, which pleased both of them. Crowds moving to and fro! Crowds of plain people; no fashion, no distinction; but respectable people, solid people; no riff-raff, no wastrels, adventurers, flighty persons.

'It *is* a very nice place," Violet repeated. "And they're much better than audiences at cinemas, I must say."

Of course, she went through the common experience of mistaking a wax figure for a human being, and called herself a silly. Suddenly she clutched Henry's arm. The clutch gave him a new, delightful sensation of owning and being owned, and also of being a protector.

"Oh, dear!" she exclaimed in alarm. "It gave me quite a turn."

"What did?"

"I thought he was a wax figure, that young man there by the settee. I looked at him for ever so long, and he didn't move; and then he moved! I wouldn't like to come here alone. No! That I wouldn't!" Thereupon, with a glance of trust, she loosed Henry.

For perhaps a couple of decades Henry had not been even moderately interested in any woman, and for over a decade not interested at all; he had been absorbed in his secret passion. And now, after a sort of Rip van Winkle sleep, he was on his honeymoon, and in full realization of the wonderfulness of being married. He felt himself to be exalted into some realm of romance surpassing his dreams. The very place was romantic and uplifted him. He blossomed slowly, late, but he blossomed. And in the crowds he was truly alone with this magical woman. He did not, then, want to kiss her. He would save the kissing. He would wait for it; he was a patient man, and enjoyed the exercise of patience. Quite unperturbed, he was convinced, and rightly, that none in the ingenuous crowds could guess the situation of himself and Violet. Such a staid, quiet, commonplace couple. He savoured with the most intense satisfaction that they were deceiving all the simple creatures who surrounded them. He laughed at youth, scorned it. Then his eye caught a sign, "Cinematograph Hall." Ha! Was that a device to conjure extra sixpences and shillings from the unwary? He seemed to crouch in alarm, like a startled hare. But the entrance to the Cinematograph Hall was wide and had no barriers. The Cinematograph Hall was free. They walked into it. A board said, to empty seats, "Next performance four o'clock."

"We must see that," he told Violet urgently. She answered that they certainly must, and thereupon, Henry having looked at his watch, they turned into the Hall of Tableaux.

A restful and yet impressive affair, these reconstitutions of dramatic episodes in English history. And there was no disturbing preciosity in the attitude of the sightseers, who did not care a fig what "art" was, to whom, indeed, it would never have occurred to employ such a queer word as "art" even in their thoughts. Nor did they worry themselves about composition, lighting, or the theory of the right relation of subject to treatment. Nor did they criticize at all. They accepted, and if they could not accept they spared their brains the unhealthy excitement of trying to discover why they could not accept. They just left the matter and passed on. A poor-spirited lot, with not the slightest taste for hitting back against the challenge of the artist. But anyhow they had the wit to put art in its place and keep it there. What interested them was the stories told by the tableaux, and what interested them in the stories told was the "human" side, not the historic importance. King John signing Magna Charta under the menace of his bold barons, and so laying the foundation stone of British liberty? No! The picture could not move them. But the death of Nelson, Gordon's last stand, the slip of a girl Victoria getting the news of her accession, the execution of Mary Queen of Scots? Yes! Hundred per cent. successes every one. Violet shed a diamond tear at sight of the last. Violet said:

"They do say, seeing's believing."

She was fully persuaded at last that English history really had happened. Henry's demeanour was more reserved, and a little condescending. He said kindly that the tableaux were very clever, as they were. And he smiled to himself at Violet's womanish simplicity—and liked her the better for it, because it increased her charm and gave to himself a secret superiority.

What all the sightseers did completely react to was the distorting mirrors, which induced a never-ceasing loud tinkle and guffaw of mirth through the entire afternoon. Violet laughed like anything at the horrid reflection of herself.

"Well," she giggled, "they do say you wouldn't know yourself if you met yourself in the street. I can believe it."

Rather subtle, that, thought Henry, as he smiled blandly at her truly surprising gaiety. He hurried her away to the cinematograph. The hall was full. He had never in his life been to a picture-theatre. Why should he have gone? He had never felt the craving for "amusement." He knew just what cinemas were and how they worked, but he did not lust after them. By long discipline he had strictly confined his curiosity to certain fields. But now that the cinema lay gratis to his hand he suddenly burned with a desire to judge it. He refrained from confessing to Violet that he had never been to a picture-theatre. As he had already decided that the cinema was a somewhat childish business, he found nothing in the show to affect this verdict. While it was proceeding he explained the mechanism to Violet, and also he gave her glimpses of the history of Madame Tussaud's, which he had picked up from books about London. Violet was impressed; and, as she had seen many films far more sensational than those now exhibited, she copied his indifference. Nevertheless, Henry would not leave until the performance was quite finished. He had a curiously illogical idea in his head that although he had paid nothing he must get his full money's worth.

It was in the upper galleries, amid vast waxen groups of monarchs, princes, princesses, statesmen, murderers, soldiers, footballers and pugilists (Violet favoured the queens and princesses) that, to the accompaniment of music from a bright red-coated orchestra, a new ordeal arose for Henry.

"I wonder where the Chamber of Horrors is," said Violet. "We haven't come across it yet, have we?"

An attendant indicated a turnstile leading to special rooms —admittance eightpence, tax included. Henry was hurt; Madame Tussaud's fell heavily in his esteem, despite the free cinematograph. It was a scheme to empty the pockets of a confiding public.

"Oh!" exclaimed Violet, dashed also. She was in a difficult position. She wanted as much as Henry to keep down costs, but at the same time she wanted her admired mate to behave in a grand and reckless manner suitable to the occasion.

Meeting her glance, Henry hesitated. Was there to be no end to disbursements? His secret passion fought against his love. He turned pale; he could not speak; he was himself amazed at the power of his passion. Full of fine intentions, he dared not affront the monster. Then, his throat dry and constricted, he said blandly, with an invisible gesture of the most magnificent and extravagant heroism:

"I hardly think we ought to consider expense on a day like this."

And the monster recoiled, and Henry wiped his brow. Violet paid the one and fourpence. They entered into a new and more recondite world. Relics of Napoleon did not attract them, but a notice at the head of a descending flight of steps fascinatingly read, "*Downstairs to the Chamber of Horrors*." The granite steps presented a grim and awe-inspiring appearance; they might have been the steps into hell. Violet shivered and clutched Henry's arm again.

"No, no!" she whispered in agitation. "I couldn't face it. I couldn't."

"But we've paid, my dear," said Henry, gently protesting.

He, the strong male, took command of the morbidly affected, clinging woman, and led her down the steps. Her arm kept saying to him: "I am in your charge. Nobody but you could have persuaded me into this adventure. . . ." Docks full of criminals of the deepest dye. The genuine jury-box from the original Old Bailey. Recumbent figures in frightful opium dens. Reconstitutions of illustrious murder scenes, with glasses of champagne and packs of cards on the tables, and siren women on chairs. Wonderful past all wondering! Violet was enthralled. Quickly she grew calmer, but she never relaxed her hold on him. The souvenirs of incredible crimes somehow sharpened the edge of his feeling for her and inflamed the romance. He remembered with delicious pain how his longing for this unparalleled Violet had made him unhappy night and day for weeks, how it had seemed impossible that she could ever be his, this incarnation of the very spirit of vivacity, brightness, energy, dominance. . . . And now he dominated her. She attached herself to him, wound round him, the ivy to his oak. She was not young. And thank God she was not young. A nice spectacle he would have made, gallivanting round at the short skirts of some girlish thing! She was ideal, and she was his. The exquisite thought ran to and fro in his head all the time.

"What murder *can* that be?" she demanded in front of a kitchen interior. She had identified the others.

Close by was a lady with a catalogue.

"Would you mind telling me what crime this is supposed to be, madam?" Henry politely asked, raising his hat. The lady looked at him with a malignant expression.

"Can't you buy a catalogue for yourself?"

"Vulgar, nasty creature!" muttered Violet.

Henry said nothing, made no sign. They walked away. He knew that he ought to have bought a catalogue at the

start, but he had not bought one, and now he could not.
No! He could not. The situation was dreadful, but Violet
enchantingly eased it.

"Everything ought to be labelled," she said. "However——" And she began to talk cheerfully as if nothing had
happened.

They passed along a corridor and through a turnstile, and
were once again in the less sensational Hall of Tableaux, and
they heard the tinkling, unbridled laughter of girls surveying
themselves in the distorting mirrors. Henry limped noticeably. Violet led the way through the restaurant towards
the main hall. Tea laid on spotless tables. Jam in saucers on
the tables. Natty, pretty and smiling waitresses.

"I could do with a cup of tea. Oh! And there's jam!"
exclaimed Violet.

Henry was shocked. More expense. Must they be eating
all day? Nevertheless, they sat down.

"I'm afraid I'm about done for," said Henry sadly, dis-
heartened. "My knee."

His knee was not troubling him in the least, but a desperate
plan for cutting short the honeymoon and going home had
seized him. He had decided that the one cure for him was to
be at home alone with her. He had had enough, more than
enough, of the licence of the West End. He wanted tranquillity. He wanted to know where he was.

"Your knee. Oh, Henry! I'm so sorry. What can we
do?"

"We can go home," he replied succinctly.

"But the big cinema, and all that?"

"Well, we've seen one. I feel I should like to be at
home."

"Oh, but——!"

Violet was strangely disturbed. He could not understand
her agitation. Surely they could visit the big cinema another
night. He was determined. He said to himself that he must
either go home or go mad. The monster had come back
upon him in ruthless might. To placate the monster he must
at any cost bear Violet down. He did bear her down, and

she surrendered with a soft and deferential amiability which further endeared her to him. They partook of tea and jam; she discharged the bill, and they departed.

"I don't want to be bothered with my lameness on my wedding-day," he said, wistfully, smiling, as they got out into the street.

CHAPTER IV

Vacuum

FOR potent municipal or administrative reasons the tram-car carrying Henry and his bride would not stop at Riceyman Steps, but it stopped fifty yards farther down the road. As Henry was whisked thunderingly past his home and the future nest of his love, he glimpsed in the Steps such a spectacle as put a strain on the credibility of his eyes. Only on the rarest occasions do men refuse to believe their eyes; they are much more likely to allow themselves to be deluded by their deceitful eyes. The vision was come and gone in a moment, and Henry, who had great confidence in his eyes, did, in fact, accept, though with difficulty, their report, which was to the effect that a considerable crowd had collected in front of his house, that the house was blazing with light, and that forms resembling engines, with serpentine hose rising therefrom, stood between the shop-door and the multitude of spectators.

"Did you see that?" he demanded, sharply but calmly.

"See what, dear?" said Violet, self-consciously.

"The house is on fire."

"Oh, no! It *can't* be on fire."

A strange colloquy! It seemed unreal to him. And the strangest thing was that he did not honestly think the house was on fire. He did not know what to think. But he suspected his angel of some celestial scheming against him; and he considered that she was beginning rather early and that his first business must be to set her in the true, wifely path. Suspicion is a wonderful collector of evidence in its own support. He recalled her agitation when he had decided to tear up the programme for the day and go home earlier; the agitation had soon passed, but during the journey to Clerkenwell it had certainly recurred, increasing somewhat as they neared the destination. Also he recalled her private chat with Elsie before leaving in the morning. At the time he had attached no significance to that whispered interview, but now it suddenly took on a most sinister aspect.

An amazing fellow was Henry. As he hurried, without a word, from the tram to the house he carefully maintained his limp, and in pushing through the crowd he was careful to avoid any appearance of astonishment or alarm. At any rate, the engines, both throbbing, were too small to be fire-engines, there were no brass helmets or policemen about, and the house was not on fire. What distressed him was the insane expenditure of electricity that was going on. And why was the shop open? The day being Saturday it ought to have been closed hours ago.

He strode over a hose-pipe into his establishment. One side of the place looked just as if it had been newly papered and painted, and all the books on that side shone like books that had been dusted and vaselined with extreme care daily for months; almost the whole of the ceiling was nearly white, and the remainder of it was magically whitening under a wide-mouthed brass nozzle that a workman who stood on a pair of steps was applying to it. And Henry heard a swishing sound as of the indrawing of wind. He went forward mechanically into his private room, which, quite unbelievably, was as clean as a new pin. No grime, no dust anywhere! And not a book displaced. The books which ordinarily lay on the floor still lay on the floor, and even the floor planks looked as if they had been planed or sandpapered. He dropped into a chair.

"Darling, how pale you are!" murmured Violet, bending to him. "*This is my wedding present to you. I wanted it to be a surprise, but you've gone and spoilt it all with coming back home so soon! And I couldn't stop you.*"

He did not realize for weeks the grandeur of his wife's act, which had outraged a thrifty instinct in her nearly as powerful as his own. But he realized at once the initiative and the talent for organized execution which had rendered her plan successful. How had she managed to accomplish the affair without betraying to him the slightest hint of what she was about? A prodigious performance! And she had suborned the faithful Elsie, too!

He could not like the cleanliness. He had been robbed of something. And the place had lost its look of home; it was bare, inhospitable, and he was a stranger in it.

"How much is it to cost?" he breathed.

"Well," Violet answered hesitatingly, "of course, vacuum-cleaning isn't what you'd call cheap. But it saves so much labour and wear-and-tear and inconvenience that it pays for itself over and over again. And you know I can't *stand* dirt. And when a thing's got to be done I'm one of those that must get it over and have *done* with it. And it's my little present to you. Shall I rub your knee with some Zam-buk? I have some."

"How much is it to cost?" he repeated.

"Well, it ought by rights only to cost ten pounds for the whole job."

"Ten pounds!"

"Yes. Only as I wanted it done in a great hurry, I knew that would mean two machines instead of one; and besides that, the men expect overtime pay for Saturday afternoons. I'm afraid it'll cost thirteen or fourteen pounds. But think how nice it's going to be. Look at this room. You wouldn't know it."

"Fourteen pounds!"

The wages of a morning charwoman for over three months! Squandered in a few hours! The potentialities of Violet's energetic brain frightened him.

"You aren't vexed, I'm sure!" said Violet.

"Of course I'm not," he replied blandly, admitting the nobility of her motives and the startling efficiency of her methods.

"Perhaps I ought to have told you."

"Yes."

"But, you see, I wanted it to be a surprise for you."

He walked back into the shop and thence outside.

"What do you do with the dirt?" he inquired of one of the men in charge of the machines.

"Oh, we take it away, sir. We shan't leave any mess about."

"Do you sell it? Do you get anything for it?"

CHAPTER V

The Priestess

WHILE Henry was inquiring into the market value of the dirt which he himself had amassed, the new Mrs. Earlforward went upstairs to inspect her best bedroom. It was empty, but electric current was burning away in a manner to call forth just criticism from her husband. The room was incredibly clean, and had a bright aspect of freshness and gaiety which delighted Violet. She said to herself: "This vacuum business was a great idea of mine. Dangerous; but it's gone off very well." Already she realized, though not quite fully, that she had passed under the domination of her bland Henry. It was as if she had entered a fortress and heard the self-locking gates thereof clang behind her. No escape! But in the fortress she was sheltered; she was safe.

According to a prearrangement, certain dispositions had been made in the bedroom. On the bed was spread a luxurious and brilliant eiderdown quilt—Violet's private possession, almost her only possession beyond clothes, cash, and money invested. Her three trunks were deposited in a corner. The wardrobe had been cleared of books, and one chest of drawers cleared of Earlforwardian oddments, and Violet, having doffed her street attire, began to unpack in the cold, which she did not notice.

She hoped that Henry would give her time to feel at home in the chamber. She was sure, indeed, that he would, for he could practise the most delicate considerations. Before deciding which drawers should hold which clothes, she laid out some of the garments on the bed, and this act seemed to tranquillize her. Then she noticed that an old slipper had been tied by a piece of pink ribbon to the head-rail of the bed. It was a much-worn white satin slipper, and had once shod the small foot of some woman who understood elegance. Elsie's thought! Elsie's gift! It could have come from none but Elsie. Elsie must have bought it, and perhaps its fellow, at the second-hand shop up the King's Cross Road, past the police-station. And Elsie must also have bought the pink ribbon.

Violet was touched. She wanted to run out and say something nice to Elsie, wherever Elsie might be, but she wanted still more to stay in the bedroom and think. She enjoyed being in the bedroom alone. She glanced with pleasure at the shut door, the drawn blind, the solidity of the walls and of the furniture. And she thought of her first honeymoon. A violent, extravagant and passionate week at Southend! What excursions! What distractions! What fishings! What tragi-comical seasickness! What winkle-eatings! What promenades and rides on the pier! What jocularities! What gigglings and what enormous laughter! What late risings! What frocks and hats! What hair-brushings! What fastening of frocks! What arrogant confidence in one's complexion! What emancipations! What grand, free, careless abandonments to the delight of life! What sudden tendernesses! What exhaustless energy! What youth! . . . And then the swift change in the demeanour of the late Mr. Arb when they got into the London train. Realization then that the man who could play and squander magnificently could also work and save magnificently! A man, in fact, the late Mr. Arb; and never without a grim humour unlike anybody else's! And he was the very devil sometimes, especially at intervals during the few days when he was making up his mind to cut his corns. . . .

She did not gaze backward on that honeymoon with pangs of regret. No! She was not that kind of woman. As she advanced from one time of life to another she had the commonsense of each age. She did not mourn the Southend hoydenish bride who knew nothing. She had a position now, both moral and material. She could put honeymoons in their right perspective. The honeymoon which she was at that moment in the midst of had certainly some remarkable

characteristics. That is to say, it was a rather funny sort
of honeymoon. But what matter? She was happy—not
as the Southend bride had been happy, but still happy. She
knew that she could comprehend Henry just as well as she had
comprehended the late Mr. Arb. On the subject of men she
was catholic. She could submit in one way to one and in another way to another; and the same for manœuvring them.
Look at what she had by audacity accomplished in the very
first hours of this second marriage! Cleanliness! The
brilliance of the results of scientific cleaning astonished even
herself, far surpassing her expectations.

And the old satin shoe influenced her. There was something absurd, charming, romantic and inspiring about that
shoe. It reminded Violet that security and sagacity and
affectionate constancy could not be the sole constituents of a
satisfactory existence. Grace, fancifulness, impulsiveness,
some foolishness, were needed too. She saw the husband, the
house, and even the business, as material upon which she had
to work, constructively, adoringly, but also wilfully, and
perhaps a bit mischievously. What could be more ridiculous
than an old shoe tied to a respectable bedstead? And yet it
had changed Violet's mood. For her it had most mysteriously
changed the mood of the domestic interior, of all Clerkenwell.
It helped Violet to like Clerkenwell, an unlikeable place in
her opinion.

After a long time, and reluctantly, she went downstairs
again. Nobody had disturbed her—neither her husband nor
Elsie nor the workmen. She had heard various movements
beyond the citadel of the bedroom—ascents, descents, bump-
ings—and she now found the upper floors in darkness; the
upper floors were finished. The shop also was apparently
finished, with the exception of the principal window. She
paused at the turn of the stairs and watched her husband
attentively watching the operation on the windowful of books.
Two workmen were engaged upon it. One handled the
books in batches of ten or a dozen; the other manipulated the
cleansing, swishing nozzle. Both men seemed to be experts,
laborious, conscientious and exact. The volumes were re-

placed with precision. Mr. Henry Earlforward, in a critical temper, as became a merchant over an important affair which affected him closely but upon which he had been in no wise consulted, stood ready to pounce upon the slightest error or carelessness. Well, he found no occasion to pounce; the bland demon in him was foiled of its spring. He moved away, disappointed, admiring, and caught sight of Violet. His face welcomed her appearance. Undoubtedly he was pleased with and impressed by her capacity, in addition to being in love with her. She looked down demurely, perturbed by the ardour of his glance.

"Been putting things to right in the bedroom?" he murmured, approaching her.

She nodded. He lifted his hand to her shoulder, and there it rested for a moment. She wished to heaven the interminable job was finished and they could walk about the transformed shop alone together.

"Look here," he murmured; the men at the window could not possibly distinguish what he was saying.

"Yes?"

He led her to a corner. One of the sacks in which books were delivered hid a fairly large cubical object. He pulled off the sack and disclosed an old safe which she had never seen before.

"I bought it yesterday," said he, "and they delivered it this morning, I suppose." Bending down, he took a key from his pocket, unlocked the safe, and swung open the massive door. "Two drawers, you see, and two compartments besides."

"Very nice, I'm sure."

He relocked the safe and handed her the key, which was very bright.

"It's for you," he said. "A little wedding-present. You must decide where you'd like to have it. If you want it upstairs, I might get some of these chaps to carry it up before they go. Cheaper than getting men in on purpose. And it's no featherweight, that safe isn't."

Violet was startled almost out of her self-possession. She

held the key as though she did not know what to do with it.
She gave a mechanical smile, very unlike the smile whose
vivacity drew crinkling lines from all parts of her face to the
corners of her eyes and of her mouth. The present was
totally unexpected. He had not said one word as to presents;
certainly he had not questioned her about her preferences, nor
shown even indirectly any kind of curiosity in this regard.
She had comprehended that he wished neither to bestow nor
to receive, and she was perfectly reconciled to his idiosyncrasy.
After all, was she not at that moment wearing, without resentment or discomfort, the wedding-ring to obtain which he had
sold its predecessor? And yet he had conceived the plan of
giving her a present and had executed it in secret, as such
plans on such occasions ought to be executed. And he was
evidently pleased with his plan and proud of it.

How many husbands would have given a safe to their wives
so that the dear creatures might really possess their property
in privacy and independence? Very few. The average good
husband would have expected his wife to hand over all that
she had into his own safe-keeping—not for his own use—but
she would have had to ask him for what was hers, and in giving
her what was hers he would have had the air of conferring a
favour. Henry was not like that. Henry, she knew, admired her for her possessions as well as for her personality.
And he had desired to insist on them in a spectacular manner.
She was touched. Yes, she was touched; because she understood his motives; saw the fineness, the chivalry, in his
motives.

When she had thanked him she said:

"I think I shall have it in the bathroom, under the window;
there is plenty of room there."

Her practical sagacity had not failed her. In the bath-room
she could employ her safe, study the contents of her safe, and
take from them or add to them, unsurveyed, according to
her most free fancy. Whereas, if the safe was in the bedroom
or in the dining-room, or side by side with Henry's safe in
the office—well, you never knew! He agreed instantly with
her suggestion.

"If I were you," said he, "I should get your things out of that Cornhill safe-deposit place at once."

The late Mr. Arb had always been in favour of a "safe-deposit place" for securities and valuables. The arrangement was beyond doubt best for a nomad, but in addition, with his histrionic temperament, he had loved the somewhat theatrical apparatus of triple security with which safe-deposit companies impressed their clients. He had loved descending into illuminated steel vaults, and the smooth noise of well-oiled locks and the signing and countersigning, and the surveillance, and the surpassing precautions. Violet had loved it also. It magnified riches. It induced ecstatic sensations.

But Mr. Henry Earlforward had other views. He held that the rent which you had to pay for a coffer in a safe-deposit was excessive, and that to pay it was a mere squandering of money in order to keep money, and quite irrational, quite ridiculous—indeed, a sort of contradiction in terms. That Mrs. Arb should patronize a safe-deposit company had seemed to offend him; that his wife should patronize a safe-deposit company gave him positive pain. Imagine having to take motor-buses and trams and spend money and half a day of time whenever you wanted to open your own coffer! Violet had listened to him at length on this topic.

She was pleasantly touched now, but simultaneously she was frightened again. Standing close to him in the gloom of the corner, dangling the key on its bit of string, glancing at his fresh, full-lipped, grey-bearded, kindly face, and at his bland little eyes which rested on her with love, she was frightened and even appalled. She had made him a present of a scientific spring-cleaning, and he had given her a safe, on their wedding day! It was terrible, it was horrible! Why? Eminently sensible gifts, both, surely! Not more prosaic than those very popular and well-accepted presents, a pair of fish carvers, a patent carpet-sweeper, a copper coal-scuttle! No, possibly not more prosaic than those. . . . And yet, terrible! No doubt she would not have thought them so horrible if she had not seen that second-hand satin shoe hanging on the bedstead by a piece of pink ribbon. She knew that the excellent, trustworthy and adoring man who was the safe-deposit in which she had deposited herself had no suspicion of the nature of her thoughts. And his innocence, his simplicity, his blindness—call it what you please—only intensified her perturbation. He turned away to speak to the workmen about moving the safe.

At a later hour, soon after the workmen and the engines and the hose and all the apparatus of purification had vanished from Riceyman Steps, to the regret of a persistent crowd which had been enjoying an absolutely novel sensation, Mr. and Mrs. Henry Earlforward, who were alone and rather self-conscious and rather at a loss for something to do in the beautiful shut shop, heard steps on the upper stairs. Elsie! They had forgotten Elsie! It was not a time for them to be thoughtful of other people. Elsie presently appeared on the lower stairs, and was beheld of both her astonished employers. For Elsie was clothed in her best, and it was proved that she indeed had a best. Neither Henry nor Violet had ever seen the frock which Elsie was wearing. Yet it was obviously not a new frock. It had lain in that tin trunk of hers since more glorious days. Possibly Joe might have seen it on some bright evening, but no other among living men. Its colour was brown: in cut it did not bear, and never had borne, any relation to the fashions of the day. But it was unquestionably a best dress. Over the façade of the front Elsie displayed a garment still more surprising; namely, a white apron. Now in Clerkenwell white aprons were white only once in their active careers, and not always even once. White aprons in Clerkenwell were white (unless bought "shop-soiled" at a reduction) for about the first hour of their first wearing. They were, of course, washed, rinsed and ironed, and sometimes lightly starched, but they never achieved whiteness again, and it was impossible that they should do so. A whitish grey was the highest they could reach after the first laundry. Elsie therefore was wearing a new apron; and, in fact, she had purchased it with her own money under the influence of her modest pride in forming a regular part of a household comprising a gentleman and lady freshly united in matrimony. She had also purchased a cap, but at the last moment, after trying it on, had lacked the courage to keep it on; she felt too excessively odd in it. She was carrying a parcel in her left hand, and the other was behind her back. Mrs. Earlforward, at sight of her, guessed part of what was coming, but not the more exciting part.

"Oh, Elsie!" cried Mrs. Earlforward. "There you are! I fancied you were out."

"No, 'm," said Elsie, in her gentle, firm voice. "But I wasn't expecting you and master home so early, and as soon as you came I run upstairs to change."

With that, Elsie, from the advantage of three stairs, suddenly showed her right hand, and out of a paper bag flung a considerable quantity of rice on to the middle-aged persons of the married. She accomplished this gesture with the air of a benevolent priestess performing a necessary and gravely important rite. Some of the rice stuck on its targets, but most of it rattled on the floor and rolled about in silence. Indeed, there was quite a mess of rice on the floor, and the pity seemed to be that the vacuum-cleaners had left early.

Violet was the first to recover from the state of foolish and abashed stupefaction into which the deliberate assault had put man and wife. Violet laughed heartily, very heartily. Her mood was transformed again in an instant into one of gaiety, happiness, and natural ease. It was as if a sinister spell had been miraculously lifted. Henry gradually smiled, while regarding with proper regret this wanton waste of a health-giving food such as formed the sole nourishment of many millions of his fellow-creatures in distant parts of the world. Sheepishly brushing his clothes with his hand, he felt as though he was dissipating good rice-puddings. But he, too, suffered a change of heart.

"I had to do it, because it's for luck," Elsie amiably explained, not without dignity. Evidently she had determined to do the wedding thoroughly, in spite of the unconventionalities of the contracting parties.

"I'm sure it's very kind of you," said Mrs. Earlforward.

"Yes, it is," Mr. Earlforward concurred.

"And here's a present from me," Elsie continued, blushing, and offering the parcel.

"I'm sure we're very much obliged," said Mrs. Earlforward, taking the parcel. "Come into the back-room, Elsie, and I'll undo it. It's very heavy. No, I'd better not hold it by the string."

And in the office the cutting of string and the unfolding of brown paper and of tissue paper disclosed a box, and the opening of the box a wedding-cake—not a large one, true, but authentic. What with the shoe and the rice and the cake, Elsie in the grand generosity of her soul must have spent a fortune on the wedding, must have exercised the large munificence of a Rothschild—and all because she had faith in the virtue of the ancient properties appertaining to the marriage ceremony. She alone had seen Mrs. Earlforward as a bride and Mr. Earlforward as a bridegroom, and the magic of her belief compelled the partners also to see themselves as bride and bridegroom.

"Well, Elsie," Violet burst out—and she was deeply affected—"I really don't know what to say. It's most unexpected and I don't know how to thank you. But run and get a knife, and we'll cut it."

"It must be cut," said Elsie, again the priestess, and she obediently ran off to get the knife.

"Well, well! . . . Well, well!" murmured Henry, flabbergasted, and blushing even more than his wife had blushed. The pair were so disturbed that they dared not look at each other.

"You must cut it, 'm," said Elsie, returning with the knife and a flat dish.

And Mrs. Earlforward, having placed the cake on the dish, sawed down into the cake. She had to use all her strength to penetrate the brown; the top icing splintered easily, and fragments of it flew about the desk.

"Now, Elsie, here's your slice," said Violet, lifting the dish.

"Thank ye, m'. But I must keep mine. I've got a little box for it upstairs."

"But aren't you going to eat any of it?"

"No, 'm," with solemnity. "But *you* must. . . . I'll just taste this white part," she added, picking up a bit of icing from the desk.

The married pair ate.

"I think I'll go now, 'm, if you'll excuse me," said Elsie. "But I'll just sweep up in the shop here first." She was standing in the doorway.

They heard her with hand-brush and dustpan collecting the scattered food of the Orient. She peeped in at the door again.

"Good night, 'm. Good night, sir." She saluted them with a benignant grin in which was a surprising little touch of naughtiness. And then they heard her receding footfalls as she ascended cautiously the dark flights of stairs and entered into her inviolable private life on the top floor.

"It would never have done not to eat it," said Violet.

"No," Henry agreed.

"She's a wonder, that girl is! You could have knocked me down with a feather."

"Yes."

"I wonder where she bought it."

"Must have gone up to King's Cross. Or down to Holborn. King's Cross more likely. Yesterday. In her dinner-hour."

"I'm hungry," said Violet.

And it was a fact that they had had no evening meal, seeing that they had expressly announced their intention of "eating out" on that great day.

"So must you be, my dear," said Violet.

There they were, alone together on the ground floor, with one electric bulb in the back-room and one other, needlessly, lighting the middle part of the cleansed and pleasant shop. They could afford to be young and to live perilously, madly, absurdly. They lost control of themselves, and gloried in so doing. The cake was a danger to existence. It had the consistency of marble, the richness of molasses, the mysteriousness of the enigma of the universe. It seemed unconquerable. It seemed more fatal than daggers or gelignite. But they attacked it. Fortunately, neither of them knew the inner meaning of indigestion. When Henry had taken the last slice, Violet exclaimed like a child:

"Oh, just one tiny piece more!" And with burning eyes she bent down and bit off a morsel from the slice in Henry's hand.

"I am living!" shouted an unheard voice in Henry's soul.

CHAPTER VI

The Next Day

THE next morning, before the first church-bells had begun to ring for early communion, and before the sun had decided whether or not it would shine upon Riceyman Square and Steps that day, Violet very silently came out of the bedroom and drew the door to without a sound; even the latch was not permitted to click. She was wearing her neat check frock, the frock of industry, and she carried in her hand a large blue pinafore-apron, clean and folded, and an old pair of gloves. Her hair, in a large cap, was as hidden as a nun's. Her face had the expression, and her whole vivacious body the demeanour, of one who is dominated by a grandiose idea and utterly determined to execute it. She went upstairs, in the raw, chilly twilight, to the narrow room over the bathroom, which, in her mind, she called the kitchen, not because it was a kitchen, but because it alone in the house served the purpose of a kitchen.

Elsie, her hair still loose, was already there, boiling water on the gas-ring. The jets of blue flame helped to light the place, and also comfortably warmed it and made it cosy. Violet greeted the girl with a kindly smile, which was entirely matter-of-fact—as though this morning was a morning just like any other morning.

"Your master's fast asleep," she solemnly whispered; from her tone she might have been saying "our master."

"Yes, 'm," Elsie whispered solemnly.

And it was instantly established that the basic phenomenon of the household was their master's heavy and sacred slumber.

"*I'll* have some of that tea, too," said Violet. "What is there for dinner?"

She had expressly refrained from showing any curiosity

whatever about domestic arrangements until she should have acquired the status entitling her to take charge; no one could be more discreet, more correct, on important occasions, than Violet.

"He told me to buy this bit of mutton," answered Elsie, indicating a scrag-end on a plate, "and then there's them potatoes and the cheese."

"But how shall you cook it?"

"Boil it, 'm. He never has flesh meat, not often that is, but when he does I boil it."

"Oh, well, that will be all right. Of course I shall have to fix things up here, Elsie, and we may as well begin as we mean to go on."

"Yes, 'm."

"And you know my ways, don't you? That's fortunate."

"Yes, 'm."

While they were drinking the tea and eating pieces of bread, Violet nicely pretending to be Elsie's equal in the sight of God, and Elsie gently firm in maintaining the theory of the impassableness of the social chasm which separated them, Violet said:

"I'm sure we shall understand one another, Elsie. Of course you've been here on and off for a long while, and you've got your little habits here, and quite right too, and I've no doubt very good habits, because I'm convinced you're very conscientious in your work; if you hadn't been I shouldn't have kept you; but we've got to start afresh in this house, haven't we?"

"Oh, *yes*, 'm!" Elsie eagerly concurred.

"Yes, and the first thing to do is to get straight and tidy. I know it's Sunday, and I'm as much for rest and church as anybody, and I hope you'll go to church yourself every Sunday evening regular. But tradespeople aren't like others, and they can't be. There's certain things that can only be done on Sundays in a place of business—same as they have to lay railway lines on Sundays, you see. And what's more, I'm one of those that can't rest until what has to be done *is* done. They do say, the better the day the better the deed, don't they?

Now all those books lying about on the floor and so on everywhere—they've got to be put right."

"Master used to say so, 'm, but somehow——"

"Yes," Violet broke in, anticipating some implied criticism of the master. "Yes. But, of course, he simply hasn't been able to do it. He's been dreadfully overworked as it is. Now there's all those books in the bath-room to begin with. I'm going to have them in the top front-room, next to yours, you know. . . . I wish there were some spare shelves, but I suppose we must arrange the books on the floor."

"There's a lot of shelves slanting down the cellar steps, 'm," said Elsie, with the joy of the bringer of glad tidings.

"Oh! I didn't know we had a cellar."

"Oh, yes, 'm, there's a cellar."

Violet enveloped herself in the pinafore-apron and put on the gloves. The bride on her honeymoon and the girl crept softly downstairs, and one by one, with miraculous success in the avoidance of any sound, the planks—they were no more than planks—were transported from the bottom of the house to the top. No uprights for the shelves could be dis- covered, but Violet, whose natural ingenuity had been intensi- fied by the resistless force of her grandiose idea, improvised supports for the shelves out of a lot of shabby old volumes of *The Illustrated London News*. She laid a shelf on three perpen- dicular tomes—one at either end and one in the middle—and then three more tomes on the shelf, and then another shelf on them, and so on, till the whole of the empty wall in the front room was a bookcase ready to receive books. Violet was well pleased, and Elsie marvelled at Violet's magical creative power.

The house was sealed up from the world. Not a door open; not a window open! Hours passed. The sun coldly shone. The faint jangle of church-bells was the only sound within the house where the two devotees laboured in a tip- toeing silence upstairs and downstairs while the master reposed unconscious. Violet filled Elsie's stout apron with books, and, bearing a handful of books herself, followed her upstairs; the books were ranged; the devotees descended again. The work was simplified by the fact that the vacuum-cleaners had remedied the worst disorder on the previous day; they had, for example, emptied the bath of all its learning. At intervals Violet listened anxiously at the bedroom door. Once she peeped in. No sign of life. And the devotees were happy because in their rage of constructive energy they had contrived not to wake the master. The bath-room was cleared; the chief obstructions on the stairs were cleared; and there was still some space available on the improvised shelves.

"We'll move on to that dark corner of the shop floor by the stairs," said Violet, triumphing more and more.

This decision meant still more stair-climbing. When Elsie, breathless, had lifted the first load out of the shop to the top floor, Violet said thoughtfully as she emptied the apron: "I suppose your master *is* still asleep? Does he ring? Is there a bell?"

"Yes, there's a bell, 'm, but it's been out of order ever since I was here, and I don't know where it would ring if it wasn't out of order. He's never slept like this before, 'm."

Anxiety passed across their intent faces. Such sleeping was unnatural. Then they heard his footsteps on the stairs. . . . He had gone down into the shop, probably into his office.

"Better go and make some more tea," said Violet gravely. "Yes, 'm."

The bride preceded the girl down the stairs. She felt suddenly guilty in well-doing. She wondered whether she was a ministering angel or a criminal. Henry stood in the bright, clean shop, gazing at the disturbed corner from which books had been taken.

"My dear, you're ruining my business," he said mildly and blandly.

"Henry!" She stopped near the foot of the stairs, as it were thunderstruck by a revelation.

"You don't understand how much of it depends on me having lots of books lying about as if they weren't anything at all. That's just what book-collectors like. If everything was ship-shape they wouldn't look twice at the place. Whenever they see a pile of books in the dark they think there must be bargains."

He did not say he was sure she meant for the best, nor praise her enterprise and energy. He merely stated baldly, simply, quietly, impartially, dispassionately a psychological fact. And he asked no questions.

"Oh, Henry! I never thought of that. I'm so sorry."

And she for her part did not try to justify herself. In her self-confident ignorance she had sinned. His perfect tranquillity intimidated her. And he was so disturbingly sure of his position. He stood there in his neat blue Sunday suit, with the necktie hiding all the shirt-front, and the shirt-cuffs quite invisible, and his leather slippers, and his trim, greying beard and full, heavy, crimson lips, and his little eyes (rather fatigued now), and he put the plain truth before her, neither accusing nor excusing. She saw that, witless, she had been endangering the security of their joint future. She felt as though she had had the narrowest escape from actually ruining the business! In her vivacity and her proud carriage she was humbled. She came forward and took his hand.

"How cold your hand is, darling!" (She had never called the late Mr. Arb "darling." She had called him "old josser" and things like that.)

"That's cold water," said he.

"You ought to have warm water to wash in."

He laughed grimly. She knew that so long as the gasmeter clicked he would never allow her to heat water on the gas-ring for him. He bent and kissed her, and kept his mouth on hers for ages of eternity. They were happy together; they were bound to be happy together. As for her, she would be happy in yielding her will to his, in adopting all his ideas, and in being even more royalist than the king. Her glance fell. She experienced a sensuous pleasure in the passionate resolution to be his disciple and lieutenant. When Elsie, celestially benevolent, appeared with a tray on the stairs, Violet seized her husband's arm to lead him to the back-room. And as she did so she bridled and slightly swayed her body, and gave a sidelong glance at Elsie as if saying: "I am his slave, but I own him, and he belongs to no woman but me."

"Elsie," she said sternly. "You'd better bring that last

lot of books down again. Mr. Earlforward thinks they should stay where they were." The indisputable fiat of the sultan, published by his vizier!

"Yes, 'm."

She sat him down in his desk-chair, and as she dispensed his tea she fluttered round him like a whole flock of doves.

"Let me see," said he, with amiable detachment. "Did you give me the account of that one pound you had for spending yesterday?"

Outside, London was bestirring itself from the vast coma of Sunday morning. But inside the sealed house London did not exist. This was the end of the honeymoon; or, if you prefer it, their life was one long honeymoon.

PART III

CHAPTER I

Early Morning

ELSIE it always was who every morning breathed the breath of life into the dead nocturnal house, and revived it, and turned it once again from a dark, unresponsive, meaningless and deathlike keep into a human habitation. The dawn helped, but Elsie was the chief agent.

On this morning, which was a Monday, she arose much earlier than in the rest of the week, and even before the dawn. She arose with her sorrow, which left her only when she slept and which was patiently and ruthlessly waiting for her when she awoke. Few people save certain bodily sufferers and certain victims of frustration know the infernal, everlasting perseverance of which pain, physical or mental, is capable. Nevertheless, Elsie's sorrow was lightening by hope. Nearly a year had passed since Joe's departure, and she had invented a purely superstitious idea, almost a creed, that he would reappear on the anniversary of his vanishing. This idea was built on nothing whatever; and although it shot her sorrow through with radiance it also terrified her—lest it should prove false. If it proved false her sorrow would close her in like the black grave.

She raised the blind of her window and dressed; she was dressed in three minutes; she propped the window open to the frosty air, lit the candle, and went downstairs to the bathroom, and as she went the house seemed to resume life under her tread. The bath-room contained nothing but Mrs. Earlforward's safe, under the window, a clothes-horse, a clothesline or two stretched from window to door, and an orangebox and an oval galvanized iron bath-tub, both of which were in the bath proper. The week's wash lay in the orangebox and in the oval bath. It comprised no large articles—

no sheets, no tablecloths, only personal linen (including one grey flannel shirt of Henry's and two collars), a few towels, aprons, cloths, and two pillow-slips. Elsie fearfully lit the ancient explosive geyser, cried "Oh!" and rushed to the window because she had omitted the precaution of opening it, put nearly all the linen into the bath, set the bath on the orange-box in the bath proper, left the bath-room, and returned to it with another "Oh!" to blow out the candle, which she had forgotten. It was twilight now.

In the first-floor front-room, which Mrs. Earlforward called the dining-room and Elsie the parlour, all objects stood plainly revealed as soon as Elsie had drawn up the two blinds. Half of the large table was piled several feet high with books, and the other half covered with a sheet of glass that was just a little small for its purpose. Elsie dusted this glass first, and she dusted it again after she had cleaned the room; not a long operation, the cleaning; she was "round" the room like an express train. When she opened one of the windows to shake her duster the sun was touching the top of the steeple of St. Andrew's, Daphut's yard was un-locked, and trams and lorries were in movement in King's Cross Road.

A beautiful October morning, thought Elsie as she naughtily lingered for ten seconds at the window instead of getting on with her job. She enjoyed the fresh, chill air blowing through Riceyman Steps. Conscience pricked her; she shut the window. Taking crockery and cutlery from the interior of the sideboard, she rapidly laid breakfast on the glass for two. The parlour was now humanised despite the unlit gas-fire. With a glance at the clock, which rivalled Green-wich in exactitude, but which had a mysterious and dis-concerting habit of hurrying when she wanted it to loiter, Elsie hastened away back to the bath-room and gave a knock on the bedroom door as she passed. The bath-room was beautifully warm. She rolled up her tight sleeves, put on a rough apron, and pushed the oval tub under the thin trickle of steaming water that issued from the burning geyser. She was absorbed utterly in her great life-work, and in the problem of fitting the various parts of it into spaces of time which would scarcely hold them. She had the true devotee's conviction that something very grave, something disastrously affecting the whole world, would happen if she fell short of her ideal in labour. As she bent over the linen in the tub she hummed "God Save the King" to herself.

In the darkened bedroom Violet leaned over from her side of the bed and placed her lips on Henry's in a long, anxious, loving kiss, and felt the responsive upward pressure of his rich, indolent lips. They were happy together, these two, so far as the dreadful risks of human existence would allow. Never a cross word! Never a difference!

"How are you?" she murmured.

"I'm all right, Vi."

"You've got a heavy day in front of you."

"Yes. Fairly. I'm all right."

"Darling, I want you to do something for me, to please me. I know you will."

"I expect I shall."

"I want you to eat a good breakfast before you start. I don't like the idea of you——"

"Oh! *That!*" he interrupted her negligently. "I always eat as much as I want. Nothing much the matter with me."

"No. Of course there isn't. But I don't like——"

"I say," he interrupted her again. "I tore the seat of my grey trousers on Saturday. I wish you'd just mend it—now. It won't show, anyhow. You can do it in a minute or two."

"You never told me."

The fact was he seldom did tell her anything until he had to tell her. And his extraordinary gift for letting things slide was quite unimpaired by the influence of marriage. Her face was still close to his

"You never told me," she repeated. Then she rose and slipped an old mantle over her night-dress.

"Oh, Harry," she cried, near the window, examining the trousers, "I can't possibly mend this now. It will take me half the morning. You must put on your blue trousers."

"To go to an auction? No. I can't do that. You'll manage it well enough."

"But you've got seven pairs of them, and six quite new!"

Years ago he had bought a job lot of blue suits, which fitted him admirably, for a song. Yes, for a song! At the present rate of usage of suits some of them would go down unworn to his heirs. He had had similar luck with a parcel of flannel shirts. On the other hand, the expensiveness and the mortality of socks worried him considerably.

"I don't think I'll wear the blue," he insisted blandly. "They're too good, those blue ones are."

"Well, I shall mend it in bed," said Violet, brightly yielding. "There must have been a frost in the night."

She got back into bed with the trousers and her stitching gear, and lit the candle which saved the fantastic cost of electric light. As soon as she had done so Mr. Earlforward arose and drew up the blind.

"I think you won't want that," said he, indicating the candle.

"No, I shan't," she agreed, and extinguished the candle.

"You're a fine seamstress," observed Mr. Earlforward with affectionate enthusiasm, "and I like to see you at it."

Violet laughed, pleased and flattered. Simple souls, somehow living very near the roots of happiness—though precariously!

CHAPTER II

After Breakfast

BY chance Violet went down into the shop just after the first-post delivery and just before Henry came. She was always later in the shop on Monday mornings than on other mornings because on that day she prepared the breakfast herself and also attended personally to other "little matters," as she called them. Henry had already been into the shop, for such blinds as there were had been drawn up, and he had replenished the bookstand, but too soon for the letters. She noticed the accumulation of dirt in the shop, very gradual, but resistless. Although the two women cleaned the shop, and, indeed, the whole establishment, section by section, with a most regular periodicity, they could not get over the surface fast enough to cope with the unceasing deposit of dirt. And they could not cope at all with, for instance, the grime on the ceiling; to brush the ceiling made it worse. In Henry's eyes, however, the shop was as clean as on the wedding night, and he was as content with it as then; he deprecated his wife's lamentations about its condition. Certainly no one could deny that it still was cleaner than before her advent, and anyhow he could never again have tolerated another vacuum-cleaning, with its absurd costliness; he knew the limits of his capacity for suffering.

Violet unlocked the door and let in the morn, and shivered at the tonic. This act of opening the shop-door, though having picked up the milk she at once closed the door again, seemed to mark another stage in the process which Elsie had begun more than two hours earlier; it broke the spell of night by letting in not only the morn but dailiness. She gathered the envelopes together from the floor, and noticed one with a halfpenny stamp, which she immediately opened—furtively.

Yes, it was the gas bill for the September quarter, the quarter which ought to be the lightest of the year. And was not! She deciphered the dread total; it affected her like an accusation of crime, like an impeachment for treason. She felt guilty, yet she had done her utmost to "keep the gas down." What would Henry say? She dared not let him see it. . . . And the electricity bill to follow it in a few days! . . . Unquestionably Elsie was wasteful. They were all alike, servants were, and even Elsie was not an exception.

At that moment Henry limped down the stairs. Violet hid the bill and envelope in the pocket of her pinafore-apron.

"Here are the letters," she said, seizing the little milk-can and moving forward to meet him. "Just put a match to the stove, will you? I'm late."

She went on towards the stairs.

"We surely shan't want the stove to-day," he stopped her. "We haven't needed it yet. It's going to be a beautiful day."

She had had the fire laid in the stove more than a week ago, perceiving, with her insight into human nature, that a fire laid is already half lighted.

"That's all very well for you—for you to talk like that," she laughed, hiding her disquiet with devilish duplicity under a display of affectionate banter. "You're going out, but *I* have to keep shop."

He was dashed.

"Well, you'll see later on. I won't light it now, at any rate. You'll see later on. Of course, you must use your own judgment, my dear," he added, courteously, judicial, splendidly fair.

"Elsie," said Violet, peeping into the bath-room on her way upstairs. "Do you really need that geyser full on all the time?" She spoke with nervous exasperation.

"Well, 'm——"

"I don't know what your master will say when he sees the gas bill that's come in this very moment. I really don't. I daren't show it him." She warningly produced the impeachment.

"Well, 'm, I must make the water hot."

"Yes, I know. But please do be as careful as you can."

"Well, 'm, I've nearly finished." And Elsie dramatically turned off the gas-tap of the geyser.

The gloomy bath-room was like a tropic, and the heat very damp. Linen hung sodden and heavy along the line. The panes of the open window were obscured by steam. The walls trickled with condensed steam. And Elsie's face and arms were like bedewed beetroot. But to Violet the excessive warmth was very pleasant.

"You didn't have any tea this morning," said she, for she had noticed that nobody had been into the kitchen before herself.

"No, 'm. It's no use. If I'm to get through with my work Monday mornings I can't waste my time getting my tea. And that's all about it, 'm."

Elsie, her brow puckered, seemed to be actually accusing her mistress of trying to tempt her from the path of virtue. The contract between employers and employed in that house had long since passed, so far as the employed was concerned, far beyond the plane of the commercial. The employers gave £20 a year; the employed gave all her existence, faculties, energy; and gave them with passion, without reserve open or secret, without reason, sublimely.

"It's her affair," muttered Violet as she mounted to the kitchen to finish preparing breakfast. "It's her affair. If she chooses to work two hours on a Monday morning on an empty stomach, I can't help it." And there followed a shamed little thought: "It saves the gas."

When the breakfast tray was ready she slipped off her blue apron. At the bedroom door she set the tray down on the floor and went into the bedroom to put on the mantle which she had already worn that morning as a seamstress in bed. Before taking the tray again she called out to Elsie:

"Your breakfast's all ready for you, Elsie."

Mr. Earlforward was waiting for her at the dining-room table. He wore his overcoat. In this manner, at his instigation, they proved on chilly mornings that they could ignore the outrageous exactions of coal trusts and striking colliers.

"What's that?" demanded Henry with well-acted indifference as he observed an unusual object on the tray.

"It's a boiled egg. It's for you."

"But I don't want an egg. I never eat eggs."

"But I want you to eat this one." She smiled, cajolingly. Useless! She was asking too much. He would not eat it.

"It'll be wasted if you don't."

It might be; but he would not be the one to waste it. He calmly ate his bread and margarine, and drank his tea.

"I do think it's too bad of you, Harry. You're wasting away," she protested in a half-broken voice, and added with still more emotion, daringly, defiantly: "And what's the use of a husband who doesn't eat enough, I should like to know?"

A fearful silence. Thunder seemed to rumble menacingly round the horizon; nature itself cowered. Henry blushed slightly, pulling at his beard. Then his voice, quiet, bland, soothing, sweet, inexorable:

"Up to thirty, eat as much as you can. After thirty, as much as you want. After fifty, as little as you can do with."

"But you aren't fifty!"

"No. But I eat as much as I want. I'm the only judge of how much I want. We're all different. My health is quite good."

"You're thinner."

"I was getting stout."

"I prefer you to *be* a bit stout—much. It's a good sign in a man."

"Question of taste," he said with a humorous, affectionate glance at her.

"Oh, Harry!" she exclaimed violently. "You're a funny man." Then she laughed.

The storm had dissipated itself, save in Violet's heart. She knew by instinct, by intuition, beyond any doubt, that Henry deprived himself in order to lessen the cost of housekeeping—and this although by agreement she paid half the cost out of her separate income! The fact was, Henry was just as jealous of her income as of his own. She trembled for the future.

Then for safety, for relief, she yielded to him in her heart; she trusted; her hope was in the extraordinary strength of his character.

Mr. Earlforward ate little, but he would seldom hurry over a meal. At breakfast he would drink several cups of tea, each succeeding one weaker and colder than the last, and would dally at some length with each. He was neither idle nor unconscientious about his work; all that could be charged against him was leisureliness and a disinclination to begin; no urgency would quicken him, because he was seriously convinced that he would get through all right; as a rule, his conviction was justified; he did get through all right, and even when he didn't nothing grave seemed to result. He loved to pick his teeth, even after a meal which was no meal. One of the graces of the table was a little wineglass containing toothpicks; he fashioned these instruments himself out of spent matches. He would calmly and reflectively pick his teeth while trains left stations without him and bargains escaped him. Violet, actuated by both duty and desire, would sit with him at meals until he finally nerved himself to the great decision of leaving the table and passing on to the next matter; but as she never picked her teeth before her public, which was himself, she grew openly restive sometimes. Not, however, this morning. No, this morning she would not even say: "I know you're never late, dear, but——"

When they did arrive in the shop Elsie, having had her breakfast and changed her apron, had already formally opened the establishment and put the bookstand outside in front of the window. The bookstand, it should be mentioned, could now be moved, fully loaded, by one person with ease, for brilliant Violet had had the idea of taking the castors off the back legs of an old arm-chair and screwing them on to two of the legs of the bookstand, so that you had merely to raise one end of the thing and it slid about as smoothly as a perambulator. Do not despise such achievements of the human brain; such achievements constituted important events in the domestic history of the T. T. Riceyman firm; this one filled Violet with exultation, Henry with pride in his wife, and Elsie with wondering admiration; Elsie never moved the bookstand without glee in the ingenious effectiveness of the contrivance.

Violet, despite the chill, had removed her mantle. She could not possibly wear it in the shop, whatever the temperature, because to do so would be to admit to customers that the shop was cold. Nor would she give an order to light the stove; nor would she have the stove lighted when the master had gone forth on his ways; after the stifled scene at breakfast she must act delicately; moreover, she contemplated a further dangerous, desperate move which might be prejudiced if she availed herself of Henry's authorization to use her own judgment in regard to the stove. So she acquired warmth by helping Elsie with the cleaning and arranging of the shop for the day. The work was done with rapidity. . . . Customers might now enter without shaming the management. An age had passed since Elsie, preceding the dawn, arose to turn night into day. Looking at it none could suppose that the shop had ever been sheeted and asleep, or that a little milk-can was but recently squatting at the foot of its locked door. Mysterious magic of a daily ritual, unperceived by the priest and priestesses!

Mr. Earlforward was writing out the tail-end of a long bill in the office. He could not use his antique typewriter for bills, because it would not tabulate satisfactorily. He wore his new eyeglasses, memorial of Violet's sole victory over him. She had been forced to make him a present of the eyeglasses, true; but he did wear them.

"My dear," he summoned her in a rather low voice, and she hastened to him, duster in hand. "Here's this bill for Mr. Bauersch; £148 18s." He blotted the bill with some old blotting-paper which spread more ink than it absorbed. "And here's the stamp. I haven't put it on in case there's any hitch. I asked him if he'd mind paying in cash. Of course he's a very big dealer, but you never know with these New Yorkers, and he's sailing to-morrow, and I've not done any business with him before. He said he wouldn't mind at all."

"I should hope not, indeed!" said Violet, who, nevertheless, was well aware that the master had asked for cash, not from any lack of confidence in the great Bauersch, but because he had a powerful preference for cash; the sight of a cheque did not rouse Henry's imagination.

"It's all ready," said Henry, pointing to two full packing-cases in front of his desk.

"But are we to nail them up, or what?"

"I haven't fastened them. He might want to run through them with the bill."

"Yes," agreed Violet, who nevertheless was well aware that the master had not fastened them because he had postponed fastening them till too late.

"He'll take them away in a car; probably have them re-packed with his other purchases. I hear he's bought over twenty thousand pounds' worth of stuff in London these last three weeks."

"Oh, my!"

"And you can put the money in your safe till I get back."

Henry stood up, took his hat from the top knob of the grandfather's clock, and buttoned his overcoat. He was going to a book auction at Chingby's historic sale-rooms in Fetter Lane. For years he had not attended auctions, for he could never leave the shop for the best part of a day; he had to be content with short visits to ragged sub-dealers in White-chapel and Shoreditch, and with such offers of "parcels" as came to him uninvited. He always bought cheap or not at all; but he would sell cheap, with very rare exceptions. If he picked up a first edition worth a pound for two shillings he would sell it for five shillings. Thus he had acquired a valu-able reputation for bargains. He was shrewd enough—shrewder than most—and ready to part with money in ex-change for stock. Indeed, his tendency was to overstock his shop. Violet's instinct for tidiness and order had combated this tendency, whose dangers he candidly admitted. He had applied the brake to buying. No longer was the staircase embarrassed with heroic and perfect girls in paper dust-jackets! And save in the shop and the office all floors had been cleared of books. A few hundred volumes, in calculated and admired

E

disorder, still encumbered the ground floor and the lower steps of the staircase, to the end explained by the master to his wife on the morrow of the honeymoon. Stock was now getting a little low, and the master went to certain sales with his wife's full encouragement. He was an autocrat, but where is the autocrat who can escape influence?

"Now do take care of yourself, darling," Violet murmured, almost in a whisper. "And if you go to that A.B.C. shop be sure to order some cold beef. What does it matter if you do miss a few lots?"

"I'll see."

They parted at the shop-door on a note of hard, cheerful indifference: note struck for the sake of the proprieties of a place of business—and utterly false. For Henry loved his wife to worry about him, and Violet's soul was heavy with apprehensions. She saw herself helpless in a situation growing ever more formidable.

CHAPTER III

International

VIOLET was attending to another customer when Mr. Bauersch came into the shop. She ignored him until she had sped the first customer, who happened also to be "in the trade." According to Violet's code, all customers were equal in the sight of the shopkeeper, and although the first customer was shabby and dirty, and carried for his acquisitions a black stuff sack which he slung over his shoulder, Violet would not abate one comma of her code. Nevertheless, while ignoring, she appraised Mr. Bauersch, whom on his previous visits she had only glimpsed once. She was confirmed in her original lightning impression that he bore a resemblance to Henry. He was of about the same age and build; he had the same sort of pointed beard, and the same mild demeanour; and also his suit was of the same kind and colour of cloth as Henry wore on Sundays. But what a different suit from Henry's! It had a waist. Violet did not like that. Unaware that Mr. Bauersch clothed himself in London, she attributed the waist to the decadent eccentricity of New York. Nor did she like the excessive width of the black ribbon which held Mr. Bauersch's pince-nez. Nor did she like the boldly exposed striped shirt—(nobody except Violet and Elsie ever saw even the cuffs of Mr. Earlforward's shirt, to say nothing of the front)—nor the elegant, carefully studied projecting curve of the necktie. In short, Mr. Bauersch failed utterly to match Violet's ideal of a man of business.

She turned to him at last, as he was strolling about curiously, and greeted him with the hard, falsely genial, horrible smile of the suspicious woman who is not going to be done in the eye in a commercial matter. This was not at all the agreeable Violet of the confectioner's shop. And the reason for the transformation was that she had a husband to protect, that the prestige and big transactions of the great Bauersch made her nervous and that Mr. Bauersch was from New York. Violet, I regret to say, had fixed and uncharitable notions about foreigners. Mr. Bauersch acknowledged her greeting with much courtesy, and with no condescension whatever.

"My name's Bauersch, Mrs. Earlforward," said he. (Why should he so certainly assume that she was Mrs. Earlforward?)

"Oh, yes!" she murmured, simpering. "You've called about the books, I suppose?" Her tone indicated that there was just a chance of his having called about the gas or the weather.

"Yes. Are they all ready for shipping?" (What did he mean by "shipping"? They were ready for him to take away, ready for dispatch.)

She nodded vaguely.

"Those are the cases, no doubt," said Mr. Bauersch, point-ing to the office, and walking into it without invitation.

"People aren't supposed to come in here," said Violet, smiling harshly, as she followed him.

He examined the packing of the cases rather negligently, and then turned to the shelves and adjusted his pince-nez.

"Mr. Earlforward left the bill. I don't know whether you'd like to check the volumes."

Mr. Bauersch appeared to be a man of few words. In an-other minute he had paid down the money in Bank Notes and Treasury Notes. Violet counted and temporarily locked the money away in a drawer of the desk. Strange that this reassuring episode did not soften her attitude!

"May I go and explore a little upstairs?" asked Mr. Bauersch while she was preparing the receipt.

Evidently Henry, as sometimes he did to customers, had given Mr. Bauersch the freedom of the house during Violet's absence. The house was still very full of books, and free exploration was good for trade; but Violet the house-mistress objected to free exploration.

"I'm afraid I can't go up with you now," said she. "I'm all alone in the shop."

"I quite see." Mr. Bauersch accepted the rebuff with grace, and turned back again to the shelves, and then to the mounds of books on the floor.

Having receipted the bill, Violet ahemmed in the direction of the absorbed Mr. Bauersch, who ignored the signal. Then two young women entered the shop, and Violet decided to punish Mr. Bauersch by attending to them. They wanted "sevenpennies." There were no sevenpennies, and Violet spent at least five minutes with them, making a profit of one penny on the sale of a soiled copy of "The Scapegoat"; she displayed no impatience, and continued to chat after the deal was done and finished; she seemed to part from them with lingering pain.

"How much is this?" Mr. Bauersch demanded, somewhat urgently, holding out a volume; he had come into the shop.

The book was a copy of an eighteenth-century Dutch illustrated edition, octavo, of La Fontaine's Tales. Violet, looking at it, inspected it. She did not know what the book was. But Henry had taught her some general principles: for instance, that any book printed before 1600 is "worth money," that any book of verse printed before 1700 is worth money and that most illustrated books printed before 1800 are worth money. Also she had learnt to read Roman date numerals. Indeed she had left Elsie out of sight in the race for knowledge. The price of the book was marked in cipher, inside the front-cover—ten shillings. In Elsie's viceroyalty all prices had been marked in plain figures—largely for the convenience of Elsie. But under Violet plain figures were gradually being abolished; there was no need for them, and they were apt to interfere with Violet's freedom of action in determining prices to suit the look and demeanour of customers.

"A pound," she answered.

"Put it in, please." Mr. Bauersch pulled out a Treasury Note. "We won't haggle. Now I must have these cases sent down to the American Express Company's at once, please, at once. I'll have the books checked there. I've got a pile of stuff collected there, and they must leave London to-night, sure."

"Mr. Earlforward told me you would take the cases away with you in your car."

"Me take them away with me! . . . Well, in the first place, I've come in a taxi. And in the second place, I couldn't put those in a car. And they won't hold in a taxi either. I'll be glad if you'll send them down."

"I'm very sorry, but I don't see how I can send them. I haven't anybody here, as I've told you." She was unhelpful, adamantine.

"Mr. Earlforward isn't in?" Mr. Bauersch's tone had begun to roughen in impatience.

"Oh no!" She swept aside such an absurd impossibility. "But I'm sure he understood you were taking them away." (She perceived, however, that Henry had involved her in this difficulty in order to escape the cost of delivery.)

"Do you know where he is?"

"I couldn't say exactly; he might be at a sale at Chingby's."

"Well, will you mind telephoning to him and saying——"

"We don't have the telephone here," she replied, with cold triumph, remembering Henry's phrase, "those New Yorkers."

"Well, can you send to a garage and get a van or something for me?"

"I couldn't unless I went myself."

"Well, where *is* the nearest garage?"

"I'm sure I couldn't tell you."

Using words in a sense in which Violet had never heard them used, Mr. Bauersch dashed out of the shop to speak to his taxi-driver. He returned in ten minutes. In the meantime Violet had hammered the lids on the two cases. In possession of both the money and the books she had maintained all her tranquillity. Mr. Bauersch had come back with a Ford van in addition to his taxi. He led the driver of the taxi and the driver of the van into the office, and instructed them to remove the cases.

"The receipt, if you please," he said dryly to Violet, who handed him the receipt, but showed none of the clemency due from a conqueror to the defeated.

Mr. Bauersch moralized (to himself) about English methods.

"Why *do* they hate the sight of a customer?" he asked himself, puzzled. "I'll never come into this damned store again!" he said to himself.

But he well knew that on his next visit he would come into the damned shop again, because the shop had the goods he wanted, and didn't care whether he bought them or not. If he could have ruined the shop by never coming into it again he would perhaps have ruined the shop. But it was the shop's cursed indifference that spiritually beat him and ensured the triumph of the astonishing system.

CHAPTER IV

Afternoon

WHEN Henry came home, limping, taciturn and absorbed, in the afternoon, Violet examined him carefully with her glance, and, asking no questions, gave him the written list of the day's transactions, which he always wanted, and which to-day was quite a good one. He, on his part, asked no questions either—he said not an inquiring word even about the visit of Mr. Bauersch; the name and the sum noted on the list sufficed his curiosity for the moment. (Out of compassion for his fatigue, Violet said not a word about his trickery in the matter of the removal of Mr. Bauersch's books.) After a sale he would sit down to his desk and study the catalogue marked with his purchases, and he would transfer the details into a special book; he must do this before anything else. Violet went upstairs, leaving him alone in the office to guard the shop.

She went upstairs to the kitchen and to her conspiracies and to the secret half of her double life which had recently commenced. Although apparently she had accomplished little in the way of modifying the daily routine of the establishment and household, that little amounted spiritually to a great deal. And it had been done almost without increased expense— save for gas. Her achievement generally was symbolized and figured in the abolition of the thermos flask from which Henry was used to take his tea, made many hours earlier when the gas was "going." The abolition of the thermos flask had been an event in the domestic annals. (Henry afterwards sold the contrivance for half a crown.) Violet would have tea set on the table in the dining-room; she would have fresh tea; she refused to drink thermos-preserved tea; she would have plates and bread and margarine on the table. And, con-

sidering that tea—now served immediately on the closing of
the shop—was the last meal or snack of the day in that abode,
none could fairly accuse her of innovating in an extravagant
manner. Still, the disappearance of the thermos flask was
regarded by everybody in the house as the crown of a sort of
revolution. Such was the force of the individuality of Mr.
Earlforward, who had scarcely complained, scarcely argued,
scarcely protested! He had opposed simply his quiet blandness and had yielded—and the revolutionary yet marvelled
at her own courage and her success, and had a sensation akin
to being out of breath.

She had never been able to reorganize the kitchen depart-
ment fundamentally; the problem of doing so was insoluble.
In the young days of the house what was now the office had
been a parlour-kitchen-scullery. The site of a little range was
still distinguishable in it. Henry's bachelor uncle had trans-
ferred the kitchen to the top floor; it could not possibly be
brought down again; there was no other room capable of
serving as a kitchen. But Violet had humanized the long,
narrow cubicle a little by means of polished utensils and white
wood, and she had hung a tiny wire-cage larder outside the
window, where it was the exasperation of foiled cats. The
gas-ring remained, solitary cooker. She had not dared to
suggest a small gas-stove or even an oil-stove, and two mere
rings would not, in her opinion, have been much better than
one. There were things she could dare and things she could
not dare. For another example, she could not dare to bring
in a plumber to cure the water-tap, which still ceaselessly
dripped on to the sink. But the kitchen, with all its defects,
had one great quality—it was gratefully warm in the cold
months. Violet came into it again now, after hours in the
haunting chill of the shop, with a feeling of deep physical
relief. Elsie stood warm and supine, her back to the window.
The two women filled the room. Violet had gradually come
to find pleasure, chiefly no doubt unconsciousness, in Elsie's
mere presence and nearness. Elsie was so young, so massive,
so mild, so honest, so calm. She might be somewhat untidy
in her methods and forgetful, but Violet was extremely well

content with her. And Elsie, though she liked Violet less, liked her. They mutually suspected one another of occasional insincerity and ruse, and for Elsie's taste Violet was a bit over-sugary when she had an end to gain; but their common self-devotion to the welfare of Henry drew them together quite as fast as suspicions pushed them apart.

"Is that all right?" Violet asked, pointing to a bright contraption perched on the gas-ring and emitting the first hints of a lovely odour.

This contraption, new in Elsie's experience, and doubtfully regarded by her, was an important item in the double life of Violet, who had bought it exclusively with her own money, and, far from letting it appear in the household accounts which Henry expected from her as a matter of course, had not even mentioned it to. him. Henry seldom or never entered the kitchen nowadays, being somehow aware that women did not welcome men in kitchens.

"Oh, yes, 'm," Elsie cheerfully and benevolently answered. She had not quite seen the point of the contraption. She knew that it was divided into two compartments, one above another, but why it should be so divided she had not fully understood, despite explanations administered to her.

Violet thought:

"How nice this is! How warm! What a comfort Elsie is! What a dear Henry is! And I shall have my way with him to-night, and having my way with him will make us both happier. And we're very happy, I'm sure; much happier than most people; and everything's so secure; and we've got plenty to fall back on. And how lovely and warm it is in here. And what a lovely smell. . . . I hope he won't smell it till I'm ready for him." She looked to see that the door was shut and the window a little open.

Thus did Violet's thoughts run. And then she noticed, by chance as it seemed, a particle of something or other detach itself from the lower rim of the contraption and fall on the wooden shelf on which the gas-ring stood. Then another particle; then another. She was spellbound for a moment.

"Elsie!" she cried, aghast, desperate, and whipped the contraption off the ring.

"What, 'm?"

"You've not put any water in the bottom part and the solder's melted. You've ruined it! You've ruined it! How any girl can be so stupid, so *stupid*—after all the trouble I took to tell you—I cannot imagine. No, I cannot!"

And she could not. She knew that Elsie was stupid. In two days Violet had learnt more about the contents of the shop than Elsie had ever learnt or ever could learn. She knew that Elsie was conservative, set hard in her ways, and opposed to new knowledge. But she had not guessed that even Elsie could be so stupid as to leave the lower compartment of the contraption without water and then stick it on a lighted gasring! The phenomenon passed her comprehension.

"Stand away, do!" she exclaimed, as Elsie, puckered and gloomy, approached the region of disaster. "I shall have to have it repaired. And I can't cook this now as I wanted to. And I shall have to begin it all over again. And your master comes home tired out and this is all you can manage to do!"

Elsie, though severely conscience-stricken, was confirmed in her opinion that these new-fangled dodges were worthless —you never knew where you were with them.

"I should like to pay for the repairing, 'm," she at last broke the silence.

"Yes! And I should think you *would* like to pay for the repairing, my girl! You *shall* pay for it, whether you like or not! But what would your master say to such careless waste if he knew?" And Violet proceeded with the heartbreaking work of salvage.

"Now pass me that saucer, do!"

Elsie passed the saucer. Violet stared at the saucer, withheld from taking it by a sudden thought.

"What did you do with that egg?"

"What egg, 'm?"

"You know what egg. The egg your master couldn't eat this morning at breakfast. I put it in that saucer, I'm sure I did."

Violet gazed formidably at Elsie. Elsie's eyes dropped and her lips fell and she crimsoned.

"Have you put it in the cage?" No answer. "You don't mean to tell me you've eaten it!"

"Well, 'm. There it was all the time. And I felt so sinking like this afternoon. And I don't know what I was thinking of——"

"Elsie, your master always did say you were greedy! And I suppose you'll say I starve you. I suppose you'll say I don't give you enough to eat."

Violet burst into tears, to her own surprise and shame. Of late she had been less gay, less vivacious and more nervous than at the beginning of the year. She had not wanted the egg for her own need. But she had wanted to eat it, warmed up afresh, so as to keep Henry company while he ate the dish which Elsie's negligence had so nearly spoilt. And now Elsie had gluttonously swallowed the egg. Nobody could make out these servants. They might be very faithful and all that, but there was always something—always something. Yes, she cried openly! She was bowed down. And Elsie, seeing the proud, commanding spirit bowed down, melted and joined her in tears. And they were very close together in the narrow, warm cubicle and in the tragedy; and the contrast between the wrinkled, slim, mature woman and the sturdy, powerful ingenuous young widowed girl was strangely touching to both of them. And twilight was falling, and the gas-ring growing brighter.

And Elsie was thinking neither of the ruined contraption nor of the egg. She was most illogically crying because of her everlasting sorrow, and because, with constant folding and unfolding, Joe's letter, which she read every night, had begun to tear at the creases. Her greed, and the accident due to her carelessness, and Mrs. Earlforward's breakdown had mystically reinforced her everlasting sorrow and eclipsed her silly, fond hope that on the approaching anniversary of his disappearance Joe would reappear.

CHAPTER V

Tea

TEA was late; it was indeed very late—for tea. But Mr. Earlforward, down in the office, gave no sign of hunger, or even of impatience. He had to be called to the meal, and he responded without any alacrity. Husband and wife, he in his overcoat and she in her mantle, took their places at the glass-covered table in the fireless room; and the teapot was there and the bread-and-margarine was there, and everything seemed as usual, save in one point—a knife and fork had been set for Mr. Earlforward and another for Violet. As a fact, the appearance of such cutlery on the tea-table was the most extraordinary phenomenon in the history of the Earlforward marriage. Violet recognized this; and beneath a superficial, cheerful calm she was indeed very nervous and very excited. Moreover, she had suffered nerve-racking ordeals from break-fast onwards. Therefore she watched anxiously for Henry's reactions to the cutlery. But she could perceive no reactions, unless his somewhat exaggerated scrutiny of the high piles of books occupying the unglazed half of the dining-table might be interpreted as a reaction.

The blinds were drawn, the curtains were drawn; electric current was burning, if not the gas-fire; despite the blackness of the hearth the room had an air, or half an air, of domestic cosiness. Violet poured out the tea, an operation simplified by the total absence of sugar.

"Come, come!" Violet murmured as if to herself, fretfully, and Henry glanced at her. Then Elsie entered.

"Come along, Elsie! Come along!" said Violet. "What have you been doing?"

She made this remark partly to prove to Mr. Earlforward that if he imagined she cared twopence for him, or that she feared for the unusualness of the plate covered by another plate which Elsie carried, or that she was not perfectly mistress of herself—if he imagined any of these things he was mistaken.

But Violet, expecting to startle Henry, was herself considerably startled. Elsie was wearing a cap. Now Elsie never wore a cap. And the sight of her in a cap was just as gravely disturbing as the impossible, incredible sight of a servant without a cap would be in the more western parts of London. In a word, it shocked. Violet could make nothing out of it at all. Where had the girl obtained the cap? And why in the name of sense had she chosen this day of all days, this evening when the felicity of domestic life was balanced perilously on a knife-edge, to publish the cap? Violet knew not that Elsie had bought the cap before the marriage, but had lacked the audacity to put it on. And Violet knew not that Elsie was now wearing it as a sort of sign of repentance for sin, and in order to give solemnity and importance to the excessively unusual tea. Elsie undoubtedly had the dramatic instinct, but the present manifestation of it was ill-timed.

"Put it here! Put it here!" said Violet, indicating the space between her own knife and fork, and stopping Elsie with a jerk in her progress towards the master of the house.

When Elsie had gone Violet displayed the contents of the under-plate, and showed that noses had not been wrong in assuming them to be a beef-steak; the steak was stewed; it was very attractive, seductive, full of sound nourishment; one would have deemed it irresistible. Violet rose and deposited the plate in front of Henry, who said nothing. She then bent over him, and with his knife and fork cut off a little corner from the meat.

"You're going to give this bit to your little wife," she whispered endearingly, and kissed him, and sat down again with the bit, which she at once began to eat. "It's very tender," said she, pretending that the steak was a quite commonplace matter, that it was not unique, breath-taking, in the annals of tea-time in Riceyman Steps.

"I don't think I can eat any," said Henry amiably.

"To please me," Violet cajoled again, as at breakfast,

changing her voice with all the considerable sexual charm at her disposition.

"I'm really not hungry," said Henry.

"I shan't finish mine till you begin yours." Her voice was now changing.

She waited for him to begin. He did not begin. The point with Henry was, not that he disliked the steak, but that for reasons of domestic policy he was absolutely determined not to eat it. Meat for tea! What an insane notion! The woman was getting ideas into her head! He saw in the steak the thin edge of a wedge. He felt that the time was crucial. He had been married for little less than a year, and he knew women. Placidly he continued with his bread-and-margarine.

"Henry!" she admonished him.

"I've got indigestion already," said he.

Strange that such a simple remark should have achieved the crisis; but it did.

"Yes. That's right!" Violet exclaimed sharply, in rasping tones. "That's right! Tell me you've got indigestion. You never have indigestion. You never have had indigestion. And you know perfectly well it's only an excuse. And you think any excuse is good enough for your wife. She's only a blind fool. Believe anything, your wife will—if *you* say it! God Almighty to your wife, aren't you!"

Just as the voyager at sea, after delighting in an utterly clear, soft sky and going below, may come on deck again to find the whole firmament from rim to rim hidden by dark, menacing clouds created inexplicably out of nothing, so did Henry find the sky of his marital existence terribly transformed in an instant. All had been well; all was ill. The bread-and-margarine stuck in his throat. Violet's features were completely altered as she gazed glassily at her plate. Henry saw in them the face of the unreasonable schoolgirl that Violet long ago must have been. He understood for the first time that her vivacity and energy had another and a sinister side. He felt himself to be amid formidable dangers; he was a very courageous man, and like nearly all courageous men in danger he was frightened.

"A nice way I'm treated!" Violet continued grimly. "All I think of is you. All I want is your happiness, and look at me! I'm always snubbed, always! So long as you do everything you want, and *I* do everything you want, it's all right. But if *I* suggest anything—look at you! I have to have my meals in my mantle because you grudge me a bit of fire! It isn't as if I.didn't pay my share of everything. I pay my share right enough, and more—you see to that, trust you! But I have to catch my death of cold every day, because we're so poor, I suppose! Oh, yes! We haven't a penny in the world to bless ourselves with!"

Henry felt in his pockets, and then left the room in silence. Alone, Violet busily fed her angry resentment. She was in a rage, and knew she was in a rage, and her rage was dear to her. She cared for nothing but her rage, and she was ready to pay for it with all her possible future happiness and the future happiness of her husband. Henry returned with a match-box and lit the gas-fire.

Still no word. No sound but the plop of igniting gas. Violet sprang up in fury, rushed to the stove and extinguished it with a vehement, vicious gesture.

"No! I couldn't have it before, and I won't have it now!" She pulled off her mantle and threw it to the floor. "If I'm to be cold I'll *be* cold. Here I've been in the shop all day, shivering. Why? How many wives would do it? There isn't another in this dreadful Clerkenwell that you're so fond of, I swear! You're the stingiest man in London, and don't you make any mistake. You think I can't see through you and your excuses! Ha!" She began to walk up and down the room now. "I'm a slave, same as Elsie is a slave. More than Elsie. She does get an afternoon off. But me? When? Night and day! Night and day! Love? A lot you know about it! Cold by day and cold by night! And so now you know! I've often wanted to tell you, but I wouldn't, because I thought it was my duty to struggle on. Besides, I didn't want to upset you. Well, now I *do* want to upset you! . . . And *why* wouldn't you eat the steak? I'll tell you. Because *I* asked you to eat it."

"You know that's rather unfair," Henry muttered.

"'Unfair,' is it? 'Unfair'? A nice word for you to use. So I know it's unfair, do I? I'm being 'unfair,' am I?" She looked straight at him. Her eyes blazed at him, and she added solemnly: "Henry, you ought to be *ashamed* of yourself, the way you go on. What do you think Elsie thinks? The marvel is that she stays here. Supposing she left us and started to talk! You ought to be *ashamed* of yourself."

She dropped back into her chair and sobbed loudly. If Elsie heard her, what matter? In her rage she had put facts into words, and thereby given them life, devastating life. In two minutes she had transformed the domestic interior from heaven into hell. She had done something which could never be undone. Words had created that which no words could destroy. And he had driven her to it. She gazed at him once more, across the ruins of their primitive and austere bliss.

"You're shortening your life. That's what you're doing," she said, with chill ferocity. "Not to speak of mine. What's mine? What did you have for your dinner out to-day? You daren't tell me because you starved yourself. I defy you to tell me."

She laid her head on the table just like a schoolgirl abandoning herself utterly to some girlish grief, and went on crying, but not angrily and rebelliously now—mournfully, self-pityingly, tragically. And then she sat up straight again, with suddenness, and shot new fire from her wet eyes at the tyrannic monster.

"Yes, and you needn't think I've been spending money on servant's caps, either! Because I haven't. I know no more about that cap of Elsie's than you do. God alone knows where she's got it from, and why she's wearing it. But I give servants up." (Here Henry had an absurd wild glimmer of hope that she meant to give Elsie up, do without a servant, and so save wages and food. But he saw the next instant that he had misunderstood her words.) "They're past me, servants are! Only, of course, you think it's me been buying caps for the girl!"

This was the last flaring of her furious resentment. Instead of replying to it, Henry softly left the room. Violet's sobs died down, and her compassion for herself grew silent, since there was no longer need for its expression. She tried hard to concentrate on the hardships of her lot, but she could not. Another idea insisted on occupying her mind, and compared to this idea the hardships of her lot were trifles.

"I've lost my power over him."

If he had only responded to her cajolings, and recognized in some formal way her power! If he had only caressed her and pleaded with her not to exercise her power too drastically upon him. If he had only said: "Vi, let me off. I'll eat just a little bit to please you, but I really can't eat it all. You know you can do what you like with me, but let me off!" That would have been marvellous, delicious, entirely satisfactory. But she had lost her power. And yet, while mourning that she had lost her power, she knew very well that she had never had any power. He was in love with her, but he was more in love with his grand passion and vice, which alone had power over him, and of which he, the bland tyrant over all else, was the slave. She had pretended to herself that she had power, and she had been able to maintain the pretence because she had never till that day attempted to put her imagined power really to the test. Twice now she had essayed it, and twice failed. Fool! She was a fool! She had irreparably damaged her prestige. She had but one refuge, the refuge of yielding. "I must yield! I must yield!" she thought passionately. And the voluptuous pleasure of yielding presented itself to her temptingly. . . . She must submit. She must cling still closer to him, echo faithfully his individuality, lose herself in him. There was nothing else.

Elsie entered to clear the table. Violet jumped up, seized the discarded mantle, and put it on. She was not young enough—that is to say, her body was not young enough—to scorn the inclement evening cold of the room. Averting her face from the cap-wearer, she departed. But at the door another idea occurred to her.

"Elsie," she said. "I must leave you to see to everything

to-night. I'm going to lie down." She spoke in a hard, dry voice, without turning her face towards Elsie. And in a few minutes she was getting into the sheetless and empty bed in the dark bedroom. She must yield! She must yield!

Elsie had had the experience of her own brief marriage, and had seen a very great deal of other people's. Mrs. Earl-forward's efforts to deceive her were a complete failure. She knew at once, on entering the dining-room, that there must have been trouble. Mr. Earlforward's visit to the office during tea was unusual. Then there was the singular spectacle of Mrs. Earlforward putting on her mantle at the end of the meal. Why had she taken it off? The only explanation that Elsie could think of was that Mrs. Earlforward had taken off the mantle in order to have a dust-up with Mr. Earlforward. That was the natural explanation, but Elsie was sure that it could not be the true one. Then there was the appearance of Mrs. Earlforward's features, and the fact that in speaking to Elsie she departed from her habit of looking Elsie straight in the face. And further, there was the uneaten steak on Mr. Earlforward's plate, and the fragment of it on Mrs. Earl-forward's plate. And further, there was the very disconcerting retirement to bed of Mrs. Earlforward. Elsie could not conceive what the trouble had been about. But she managed to think that both the antagonists were in the right, and to feel sorry for both of them—and so much so that her eyes filled with tears.

When she reached her kitchen with the remains of tea, the steak was to her a sacrosanct object. Even the fragment of it was a sacrosanct object; she put the fragment with her fingers on the same plate as the steak, and then she licked her fingers—not a very wise action—and proceeded to wash up. She was still full of remorse for the theft—yes, it was a theft!—of the egg. That incident was to be a lesson to her; it was to teach her the lamentable weakness of her character. Never again would she fall into sin. Absurd to fancy that she did not have enough to eat at Riceyman Steps, and that she was continually hungry! She had more to eat, and more regularly, than many persons in her experience. Appetite was a sign of good

health, and she ought to be thankful for good health; good
health was a blessing. She ought not to be greedy, and above
all she ought not to seek to excuse her greed by false excuses
about appetite and lack of food. She continued calmly with
her washing up.

The steak, during its cooking, had caused her a lot of inconvenience; the smell of it had awakened desires which she
had had difficulty in withstanding; it had made her mouth
water abundantly; and she had been very thankful to get the
steak safely into the dining-room without any accident happening to it. But now the steak did not challenge her weakness. Resolution had triumphed over the steak. Her too
active and ingenious mind became, however, entangled in the
conception of the tiny fragment lying by the steak itself.
She examined the fragment. A mouthful; no more! In the
morning it would be dried up and shrunk to nothing. It
would be wasted. She picked up the fragment out of curiosity, just to see exactly what it was like, and in an instant the
fragment had vanished. The fragment did not seem to go
into her stomach; it sub-divided itself into a thousand parts,
which ran through all her veins like fire, more potent than
brandy, more dreadfully inspiring than champagne.

From this moment the steak was turned into a basilisk,
with a devilish, sinister fascination for her. She ceased to
wash up. She was saddened by the domestic infelicity of her
employers; she was cast down and needed a tonic. She felt
that without some pick-me-up she could not bear the vast
grief of the world. She went through the agonies of the
resisting drunkard dragged by ruthless craving nearer and
nearer to the edge of the fatal precipice. Would her employers themselves eat the steak on the morrow? Very probably not. Very probably Mrs. Earlforward on the morrow
would authorize her, Elsie, to eat the steak. If she might eat
it to-morrow she might eat it to-night. What difference to
her employers whether she ate it to-morrow or to-night?
Moreover, if Mrs. Earlforward had not been upset she would
quite possibly have given Elsie express permission to eat the
steak. Elsie began to feel her self-respect slipping away, her

honour slipping away, all right-mindedness slipping away, under the basilisk's stare of the steak. A few minutes later she knocked at the bedroom door, and, receiving no answer, went in. The room was dark, but she could distinguish the form of Mrs. Earlforward in the bed.

"What is it? What is it?" demanded a weak, querulous, mournful voice.

Mrs. Earlforward vaguely extended her hand, and it touched something which for several seconds she could not identify. It touched Elsie's cap. Elsie had sunk to her knees by the bedside. She burst into weeping.

"Oh, 'm!" sobbed Elsie. "Oh, 'm! I've gone and eaten the steak. I don't know what made me do it, 'm, but I've eaten the steak and I run straight in to tell you, 'm."

CHAPTER VI

Evening

VIOLET laughed in the dark: an unusual laugh, not vivacious nor hearty, but a laugh.

"I'm glad, Elsie," she said, withdrawing her hand as though
Elsie's cap had been red-hot.

Elsie, dismissed, felt relieved, but at the same time she was
disappointed of her rich, tearful penitence, and she went away
with the sensation that the world was an incomprehensible and
arid place. Violet got out of bed and turned on the light, and
the light somehow cured her perspective of a strange distortion.
What! Make a tragedy because a man preferred not to eat a
bit of steak for his tea! Absurd! Childish! Surely he had
the right to refuse steak without being insulted, without being
threatened with the destruction of his happiness! It was not
as if he had forbidden his wife to eat steak. Thus did Violet
try to nullify to herself the effect of her wild words in the
dining-room and to create that which they had destroyed.
Fortunately, Henry did not know that she had retired to bed,
and so she could rise again without loss of dignity. She was
very courageous at first, but when she had finished dressing,
and was ready to go downstairs and face Henry once more,
she was no better than a timorous young thing, defenceless
and trembling.

As for Henry, he was working, and really working, in his
office; but, as he worked, the idea pervading his mind was
that he had had a serious shock. He had won; but had he
won? He had deemed himself to be secure on the throne, and
the throne was shaking, toppling. He had miscalculated
Violet and under-estimated the possibilities of the married
state. He saw, for the first time clearly, that certain conjugal
problems are not to be solved by reason, and that if he wished

to survive the storms of a woman's temperament he must be a traitor to reason and intellectual uprightness. In brief, the game must obviously be catch-as-catch-can. Ah! He was deceived in Violet. Because she would not pay more than sixpence for a needed book, and because she had surpassed himself in sweating a charwoman, he had been fool enough to believe that she was worthy to be his partner in the grand passion of his life. Well, he was wrong. He must count her in future as the enemy of his passion, and plot accordingly.

Then at length the weak creature, the broken reed upon which he had depended, reappeared in the doorway of his office, and she was not wearing her mantle. Henry had in that moment a magnificent inspiration. He limped from his chair at the desk and put a match to the fire, which was laid —which had been laid for many months. The fuel seemed anxious to oblige, and flared up eagerly. Violet was touched by the attention, whose spirit she comprehended and welcomed. All warm and melting from the bed and her tears, she let him masterfully take her in his clasp. And he felt her acquiescence, and the moment was the most exquisite of his whole life. Her frailty, her weakness, merely adorned and enhanced her—were precious, were the finest part of her charm. Reason was not. But whether he had won, or she, he could not decide; he could only hope for the best. Not a word said! They held each other near the warmth of the mounting fire in the office, with the dark shop stretching behind for a background. And Violet remembered how once she had jauntily told herself that at any rate she possessed one advantage over him—her long experience of marriage against his inexperience—and she saw that the advantage was quite illusory, and she was humbled, deliciously rueful! He said:

"I think you've got the key of my desk, haven't you?"

She nodded, gave a precarious smile, and ardently produced the key. The next moment he had taken the day's receipts, save Mr. Bauersch's money, from the tin box which was their appointed place in the top middle drawer, and husband and wife counted them together, checking one another, and

checking the total with the written list of sales already delivered
to Henry by Violet.

"Correct," said he, and was about to open his safe, when
he stopped and added:

"Better get that Bauersch money first. I suppose you
put it in your safe?"

"Yes. I'll run up for it." As instructed, she had trans-
ferred the important sum for safety during the day from the
drawer to her own safe.

"I'll go with you," said he, as if anxious not to deprive himself of her society even for one minute. As they were entering
the bath-room he saw Elsie in the obscurity of the upper stairs.

"Elsie," he called, "run out and buy me the *Evening Standard*, will you? You'll get it opposite the Rowton House, you
know. Here's a penny." His tone was carefully matter-of-
fact. Both women were astounded; they were almost
frightened. Violet had never known him to buy a paper, and
Elsie scarcely ever. Violet was grateful for this proof that
when the greatness of the occasion demanded it he was capable
of sublime extravagance. First the fire! Now the paper!
It was not credible.

In the bath-room, where nobody ever had a bath, but of
which the bath was at any rate empty of books, and very
clean, Henry bent his head to avoid the clothes-lines, and
Violet kneeled down and unlocked her safe. It was like a
little picnic, a little pleasure excursion. It was the first time
Henry had been present at the opening of Violet's battered old
safe. She swung the steel door; the shadow of her head
remained stationary, though the door swung, and fell across
the pale interior of the safe in a shape as distorted as Violet's
perspective had been half an hour earlier. A fair pile of
securities tied up with white tape lay in the embrasure above
the twin drawers. Violet drew forth the right-hand drawer:
there was nothing in it but Mr. Bauersch's money—ten-
pound notes, five-pound notes, one-pound Treasury Notes, all
new and lovely, with a soiled ten-shilling Treasury Note, and
some silver wrapped in a bit of brown paper. Violet placed
the entire mass on the top of the safe, and Henry, settling his

spectacles more firmly on his nose, began to count slowly, accurately, passionately. Violet watched him.

"Why!" he exclaimed with a contented smile, after two countings, "he's given you a pound too much. The bank-notes are all right, but there's nine pound notes instead of eight. One, two, three, four, five, six, seven, eight, nine. Only ought to be eight. One hundred and forty-eight pounds, eighteen shillings, it ought to be all together."

"Well, that's funny, that is," said Violet. "I made sure I counted them right. Oh, I know! There was another pound for a French book I sold him. I forgot to enter it in the list. It was marked ten shillings, but I asked him a pound and he took it."

"Oh!" murmured Henry, disillusioned.

"Yes."

"And he took it at a pound, did he? Well, then, you made ten shillings for yourself that time, Vi." And he gave her the ten-shilling note, a glint of humour in his voice and glance.

Princely munificence! She was deliciously dumb-founded. She had misjudged him. Heaven was established again in the sealed home. She thanked him with a squeeze of the arm, and then put the note in the left-hand drawer of the safe, where were a lot of other notes.

"So that's your stand-by, in case?" said Henry.

"That's my stand-by, in case," said Violet, pleased by the proud approval in his voice, and she snapped-to the drawer and the brass handle rattled against the front of it.

"And I suppose those are your securities?"

"Like to look at them, darling?" She was still warm and melting.

He nodded. He undid the binding tape and examined the securities one by one, unfolding them, reading, scrutinizing, with respect—with immense respect. In each instance her surname had been altered from Arb to Earlforward in an official hand and initialled. She gazed up into his face like a satisfied child who has earned good marks.

"Well," he murmured at last, re-tying the tape. "For gilt-edged, fixed-interest-bearing securities. . . ."

He nodded, several times, almost ecstatic. Yes, he was as proud of her possessions as of herself. Violet was exceedingly happy. He then examined the few oddments in the safe, such as certain receipts, some coupons, the marriage-certificate, the birth-certificate. He smiled benignantly as in a sort of triumph she locked the safe. He was a wonderful husband. No covetousness, no jealousy in his little eye. They departed from the bath-room, leaving the magical income-producing apparatus inviolate in the eternal night of its tomb.

When they had felt their way downstairs again Violet exclaimed, happy and careless:

"I wonder what's happened to Elsie all this time?" Few things could have worried her then.

Mr. Earlforward, having lighted the office, limped through the gloom of the unlit shop to the entrance-door.

"Tut, tut!" His tongue clicked against the back of his teeth. "She's left this door unlocked. She knew perfectly well she ought to have taken the key with her. Leaving the door unfastened like that! One of these nights we shall be let in for it." He locked the door sharply.

"Oh, Henry!" Violet laughed easily; but a minute later she exclaimed again, with the faintest trace of apprehension in her voice: "I wonder what *has* happened to that girl?"

Husband and wife could "settle to nothing" until Elsie came back. The marvel of Henry sending for a paper at all returned upon Violet, and she began to imagine that he had some very special purpose in doing so. She felt the first subtle encroachments of the fear without a name.

"*Well!*" she burst out later, and went to the door and opened it, and looked forth into King's Cross Road. No Elsie. She came in again and secured the door, and entered the office humming. Henry stood with his back to the fine fire, luxuriating grandly in its heat and in his own splendid extravagance. His glance at Violet seemed to say:

"See how I prove that I can refuse you nothing! See what follies I will perpetrate to please you!"

Then the shop-door shook, and the next instant there was a respectful tap-tap on it. Violet ran like a girl.

"Elsie, you know perfectly well you ought to have taken the key with you."

Elsie apologized. She was out of breath.

"You've been a long time, Elsie. We couldn't think what had happened to you!" added Violet, locking the door finally for the night.

"I couldn't get no paper, 'm," Elsie explained. "I had to go down nearly to the Viaduct before I could get one. And now it isn't the *Evening Standard*—it's the *Star*. They were all sold out, 'm."

She advanced towards the office, and in her deferential hands the white newspaper became the document of some mysterious and solemn message to the waiting master. Her demeanour, indeed, showed that she knew it to be such. She had not been reading the paper—that, somehow, for her, would have been to pry—but as she passed under the sole gas-lamp of Riceyman Steps she had by accident noticed one word on the *Star's* front page. That word was "Clerkenwell." Something terrible had been occurring in Clerkenwell. Mr. Earlforward whose habits she knew well, must have seen a reference to Clerkenwell on the *Evening Standard's* poster on his way home, and after careful reflection he had decided to buy a copy of the paper.

"Wait a moment! Wait a moment!" said Mr. Earlforward to Elsie as she turned to leave the office. Elsie stood still. Violet sat on the chair behind the desk. Mr. Earlforward maintained his position by the fire, and created expectancy.

"'Further slump in the franc,'" he read, his eye negligently wandering over the paper.

Elsie had not the least idea what this meant or signified. Violet was by no means sure of its import, but she knew positively that it was bad news for decent investing persons.

"'Belgian franc falls in sympathy.'"

Happily Elsie did not even know what a franc was; but whatever a franc might be she vaguely wondered in the almost primeval night of her brain how its performances could be actuated by such a feeling as sympathy. For Violet the financial situation grew still gloomier.

"'Over a million doomed to starvation in the Volga region.' That's communism, I'd like you to know; that's the result of communism, that is," observed Mr. Earlforward, looking over his glasses and including both women in an equal glance. "That's what communism leads to. And what it must lead to wherever it's tried."

He had suddenly become an oracle. The women were impressed. They felt as if they had been doing something wrong, perhaps defending communism or trying to practise it. Elsie could not believe that he had bought the paper in order to obtain the latest results of communism. She waited for the word "Clerkenwell," but Mr. Earlforward was never in a hurry and could not be hurried. As usual he was postponing.

"'Fatal Affray in a Clerkenwell Communist Club,'" he announced at length. "Ah! So that's it ... Great Warner Street. Just across the road from here. Not five minutes away. 'The Millennium Club'...." He nodded scornfully at the name. "'Girl's heroism'.... Girls in it, too!... Oh! She was the waitress. 'Threw herself very courageously between the assailants and seized the revolver, which, however, Vicenza wrenched from her and then fired, wounding Arthur Trankett in the abdomen. When the police effected an entrance at midnight'—that's last night—'Smith was lying dead on the floor in front of the bar, and Trankett was unconscious by his side.... Vicenza was subsequently apprehended in a house in Coldbath Square.'"

Mr. Earlforward continued calmly and intimidatingly to read the account of the police-court proceedings, and then went on:

"There you are, you see. At our door, as you may say! But don't think Clerkenwell's the only place. It's everywhere, communism is. Ask Glasgow. It's what we're coming to. It's what all Europe's coming to. You may be sure if it's as bad as this in England, it's far worse on the Continent.... Oh, yes! 'The magistrate warmly commended the girl Pieta Spinelly for her heroism and congratulated her on her lucky escape'.... Yes, but she won't always be so lucky. And will any of us?"

Violet was just reflecting that to eat steaks with communism at the door was an act showing levity of mind and not seriously to be defended, when Elsie remarked, with surprising equanimity:

"Pieta Spinelly. That's my cousin."

Mr. Earlforward, profoundly agitated, crushed the paper together.

"Your cousin?"

"Your cousin, Elsie?" Mrs. Earlforward stood up.

The shock of learning that Elsie had any relatives or connexions of any kind, that she had any human interests outside Riceyman Steps, that she was not cut off utterly from the world and devoted exclusively to themselves—this alone would have sufficed to overthrow her employers, who had never since she entered their house, as a novice enters a nunnery, thought of her as anything but a "general." But that she should be connected by blood with communists and foreigners! . . . Communists seemed to have invaded the very house, and civilization itself was instantly threatened.

"Yes, 'm. She's my Aunt Maria's daughter. My Aunt Maria married an Italian, an iceman, and his name was Spinelly. . . . Not as I ever saw them."

"Oh! So you don't see this girl what's-her-name?"

"Shouldn't know her if I saw her, 'm. But I know they always had to do with clubs like. There's a lot of clubs round here. But I'm glad she's not dead or anything. You see, 'm, her being half Italian I *shouldn't* see her! . . . And my Aunt Maria's been dead nearly five years. It must be Pieta, that must. There couldn't be two of 'em. And it was just like her too, because I remember her at school. Oh, she was a one? But then what could you expect, poor thing? But I'm glad she's not dead, nor cut about. Fancy her being in the papers!"

Elsie showed no perturbation. In spite of herself she felt pride in a foreign connexion and the appearance of a heroic cousin in the papers; but the more serious part of her was rather ashamed of the foreign connexion. Mrs. Earlforward informed her that she might retire to bed if she had left the kitchen all straight and ready for to-morrow morning. She retired, quite unaware of the fact that practically she had brought communism right into the house.

All this while the day's takings had lain on the desk, unprotected and unconcealed! Even during the unlocked shopdoor interval they had lain there! The little heaps of paper and coins seemed to accuse somebody of criminal negligence, almost of inviting communism to ruin the structure of society. Husband and wife were still gravely under the shock of the communist murder (of course communists would be murderers—they always killed everyone who had the misfortune to disagree with them) so near to Riceyman Steps, and the shock of Elsie's evil communications; and as for Violet herself, she was further thrilled by the perception of the deliberate dramatic quality of Henry's purchase of the paper and announcement of the news, and by the mysterious man's power of biding his time, and by his generosity in the fire gift and the money gift, and by his loving embrace—all these matters working upon the embers of the burning episode of the steak. Violet, indeed, that sagacious, bright, energetic and enterprising woman of the world, was in a state of quivering, confused emotion whose intensity she scarcely realized. When Henry brought out his safe-key she was strangely relieved, and her glittering eyes seemed to say: "This money's been lying here on the desk too long. Hide it quickly, quickly! Secure it without another moment's delay, for heaven's sake!"

Having unlocked his safe, Henry pulled out two of the drawers (it was a much larger safe than Violet's, with four drawers), and placed them on the desk. One of them was full of pound notes and the other of ten-shilling notes, and all the notes were apparently equal to new. He never kept a dirty note for more than a few days, and usually he managed to exchange it for a clean one on the day of receipt. At the bottom of the drawer containing the Treasury notes lay a foolscap linen envelope which he had once had by registered post. It bulged with bank-notes. Into this he forced Mr. Bauersch's excellent tale of bank-notes. As he dealt method-

ically, slowly, precisely with the rest of the money Violet
wondered how much cash the drawers held. It might be
hundreds, it might be thousands of pounds; she could not
estimate. It was a very marvellous and reassuring sight. She
had seen it before, but not in such solemn circumstances nor
so fully. It reassured her against communism. With that
hoard well gripped, what could communists do to you after
all? Of course to keep the cash thus was to lose interest, but
you couldn't have it both ways. And the cash was so beautiful
to behold. . . . Stocks! Dead flesh! Bodily desires, appe-
tites! . . . Negligible! This lovely cash satisfied the soul.
Ah, how she admired Henry! How she shared his deepest
instincts! How she would follow his example! How right
he was—always!

He said suddenly, but with admirable calm:

"Of course if things do come to the worst, as they certainly
will, in my opinion, all this will be worth nothing at all!"
"This" was the contents of the two drawers. "Nothing.
Or just as much as a Russian rouble. If some of those fellows
across the road in Great Warner Street get their way a five-
pound note won't buy a loaf of bread. I'm not joking. It's
happened in other countries, and it'll happen here. And the
first thing will be the banks closing. And then where will
you be, with your gilt-edged securities? Where will you be
then? But I'll tell you one thing that communism and
socialism and murder and so on won't spoil, and it'll always be
good value."

He took a third drawer out of the safe, lifting it with both
hands because of its weight, and put it on the table. It was
full of gold sovereigns. Violet had never seen this gold
before, nor suspected its existence. She was astounded,
frightened, ravished. He must have kept it throughout the
war, defying the Government's appeal to patriots not to hoard.
He was a superman, the most mysterious of supermen. And
he was a fortress, impregnable.

"Nothing like it!" he said blandly, running his fingers
through the upper sovereigns as through water that tinkled
with elfin music.

She too ran her fingers through the gold. A unique sensation! He had permitted it to her as a compensation for her silly sufferings in regard to the steak. She looked down, moved. . . . With regret she saw him put the drawers back and close the safe. They stayed a very long time in the office. Henry had clerical work to do, and she helped him, eagerly, in a lowly capacity. . . . The crumpled newspaper was carefully folded. The light was extinguished. They climbed the dark stairs, leaving behind them the shop, with the faint radiance near the window from the gas-lamp. She slipped. She grasped his arm. He knew the stairs far more intimately than she did. On the first landing she exclaimed:

"Now, has that girl fastened the dining-room windows? Or hasn't she?"

She had new fears for the security of the house. Not surprising that he had previously breathed no word as to the golden contents of his safe! What a proof of confidence in her that he had let her into the dangerous secret! Suppose that the truth should get about? Burglars! Homicides! (Madame Tussaud's!) She shut her knowledge up with triple locks in herself. They passed into the dining-room groping. The windows had been duly fastened. There was plenty of light through them. The upper windows of the confectioner's nearly opposite, her old shop, were blazing as usual with senselessly extravagant illumination. That business would not last long. She had been fortunate to get the last instalment of her money. The purchaser was a middle-aged man with a youngish wife. Fatal combination! Violet had not found him directly through her advertisement in the *News of the World*, but through one of those business-transfer agents, who had written to her about the advertisement. How right Henry had been in insisting that she should not pay the agent's commission until she had received the last instalment of the purchase-money! Henry had told her that most business-transfer agents were quite honest, but that a few weren't, because it was a calling that could be embraced without any capital and therefore specially tempting to the adventurer. Henry knew all those things.

A tramcar thundered up King's Cross Road, throwing sparks from its wheels and generally glowing with electricity. It was crammed and jammed with humanity—exhausted pleasure-seekers, returning home northwards from theatre, music-hall, cinema and restaurant. Pathetic creatures; stupid, misguided, deluded, heedless, improvident—sheltered in no strong fortress, they! Violet thought of the magic gold.

"Come. Come to bed," she said. "It's very cold here after the office."

He obeyed.

F

PART IV

CHAPTER I

At the Window

ELSIE was cleaning the upper windows of T. T. Riceyman's, and she had arrived at the second-floor spare-room, which had two windows, one on King's Cross Road and the other on Riceyman Steps. (A third window, on Riceyman Steps, had been bricked up, like two first-floor windows on King's Cross Road, in the prehistoric ages of the house.) Two-thirds of her body was dangerously projected over King's Cross Road, above the thunder of the trams and the motor-lorries and the iron trotting of cart-horses; the inferior third dangled within the room. She clung with one powerful arm to woodwork or brickwork, while with the other she wiped and rubbed the panes; the window-sill was the depository of a tin can, a leather, and a cloth, each of which had to be manipulated with care, lest by falling any of them should baptize or injure the preoccupied passers-by whose varied top-knots and shoulders Elsie glimpsed when she happened to look down. The windows of the house were all sashed; to clean the upper half was fairly easy, but the lower half could only be done by lifting it bit by bit into the place of the upper half and pulling the latter down on to Elsie's legs. A difficult operation, this cleaning, in addition to being risky to limb or even to life. Elsie performed it with the exactest conscientiousness in the dusty and cold north wind that swept through the canyon of King's Cross Road.

She could see everything within the room. The orderly piles of books ranged on the floor, and the array of provisional shelves which she and her mistress had built upon odd volumes (still unsold) of *The Illustrated London News*. The top or covering plank had disappeared, having been secretly removed, during the master's absence, and sawn and chopped up for firewood in the cellar; for the master had decisively dis-countenanced the purchase of more firewood, holding that somehow or other the women could "manage"; they had managed. Elsie saw the door open and her mistress enter with a plant-pot in either hand. Violet, all aproned and wearing a renovated check frock, gave a start at the sight of Elsie's legs.

"So here you are!" Elsie heard her voice coming weakly through the glass into the uproar of the street. "And I've been looking for you everywhere!"

That Elsie had been engaged upon the windows for quite three-quarters of an hour was proof that a servant might go her own ways without attracting the attention even of an employer who flattered herself on missing nothing. Elsie wormed her body back within the room.

"Didn't you see me cleaning the outside of the shop win-dows, 'm?" she asked, sedately benevolent. (She could clean the inside of the shop windows only by special arrangement with the proprietor.)

"No, I did not. It's true I've had other matters to think about this morning. Yes, it is! And why must you choose this morning for your windows? You know it's your after-noon out, and there's a lot to do. But perhaps you aren't going out, Elsie?"

"Well, 'm, I was thinking of going out," Elsie answered, bringing in the tin can. "But I thought they looked so dirty."

Here Elsie was deceitful, or at best she was withholding part of the truth. Mrs. Earlforward would not have guessed in a million guesses Elsie's real reason for cleaning the windows on just that morning. The real reason was that the vanished Joe had been famous for the super-excellence of his window-cleaning. This day was the anniversary of his disappearance. Elsie had no genuine expectation that he would reappear. The notion of his return after precisely a year was merely silly. She admitted it. And yet he might come back! If he did he would find her in half an hour by inquiry, and if he did find her, she could not tolerate that he should find "her" windows dirty. He had an eye for windows, and windows must shine for him. Thus mysteriously, mystically, poetically, passionately did Elsie's devotion express itself.

"Now don't *shut* the window!" Violet admonished her sharply. "You know I want to put these plants out."

Elsie's eyes grew moist.

"How touchy the girl is this morning!" thought Violet. "If she had to put up with what I have——"

And perhaps Violet was to be excused. How could she, with all her commonsense and experience of mankind, divine that stodgy Elsie's equanimity was at the mercy of any gust that windy morning? She could not.

She established the plant-pots on the window-sill. She had bought bulbs with the ten shillings so startlingly given to her by her husband, and with his reluctant approval. She had scrubbed the old plant-pots, stirred the soil in them, and embedded the bulbs. She put the pots out in the day-time and brought them in at night; she watered them when necessary in the bath-room. She tended them like a family of children. All unseen, they were the romance of her daily existence, her refuge from trouble, the balm of her anxieties. The sight of the clean, symmetrically arranged pots on the sills might have given the idea that a new era had set in for T. T. Riceyman's, that the terror of the curse of its vice had been exorcized by the secret workings within those ruddy pots. Violet hoped that it was so. But it was not so, and Elsie, in the primeval quality of her instincts, knew that it was not so. The bulbs were not pushing upwards to happiness; they were pushing upwards to sinister consummations, the approach of which rendered them absurd. And Elsie felt this too.

"Were you wanting me for anything particular, 'm?" Elsie asked, rather contrite about her windows and eager to appease.

"Yes, I should think I *was* wanting you for something! How dare you give me this money you put on my dressing-table?" She spoke with nervous exasperation, and produced from her pocket some coins wrapped in the bit of paper in which Elsie had wrapped them an hour or two earlier—the price of the ruined double saucepan, now replaced by Violet.

"Take it back. You ought to have known I should never let
you pay for it."

This after she had most positively insisted that Elsie should
repair out of her resources the consequence of her unparalleled
stupidity! The fact was that Violet, unsentimental and hard
as she could be, and generally was, in "practical" matters, had
been somewhat moved at the sight of the poor little coins in
the dirty paper, deposited in the bedroom dumbly, without a
word written or spoken. Also she happened that morning to
be in a frame of mind favourable to emotion of certain sorts.
She sniffed ominously, glancing at Elsie's face and glancing
away. She could not bear to think that the lovable, loyal,
silly creature had seriously intended to settle for the saucepan
out of her wages.

Elsie, astonished and intimidated, took the money back as
dumbly as she had paid it out.

"I'm that sorry, 'm," she murmured simply.

The little episode was closed. And yet Violet sniffed again,
and her features slowly suffered distortion, and she began to
cry. She was one who "never cried," and this was her third
crying within a week! In truth it was not about the money
at all that she had wanted to speak to Elsie. She said
indistinctly through her tears:

"He's not gone out this morning, Elsie; and he's not going
out. He's missing the sale. He says himself he's not well
enough; that just means not strong enough. And now he's
sitting in the office trying to type, and customers just have to
come to *him*."

The secret that was no secret was suddenly out. There was
in Elsie's ingenuous dark-blue eyes such devotion, such reliability, such an offering of soft comfort as Violet could not
resist. The deep-rooted suspiciousness which separates in
some degree every woman from every other woman dissolved away, and with it Violet's pride in her superior station
and Violet's self-sufficiency. The concealed yet notorious
fact that Violet lived in torment about her husband, that all
was not well in the placid household, was now openly admitted. In an instant Elsie, ardently yielding herself to an-

other's woe, quite forgot the rasping harshness of Violet's recent onslaught. She was profoundly flattered. And she was filled with an irrational gratitude because Violet had given her the shelter of a sure, respectable home which knew not revolutions, altercations, penury, debauchery, nor the heart-rending stridency of enervated mothers and children.

"He's not himself, master isn't," she said gently.

"What do you mean—he's not himself?"

"I mean, he's not well, 'm."

"He'd be all right if he'd eat more—you know that as well as I do."

"Perhaps he hasn't got no appetite, 'm."

"Why shouldn't he have an appetite? He's never suffered from indigestion in all his life; he says so himself."

"Yes, 'm. Not till lately."

"All this talk about saving . . . !" said Violet, shrugging her shoulders and wiping her eyes.

It was a curious thing to say, because there had never been any talk about saving, and, even if there had been, clearly Elsie ought not to have heard it. Nevertheless, she received the remark as a matter of course, nodding her head.

"What's the use of saving if you're killing yourself to do it?" Violet proceeded impatiently.

Violet was referring, and Elsie knew that she was referring, to the master's outburst on communism, with all its unspoken implications. They had both been impressed at the time; Mr. Earlforward had convicted them of sin. But now they were both femininely scornful of the silent argument of the illogical male. What, indeed, was the use of fatally depriving yourself now in order not to have to deprive yourself later on? There was something wrong in the master's mysterious head.

"If you could get somebody to talk to him, 'm, *somebody from outside.*"

Elsie stressed these last three words, thereby proving that her simplicity had led her straight to the heart of the matter. The atmosphere of the sealed house was infected by the strangeness of the master, who himself, in turn, was influenced by it. Fresh air, new breath, a great wind, was needed to dispel the corruption. The house was suffocating its owners. An immense deterioration had occurred, unperceived till now. Violet was afraid; she was aghast; she realized the change, not fully, but sufficiently to frighten her. The gravity of the danger dried up her tears.

"Yes," she assented.

"The doctor—Dr. Raste."

"But do you think he'd let me send for the doctor—for one moment? And if I did send, do you think he'd see him? It's out of the question!"

"You might have the doctor for yourself, 'm. You might send me for him, and then he could see master by accident like."

"But I'm not ill, my girl," Violet protested, though she was impressed by the kind creature's resourcefulness.

"Oh, *mum!* Why, you've been ill for weeks!"

Violet blushed like a culprit.

"What in the name of goodness are you talking about?" she demanded. "Of course, I'm not ill!" They were all the same, servants. They never understood that familiarity from an employer should not be answered by familiarity.

"Sorry, 'm," said Elsie meekly, but still with a very slight benevolent obstinacy, as one who would withdraw and wouldn't withdraw.

Violet stared half a moment at her, and then abruptly walked out of the room. The interview was getting to be too much for her. She could not stand any more of it—not one more word of it. She foresaw the probability of a complete humiliating breakdown if she tried herself too far. A few seconds later she popped her head in at the door again and said firmly but quite pleasantly:

"Now, Elsie, you'd better be coming downstairs. There's nothing else up here to keep you."

As a fact, Elsie was dawdling, in reflection.

CHAPTER II

Elsie's Motive

THERE was only one exit from the T. T. Riceyman premises—through the shop. Once a door had given direct access to King's Cross Road, but so long ago that the new bricks which had bricked it up were now scarcely distinguishable from the surrounding bricks. No one could have guessed at a glance that the main façade of the building had been shifted round, for some reason lost in antiquity, from King's Cross Road to Riceyman Steps; or that the little oblong, railing-enclosed strip of grass, which was never cut nor clipped nor trodden by human foot, had once been a "front garden." The back parts of T. T. Riceyman's provided no escape save through a little yard, over high brick walls, into the back parts of other properties inhabited by unknown and probably pernickety persons and their children.

As there was only the shop exit from the T. T. Riceyman premises, it could not be concealed from the powers that Elsie went forth that same afternoon dressed in her best. Unusual array, for the girl generally began half-holidays by helping her friends, to whom she was very faithful, in Riceyman Square, either by skilled cleansing labour in the unclean dirty house, or, as occasion might demand, by taking children out for an excursion into the more romantic leafy regions of Clerkenwell up towards the north-east, such as Myddelton Square, where there was room to play and opportunity for tumbling about in pleasant outdoor dirt. Mrs. Earlforward nodded to Elsie as she departed, and Elsie blushed, smiling. But Mrs. Earlforward asked no curious question, friendly or inquisitive. She knew her place, as Elsie knew Elsie's. She knew that it was not "wise" to meddle. Servants must do what they liked with their own; they were mighty independent, even the best of them, these days. Not a word, save on household matters, had passed between the two women since the scene of the morning. Mr. Earlforward was still dealing with customers in the office; his voice, rather enfeebled, seemed blander than ever.

"I hope it will be fine for you," Violet called after Elsie at the shop-door. Wonderful, the implications in the tone of that briefly-expressed amiability! It was as if Violet had said: "I know you're up to something out of the ordinary. I don't know what it is, and I don't seek to inquire. I believe in people minding their own business. But you might have given me a hint, and anyhow I can see through you, though you mayn't think it. Anyhow, in spite of the cold wind and the big moving clouds, I hope you won't be inconvenienced in your very private affairs by the weather."

Elsie comprehended all that Violet had not said, and her blushes flared out again.

No sooner had she turned the corner into the King's Cross Road than she ceased to be the "general" at T. T. Riceyman's, and became the image of the wife of a superior artisan with a maternal expression indicating a small family left at home, a sense of grave responsibilities, an ability to initiate and execute, considerable dignity. She had put her gloves on. She carried her umbrella. She had massiveness, and looked more than her age; indeed, she looked close on thirty. If she had blushed to Violet, it was because of her errand, which, had Violet known of it, would have set up serious friction. Elsie was going to see Dr. Raste about the state of health of T. T. Riceyman's. An impossible errand, of course! Fancy a servant interfering thus in the most intimate affairs of her employers. But the welfare of her employers was as dear to Elsie as her own. Her finest virtue was benevolence, and she was quite ready to affront danger to a benevolent end. At the same time it has to be admitted that Elsie's motive in going to Myddelton Square, without a train of children, to see Dr. Raste, was not a single motive. Probably in human activity there is no such a thing as a single motive. For Elsie this day was not chiefly the day on which Mrs. Earlforward had so piteously broken down before her as to Mr. Earlforward's physical and mental condition—it was chiefly the anniversary of Joe's disappearance. The fact of the anniversary filled all the horizon of Elsie's thoughts, and at intervals it surged inwards upon her from every quarter of the compass and overwhelmed her—and then it would recede again. Joe had been in the service of Dr. Raste. He had lived at Dr. Raste's. Therefore, it would be natural for him, if he reappeared, to reappear first at Dr. Raste's. He would not reappear; it was inconceivable that he should reappear. This anniversary notion of hers, as she had often said to herself, was ridiculous. Much more likely that Joe had married some other girl by this time, for Elsie knew that he was not a man capable of doing without women. He had probably settled down somewhere. Where? Where could he be? . . . And yet he *might* reappear. The anniversary notion might not be so ridiculous after all. You never knew. And herein was part of her motive for going to Dr. Raste's.

The doctor's house—or, rather, the house of which he occupied the lower part—was one of the larger houses in the historic Myddelton Square, and stood at the corner of the Square and New River Street. The clock of St. Mark's showed two minutes to the hour, but already patients had collected in the ante-room to the surgery in the side-street. Elsie hesitated exactly at the corner. From details and absorbing talks about nothing with Joe, she knew the doctor's habits pretty well. The doctor was due to be entering his surgery for the afternoon session. And there he was—it seemed almost a miracle—approaching from the eastward! A little girl, all thin legs and thin arms, was trotting by his side, and the retinue consisted of a fox-terrier, who was joyfully chasing a few selected leaves among the thousands blown across the square by the obstreperous wind. The doctor and his little girl stopped at their front-door.

"Very well," Elsie heard the doctor say, "you can give Jack his bath, but you must change your frock first, and if there's any mess of any sort I shan't take your part when mummy comes home."

The dog stood still, listening, and the doctor turned to him and ejaculated loudly and mischievously:

"Bath! Bath!"

Jack's tail dropped, and in deep sulks he walked off towards the railings in the middle of the square.

"Come here, sir!" commanded the doctor firmly.

"Come here, sir!" shrieked the little girl in imitation.

Jack obeyed, totally disillusioned about the interestingness of dead leaves, and slipped in a flash down the area steps, the child after him. Dr. Raste moved towards the surgery, and saw Elsie in his path.

"No! No!" he said to her, kindly, humanly, for he had not yet had time to lose his fatherhood. "This won't do, you know. You must take your turn with the rest." He raised his hand in protest. He was acquainted with all the wiles of patients who wanted illicitly to forestall other patients.

"It isn't for myself, sir," said Elsie, with puckered brow, very nervous. "It's for Mr. Earlforward—at least, Mrs. Earlforward."

"Oh!" The doctor halted.

"You don't remember me, sir. Mrs. Sprickett, sir. Elsie, sir."

"Yes, of course." He ought to have proceeded: "By the way, Elsie, Joe's come back to-day." It would have been too wonderful if he had said that. But he didn't. He merely said: "Well, what's it all about?" somewhat impatiently, for at that moment the clock struck.

"Mr. Earlforward's that bad, sir. Can't fancy his food. And Mrs. Earlforward's bad, too——"

"Mrs. Earlforward? Is he married, then?"

"Oh, yes, sir. He married Mrs. Arb, as was; she kept that confectioner's shop opposite in the Steps. But she sold it. And I'm the servant, sir, now. It'll soon be a year ago, sir."

"Really, really! All right. I'll look in—some time before six. Tell them I'll look in."

"Well, sir," said Elsie, hesitating and blushing very red, "missis didn't exactly send me, in a manner of speaking. She says master won't have a doctor, she says. But I was thinking if you could——"

"Do you mean to say you've come up here to tell me about your master and mistress without orders?"

" Well, sir——"

"But—but—but—but—but," Dr. Raste spluttered with the utmost rapidity, startled for once out of his inhuman imperturbability by this monstrous act of Elsie's. He had no child nor dog now. He was the medico chemically pure. "Did you suppose that I can come like that without being called in? I never heard of such a thing. What next, I wonder?"

"He's very bad, sir, master is."

The slim little man stood up threateningly against Elsie's mighty figure.

"What do I care? If people need a doctor, they must send for him."

Dr. Raste walked off down New River Street, but after a few steps turned again.

"Haven't they got any friends you could speak to?" he asked in a tone still hard, but with a touch of comprehending friendliness in it. This touch brought tears to Elsie's silly eyes.

"No, sir."

"No friends?"

"No, sir."

"Nobody ever calls?"

"No, sir."

"And they never go out?"

"No, sir."

"Not even to the cinema, and so on?"

"Oh, never, sir."

"Well, I'm very sorry, but I can't do anything." He left her and leapt up his surgery steps.

Not a word about Joe. Not a word, even, of inquiry! And yet he knew that Joe and she had been keeping company! And he had been so fond of Joe. He had thought the world of Joe. He might, at least, have said: "Seen anything of poor

Joe lately?" But nothing! Nothing! Joe might never have existed for all the interest the doctor showed in him. It was desolating. She was a fool. She was a fool to try to get the doctor to call without a proper summons, and she was thrice a fool to have hoped or fancied that Joe would turn up again, on either the anniversary of his vanishing or any other day. The reaction from foolish hope to despair was terrible. She had known that it would be. The whole sky fell down on her and overwhelmed her in choking folds of night, and there was not a gleam anywhere. No glimmer for T. T. Riceyman's. No glimmer for herself. . . . And then she did detect a pin-point of light. The day was not yet finished. Joe might still . . . Renewal of utter foolishness!

CHAPTER III

Charity

A DRAMATIC event occurred that same afternoon at the
shop. Violet and Henry were together in the office,
where the electricity had just been turned on; the shop itself
was still depending on nature for light, and lay somewhat
obscure in the dusk. Husband and wife were in an affectionate mood, for Violet as usual had been beaten by the man's
extraordinary soft obstinacy. She had had more than one
scene of desperation with him about his health and his treatment of himself, but nobody can keep on fighting a cushion for
ever. Henry had worn her down into a good temper, into
a condition of reassurance and even optimism. He had, in
fact, by patience convinced her that his indisposition was
temporary and such as none can hope to escape; and that he
undoubtedly possessed a constitution of iron. The absence
of Elsie helped the intimacy of the pair; they enjoyed being
alone, unobserved, free from the constraint of the eyes of a
third person who was here, there and everywhere. The
trouble was that as soon as the affectionate mood had been
established Violet wanted to begin her tactics and her antics all
over again.

"You know, darling," she said, playful and serious, sitting
on the edge of the desk by his side in a manner most un-
matronly. "Either you eat to-morrow, or I shall have the
doctor in. Oh! I shall have the doctor in! It's for you to
decide, but I've made up my mind. You must admit——"

And then the shop door opened and someone entered.
Violet sprang off the desk to the switches, illuminated the shop,
and beheld Dr. Raste. Henry also beheld Dr. Raste. Although a perfectly innocent woman, Violet's face at once
changed to that of a wicked conspirator who has been caught

in the act. Try as she would she could not get rid of that demeanour of guilt, and the more she tried the less she succeeded. She dared not look at Henry. Certainly she could not murmur to Henry: "I swear to you I didn't send for him. His coming's just as much a surprise to me as it is to you." She thought: "This is that girl Elsie's doing." And she was angry and resentful against Elsie, and yet timorously glad that Elsie had been interfering. What Henry was thinking no one could guess. Henry's mind to him a kingdom was, and a kingdom never invaded. All that could be positively stated of Henry was that the moment he recognized the doctor he rose vigorously from his chair and limped about with vivacity to prove that he was not an invalid, or in any way in need of any doctor. And, strange to say, he really felt quite well. Dr. Raste startled Violet by offering to shake hands.

"Ha! How d'ye do, Mrs. Earlforward," said he, in his sprightly, professional, high-voiced style. "Not seen you for a long time."

Violet recalled the Sunday morning in Riceyman Square when he had spoken to Henry on the pavement. She was happy then, and expectant of happiness. She was girlish then, exuberant, dominating, self-willed, free. None could withstand her. A year ago! The change in twelve months suddenly presented itself to her with a sinister significance; but she imagined that the change was confined to her circumstances, and that an unchanged Violet had survived.

The doctor with his fresh eyes saw a shrunken woman, subject to some kind of neurosis which he could not diagnose. He greeted the oncoming Mr. Earlforward, and shook a hand of parchment. Mr. Earlforward's appearance indeed astonished him, and he said to himself that perhaps he had done well to call, and that anyhow Elsie had not exaggerated her report. Mr. Earlforward was worse than shrunken—he was emaciated; his jaws were hollowed, his little eyes had receded, his complexion was greyish, his lips were pale and dry—the lower lip had lost its heavy fullness; his ears were nearly white. And there he was moving nervously about in the determination to be in excellent health in the presence of the doctor.

Amazing, thought Dr. Raste, that Mrs. Earlforward had not summoned medical assistance weeks earlier! But then Mrs. Earlforward saw her husband every day and nearly all day. Amazing that no customer had dropped a word of alarm! But then Mr. Earlforward's amiable and bland relations with customers were not such as to permit any kind of intimacy. You got a certain distance with Mr. Earlforward, but you never got any further.

"You remember I bought a Shakspere here last year," Dr. Raste began cheerily, and somewhat loudly. (He often spoke more loudly than he need: result of imposing himself on the resistant stupidity of the proletariat.) Relief spread through the shop like a sweet odour. The professional man's visit was a pure coincidence after all. Violet ceased to look guilty. Henry ceased to ape the person of vigorous health.

"Yes, yes," said Mr. Earlforward; and to his wife: "Just reach down that 'Shakspere with Illustrations,' will you?"

"Shakspere with Illustrations," was the shop's title for the work (Valpy's edition of Shakspere's plays and poems), because these three words were the only words on the binding.

"You don't mean to say you've not sold it yet—a year, isn't it?" cried Dr. Raste.

And Mr. Earlforward recalled from their previous interview in the shop an impression that the doctor was apt to be impudent. What right had the man to express surprise at the work not having been sold? Mr. Earlforward had in stock books bought ten years ago, fifteen years ago.

"I could have sold it," said he. "But the truth is I've been keeping it for you. I felt sure you'd be looking in one of these days. I meant to drop you a postcard to say I'd found it; but somehow——"

All this was true. For at least ten months Mr. Earlforward had intended to drop the postcard, and had never dropped it. Yet his conviction that one day he would drop it had remained fresh and strong throughout the period.

"Here! It's up in that corner, my dear," said Mr. Earlforward.

"Yes, I know. I'm just going to get the steps."

"Where are they? They ought to be here."

"I don't know. Elsie must have had them for her windows, and forgotten to bring them back."

"Tut, tut!" Mr. Earlforward blandly expostulated.

"Shakspere's been having considerable success in my house," Dr. Raste went on, when the two men were alone, with an arch smile at his own phrasing. "You'd scarcely believe it, but my little daughter simply devours him. And as it's her birthday next week I thought I'd give her my Globe edition for herself, and get another one with a wee bit larger type for myself. My eyes aren't what they were. . . . Simply devours him! Scarcely believe it, would you?" The doctor was growing human. His eyes sparkled with ingenuous paternal pride. Then he checked himself.

"I notice your old clock isn't going," said he, in a more conventional, a conversation-making tone, and glanced at his wrist.

"No," Mr. Earlforward quietly admitted, thinking: "What's it got to do with you—my 'old clock' not going?" The clock had not gone for months.

Violet, who had further illuminated the shop as she passed out, was rather long in returning, partly because she had had to hunt for the steps, and partly because she had popped into the bedroom to see that it was in order. Dr. Raste gallantly took the volumes from her as she stood half-way up the steps.

"Fifteen volumes—that's right," said Mr. Earlforward. "I told you there were eight, didn't I?"

"Did you?" said Dr. Raste, wondering at the bookseller's memory.

"Yes. I was mixing it up with another edition. Easy to make a mistake of that kind. Well, just look at it. Biography. Notes. Beautiful clear type. Nice, modest binding, in very good taste. Light and handy to hold. Clean as a pin. Nearly two hundred illustrations—from the Boydell edition. I told you Flaxman's illustrations, didn't I? Yes, I did. That was wrong. I somehow got the idea they were Flaxman's because they're in outline. But I see there's quite a selection of artists." He peered at the names engraved in microscopic characters under the illustrations, and passed one volume after volume to the prospective customer. "Pretty edition."

A silence. Violet stood attendant—an acolyte, submissive, watchful—while Henry did business.

"I'm afraid it'll be too dear for my purse," said the doctor, affrighted by the thought of nearly two hundred illustrations from Boydell.

"Twenty-five shillings."

"I'd better take it," said the doctor, looking up from the books into Mr. Earlforward's little eyes; he was startled at the lowness of the price, and immediately counted out the money—two notes and two new half-crowns, which Mr. Earlforward gazed at passionately, and in a bravura of self-control left lying on the desk.

"Make them up into two parcels, will you?" said the doctor. "I'll carry them home myself. I suppose you wouldn't be able to deliver to-night? Too late?"

"Yes. Too late to-night, I'm afraid," answered Mr. Earlforward calmly, well aware that he had long since ceased to deliver any goods under any circumstances. "My dear, some nice brown paper and string. Oh! The string's here, isn't it?" He bent down to a drawer of the desk, and drew out a tangle of all manner of pieces of string.

Violet now became important in the episode, and took charge of the wrapping; her mien showed a conviction that she could make up a parcel as well as her husband.

"Hospitals are getting in a bad way," said Dr. Raste, and Mr. Earlforward thought to himself that the doctor was one of those distressing persons who from nervousness could not endure a silence.

"Yes?"

"Yes. Haven't you read about it in the papers?"

"Well, I may have seen something about it," said Mr. Earlforward. But he had not seen anything about it, nor did he care anything about it. He held the common view that hospitals were maintained by magic, or if not by magic, then by the cheques of millionaires in great houses in the West

End who paid subscriptions as they paid their rates and taxes.

"Yes. The London Hospital—our largest hospital—unparalleled work in the East End, you know—the London's thinking of closing a hundred beds. A calamity, but there seems to be no alternative. My wife's interesting herself in Lord Knutsford's special effort to save the beds; she used to be on the staff. I was just wondering whether you'd care to give me something for her list. . . . I thought I might mention it—as I'm not here professionally. Here as a customer, you see." He gave one of his little, nervous laughs.

Mr. Earlforward perceived that the doctor had not been merely breaking a silence. He perceived also that Violet, mysteriously excited by the name of the legendary subscription-collecting peer who directed the London Hospital, was "willing" him to practise charity on this occasion. He keenly regretted, as the doctor developed his subject, that he had left the price of the Shakspere on the desk. There it lay, waiting to be given, asking to be given! There it lay and could not be ignored. The doctor was, of course, being impudent again; but there the money lay. Half a crown? Too little. Two half-crowns, those bright and lovely objects? Too little—or at any rate too little so long as the notes lay beside them. A note? Impossible! Fantastic! The situation was desperate, and Mr. Earlforward in agony. He could not in decency refuse—he a Londoner, fond of London and its institutions—he an established tradesman; neither could he part with his money. He was about to martyrize himself; his hand, each finger separately suffering, hovered over one of the notes, when deliverance occurred to him.

"I'll tell you what I'll do," said he, and picked up a thin, tattered, quarto volume that was lying on the desk. "I'll make you a sporting offer. Here's one of the earliest collected editions of Gray's Poems."

"Gray? Gray?" reflected the doctor, and aloud: "Elegy in a Country Churchyard sort of thing?"

"Yes. This is the Glasgow edition, and I can't remember now whether it or the London edition was the first—the first collected edition, I mean. They are both dated 1768. I'll give you this for your hospital. You take it to Sotherans or Bain, and see what it'll fetch."

The doctor opened the book.

> "'Full many a flower is born to blush unseen
> And waste its sweetness on the desart air.'"

he read. "Funny way of spelling 'desert,' *a*, r, t. But this is very interesting. 'Full many a flower——' So that's Gray, is it? Very interesting." He was quite uplifted by the sight of familiar words in an old book. "It's very clean *in*side. Suppose it's worth a lot of money. I'm sure you're very generous, very generous indeed." Violet paused in making up the second parcel.

"Well," said Mr. Earlforward, uplifted in his turn by reason of the epithet "generous" applied to him. "I don't know without inquiring just what it *is* worth. That's the sporting offer."

"I wouldn't mind giving a couple of pounds for it myself. I should like it.

> "'Far from the madding crowd——,'

"Well, well! And one of the earlier editions, you say?"

"Not earliest of the Elegy. Earliest of the collected poems."

"Just so! Just so! Two pounds a fair price?"

"I'm afraid it's worth more than that, at the worst," said Mr. Earlforward, suddenly grieved. He saw to what an extent he was making a fool of himself—losing pounds in order to save a ten-shilling note! Ridiculous! Idiotic! Mad! True, he had bought the book for ten shillings, and he strove to regard the transaction from the angle of his own disbursement. But he could not deny that he was losing pounds. Yes, pounds and pounds. Still, he could not have let the ten-shilling note go. A ten-shilling note was a treasure, whereas a book was only a book. Illogical, but instinct was more powerful than logic.

"Ah!" said the doctor. "If it's worth more than two

pounds I must sell it. You're generous. Mr. Earlforward, you're generous. Thank you."

Violet rearranged the second parcel, including the Gray in it, while Dr. Raste expanded further in gratitude.

"That type won't strain anybody's eyes," Mr. Earlforward commented on the Gray as it disappeared within brown paper.

"No."

"I'm thankful to say *my* eyesight doesn't give me any trouble now."

"Um!" said the doctor, gazing at the bookseller, and taking the chance to feel his way towards the matter which had brought him into the shop. "I shouldn't say you were looking *quite* the man you were when I saw you last."

"No, he is not!" Violet put in eagerly.

"Oh! I'm all right," Mr. Earlforward, defending himself against yet another example of the doctor's impudence. "All I want is more exercise, and I can't get that because of my knee, you know."

"Yes," said the doctor. "I've always noticed you limp. You ought to go to Barker. I shouldn't be surprised if he could put you right in ten minutes. Not a qualified man, of course; but wonderful cures! . . . You might never limp again."

"But he charges very heavy, doesn't he? I've heard of fifty pounds."

"I don't know. Supposing he does? Well worth it, isn't it, to be cured? What's money?"

Mr. Earlforward made no reply to this silly question. Fifty pounds, or anything like it, for just pulling your knee about! "What was money," indeed! He seized the money on the table. The doctor understood himself to have been definitely repulsed. Being a philosopher, he felt resigned. He had done what he could at an expense of twenty-five shillings. He lodged one of the parcels under his left arm and he took the other in his left hand and assumed a demeanour, compulsory in a gentleman, to indicate to the world that the parcels were entirely without weight, and that he was carrying them out of caprice and not from necessity.

"Here, doctor," Violet most unexpectedly exclaimed. "As you are here I think I'll consult you."

"Not about me! Not about me!" Mr. Earlforward protested plaintively, imploringly, and yet implacably.

Violet leaned over him with an endearment.

"No, darling, not about you," she cooed. "About myself."

"I didn't know there was anything particular wrong with you."

"Didn't you?" said Violet in a strange tone at once dry and affectionate. "Elsie did. Will you come upstairs, doctor?" She was no longer the packer of books. She had initiative, authority, dominion. Horribly suspecting her duplicity, Henry watched her leave the office in front of the doctor, who had set down his parcels. Never, never, would he have a doctor!

CHAPTER IV

No Verdict

"WHAT do you think of Mr. Earlforward's health?"
Violet demanded peremptorily, in the bedroom.
Her features were alive with urgent emotion. She almost
intimidated the doctor.

"Ha!" he retorted defensively, with an explosive jerk.
"I haven't examined him. I have—not—examined him.
He strikes me as under-nourished."

"And he is. He refuses food."

"But why does he refuse food? There must be some cause."

"It's because he's set on being economical. He's got
drawers full of money, and so have I—at least, I've got a good
income of my own. But there you are. He won't eat, he
won't eat. He won't eat enough, do *what* I will."

"Is that the only reason?"

"Of course it is. He's never had indigestion in his life."

"Um! Your maid, what's her name, seems to be pretty
well nourished, at all events."

"Have you been seeing her?" Violet inquired sharply,
her suspicion leaping up.

The doctor appreciated his own great careless indiscretion,
and answered with admirable deceitful nonchalance:

"I noticed her one day last week in passing. At least, I
took it to be her."

Violet left the point there.

The electric light blazed down upon them; it had no shade;
not a single light in the house had a shade. It showed harshly,
realistically, Violet half leaning against the foot of the bed, and
Dr. Raste, upright as when in uniform he used to give orders
in Palestine, on the rag hearthrug. Violet's baffled energy
raged within her. She had at hand all the materials for tranquil happiness—affection, money, temperament, sagacity, an

agreeable occupation—and they were stultified by the mysterious, morbid, absurd, inexcusable and triumphant volition of her loving husband. Instead of happiness she felt doom— doom closing in on her, on him, on the sentient house.

"My husband is a miser. I've encouraged him for the sake of peace. And so now you know, doctor!"

An astounding confession to a stranger, a man to whom she had scarcely spoken before! But it relieved her. She made it with gusto, with passion. She had begun candour with Elsie in the morning; she was growing used to it. The domestic atmosphere itself had changed within six hours. That which had been tacitly denied for months was now admitted openly. Truth had burst out. A few minutes earlier—vain chatter about hospitals, trifling and vain commercial transactions, make-believes, incredible futilities, ghastly nothings! And now, the dreadful reality exposed! And at that very moment, Henry in his office, to maintain to himself the frightful pretence, was squandering the remains of his vitality in the intolerably petty details of business.

"Well," said Dr. Raste primly—the first law of his actions was self-preservation—"there isn't a great deal to be done until you can persuade him to have professional advice. . . . And you? What is it with you? You don't look much better than your husband."

"Oh, doctor!" Violet cried, suddenly plaintive. "I don't know. You must examine me. Perhaps I ought to have come to you before."

At this point the light went out and they were in darkness.

"Oh dear!"—a sort of despair in Violet's voice now—"I knew that lamp would be going soon." The fact was that the lamps in the house generally had begun to go. All of them had passed their allotted span of a thousand burning hours. Two in the shop had failed. Henry possessed no reserve of lamps, and he would not buy, and Violet had not yet wound herself up to the resolve of buying in defiance of him. Once a fuse had melted. For two days they had managed mainly with candles. Violet, irritated, went forth secretly to buy fuse wire. She returned, and with a half-playful, half-resentful gesture threw the wire almost in his face; but it had happened that during her absence he had inserted a new fuse made from a double thickness of soda-water-bottle wire which he had picked up from somewhere. His reproaches, though unspoken, were hard for her to bear.

The doctor promptly struck a match, and Violet lit the candle on the night-table.

"I'm afraid I can't examine you by *that* light," said the doctor.

"Oh, *dear!*" She nearly wept, then masterfully took hold of herself. "I know!" she rushed to the bath-room, stood on the orange-box, and detached the bath-room lamp, and returned with it to the bedroom. "Here! This will do."

The doctor climbed on to a chair. As soon as he had fixed the new lamp Violet economically blew out the candle; and then, quaking, she yielded up her body, in the glacial chill of the room, for the trial and verdict which would reassure or agonize her. However she was neither reassured nor agonized; there was no verdict.

When Dr. Raste redescended the dark stairs the shop lay in darkness and the bookseller was wheeling in the bookstand. The doctor entered the still lighted office to get his two parcels, which he arranged on his left side exactly as before.

"Oh?" said Mr. Earlforward, approaching him. It was an interrogation.

"I should prefer not to say anything at present," the doctor announced in loud, prim, clearly articulated syllables. "There may be nothing abnormal, nothing at all. At any rate, it is quite impossible to judge under existing conditions. I shall call again in a week or ten days—perhaps earlier. No immediate cause for anxiety."

He had been but little more communicative than this to Violet herself. He was inhuman again—for his patients. Within him, however, glowed the longing to see his child's eyes kindle when he presented her with the Globe Shakspere for her very own.

That night, contrary to custom, Henry went to bed earlier than Violet. He stated that he felt decidedly better, but that he had finished all his book-keeping and oddments of work, and that it would be a pity to keep the office fire alive for nothing. Violet, in her mantle, had to darn a curtain in the front-room. When she went into the bedroom and switched on the light she saw him, with the counterpane well up to his chin, lying flat on his back, eyes shut, but not asleep. He had the pallor of a corpse, and the corpse-like effect was enhanced by the indications of his straight, thin body under the clothes. She stood bent by the side of the bed and looked at him, as it were passionately, but vainly trying by the intensity of her gaze to wrench out and drag up from hidden paths the inaccessible secrets of his mind.

Though saying little to her about her trouble he had behaved to her through the evening with the most considerate kindliness. He had caressed her with his voice. And about her trouble she had not expected him to say much. He had a very inadequate conception of the physical risks which women by nature are condemned to run. And she had never talked much in such directions, for not only was he a strangely modest man, but she deliberately practised the reserve which he himself practised. She argued, somewhat vindictively: "He tells me nothing. I will tell him nothing." Moreover, the doctor's calm non-committal attitude had given Henry an exceptional occasion to exercise his great genius for postponement. Never would Henry go half-way to meet an ordeal of any sort. Lastly, his reactions were generally slow. Fear, anxiety, seemed to come late to him.

He opened his eyes. She gave him one of the long kisses which he loved. Could he guess (she wondered) that her kiss was absent-minded that night, perfunctory, a kiss that emerged inattentive to him from the dark, virginal fastnesses of her being, which neither he nor any other would or could invade. With intention she pressed her lips on his.

"Come to bed," he murmured gently, "and get that light out."

Half undressed she looked carefully at herself in the mirror of the perfectly made, solid, everlasting Victorian wardrobe. Yes, her face showed evidence of illness; it frightened her. No, she was merely indisposed; she was frightening herself. She had no pain, or extremely little. She thought, as she regarded herself in the glass, how inscrutable, how enigmatic, how feminine she was, and how impossible it was for him to comprehend her. She felt superior to him, as a complex mind to a simple one. She thought that she, far better than he, could appreciate the significance of the terrible day. She was overwhelmed by it. Situations were evolving one out of another. Nothing had happened, and yet all was changed. The night was twenty years away from the morning.

"Do you know about that girl?" he asked with soft weariness when she had slipped into bed and the light was out.

"No. Elsie? What?"

"She's eaten two-thirds of the cheese in the cage—at least two-thirds. Must have eaten it before she went out."

The "cage" was the wire-netted larder hung outside the kitchen window. Henry had taken to buying cheese, because it was as nourishing as meat, and cheaper. He had "discovered" cheese as a food—especially a food for servants. Violet said no word, but she sighed. She was staggered, deeply discouraged, by this revelation of Elsie's incredible greed and guile; it was a blow that somehow finished her off.

"Yes," Henry went on, and his mild voice passed through the darkness into Violet's ear with an uncanny effect. "I happened to go up into the kitchen just before I came to bed." (And he had not rushed back to tell her of the calamity. He had characteristically kept it to ripen in his brain. And how characteristic of him to wander ferreting into the kitchen! Naught could escape his vigilance.) "Did you see her when she came home?"

"Yes. She went straight to bed."

A silence.

"Something will have to be done about that girl," he said at length.

"What does he mean?" thought Violet, alarmed anew. "Does he mean we must get rid of her? No, that would be too much." But she was not afraid of the extra work for herself which getting rid of Elsie would entail. She was afraid of being left to live all alone with Henry. She trembled at such a prospect.

CHAPTER V

Midnight

ELSIE, straight from the street, sat down on the edge of her creaking bed on the second floor and looked at her best boots, which had lost their polish during the course of the afternoon and were covered with dust. She had paid various brief calls, and in her former home in Riceyman Square she had taken off her jacket and put on a pinafore-apron and vigorously helped with housework in arrear. But most of the time she had spent in walking certain streets. Though she ought to have been tired—what with the morning's labour, the calls, the episode in the pinafore, the long walking—she had almost no sensation of bodily fatigue. Her mind, however, was exhausted by the monotony of thinking one importunate thought, which refused to be dismissed, and which indeed she did not sincerely want to dismiss.

When, on her way upstairs, she had spoken to Mrs. Earl-forward at the door of the dining-room, she had hoped that her employer would say: "There's someone been inquiring for you," or, "Elsie, *that man* has come pestering again." But no! Nothing but a colourless, pre-occupied "Good night." An absurd hope, naturally! She knew it was an absurd hope —and yet would not let it go. She had had the same silly hope upon entering each of the houses which she had visited. She had had it constantly as she walked the streets, examining every distant male figure. The silence of Dr. Raste had nearly killed it, but it could not be killed; it had more lives than a cat.

She had been sitting on the bed for a century when a church clock struck. Eleven! Still another hour! Why exactly an hour? Well, midnight was midnight. She must give him till twelve. An hour was an enormous period, full of chances.

Suddenly she bent to take off her boots. They were not comfortable, never had been, but she took them off for another
reason: so that she might move about noiselessly. She extinguished the candle and passed into the empty front-room,
and after some struggles with the front window posted herself
at the side window. It was unfortunate that the window
giving on to Riceyman Steps simply would not open on just
this night, for if Joe came he would probably come by way of
the steps, having first called at the house in the Square to get
news of her. Nevertheless, he might come along King's Cross
Road *en route* for the Square.

King's Cross Road was preparing to go to sleep for the
night. No lorries. Not a taxi—even in the daytime taxis
were few in King's Cross Road. A tram-car, two tram-cars
crammed with passengers. A few footfarers, mostly couples.
The Nell Gwynn Tavern was dark, save for a window in the
top storey where the barmaids slept. Down to the left a cold,
vague glare showed the locality of the loading yard of the big
post office. She could not see the pavement beneath the window; thus she might miss him. Cautiously and silently she
opened the window wider. The bulb-pots were on the sill.
Mrs. Earlforward had forgotten to bring them in. Elsie
brought them in. (A transient, sympathetic thought for Mrs.
Earlforward in her trouble.) She leaned her body out of the
window, and felt the modest feather of her hat brush against
the window-frame. She could see everything perfectly now
—north and south. No wanderer could escape her vision.
At intervals, not a sign of either vehicle or footfarers! The
road would be utterly deserted, and the street lamps seemed to
be wasted. Then a policeman; he never looked up, never
suspected that Elsie had her eye on him. Then a tram-car,
empty save for a few woeful figures, a vast waste of tram-car.

She fancied she saw him approaching from the direction
of the police-station. No, not a bit like him. She fancied she
heard a sound in the room behind her. Incredible that her
first notion should be that Joe had somehow entered the house
and meant to surprise her with a long hug; and that the far
more obvious explanation of surveillance by Mr. or Mrs.

Earlforward should come to her only second! But so it was.
Neither was correct. In the excited tension of her nerves she
had merely imagined the sound. This delusion made her
ashamed of her infatuated vigil. She had withdrawn into the
room, but after a moment, despite shame, she resumed her
post.

The night was calm and not very cold, but no frost would
have driven her inside. The sky was thickly clouded; she
did not raise her eyes to it. Weather did not exist for her.
Another tram-car thundered past; she did not hear it—only
saw it. And, as a fact, nobody in the house ever heard the
tram-cars nor felt, save rarely, the vibrations which they
caused. Elsie was far gone now in her madness, and yet more
sane every minute. She felt herself in Joe's arms, heard herself
murmuring to him—and he mute and passionate; and at the
same time she well realized that she was merely indulging
herself in foolishness. She was happy in the expectation of
bliss, and wretched in the assurance of its impossibility.

The church clock began to strike. Could a whole hour
have gone by? It seemed more like a quarter of an hour.
She had her great sorrow, and superimposed on it a childish
regret that the expectant watching was over; she had enjoyed
the vigil, and it appeared now that no balm whatever remained
to her. Reluctantly she drew in her body and shut the window softly, shutting out the last vestige of hope, and carrying
with her, as she padded back to her bedroom, the full sense of
her unbelievable silliness. Her mind swerved round to Mrs.
Earlforward's ordeal; her heart overflowed with benevolence
towards Mrs. Earlforward, and with a sublime determination
to stand by Mrs. Earlforward in any crisis that might arise.
She forgot herself for a space, and became tranquil and cheerful
and uplifted.

Then she felt hungry. Since midday she had eaten little,
having refused offers of meals on her visits, and accepted only
snacks, lest she might deplete larders already very inadequate.
She took the candle into the kitchen cautiously, but also with
a certain domination; for at nights the entire second floor was
her realm. She opened the kitchen window and the cage,

and procured for herself more of the diminished cheese and one or two cold potatoes and a piece of bread crust. Then she arranged the side-flap of sacking on the cage to protect it against possible rain. She ate slowly, enjoying with deliberation each morsel. After all, she had one positive pleasure in life. She knew she was wicked; she knew she was a thief; she did not defend herself by subtle arguments. Of late she had been stealing more and more, and had received no reproach. She thought "they" had given up taking stock of the larder. She was becoming a hardened criminal.

CHAPTER VI

Henry's Plot

WHEN Violet awoke the next morning at the appointed time for waking, and heard the familiar muffled sounds of Elsie's activity, she was tempted to stay in bed; she had not had a good night, and she felt quite disturbingly unwell; indeed, her physical sensations, although not those of acute pain, alarmed her by a certain fundamental quality involving the very basis of her vitality. But she resisted the temptation, apprehensive of the results, on herself and on the household organism, of any change of habit. The upset would be terrible if she failed in her daily role; Henry would maintain his calm, but beneath the calm "what a state he would be in!" She knew him (she said to herself). "I shall be better on my feet, and I shall worry less." So she arose to the cold room and to the cold water. Henry was quite bland and cheerful, and said that he had slept well. It was his custom to get up as soon as Violet had washed. He did not get up.

"Aren't you going to get up? I've finished here." She was folding the towel.

"I think I shall stay where I am for a bit," he announced with tranquillity.

It was just as if he had given her a dizzying blow. This, then, was the beginning of the end. She crossed the room to the bed, and gazed at him aghast.

"Now, Vi!" he admonished her, pulling at his short beard. "Now, Vi!"

There was so much affection, so much loving banter, in his queer tone, that her glance fell before his, as it had not fallen for months. She covered her exposed throat with her cold, damp hands.

G

"I shall send for the doctor at once," she announced with vivacity, all her body tingling in sudden energy.

"You'll do nothing of the sort," he said. "I've told you I'm all right. But I'll promise you one thing. Next time the medicine-man comes to see you he shall see me as well, if you like. . . . Now"—he changed his tone to the practical—"you can attend to everything in the shop. Surely it can manage without me for a day or two."

"A day or *two*!" she thought. "Is he taking to his bed permanently? Is that it?"

"And I shall save a clean shirt," he said reflectively.

"But, darling, if you're all right, why must you stay in bed? Please, please, do be open with me. You never are—if you know what I mean." She spoke with a plaintive and eager appeal, as it were girlishly. Her face, with an almost forgotten mobility, showed from moment to moment the varying moods of her emotion; tears hung in her eyes; and she was less than half-dressed. She looked as if she might sob, shriek, and drop in a hysterical paroxysm to the floor.

"Something has to be done about that thief of an Elsie." Henry very calmly explained. "Of course, I could put a lock on the cage, but that might seem stingy, miserly, and I should be sorry if anybody thought we were that. Besides, she's a good sort in some ways. She's got to be frightened; she's got to be impressed. You send her in to me. You can talk to her yourself as much as you like afterwards, but send her in to me first. I'll teach her a lesson."

"How? What are you going to say to her?"

"I shall tell her we've had the doctor, and make out I'm very ill indeed. And we'll see if that won't shake her up! We'll see if she'll keep on picking and stealing after that! That ought to sober her down. And it will, too. Something must be done."

Violet was amazed at this revelation of his mentality. She had a new source of alarm now. No doubt the plan would work; but what a plan! How *funny*! (She meant morbid.) Could she cross him? Could she deride the plan? She dared not. She dared not trifle with a man in his condition.

And the worst was that he might, after all, be only pretending to pretend he was very ill. He might really be very ill.

"Elsie," she said shortly in the kitchen, "go to your master. He wants to speak to you."

"Is he in the office already, 'm?"

"No, he isn't in the office already. He's in bed. Now run along, do!"

As soon as Elsie was gone, Violet examined the hanging larder. The ravage was appalling. Where in heaven's name did the girl stow the food? Well might the doctor say that she was well nourished. A good thing if she *was* to be frightened? She deserved it. . . . Ah! Violet did not know which way to turn in the moil of Henry's illness, Henry's morbidity, her own unnamed malady, and Elsie's shocking and incredible vice.

Elsie entered the bedroom with extreme apprehension, as for an afflicting solemnity. She thanked God she had had the wit to remove her working apron. Mr. Earlforward was staring at the ceiling. Nothing of him moved except his eyelids, and he appeared not to notice her presence. She waited, twitching her great, red hands. Violet had seemed like a girl before him. But here was the genuine girl. Elsie's hard experience of life and disaster fell away from her. She was simple and intimidated. Youthfulness was her chief characteristic as she stood humbly waiting. Her candid youthfulness accused the room of age, decay and distemper.

"Elsie, has Mrs. Earlforward told you anything?"

"No, sir."

"Listen." He still did not shift his eyes from the ceiling. "We had the doctor in yesterday afternoon." Elsie's heart thumped. Had the doctor betrayed her meddling? "He came to buy a book, and we kept him." Elsie thought the worst was over. "I'm very ill, Elsie, and I shall probably never get up again. Do you think it's right of you to go on stealing food as you do, with a dying man in the house?" He spoke very gently.

Elsie gave a sob; she was utterly overwhelmed.

"Now you must go. I can't do with any fuss, Elsie!"

He stopped her at the door. "Do we give you enough to eat? Tell me at once if we don't."

"Yes, yes. Quite enough!" Elsie cried, almost in a shriek, hiding her face in her hands. Her condition was so desperate that she had omitted the ceremonial "sir." The rushing tears ran between her fingers as she escaped. She sat a long time in the kitchen sobbing, sobbing for guilt and sobbing for sorrow at her master's fate.

CHAPTER VII

The Night-Call

"HERE," said Mrs. Earlforward frigidly to Elsie, handing her two coins. "Slip out now and buy half a pound of bacon and the same quantity as before of that cheese. And please hurry back so as you can take your turn in the shop. Not that you're in a state to be in charge of any shop. You're a perfect sight and a fright. However, they do say it's an ill-wind that blows nobody any good."

Mrs. Earlforward called Elsie a perfect sight and a fright because of her countenance, swollen and blotched with violent weeping. She had not deigned to share with Elsie her fearful anxieties. Elsie was unworthy to share them. She had indeed said not a single word to Elsie about the condition of the sick man. She rarely confided in a servant; servants could not appreciate a confidence, could not or would not understand that it amounted to an honour. . . . Do Elsie good to believe for a bit that her master was dying! Serve her right! (And supposing Henry really *was* dying!) Nevertheless, Mrs. Earlforward could not be, did not desire to be, too harsh with a girl of Elsie's admirable character. Elsie, even when convicted of theft, inspired respect, willing or unwilling. She had never read the Sermon on the Mount, but without knowing what she was doing she practised its precepts. No credit to her, of course; she had not reasoned her conduct out; it was instinctive; she had little consciousness of being righteous, and much consciousness of sin; and the notion of behaving in such and such a way in order to get to heaven simply had not occurred to her.

It was humiliating for her to go shopping with such a woe-puffed face as she had. But she went, and the mission was part of her penance. The shop-keeping community of the neighbourhood, though they held Mr. and Mrs. Earlforward in scorn, and referred to them with contumely and even detestation, were friendly to Elsie, and privately sympathized with her because she had to do Mr. and Mrs. Earlforward's dirty little errands. Not that Elsie was ever in the slightest degree disloyal to her master and mistress! On the contrary, her loyalty touched the excessive.

"Anything wrong?" the cheesemonger's assistant murmured to her in a compassionate tone, as he was cutting the bacon.

Elsie did not take the inquiry amiss. But unfortunately in her blushing answer she lapsed from entire honesty. She ought to have said: "I've been crying partly because I'm a thief, and partly because Mr. Earlforward is very seriously ill." But with shameful suppression of truth she replied in these words:

"Master's that ill!"

And her tears fell anew.

Within an hour the district had heard that the notorious old skinflint Earlforward of Riceyman Steps was dying at last!

Elsie ate no dinner. She tried to eat but could not. Then it was that she devised an expiatory scheme for fasting until the total amount of her thefts should be covered. She had admitted to Mr. Earlforward that she got enough to eat. She could not possibly deny that her employers allowed her more food, or at any rate more regular food, than many of her acquaintances managed to exist on from day to day. With an empty stomach and a tight throat she toiled upon her routine conscientiously, and more than conscientiously, because she felt herself in the presence of final calamity. For her the house and shop had become "the pale court of kingly death"; though she was as ignorant of the mighty phrase as of the Sermon on the Mount, and even less capable of understanding it. The bedroom was sealed against her. Mrs. Earlforward herself went out to purchase special light food. Afterwards she cooked some of the light food and carried it into the bedroom—and carried it out again untouched. Only towards evening did Mrs. Earlforward leave the mysterious and terrible bedroom with an empty basin. Elsie could not comprehend why the doctor had not come, or why, not having come, he had not been fetched. And she dared not ask. No! And she dared not ask how Mr. Earlforward was going on. And Mrs. Earlforward vouchsafed nothing. This withholding of news was Violet's punishment for Elsie. She wore a mask, which announced to Elsie all the time that Elsie was for the present outside the pale of humanity. Elsie had an intense desire to share fully Violet's ordeal, to suffer openly with her; she admitted that the frustration of this desire was no more than her deserts.

At five o'clock, in a clean apron, she was put into the shop. The stove was black out. The shop was full of the presence and intimidation of death. Customers seemed to have avoided it that day, as if they had been magically warned to keep away. Business had been negligible. Elsie hoped much that none would come in the last hour. She had lost the habit of serving in the shop, and was uncertain of her capability to handle the humblest customer without making a fool of herself. Then an old gentleman entered and stood silent, critically surveying her and the shop.

"Yes, sir? What can I——"

The old gentleman saw a fat, fairly sensible face, and young, timid, kind eyes, and was rather attracted and mollified by the eyes; but he did not allow Elsie's gaze to soften more than a very little his just resentment at the spectacle of an aproned charwoman, or at best a general servant, in charge of a bookshop.

"You can't!" he said sharply, moving his ancient head slowly from side to side in a firm negative. "I must see Mr. Earlforward."

"The master isn't very well, sir."

"Oh! Then Mrs. Earlforward."

"Missis is looking after master, sir."

"You don't mean to say he's ill?"

"Yes, sir."

"Ill in bed?"

"Yes, sir."

"Good God! I've known him for over twenty years, and never knew him ill yet. What's the matter? What's the matter with him?"

"I couldn't exactly say, sir."

"What do you mean—you couldn't exactly say?"

"He's very ill indeed, sir."

"Not seriously ill?"

Elsie drooped her head and showed signs of crying.

"Not in danger?"

Elsie replied with a sob: ·

"He'll never get up again, sir."

"Good God! Good God! What next? What next? Er—I—er—I'm sorry to hear this. I'm—er—tell him, tell Mrs. Earlforward, I——" And, murmuring to himself, he walked rapidly out of the dim shop. He was at an age when the distant shuffling and rumbling of death could positively frighten. In an instant he had seen the folly, the futility, of collecting books. You could not take first editions with you when you—went. Death loomed enormous over him, like a whole firmament threatening to fall.

Elsie heard a footfall on the stairs, and Mrs. Earlforward came with deliberation down to such light as there was, her fixed eyes glinting and blazing on the sinner submissive in disgrace. Elsie stood tremulous before those formidable eyes. She could scarcely believe that they were the same eyes which had melted in confidences to her on the previous morning. And they were not the same eyes. They were the eyes of an old woman with harsh, implacable features, petrified and incapable of mobility.

"What were you saying to that gentleman?"

"I was only telling him he couldn't see you or master because master was ill, 'm."

"But didn't I hear you say your master would never get up again?"

Elsie quivered and made no response, no defence.

"What do you mean by saying such a thing? How dare you say such a thing? It isn't true; it isn't true! And even if it was true, do you suppose I want everybody to know about our private affairs? You must have gone out of your mind!"

She waited for an answer from Elsie. None came. Elsie could not articulate. Then Mrs. Earlforward finished, abrupt and tyrannical:

"Shut the shop!"

Elsie found speech:

"It's only a quarter to six, 'm. There's a quarter of an hour yet," she said weakly, but bravely.

"Shut the shop, I tell you!"

Elsie went outside and began to wheel in the bookstand. A vision of Joe leaped up in her mind, and she gazed east and west to see if by chance he might be arriving a day late at that moment. The vision of Joe vanished from her mind. She thought: "This will be the last time I shall ever wheel in the bookstand." Then, from habit, she raked down the ashes from the stove.

"What's the good of raking the stove when you know it's out!" Mrs. Earlforward exclaimed. "Nothing can burn away if it's out. Where are your brains, wasting time?" Mrs. Earlforward marched across the shop, banged the door to, and fastened it violently, definitely. And Elsie thought: "That door 'll never open for master's customers again."

"Get upstairs!" ordained Mrs. Earlforward. Within ten seconds the shop and the office were in darkness.

That evening Elsie had none but strictly official communication with Mrs. Earlforward, who never once removed her mask, nor by any sign invited Elsie to come back within the the warm pale of humanity. The girl did not even know whether she was at liberty to retire to bed, or whether, in the exceptional circumstances, she ought to stay up on the chance of being needed. At last, in the soundless house, her common-sense told her to go to her room. If she was required she could dress in a minute, and it would be just as easy for Mrs. Earlforward to call her in the bedroom as in the kitchen. She had certainly no clear intention, as she closed the bedroom door, of disturbing the ashes of her passion for Joe; and it was almost mechanically, or subconsciously, that she got his letter from its safety in a drawer. Of late she had not been reading it so often. The envelope was no longer an envelope, but two separate pieces of paper held together only by the habit of association. The letter itself was very dirty and worn out at all the creases, some of which were no longer creases but rents. As she held it gingerly in her hands, one of the squares into which the creases divided it fell off from the main body, and sank with flutters to the floor. For weeks she had feared that this would happen. Necessarily she took it for an omen. Something had to be done at once if destiny was to be countered. Her thoughts ran down to the office for aid. But the office was two floors away, and in the night, off duty, she had no right to leave the top floor. Still less had she the right to leave the top floor in order to commit a theft. And she might be heard by the sharp, exasperated ears of her mistress and caught. But the letter was so pathetic that she could not resist its appeal. She seized the candle, and in stockinged feet, slowly and with every precaution against noise, descended the stairs like the thief she was.

On the desk in the office was a small cardboard box in which somebody at some time in history had once received false teeth from a dentist. This box was the receptacle for stamp-paper. In the shadowy and reproachful and menacing office Elsie slid open the box and stole from it quite six good inches of stamp-paper. Contrition for sin had perished in her. She was the hardened sinner. She could not learn from experience. It seemed to her that she sinned nightly now. Here her master was dying, her mistress ill and in misery, and she was thieving stamp-paper! She arrived upstairs again without discovery. Her nerves were as shaken as if she had crossed Niagara on a tight-rope.

Mr. Earlforward could do marvels of repair with stamp-paper, but Elsie had not his skill. Working on the emptied toilet-table, she did little but make the letter adhere to the surface of the table. Then through a too brusque movement she seriously tore the letter, and not in the line of a crease either. The paper was worn out by use, and had no virtue left. This was too much for Elsie's self-control. She had stood everything, but she could not stand the trifling accident. She scrunched the pieces of the letter in her powerful hand. Why should she keep the letter? She was a perfect fool to keep the letter, reminding her and reminding her. . . . She held the ball of paper to the candle. It lit slowly, but it lit. The paper spread a little with the heat. She could read: "I know I shall get better." She dropped the burning letter, and it smoked and blackened and writhed on the floor, and nothing survived of it save some charred corners, a lot of smoke, and a strong smell of fire.

Elsie now had the sensation of being alone in the world. The reaction was hunger. Hunger swept over her like a visitation. For twenty-four hours she had not eaten enough to satisfy a cat, to say nothing of a robust and active young woman. Her fancy could taste the lovely taste of bacon. She thought of all other lovely tastes, and there were many. She thought obscurely, perhaps not in actual words:" Eating is my only joy now. All else is vain, but eating is real." She thought of the cage and its contents. But Mr. Earlforward was dying, and Mrs. Earlforward in misery. And death was waiting to spring out from some dark corner of the house. The house was peopled with the mysterious harbingers of death. Still, the idea of the bacon bewitched her.

She raised the candlestick again. She passed out of the bedroom and crept, guilty and afraid, towards the kitchen. She knew the full enormity of her offence, could never, afterwards, offer the excuse that she did not realize it. On the other hand, she was helpless in the grip of the tyrannical appetite which drove her on. At the open door of the narrow kitchen she listened intently, with a guilty and fearful eye on the shadowy staircase, trying to see what was not there. Not a sound. Not a vibration. The last tram-car and the last Underground train had gone. She entered the kitchen, closed the door softly, and shut herself up with her sin. "I will not do it. I cannot do it!" she thought, but she knew that she would do it, and that she was appointed to do it. Her mouth watered; her stomach ravened within her like a tiger.

Ten minutes later the door opened suddenly. Mrs. Earlforward, a mantle over her night-dress, stood in the doorway.
In the flickering light of the candle Mrs. Earlforward caught
the gluttonous, ecstatic expression on Elsie's face and the
curve of her pretty lips before the corners of the lips fell to
dismay, and the rapt expression changed to despairing delin-
quency. Mr. Earlforward's grand bluff had failed after all.
Apparently not the atmosphere of death could cure Elsie of
her vice. Mrs. Earlforward, on the top of her other thrilling
woes, was horrified to see Elsie not merely eating bacon, but
eating bacon raw. But in this particular Mrs. Earlforward
was unreasonable. The girl could not cook the bacon. To
do so would have caused throughout the house a smell to
wake even the dead. She had no alternative but to eat the
bacon raw. Moreover, it was very nice raw. Mrs. Earlforward tried to speak about the bacon, but failed. Elsie,
with her mouth full and no chance of emptying it, could not
speak either. The tap, dripping much faster now than aforetime, talked alone. At last Mrs. Earlforward gasped:

"You're dressed. Run for the doctor."

CHAPTER VIII

On the Landing

DURING the day Henry had asked several times for bulletins as to Elsie's consumption of food, and he received them with satisfaction, but also with a certain sardonic air new in Violet's experience of him. This demeanour was one of the things that disquieted Violet. Another was that, contrary to his habit of solicitude for her, he made absolutely no inquiry as to her own health, though he surely ought to have been ever so little disturbed about it. And another was that he no longer showed his customary quiet pleasure in being worried over her. After taking some soft food he demanded a toothpick, and had employed himself with it in the most absurd way for quite an hour. In answer to her questions he said blandly again and again that he was all right. Soon after nightfall he insisted that the electricity should be switched off. Violet refused, as she was determined to watch him carefully. He said that the light hurt his eyes. She took the paper lining from a tray in her wardrobe and fashioned a shade for the lamp—the first shade ever known in that house.

At ten o'clock, feeling cold and ill, she undressed and got into bed, but kept the light burning. Henry was perfectly tranquil. The trams seemed to make a tremendous uproar. She could not sleep, but Henry apparently dozed at intervals. Then she had a severe shock. He was violently sick.

"What's this? What's this?" he murmured feebly and sadly.

He did not know what it was; but Violet, who had witnessed a deal of physical life during her peregrinations with the clerk of the works, knew what it was. It was what Violet's varied acquaintances had commonly called, in tones of awe on account of its seriousness, the "coffee-grounds vomit." It was, indeed, a sinister phenomenon.

Henry had dropped back exhausted. His forehead was wet, and his hair damp with perspiration. Also he seemed to be terrorized—he who was never afraid until hours or days after the event! At this point it was that Violet went out of the bedroom to send Elsie for the doctor.

As soon as Elsie was gone Violet dressed. She still felt very cold and ill. The minutes dragged. Henry lay inert. His aspect had considerably worsened. The facial emaciation was accentuated, and the pallor of the ears and the lips, and even his beard and hair were limp as if from their own fatigue. Elsie's greed was now an infinitesimal thing in Violet's mind, and the importance attached to it struck her as wildly absurd. Yet she had a strange, cruel desire (which she repressed) to say to Henry: "Your bluff has failed! Your bluff has failed! And look at you!" She thought of the approaching Christmas, for which she had secretly been making plans for merriment; she had meant to get Elsie's aid, because she knew that Elsie had in her the instincts of fancy and romance. Pathetic! She thought of her anger at Elsie's indiscretion in telling a customer that the master would never get up again. Ridiculous anger! He never *would* get up again; and what did it matter if all Clerkenwell knew in advance? The notion of Henry spending money on the cure of his damaged knee seemed painfully laughable. His dread, genuine or affected, of communism, seemed merely grotesque. She saw a funeral procession, consisting of a hearse and one coach, leave Riceyman Steps. The coffin would have to be carried across the space from the shop-door to the main road, as no vehicle could come right to the door. Crowds! Crowds of gapers!

Then she heard a noise below. Elsie, who had run all the way to Myddelton Square and all the way back, tapped with tremulous eagerness.

"He's coming, 'm." She was panting.

Dr. Raste arrived, but only after an interval of nearly half an hour, which seemed to Violet like half a night. The fact was that, despite much practice, he could not dress in less than about twenty minutes; nor was it his habit to run to his patients, whatever their condition. He came with the collar of his thick overcoat turned up. Violet met him on the landing; she had shut the bedroom door behind her. He was calm; he yawned; and his demeanour hovered between the politely indifferent and the politely inimical. He spoke vaguely, but in his loud tone, in reply to Violet's murmur: "I was afraid you weren't coming, doctor."

Violet had by this time lost her sense of proportion. She was incapable of bearing in mind that the doctor lived daily and nightly among disease and death, and that he was more accustomed to sick people than to healthy. She did not suspect that in the realism of his heart he regarded sick people and their relations in the mass as persons excessive in their fears, ruthless in their egotism, and cruel in their demands upon himself. She had no conception that to him a night-call was primarily a grievance and secondarily an occasion to save life or pacify pain. She might have credited that fifty per cent. of his night-calls were unnecessary, but she could never have guessed that he had already set down this visit to Riceyman Steps as probably the consequence of a false, foolish, feminine alarm. She began to explain to him at length the unique psychology of the sufferer, as though the doctor had never before encountered an unwilling and obstinate patient. The doctor grew restless.

"Yes. Just so. Just so. I'd better have a look at him."

"I haven't dared to tell him I've sent for you," said Violet piteously, reproachful of the doctor's inhumanity.

"Tut-tut!" observed the doctor, and opened the bedroom door.

He sniffed on entering, glancing placidly at Henry, then at the fireplace, and then went to the window and drew the curtains and blind aside.

"I should advise you to have a fire lighted at once, and we'll open the window a bit."

He put his hat carefully on the chest of drawers, but did not even unbutton his overcoat or turn down his collar. Then he removed his gloves and rubbed his hands. At last to Henry:

"Well, Mr. Earlforward, what's this I hear?"

No diplomacy with the patient! No ingenious excusing of

his presence! The patient just had to accept his presence; and the patient, having no alternative, did accept it.

"Shall I light the fire now, 'm?" asked Elsie timidly at the door.

"Yes," said the doctor shortly, including both the women in his glance.

"But won't she be disturbing you while you're . . ." Violet suggested anxiously. She was afraid that this unprecedented proceeding would terribly upset Henry and so make him worse.

"Not at all."

"I don't think we've ever had this fire lighted," said Violet, to which the doctor deigned no reply.

"Run along, Elsie. Take your things off and be quick. The doctor wants a fire immediately."

Before the doctor, changed now from an aggrieved human being into a scrupulously conscientious professional adviser, had finished his examination, the room was half full of smoke. Violet could not help looking at Elsie reproachfully as if to say: "Really, Elsie, you should be able to control the chimney better than this—and your master so ill!"

The patient coughed excessively, but everyone knew that the coughing was merely his protest against the madness of lighting a fire.

"I'm too hot," he muttered. "I'm too hot."

And such was the power of auto-suggestion that he did in fact feel too hot, though the fire had not begun to give out any appreciable heat. He privately determined to have the fire out as soon as the doctor had departed; a limit must be set to folly after all. However, Henry was at once faced with a great new crisis which diminished the question of the fire to a detail.

"I can't come to any conclusion without washing out the stomach," said Dr. Raste, turning to Violet, and then turning back quickly to Henry: "You say you've no pain there? You're sure?" And he touched a particular point on the chest.

"None," replied Henry.

"The fellow is lying," thought the doctor. "It's amazing how they will lie. I bet anything he's lying. Why do they lie?"

Nevertheless, the doctor could not be quite sure. And he had a general preference for not being quite sure; he liked to postpone judgment.

"*I* don't mind having my stomach washed out," Henry murmured blandly.

"No, of course not. I'll telephone to the hospital early to-morrow, and Mrs. Earlforward will take you round there in a cab." And to Violet: "You'll see he's well covered, won't you?"

"I will," Violet weakly agreed.

"But I don't want to go to any hospital," was Henry's second protest. "Why can't you do the business here?"

"Impossible in a house!" the doctor announced. "You can only do that sort of thing where you've got all the apparatus and conveniences. But I'll make it all smooth for you."

"Oh, no! Oh, no! Not to a hospital!"

The doctor said callously:

"I doubt whether you realize how ill you are, my friend."

"I'm not *that* ill. When should I come out again?"

"The moment you are better."

"Oh, no! No hospital for me. There's two of them here to nurse me."

"Your wife is not in a condition to nurse you. You must remember that, please. . . . Better get him there by eleven o'clock. I shall probably be there first. I'll give you the order—to let you in."

Henry ceased to cough; he ceased to feel hot. His condition suddenly improved in a marvellous way. He had been ill. He admitted now that he had been chronically ill. (He had first begun to feel ill either just before or soon after the eating of the wedding-cake on his bridal night.) But he was now better, much better. He was aware of a wonderful amelioration, which surprised even himself. At any rate, he would not go into a hospital. The enterprise was too enormous and too perilous. Once in, when would he get out again? And

nurses were frightful bullies. He would be helpless in a
hospital. And his business? It would fall to ruin. Everything would get askew. And the household? Astounding
foolishness would be committed in the house if he lost his
grip on it. He could manage his business and he could manage
his household; and nobody else could. Besides, there was no
sound reason for going into a hospital. As for washing out
his stomach, if that was all, give him some mustard and some
warm water, and he would undertake to do the trick in two
minutes. The doctor evidently desired to make something
out of nothing. They were all the same. And women were
all the same, too. He had imagined that Violet was not like
other women. But he had been mistaken! She had lost
her head—otherwise she would never have sent for the doctor
in the middle of the night. The doctor would undoubtedly
charge double for a night visit. And the fire, choking and
roasting him! He saw himself in the midst of a vast general
lunacy and conspiracy, and he alone maintaining ordinary
common-sense and honesty. He felt the whole world against
him; but he could fight the whole world. He had perfect
confidence in the fundamental hard strength of his nature.

Then he observed that the other two had left the room.
Yet he did not remember seeing them go. Elsie came back,
her face smudged, to watch the progress of the fire, which
was no longer smoking.

"Where's your mistress, my girl?"

"She's talking to the doctor on the landing, sir."

"You see," the doctor was saying in a low voice to Violet,
"it may be cancer at the cardiac end of the stomach. I don't
say it is. But it may be. That would account for the absence
of appetite—and for other symptoms." In the moonlight he
saw Violet wiping her eyes. "Come, come, Mrs. Earlforward, you mustn't give way."

"It's not that," Violet spluttered, who was crying at the
thought that she had consistently misjudged Henry for many
months past. Not from miserliness, but from illness, he had
been refusing to eat. He *could* not eat normally. He was a
stricken man, and to herself she had been accusing him of the

meanest avarice and the lowest stupidity. She now in a flash acquitted him on every charge, and made him perfect. His astounding secretiveness as to his condition she tried to attribute to a regard for her feelings.

"What are we to do? What am I to do?"

"Oh!" said Dr. Raste. "Don't let that worry you. We'll get him away all right to-morrow morning. I'll come myself and fetch him."

At the same moment they both saw the bedroom door open and the lank figure of the patient in his blue-grey night-shirt emerge. The light was behind him, and threw his shadow across them. Elsie stood scared in the background.

"It's not the slightest use you two standing chattering there," Henry muttered bitterly. "I'm not going into a hospital, so you may as well know it."

"Oh, Henry!"

"Better get back to bed, Mr. Earlforward," said the doctor rather grimly and coldly.

"I'm going back to bed. I don't need you or anybody else to tell me I oughtn't to be out here. I'm going back to bed." And he limped back to bed triumphant.

Dr. Raste, who thought that he had nothing to learn about the strange possibilities of human behaviour, discovered that he had been mistaken. He could not hide that he was somewhat impressed. He again assured Violet that it would be all right in the morning, but he was not very convincing. As for Violet, since Dr. Raste was a little man, she did not consider that he had much chance, morally, against her husband, who was unlike all other men, and, indeed, the most formidable man on earth.

CHAPTER IX

Violet's Victory

"HOW do you feel, my girl?" Henry asked.

They lay again in bed together. Before leaving the doctor had given, with casualness, certain instructions, not apparently important, which Violet had carried out, having understood that there was no immediate danger to her husband and also that there was nothing immediately to be done. Dr. Raste's final remarks, as he departed, had had a sardonic tone, almost cynical, which had at first abraded Violet's sensitiveness; but later she had said to herself: "After all, with a patient like Henry, what *can* you expect a doctor to do?" And she had accepted, and begun to share, the doctor's attitude. A patient might be very seriously ill, he might be dying of cancer, and yet by his callous and stupid obstinacy alienate your sympathies from him. Human sympathies were as precarious as that! She admitted it. A few minutes earlier she had lifted Henry to a pedestal of perfection. Now she dashed him down from it. "I know I oughtn't to feel as I do, but I *do* feel as I do." And she even confirmed herself in harshness. She had sent Elsie to bed for the few remaining hours of the night. She had undressed once more and got into bed herself.

The light of the fire played faintly at intervals on the astonished ceiling, and sometimes shafts of moonlight could be discerned through an aperture in the thick, drawn curtains. Behind the curtains the blind could be heard now and then answering restlessly to the north breeze. The room was so warm that the necessity to keep the bedclothes over the shoulders and up to the chin had disappeared. Violet had a strange sense of luxury. "And why shouldn't we have a fire *every* night?" she thought, and added, somewhat afraid of the extravagance of the proposition: "Well, anyhow, *some* nights

—when it's very cold." She gave no reply to Henry's question about her health.

Henry felt much better. He had scarcely any pain at the spot which the doctor had indicated; he was as sure as ever that he had done right in refusing to enter a hospital, and as determined as ever that he never would enter a hospital. None the less, he was disturbed; he was a bit frightened of trouble in the bed. He had noted his wife's face before she turned the light out, and seen rare and unmistakable signs in it. His illness was not now the important matter, nor her illness either. The important matter was their sentimental relations. He knew that he had estranged her. Convinced of the justice of his own cause and of the folly of doctors and wives, he was yet apprehensive and had somehow a quite illogical conviction of guilt. Violet had wanted to act against his best interests, and yet he must try to appease her! It was more important to appease her than to get well!

Dr. Raste, or anybody else, looking at the couple lying beneath Violet's splendid eiderdown (which still by contrast intensified the dowdiness and shabbiness of the rest of the room) would have seen merely a middle-aged man and a middle-aged woman with haggard faces worn by illness, fatigue, privations and fear. But Henry did not picture himself and Violet thus; nor Violet herself and Henry. Henry did not feel middle-aged. He did not feel himself to be any particular age. His interest in life and in his own existence had not diminished during the enormous length of time which had elapsed since he first came into Riceyman Steps as a young man. In his heart he felt no older than on that first night. He did not feel that he now in the least corresponded to his youthful conception of a middle-aged man. He did not feel that he was as old as other men whom he knew to be of about his own age. He thought that he alone had mysteriously remained young among his generation. For him his grey hairs had no significance; they were an accident. Then in regard to his notion of Violet. He knew that all women were alike, but with one exception—Violet. Women were women, and Violet was thrice a woman. He was aware of her age arithmetically, for he had seen her birth-certificate. But in practice she was a girl—well, perhaps a little more than a girl, but not much more. And she had for him a romantic quality perceptible in no other woman. He admired certain efficiencies in her, but he could not have said why she was so important to him, nor why he was vaguely afraid of her frown —why it was so urgent for him to stand well with her. He could defeat her in battle. He had more common-sense than she had, more authority, a surer grasp of things; he could see farther; he was more straightforward. In fact, a superior being! And she had crossed him, sided with the doctor against him, made him resentful. Therefore, if justice reigned, she ought to be placating him. Instead, he was anxious to placate her.

And, on her part, Violet saw in Henry a man not of any age, simply a man: egotistic, ruthless, childish, naughty, illogical, incalculable, the supreme worry of her life; a destroyer of happiness; a man indefensible for his misdeeds, but very powerful and inexplicably romantic, different from all other men whatsoever. She hated him; her resentment against him was very keen, and yet she wanted to fondle him, physically and spiritually; and this desire maintained itself not without success in opposition to all her grievances, and, compared to it, her sufferings and his had but a minor consequence.

"Well, how do you feel?" he repeated.

The repetition aroused Violet's courage. She paused before speaking, and in the pause she matured a magnificent, a sublime enterprise of attack. She had a feeling akin to inspiration. She flouted his illness, his tremendous power, her own weakness and pain. She did not care what happened. No risk could check her.

"You don't care how I am!" she began quietly and bitterly. "Did you show the slightest interest in me all yesterday? Not one bit. You thought only of yourself. You pretended you were ill. Well, if you weren't, why couldn't you think about me? But you were ill. Not that that excuses you! However ill *I* was, I should be thinking about you all the time.

But I say you were ill, and I say it again. You only told me a lot of lies about yourself, one lie after another. Why *do* you keep yourself to yourself? It's an insult to me, all this hiding, and you know it. I suppose you think I'm not good enough to be told! I can tell you one thing, and I've said it before, and this is the last time I ever shall say it—you've taught me to sew my mouth up, too; that's what you've done with your everlasting secrecy. I always said you're the most selfish and cruel man that ever was. You're ill, and the doctor says you ought to go to a hospital—and you won't. Why? Doesn't everybody go into a hospital some time or another? A hospital's not good enough for you—that's it. It suits you better to stop here and be nursed night and day by your wife. Don't matter how ill *I* am! I've got to nurse you *and* look after the shop as well. It'll kill me; but a fat lot you care about that. And if you hadn't deceived me and told me a lot of lies you might have been all right by this time, because I should have had the doctor in earlier, and we should have known where we were then. But how was I to know how ill you are? How was I to know I'd married a liar besides a miser?"

Henry interjected quietly:

"I told you long ago that the reason I didn't eat was because I'd got indigestion. But you wouldn't believe me."

Violet's voice rose:

"Oh, you did, did you? Yes, you did tell me once. You needn't think I don't remember. It was that night I cooked a beautiful bit of steak for you, and you wouldn't touch it. Yes, you did tell me, and it *was* the truth, and I didn't believe it. And you were glad I didn't believe it. You didn't want me to believe it. You're very knowing, Henry, aren't you? You say a thing once, and when it's been said, it's finished with. And then afterwards you can always say: 'But I told you.' And you're always so polite! As if that made any difference! I wish to God often you weren't so polite. My first husband wasn't very polite, and I've known the time when he's laid his hand on me, knocked me about—yes, and more than once. I was young then. Disgusting, *you'd* call it.

And I've never told a soul before; not likely. But what I say is I'd sooner be knocked about a bit and know what my man's really thinking about than live with a locked-up, cast-iron safe like you! Yes, a hundred times sooner. There's worse things than a blow, and every woman knows it. Well, you won't go to the hospital! That's all right. You won't go and you won't go. But I shall go to the hospital! The doctor'll tell me to go, and the words won't be out of his mouth before I shall be gone. I can feel here what's coming to me. I shall go, and I shall leave you with your Elsie, that eats you out of house and home. She was here before I came. I'm only a stranger. You pretend to be very stiff and all that with her, but you and her understand each other, and I'm only a stranger coming between you. Are you asleep?"

"No."

Violet rose up and slipped out of bed. Henry heard the sound of her crying. She seemed to rush at the fire. She poked it furiously, not because it needed poking, but because she needed relief.

"Come back to bed, Vi," said Henry kindly.

She dropped the poker with a clatter on the fender, and Henry saw her, a white creature, moving towards him round by his side of the bed. She bent over him.

"Why should I come back to bed?" she asked angrily, her voice thickened and obscured by sobs. "Why should I come back to bed? You're ill. You've got no strength, and haven't had for weeks. What do you want me to come back to bed for?"

He felt her fingers digging into the softness of his armpits. He felt her face nearer his. She mastered herself:

"Listen to me, Henry Earlforward," she said in a low, restrained, trembling voice: "You'll go into that hospital to-morrow morning. You'll go into that hospital. You'll *go* into it when the doctor comes to fetch you. Or, if you don't, I'll—I'll—I'll——"

He felt her lips on his in a savage, embittered and passionate kiss. She was heroical; he a pygmy—crushed by her might. He was afraid and enchanted.

"No," he thought, "there never was another like her."

"Will you, will you, will you, will you?" she insisted ruthlessly, and her voice was smothered in his lips.

"Very well. I'll go."

Her body fell limp upon his. She was not sobbing now, but feebly and softly weeping. With a sudden movement she stood upright, then ran to the door, just as she was, fumbled for the knob in the darkness, and rushed out of the room, banging the door after her with a noise that formidably resounded through the whole house. Her victory was more than she could bear.

CHAPTER X

Departure

IN the morning Dr. Raste, unusually interested in the
psychological aspect of the Earlforward affair, arrived at
about ten o'clock in a taxi-cab, prepared and well-braced to
make good his word to Violet. He remembered vividly his
own rather cocksure phrase: "We'll get him away all right
to-morrow." He was tired and overstrung, and therefore
inclined to be violent and hasty in endeavour. He had his
private apprehensions. He asked the driver to wait, meaning
to have Henry captive and downstairs in quite a few minutes.
His tactic was to take the patient by storm. He had disorganized his day's work in order to deal with the matter,
and for the maintenance of self-respect he was bound to deal
with it effectively. Further, he had arranged by telephone
for a bed at the hospital.

The front of the shop dashed him. The shop had not been
opened. The milk-can had not been brought within. There
it stood, shockingly out of place at ten a.m., proof enough
that something very strange had happened or was happening
at T. T. Riceyman's. He tried to open the door; it was
locked. Then he noisily shook the door, and he decided to
adopt the more customary course of knocking. He knocked
and knocked. Little Mr. Belrose, the proprietor of the confectioner's opposite, emerged to watch the proceedings with
interest, and two other people from the houses farther along
the steps also observed. Evidently Riceyman Steps was agog
for strange and thrilling events. Dr. Raste grew self-
conscious under the gaze of Clerkenwell. No view of the
interior of the shop could be had through the book-filled
windows, and only a narrow slit of a view between the
door-blind and the frame of the door. Dr. Raste peered

through this and swore in a whisper. At length he saw Elsie approaching.

"Isn't it about time you took your milk in?" he greeted her calmly, presenting her with the can when she opened the door. Elsie accepted the can in silence; the doctor entered the shop; Elsie shut and bolted the door. The morning's letters lay unheeded on the unswept floor at her feet. The doctor had the sensation of being imprisoned with her in the sombre and chilly shop. A feeling of calamity weighed upon him. The stairs in the thick gloom at the back of the shop seemed to be leading upwards to terrible affairs. He thought of the taximeter ticking away threepences.

"Well?" he inquired impatiently of the still silent Elsie. "Well? How's he getting on?"

Elsie answered:

"Missis must have been took bad in the night, sir. When I came down this morning, she was lying on the sofa in the parlour, and I thought she was dead. Yes, I did, sir. She was that cold you wouldn't believe. Not a stitch on her but her night-things. And she *was* in a state, too!"

"I hope you got her back to bed at once," said the doctor.

"I got her up to my bed, sir, and I half-carried her. She wouldn't go to their bedroom for fear of frightening master, and him so bad, too!"

"Of course, you couldn't send for me because you'd no one to send, had you?" The doctor began to move towards the stairs.

"Oh, I could have sent someone, sir. There's several about here could have gone. But I understood you were coming, and I said to myself half an hour more or less, like, that can't make much difference. And missis didn't want me to send anyone else, either; she didn't want it to get about too much, sir. Not that that would have stopped me, sir. Soon as I see her really ill, I says I'*m* responsible now, I says—of course, under you, sir, and I shouldn't have listened to her. No, sir."

The doctor was very considerably impressed, and relieved, by Elsie's dignity, calm and power. An impassible commonsense had come to life in the sealed house. Elsie was tidy, too;

no trace on her of a disturbed night and morning, and she was even wearing a clean apron. No wearisome lamentation about the shop having to be closed! Elsie had instinctively put the shop into its place of complete unimportance.

As they passed the shut door of the principal bedroom the doctor, raising his eyebrows, gave an inquiring jerk.

"I did knock, sir. There was no answer, so I took the liberty of looking in. He seemed to be asleep."

"You're sure he was *asleep*?"

"Well, sir," said Elsie, stolidly and yet startlingly, "he wasn't dead. I'll say that."

They passed to the second floor. There lay the mistress on the servant's narrow bed, covered with Elsie's half-holiday garments on the top of the bed-clothes. That Violet was extremely ill and in pain was obvious from the colours of her complexion and the sharp, defeated, appealing expression on her face. The doctor saw Elsie smile at her; it was a smile beaming out help and pure benevolence, and it actually brought some sort of a transient smiling response into the tragic features of the patient; it was one of the most wonderful things that the doctor had ever seen. Nobody could have guessed that only thirty-six hours before Elsie had been a thief convicted of stealing and eating raw bacon. And, indeed, the memory of the deplorable episode was erased as completely from Elsie's mind as from her mistress's.

"I shall take you to the hospital at once, Mrs. Earlforward," the doctor said in his prim, gentle tone, after the briefest examination. He added rather abruptly: "I've got a taxi waiting. I think you've borne up marvellously." In a few moments he had changed his plans to meet the new developments, and he was now wondering whether he might not have difficulty in securing a bed for Mrs. Earlforward.

"I shall see properly to master, 'm," Elsie put in. "I mean if he doesn't go to the hospital himself."

Violet nodded acquiescence. She did not want to waste her strength in speech, or she might have told them of Henry's promise to her to go into hospital. Moreover she was suffering too acutely to feel any strong interest in either Henry or anybody else.

"We'll carry you to the cab," said the doctor, and to Elsie: "She must be dressed, somehow—doesn't matter how."

Violet murmured:

"I'd sooner walk to the cab, doctor, if you know what I mean. I can."

"Well, if you *can*——" he concurred in order not to upset her.

When the summary dressing was done, Elsie having made two journeys to her employer's bedroom to fetch garments and hat, the doctor said to her confidentially:

"We shall want some money. Have you any? Where is the money kept?"

Experience had taught him never to disburse money for patients; and he had a very clear vision of the threepences ticking up outside in King's Cross Road.

"My purse. On the chest of drawers," whispered Violet, who had heard.

Elsie made a third journey to the state-bedroom. Oblivious of the proprieties, she had not knocked before, and she did not knock now. On the previous occasion Mr. Earlforward had merely watched her with apparently dazed, indifferent eyes. But the instant she picked up the purse from the chest of drawers he exclaimed:

"Here! Where are you going with that purse?"

"Missis sent me for it," Elsie replied.

From prudence she would give him no more news than that of the situation. No knowing what he might attempt to do if he was fully apprised!

Violet was carried downstairs and through the shop, and at the shop-door she was set on her insecure feet, and Dr. Raste held her while Elsie unbolted. And she managed to walk, under the curious glances of a few assembled quidnuncs, along the steps to the taxi, Dr. Raste on one side of her and Elsie on the other. She had foretold that the moment the doctor ordered her to the hospital she would go to the hospital.

She had foretold true. She was gone. The taxi made a whir and moved. She was gone.

"I'll call this afternoon!" the doctor shouted from the departing vehicle.

In the shop again, the encouraging smile with which she had speeded her mistress still not yet expired from her round, fat face, Elsie picked up the milk-can. The letters on the floor were disdained. She thought of her presentiment of the previous evening but one: "This will be the last time I shall ever wheel in the bookstand." And she had a firm conviction that in that presentiment she had by some magical power seen acutely into the future.

PART V

CHAPTER I

The Promise

ELSIE was forgetting to fasten the shop-door. With a little start at her own negligence she secured both the bolt and the lock. She thought suddenly of the days—only a year away, yet far, far off in the deceiving distances of time —when Mr. Earlforward and she had the place to themselves. Mrs. Earlforward had come, and Mrs. Earlforward had gone, and now Elsie had sole charge—had far more responsibility and more power than ever before. The strangeness of quite simple events awed her. Nor did the chill of the thin brass handle of the milk-can in her hand protect her against the mysterious spell of the enigma of life.

She "knew" that the shop would never open again as T. T. Riceyman's. She "knew" that either Mr. or Mrs. Earlforward would die, and perhaps both; and she was very sad because she felt sorry for them, not because she felt sorry for herself. In the days previous to the amazing advent of Mrs. Earlforward Elsie had had Joe. Joe was definitely vanished from her existence. Nothing else in her own existence greatly mattered to her. She would probably lose a good situation; but she was well aware, beneath her diffidence and modesty, that by virtue of the knowledge which she had acquired from Mrs. Earlforward she could very easily get a fresh situation, and from the material point of view a better one. Professionally she had one secret ambition, to be able to say to a prospective employer that she could "wait at table." There would be something grand about that, but she saw no chance of learning such an intricate and rare business. She had never seen anybody wait at table. In the little pewed eating-houses to which once or twice Joe had taken her, or she had taken Joe, the landlady or a girl brought the food to you and took

your plate away, and whisked crumbs on to the floor and
asked you what else you wanted; but she felt sure that that
was not waiting at table, nor anything like it. . . . So the
ideas ran on in her mind—scores of them following one
another in the space of a few seconds, until she shut off the
stream with a murmured: "I'm a nice one, I am!" The
solitary dæmonic figure of Mr. Earlforward, fast in bed, was
drawing her upstairs. And the shop was keeping her in the
shop. And the plight of Mrs. Earlforward was pulling her
away towards St. Bartholomew's Hospital. And there she
stood like a regular hard-faced silly, thinking about waiting at
table! She must go to Mr. Earlforward instantly, and tell
him what had happened.

When she reached the first floor she said to herself that she
might as well take the milk into the kitchen first, and when
she reached the kitchen she remembered poor Mrs. Earlforward's bulbs. The precious bulbs had been neglected. Out
of kindness to Mrs. Earlforward she went at once and watered
the soil in which they were buried, and put the pots out on
the window-sill. It was an act of piety, not of faith, for Elsie
had no belief in the future of those bulbs. Indeed, she counted
them among the inexplicable caprices of employers. If you
wanted a plant, why not buy one that you could see, instead of
interring an onion in a lot of dirt? Still, for Mrs. Earlforward's sake, she took great pains over the supposed welfare
of the bulbs. And yet—it must be admitted, however reluctantly—her motive in so meticulously cherishing the bulbs was
by no means pure. She was afraid of the imminent interview
with Mr. Earlforward, and was delaying it. If she had been
sure of herself in regard to Mr. Earlforward, she would not
have spent one second on the bulbs; she would have disdained
them utterly.

Mr. Earlforward was somewhat animated.

"I didn't sleep much the first part of the night," he said,
"but I must have had some good sleeps this morning."

Elsie thought he was a little better, but he still looked very
ill indeed. His pallor was terrible, and his eyes confessed
that he knew he was very ill. He was forlorn in the disordered

and soiled bed; and the untidy room, with its morsel of dying fire, was forlorn.

"Well," said Elsie nervously, in a tone as if she was repeating a fact with which both of them were familiar, "well, so missis has gone to the hospital!"

She had told him. She trembled for his exclamation and his questions. He made no sound, no movement. Elsie felt extremely uncomfortable. She would have preferred any reply to this silence. She was bound to continue.

"Yes. Missis was that ill that when doctor came for you he took *her* off instead. I told her I'd see after you properly till you was fetched too, sir." She gave no further details. "I'm that sorry, sir," she said.

Mr. Earlforward maintained his silence. He did not seem to desire any details. He just lay on his back and stared up at the ceiling. The expression on his hollowed face, now the face of a man of seventy, drew tears to Elsie's eyes, and she had difficulty in restraining a sob. The aspect of her employer and of the room, the realization of the emptiness of the rest of the house, the thought of Mrs. Earlforward snatched away into the mysterious and formidable interior of the legendary hospital, were intolerable to Elsie, who horribly surmised that "they" must be cutting up the unconscious form of her once lively and impulsive mistress. To relieve the tension which was overpowering her Elsie began to straighten the rumpled eiderdown.

"I'll run and make you some of that arrowroot, sir," she said. "You must have something, so it's no use you——"

Mr. Earlforward said nothing; then his head dropped on one side, and his eyes met hers.

"Elsie," he murmured plaintively, "you won't desert me?"

"Of course not, sir. But the doctor's coming for you."

"Never!" Mr. Earlforward insisted, ignoring her last sentence. "You'll never desert me?"

"Of course not, sir." His weakness gave her strength.

H

In order to continue in activity, she went to mend the fire.

"Let it out," said Mr. Earlforward. "I'm too hot."

She desisted, well knowing that he was not too hot, but that he hated to see good coal consumed in a grate where it had never been consumed before. From pity she must humour him. What did it matter whether the fire was in or out?—the doctor would be coming for him very soon. Then a flicker of thought for herself: after the departure of Mr. Earlforward, would she have to stay and mind the place till something else happened, or would she be told to go, and let the place mind itself? Very probably she would be told to stay. She opened the door.

"Where are you going now?"

"I was just going to make your arrowroot, sir. That was what missis was giving you. At least, it looks like arrowroot."

"Come here. I want to talk to you. Have you opened the shop?"

"No, sir."

A long pause.

"Bring me up the letters, and let me have my glasses."

He had accepted, in his practical, compromising philosophy, the impressive fact that the shop had not been and would not be opened.

Without saying anything Elsie went downstairs into the shadowy shop. A dozen or so letters lay on the floor. "I'll give him two or three to quiet him," she thought, counting him now as a baby. She picked up three envelopes at random. "He'd better not have them all," she thought. The others she left lying. She had no concern whatever as to the possible business importance of any of the correspondence. Her sole concern, apart from the sick-room, was the condition of the shop. Ought she to clean it, or ought she to "let it go"? She wanted to clean it, because it was obviously fast returning to its original state of filth. On the other hand, while cleaning it she might be neglecting her master. None but herself had the power to decide which course should be taken. She perceived that she was mistress. Naïvely she enjoyed the strange sensation of authority, but the responsibility of authority dismayed her.

"Are these all?" Mr. Earlforward asked indifferently, as she put the three letters into his limp, shiny hand.

"Yes, sir," she said without compunction.

He allowed the letters to slip out of his hand on to the eiderdown. She was just a little afraid of being alone with him.

CHAPTER II

The Refusal

IN the early dusk of the afternoon, about four o'clock, there was a banging on the shop-door, and the short bark of a dog, who evidently considered himself entitled to help in whatever affair was afoot. Elsie was upstairs. During the morning several persons, incapable of understanding that when a shop is shut it is shut, had banged on the door, and at last Elsie, by means of two tin tacks, had affixed to the door—without a word to her master—a dirty old card on which she had scrawled in large pencilled letters the succinct announcement, "Closed." This had put an end to banging. But now more banging!

"The doctor!" Elsie exclaimed, and ran down.

Not the doctor, but a lanky and elegant little girl, accompanied by a fox-terrier, stood at the door. As soon as the door opened and she saw Elsie the little girl blushed. The fact was that this was her very first entry into the world of affairs, and she felt both extremely nervous and extremely anxious not to show her nervousness to a servant. The dog, of course, suffered.

"Be quiet, sir!" she said very emphatically to the restless creature, addressing him as a gentleman, and the next minute catching him a clout on his hard head. "Papa can't come, and he told me to say——"

"Will you please step inside, Miss Raste?" Elsie suggested.

Nobody was about, but Elsie with a servant's imitativeness had acquired her mistress's passion for keeping private business private. The little girl, reassured by the respectful formality of her reception, stepped inside with some dignity, and the dog, too tardily following, got himself nipped in the closing door and yelped.

"Serves you right!" said Miss Raste; and to apologetic Elsie: "Oh, not at all! It's all his own fault. . . . Papa says he's so busy he can't come himself, but you are to get Mr. Earlforward ready to go to the hospital, and wrap him up well; and while you're doing that I am to walk towards King's Cross and get a taxi for you. I may have to go all the way to King's Cross," Miss Raste added proudly and eagerly. "But it will be all right. I got a taxi for papa yesterday; it was driving towards our Square, but I stopped it and got in, and told the chauffeur to drive me to our house—not *very* far, of course. Papa said I should be quite all right, and he's teaching me to be self-reliant and all that." Miss Raste gave a little snigger. "Jack! You naughty boy!"

Jack was examining in detail the correspondence which Elsie had neglected and told lies about. At his mistress's protest he ran off into the obscure hinterland of the shop to stake out a claim there.

"And after I've got you the taxi I am to walk home. Oh, and papa said I was to say you were to tell Mr. Earlforward that Mrs. Earlforward will have an operation to-morrow morning."

Miss Raste was encouraged to be entirely confidential, to withhold nothing even about herself, by the confidence-inspiring and kindly aspect of Elsie's face. She thought almost ecstatically to herself: "How nice it would be to have *her* for a servant! She's heaps nicer than Clara." But she had some doubt about the correctness of Elsie's style in aprons.

"Oh dear! Oh dear!" Elsie murmured.

"And they'll be expecting Mr. Earlforward at Bart's. It's all arranged."

Having impinged momentarily upon a drab tragedy of Clerkenwell and taken a considerable fancy to Elsie, and having imperiously summoned her dog, Miss Raste, who was being educated to leave Clerkenwell one day and disdain it, departed on her mission with a demeanour in which the princess and the filly were mingled.

"What's the matter? What have you turned the light on

for?" Mr. Earlforward demanded when Elsie, much agitated, entered the bedroom. "What *is* the matter?"

Elsie tried to compose her face.

"How do you feel now, sir?" she asked, serpent-like in spite of her simplicity and nervousness.

"I feel decidedly better. In fact, I was almost thinking of getting up."

"Oh! That's good. Because the doctor's sending a taxi for you, and I am to take you to the hospital at once. Here's all your things." She fingered a loaded chair. "And while you're putting 'em on I'll just run upstairs and get my things."

"Is the doctor here?" Henry cautiously inquired.

"No, sir. He says he's too busy. But he's sent his little girl."

"Well, I'm not going to the hospital. Why should I go to the hospital?" Mr. Earlforward exclaimed with peevish, rather shrill obstinacy.

She had "known" he would refuse to go to the hospital. She was beaten from the start.

"But you said you *would* go to the hospital, sir."

"When did I say I would go to the hospital?"

"You said so to missis, sir."

"And who told *you*?"

"Missis, sir."

"Yes, but I didn't know then that your mistress would have to go. The place can't be left without both of us. You aren't expecting I should leave *this* place in your charge. Besides, I'm not really ill. Hospital! I never heard of such a thing. I should like to know what I've got—to be packed off to a hospital! I should feel a perfect fool there. I'm not going. And you can tell everybody I'm not going." He rolled over and hid his face from Elsie, and kept on muttering, feeble-fierce. He had no weapon of defence except his irrational obstinacy; but it was sufficient, and he knew it was sufficient, against the entire organized world. If he had had an infectious disease the authorities would have had the right to carry him off by force; but he had no infectious disease, and therefore was impregnable.

"Now, it's no use you standing there, Elsie. I'm not going. You think because I'm ill you can do what you like, do you? I'll show you!"

Elsie could see the perspiration on his brow. He looked desperate. He was a child, a sick man, a spoilt darling, a martyr to anguish and pain, a tiger hunted and turning ferociously on his pursuers. His mind as much as his body was poisoned. Elsie said quietly:

"Missis is to have an operation to-morrow morning, sir."

A silence. Then, savagely:

"Is she? Then more fool her!"

Elsie extinguished the light, shut the door and descended the stairs, wondering what brilliant people, clever people, people of resource and brains, would have done in her place.

When Miss Raste came back with the taxi in the gathering night, having accomplished a marvellous Odyssey and pretending grandly that what she had done was nothing at all, it was Elsie who blushed in confusion.

"I can't get him to go to the hospital, Miss Raste. No, I can't!"

"Oh!" observed Miss Raste uncertainly. "Well, shall I tell papa that?"

"Yes, please. . . . Do *what* I will!"

"I'm afraid the taxi will have to be paid. I've left Jack in it. He's so naughty. A shilling I saw on the dial. But, of course, there's the tip."

Elsie hurried upstairs to her own room and brought down one and twopence of her own money. Another minute and she had locked herself up alone once again with her master.

CHAPTER III

The Message to Violet

"I'M raging in my heart! I'm raging in my heart!" Elsie said to herself. "It makes me gnash my teeth!" And she did gnash her teeth all alone in the steadily darkening shop. "I'm that *ashamed*!" she said out loud.

The origin of her expostulation was Mr. Earlforward's obstinacy. She was humiliated on his behalf by his stupidity, and on her own behalf by her failure to get him to the hospital. The incident would certainly become common knowledge, and ignominy would fall upon T. T. Riceyman's. What preoccupied her was less the danger to her employer's health, and perhaps life, than the moral and social aspects of the matter. She would have liked to give her master a good shaking. She was losing her fear of the dread Mr. Earlforward; she was freely criticizing and condemning him, and, indeed, was almost ready to execute him—she who, under the continuous suggestion of Mrs. Earlforward, had hitherto fatalistically and uncritically accepted his decrees and decisions as the decrees and decisions of Almighty God. He had argued with her; he had defended himself against her; he had shown tiny glimpses of an apprehension that she might somehow be capable of forcing him to go to the hospital against his will. He had lifted her to be nearly equal with him. The relations between them could never be the same again. Elsie had a kind of intoxication.

"Well, anyway, something's got to be done," she said, with a violent gesture.

She rushed for her tools and utensils, she found a rough apron and tied it tightly with a hard, viciously-drawn knot over her white one, and began to clean the shop. If seen by nobody else the shop was seen by her, and she could no longer stand the sight of its filth. She ranged about like a beast of prey. She picked up the letters from the floor and ran with them into the office and dashed them on to the desk. And at that moment a postman outside inconsiderately dropped several more letters through the flap. "Of course you *would*!" Elsie angrily protested, and picked them up and ran with them into the office and dashed them on to the desk.

"Oh! This is no use!" she muttered, after a minute or so of sweeping in the gloom, and she turned on the electric lights. Only two sound lamps were now left in the shop, and one in the office. She turned them all on—the one in the office from sheer naughtiness. "I'll see about his electric light!" she said to herself. "I'll burn his electric light for him—see if I don't!" She was punishing him as she cleaned the shop with an energy and a thoroughness unexampled in the annals of charing. This was the same woman who a short while ago had trembled because she had eaten a bit of raw bacon without authority. And when, having finished the shop, she assaulted the office, she drowned the floor in dust-laying water, and she rubbed his desk and especially his safe with a ferocity calculated to flay them. For there was not only his obstinacy and his stupidity—there was his brutality. "Then more fool her!" he had exclaimed about his wife, soon to be martyrized by an "operation." And he had said nothing else.

Then Elsie began to think of Dr. Raste. Of course, she had been mistaken about Dr. Raste. On the pavement in front of his house he had been very harsh, with his rules about what he ought to do and what he ought not to do. And before that, long before that, when he had given a careless look at her in the house in Riceyman Square upon the occasion of Joe's attack on her—well, he hadn't seemed very human. A finicking sort of man—that was what she called him—stand-offish, stony. And yet he had got out of bed in the middle of the night for the old miser, and he must have known he could never screw much money out of him. And fancy the doctor coming with a taxi himself to take away the master! Elsie had never heard of such a thing. And him taking the mistress instead! It was wonderful. And still more wonderful was the arrival of his little girl—a little queen she was, and knew her way about. And he'd arranged things at the hospital, too. (Oh! As she reflected, her humiliation at the failure to "manage" Mr. Earlforward was intensified. She could scarcely bear to think of it.) No doubt at all she had been mistaken about Dr. Raste. Joe had always praised Dr. Raste, and she had been putting Joe down for a simpleton, as indeed he was; but in this matter Joe had been right and she wrong. In repentance, or in penance, she extinguished the two lights in the shop, which she was not using; her mind worked in odd ways, but it had practical logic. The cleaning done, she doffed the rough apron.

She was somewhat out of breath, and she seated herself in the master's chair at his desk. An audacious proceeding, but who could say her nay? She looked startlingly out of place in the sacred chair as she gazed absently at the sacred desk. The mere fact that nobody could say her nay filled her with sadness. Tragedy pressed down upon her. Life was incomprehensible, and she saw no relief anywhere in the world. That man upstairs might be dying, probably was dying. And no one knew what was his disease, and no one could help him without his permission. He lay over the shop-ceiling there, and there was nothing to be done. As for mistress, the case of her mistress touched her even more closely. Mistress was a woman, and she was a woman. She had known a dozen such cases. Women fought their invisible enemy for a time. Then they dropped, and they were swept off to a hospital, and the next thing you heard they were dead. . . . Mrs. Earlforward alone in a hospital—all rules and regulations! And her husband very ill in bed at home here! Nobody to say a word to Mrs. Earlforward about home, and she fretting her heart away because of master, and the operation to-morrow morning and all! *He* was very ill, and people were often queer while they were ill. They weren't rightly responsible; you couldn't really blame them, could you? He must be terribly worried about everything. It was a pity he was obstinate, but there you were. Elsie was overwhelmed with affliction, misery, anguish. Her features were most painfully discomposed under the lamp.

But when Mr. Earlforward, answering her tap at the bed-room-door, roused himself to make a fresh and more desperate defence against a powerful antagonist who was determined to force him to act contrary to his inclination and his judgment, he saw, as soon as his eyes had recovered from the dazzle of the sudden light, a smiling, kind and acquiescent face. His relief was intense, and it flowered into gratitude. He thought: "She promised she would never desert me, and she won't." He was weak from his malady and from lack of nourishment; he was in pain; he had convinced himself that he was better, but he could not deny that he was still very ill—and Elsie was all he had. She could make his existence heaven or hell; he perceived that she meant to make it as nearly heaven as she could. She was not going to bully him. She had no inten-tion of disputing his decision about the hospital business. She had accepted her moral defeat, and accepted it without reserve and without ill-will. She was bringing liquid food for him, in an attractive white basin. He had, as usual, little desire for food, but the sight of the basin and the gleaming spoon on the old lacquer tray tempted him, and he reflected that even an abortive attempt at a meal would provide a change in the awful monotony of his day. Moreover, he wanted to oblige her.

As, angelically smiling, she walked round the bed to his side and stood close to him, a veil fell from his eyes, and for the first time he saw her, not as a charwoman turned servant, but as a girl charged with energetic life; and her benevolence had rendered her beautiful. He envied her healthy vigour. He relied on it. The moment was delicious in the silent and curst house.

"I'll try," he said pleasantly, raising his body up and gazing at her.

"Why!" she exclaimed. "If you haven't been making your bed!"

No disapproval in her voice. No warning as to the evil consequences of this mad escapade of making his bed.

"Any more letters?" he inquired, after he had swallowed a mouthful.

"I believe there was one," she answered vivaciously. "Shall I run and get it for you?" Down she ran and picked up a letter at random off the desk in the office. And she brought back also a sheet of notepaper and an envelope, a millboard portfolio and a pencil.

"What's all that?" he asked mildly, opening the letter.

"Well, you want to write to missis, don't you?"

"Um!" he murmured as he read the letter, affecting not to have heard her. He was ashamed and self-conscious because he had not himself had the idea of writing to Violet.

"You'll be sending a note to missis at the hospital. It'll give her a good lift-up to hear from you."

"Yes," he said. "I was going to write."

"Here! I'll take that letter. You can do with some of this food. I shouldn't like you to let it get cold." She stayed near him and held a corner of the insecure tray firmly. "You can't take any more? All right."

She removed the tray, and replaced it by the portfolio which was to serve as a writing-desk on the bed. It was always marvellous to Elsie to see the ease with which her master wrote. She admired. And she was almost happy because she had resolved to smile cheerfully and give in to him and do the best she could for him on his own lines and be an angel.

"Shall I read you what I've written?" he suggested, with a sudden upward glance.

"Oh, sir!"

The astounding, the incredible flattery overthrew her completely. He would read to her what he had written to the mistress, doubtless for her approval. She blushed.

"'My dear Wife,—As you may guess, I am torn with anxiety about you. It was a severe shock when Elsie told me the doctor had taken you off to the hospital without a moment's delay. However, I know you are very brave and have an excellent constitution, and I feel sure that before a week is out you will be feeling better than you have done for months. And, of course, the hospital is a very good one, one of the best in London, if not the best. It has been established for nearly eight hundred years. If it was only to be under the same roof as you I should have come to the hospital myself to-day, but I feel so much better that really it is not necessary, and I feel sure that if you were here to see me you would agree with me. There is the business to be thought of. I am glad to say that Elsie is looking after me splendidly, but, of course, that does not surprise me. Now, my dear Violet, you must get better quickly for my sake as well as your own. Be of good courage and do not worry about me. My little illness is nothing. It is your illness that has made me realize that.—Your loving Husband, H. EARLFORWARD.'"

He read the letter in a calm and even but weak voice, addressed the envelope, and then lay back on the pillows. (He was now—since he had made the bed—using Violet's pillow as well as his own.) He did not finish his food. He left Elsie to fold the letter, stick it in the envelope, and lick and fasten the envelope. She did these things with a sense of the honour bestowed upon her. It was a wonderful letter, and he had written it right off. No hesitation. And it was so nice and thoughtful; and how it explained everything. She had to believe for a moment that her master really was better. The expressions about herself touched her deeply, and yet somehow she would have preferred them not to be there. What touched her most, however, was the mere thought of the fact that once, and not so long ago either, her master had been a solitary single man, never troubling himself about women and no prospect of such; and here he was wrapped up in one, and everything so respectable and nice. . . . But he was very ill. His lips and cheeks were awful. Elsie recalled vividly the full rich red lips he once had.

She had moved away from the bed, taking the basin and putting it on the chest of drawers. The contents of her master's pockets were on the chest of drawers, where he laid them every night, in order better to fold his carefully creased clothes.

"I do fancy I haven't got any money," she said diffidently, after a little while.

"Why, it isn't your wages day—you don't mean?"

"Oh, no, sir."

She had deposited nearly all her cash in the Post Office Savings Bank during her afternoon out, and the bit kept in hand had gone to pay for the unused taxi.

"Why, Elsie! You must be a rich woman," said Mr. Earlforward. "What with your wages and your pension!" He spoke without looking at her, in a rather dreamy tone, but certainly interested.

"Well, sir," Elsie replied, "it's like this. I give my pension to my mother. She's a widow, same as me, and she can't fend for herself."

"All of it? Your mother?"

"Yes, sir."

"How much is your pension?"

"Twenty-eight shillings and elevenpence a week, sir."

"Well, well." Mr. Earlforward said no more. He had often thought about her war pension, but never about any possible mother or other relative. He had never heard mention of her mother. He thought how odd it was that for years she had been giving away a whole pension and nobody knew about it in Riceyman Steps.

"Could you let me have sixpence, sir?" Elsie meekly asked, coming to the point of her remark concerning money.

"Sixpence? What do you want sixpence for? You surely aren't thinking of buying food to-night!" Mr. Earlforward, who had been lying on his right side, turned with a nervous movement on to his back and frowned at Elsie.

"I wanted it to give to Mrs. Perkins's boy in the Square to take your letter down to missis at the hospital." In spite of herself she felt guilty of a betrayal of Mr. Earlforward's financial interests.

"What next?" he said firmly. "You must run down with it yourself. Won't take you long. I shall be all right."

"I don't like leaving you, sir. That's all."

"You get off with it at once, my girl."

She was reduced to the servant again, she who had just been at the high level of a confidante. The invalid turned again to his right side and pushed his nose into the pillow, shutting his eyes to indicate that he had had enough of words and desired to sleep. His keys were on the chest of drawers and several other things, including three toothpicks, but not money. He seldom went to bed with money in his pockets.

Elsie, with a swift gesture, silently picked up the bunch of keys and left the room, a criminal; she had no intention of taking the letter to the hospital herself. She went downstairs quite cheerful; she still felt happier because she had been smiling and benevolent and yielding after her mood of revolt, and because the letter to Mrs. Earlforward was her own idea. In the office she knelt in front of Mr. Earlforward's safe. No fear accompanied the sense of power which she felt. There was nobody to spy upon her, to order her to do one thing, to forbid her to do another. Her omnipotence outside the bedroom could not be disputed.

Although she was handling the bunch of keys for the first time, she knew at once which of the keys was the safe-key and how to open the safe, from having seen Mr. Earlforward open and close it. He would have been extremely startled to learn the extent of her knowledge, not only about the safe, but about many other private matters in the life of the household; for Elsie, like most servants, was full of secret domestic information, unused, but ready at any time for use. She unlocked the safe and swung open the monumental door of it and pulled out a drawer—and drew back, alarmed, almost blinded. The drawer was full of gold coins—full! Her domestic information had not comprised this dazzling hoard. In all her life Elsie had scarcely ever seen a sovereign. Years ago, in the early part of the war, she had seen a half-sovereign now and then. She shut the drawer quickly. Then she looked round, scared of possible spies after all. She thought she could hear creepings on the stairs and stirrings in the black corners of the mysterious shop. Not even when caught in the act of eating stolen raw bacon had she had such a terrifying sense of monstrous guilt. Her impulse was to shut the safe, lock it, double-lock it, treble-lock it, and try to erase the golden vision utterly from her memory. She would not on any account have pulled out another drawer.

But, lying on the ledge above the nest of drawers, she saw a canvas bag. This bag was familiar to her; it held silver. She loosened its string and drew forth sixpence. Then she rose, tore the wrapper off a circular among the correspondence on the table, wrote on the inside of the wrapper "6d.," and put it in the bag. Such was her poor, her one feasible, inadequate precaution against the tremendous wrath to come. She had done a deed unspeakable, and she could perfectly imagine what the consequences of it might be.

She was still breathing rapidly when she unbolted the shop-door. Rain was falling—rather heavy rain. Securing the door again, she ran upstairs to get her umbrella, which lay under her bed wrapped in newspaper. She had to grope for it in the dark. Roughly she tore off the newspaper. Downstairs she could not immediately find the door-key and decided to risk leaving the door unlocked. She would be back from the Square in a minute, and nobody would dream of breaking in. She ran off and up the Steps towards the Square.

CHAPTER IV

Out of the Rain

M RS. PERKINS'S boy, who lived with Mrs. Perkins in the house next door to Elsie's old home in Riceyman Square, and who had a chivalric regard for Elsie, fortunately happened to be out in the Square. In the darkness he was engaged in amorous dialectic with a girl of his own age—fourteen or fifteen—and they were both imperfectly sheltering under the eve of an outhouse (church property) at the northeast corner of the churchyard. Their voices were raised from time to time, and Elsie recognized his as she approached the house. Mrs. Perkins's boy wore over his head a sack which he had irregularly borrowed for the night from the express parcel company in the tails of whose vans he spent about twelve hours a day hanging on to a piece of string suspended from the van roof. That he had energy left in the evening to practise savagely-delicate sentimental backchat in the rain was proof enough of a somewhat remarkable quality of "brightness."

Elsie had chosen him for her mission because he was hardened to the world and thoroughly accustomed to the enterprise of affronting entrance-halls and claiming the attention of the guardians thereof. She now called to him across the roadway in an assured, commanding tone which indicated that she knew him to be her slave and that, in spite of her advanced years, she could more than hold her own with him against any chit in the Square. There was an aspect of Elsie's individuality which no living person knew except Mrs. Perkins's boy. He went hurrying to her.

"I want you to run down to the hospital with this letter and be sure to tell the porter it is to be given to Mrs. Earlforward to-night. She's in there. And here's sixpence for you, and

I

I'll lend you my umbrella and I'll get it again from your mammy to-morrow morning; but you must just walk to the Steps with me first because I don't want to get wet."

"Right-o, Elsie!" he agreed in his rough, breaking voice, and louder: "So long, Nell!"

"Put it in your pocket now," Elsie said, handing him the letter. "No, don't take the keys." She was still carrying Mr. Earlforward's bunch of keys.

The boy insisted on taking the umbrella, which gave him almost as much happiness as the sixpence. Never before had he had the opportunity to show off with an umbrella. He wished that he could get rid of the sack, which did not at all match the umbrella's glory.

"Here, hold on!" He stopped her and threw the sack over the railings into his mother's area. They walked together towards the Steps.

"Your Joe's been asking for you to-night," he said suddenly.

"My Joe!" She stood still, then leaned against the railings.

"Here! Come *on*!" he adjured her, nervously sniggering in a cheeky way to hide the emotion in him caused by hers.

Elsie obeyed.

"How do you know?"

"Nell just told me. It's all about."

"Where'd 'e call?"

"Hocketts's."

"What'd they tell him?"

"Told him where you was living, I suppose."

"D'you know when he was inquiring?"

"Oh, some time to-night, I s'pose."

"Now you hurry with that letter, Jerry," she said at the shop-door. Mrs. Perkins's boy sailed round the corner into King's Cross Road with the umbrella on high.

Elsie had the feeling that she had not herself spoken to Jerry at all, but that she had heard someone else speaking to him with her voice. And she was quite giddy between the influences of fear and of happiness. Her hands and feet were very cold. All kinds of memories and hopes which she had murdered in cold blood and buried deep came rushing and thronging out of their graves, intensely alive, and overwhelmed her mind. The anarchy within her was such that she had to think painfully before she could even command her fingers to open the shop-door.

Entering from the street, you had to cross the full length of the shop to the wall between it and the office in order to turn on the electric light. As Elsie passed gropingly between the bays of shelves she thought that she heard a sound of movement, and then the question struck and shook her: "Was the door latched or unlatched when I opened it?" She could not be sure, so uncertain and clumsy had been her hands. She dared not, for a moment, light the shop lest she should see something sinister or something that she wanted too much to see.

Turning the switch at last, she looked and explored with apprehensive eyes all of the shop that could be seen from the office doorway. Nothing! But the recesses of the bays nearest the front of the shop were hidden from her. She listened. Not a sound within the shop, and outside only the customary sounds which she never noticed unless attentively listening. She would go upstairs. She would extinguish the light and go upstairs. No! She could not, anyhow, leave the shop. She must wait. She must open the door and look forth at short intervals to see if Joe was coming. She must even leave the door ajar for him. He was bound to come sooner or later. He knew where she was, and it was impossible that he should not come. She heard a very faint noise, which sounded through the shop and in her ears like the discharge of a gun or the herald of an earthquake. Then a silence equally terrifying! The faint noise appeared to come from the bay at the end of which was the window giving on King's Cross Road. She could see about half, perhaps more, of this bay, but not all. She must go and look. Her skin crept and tingled. The shop was now for her peopled with invisible menaces. Mr. Earlforward was so forgotten that he might have been dead a hundred years. She must go and look. She did go and look. Her heart faltered horribly. There was indeed a heap of something lying under the side-window.

"Joe!" she cried, but in a whisper, lest by some infernal magic Mr. Earlforward up in his bedroom should overhear.

Joe was a lump of feeble life enveloped in loose, wet garments. His hat had fallen on the floor and was wetting it. He had grown a thin beard. Elsie knelt down by him and took his head in her arms and kissed his pale face; her rich lips found his dry and shrivelled up. He recognized her without apparently looking at her. She knew this by the responsiveness of his lips.

"I'm very thirsty," he murmured in his deep voice, which to hear again thrilled her. (Strange that, wet to the skin, he should be thirsty!)

Though she knew that he was ill, and perhaps very ill, she felt happier in that moment than she had ever felt. Happiness, exultant and ecstatic, rushed over her, into her, permeating and surrounding her. She cared for nothing save that she had him. She had no curiosity as to what he had been doing, what sufferings he had experienced, how his illness had come about, what his illness was. She lived exclusively in the moment. She did not even trouble about his thirst. Then gradually a poignant yet sweet remorse grew in her because, a year ago, before his vanishing, she had treated him harshly. She had acted for the best in the interests of his welfare, but was it right to be implacable, as she had been implacable, towards a victim such as he unquestionably was? Would it not have been better to ruin and kill him with kindness and surrender? For Elsie kindness had a quality which justified it for its own sake, whatever the consequences of it might be. And then she began to regret keenly that she had destroyed his letter; she would have liked to be able to show it to him to prove her constancy. Supposing he were to ask her if she had received it, what she had done with it. Could she endure the shame of answering: "I burnt it"?

"I'm so thirsty," he repeated. He was a man of one idea.

"Stay there," she whispered softly, squeezing him, and damping her dress and cheeks before loosing him.

She ran noiselessly upstairs and came back with a small jug of cold water from the kitchen. As seemingly he could not clasp the handle, she held the jug to his lips. He swallowed the water in large, eager gulps.

"Wait a bit now," she said, when he had drunk half of it, and pulled the jug away from him. After twenty or thirty seconds he drank the rest and sighed.

"Can you walk, Joe? Can you stand?"

He shook his head slowly.

"I dropped down giddy. . . . Door was unlatched, I came in out of the rain and dropped down giddy."

She ran upstairs again, lit her candle, and set it on the floor by her bedroom door. When she had descended once more she saw that the candle threw a very faint light all the way down the two flights of stairs to the back of the shop. She seized Joe in her arms—she was very strong from continual hard manual labour, and he was very thin—and carried him up to her room, and, because he was wet, put him on the floor there. Breathless for a minute, she brought in the candle and closed and locked the door. (She locked it against nobody, but she locked it.)

She was nurse now, and he her patient. She began to undress him, and then stopped and hurried down to the bathroom, where Mr. Earlforward's weekly clean grey flannel shirt lay newly ironed. She stole the shirt. Then, having secured her door again, she finished undressing the patient, taking every stitch off him, and rubbing him dry with her towel, and rubbed the ends of his hair nearly dry, and got the shirt over his shoulders, and turned down the bed, and lifted him into her bed, and covered him up, and threw on the bedclothes the very garments which in the early morning she had used for Mrs. Earlforward's comforting. There he lay in her bed, and nobody on earth except those two knew that he was in her room with the door locked to keep out the whole world. It was a wondrous, palpitating secret, the most wonderful secret that any woman had ever enjoyed in the history of love. She knelt by the bed and kissed him again and again. He smiled; then a spasm of pain passed over his face.

"What's the matter with you, Joe, darling? What is it you've got?" she asked gently, made blissful by his smile and alarmed by his evident discomfort.

"I ache—all over me. I'm cold." His voice was extremely weak.

She ran over various diseases in her mind and thought of rheumatic fever. She had not the least idea what rheumatic fever was, but she had always understood that it was exceedingly serious.

"I shall light a fire," she said, announcing this terrific decision as though it was quite an everyday matter for a servant, having put a "follower" in her own room, to light a fire for him and burn up her employer's precious coal.

On the way downstairs to steal a bucket of coal she thought: "I'd better just make sure of the old gentleman," and went into the principal bedroom and turned on the light. Mr. Earlforward seemed to be neither worse nor better. She was reassured as to him. He looked at her intently, but could not see through her body the glowing secret in her heart.

"You all right, sir?" she asked.

He nodded.

"Going to bed?"

"Oh, no! Not yet!" she smiled easily. "Not for a long time."

"What's all that wet on your apron, Elsie?"

She was not a bit disconcerted.

"Oh, that's nothing, sir," she said, and turned out the light before departing.

"Here! I say, Elsie!"

"Can't stop now, sir. I'm that busy with things." She spoke to him negligently, as a stronger power to a weaker— it was very queer!—and went out and shut the door with a smart click.

The grate and flue in her room were utterly unaccustomed to fires; it is conceivable that they had never before felt a fire.

But they performed their functions with the ardour of neo-phytes, and very soon Mr. Earlforward's coal was blazing furiously in the hearth and the room stiflingly, exquisitely hot—while Mr. Earlforward, all unconscious of the infamy above, kept himself warm by bedclothes and the pride of economy alone. And a little later Elsie was administering to Joe her master's invalid food. The tale of her thefts was lengthening hour by hour.

CHAPTER V

The Two Patients

TOWARDS four o'clock in the morning Joe woke up from a short sleep and suddenly put questions to Elsie about his safety in that strange house, and also he inquired whose bed he was in.

"You're in my bed, Joe," she answered, kneeling again by the bedside, so as to have her face close to his, and to whisper more intimately; and she told him the situation of the household and how her mistress had been carried to the hospital for an operation, and how her master was laid up with an unascertained disease, and how she alone had effective power in the house.

Then Joe began excitedly to talk of his adventures in the past twelve months, and she perceived that a change for the worse had come over him and that he was very ill. Both his voice and his glance indicated some development of the malady.

"Don't tell me now, Joe dear," she stopped him. "I want to hear it all, but you must rest now. To-morrow, after you've had another good sleep. I must just go and look at Mr. Earlforward for a minute."

She offered him a drink of water and left him, less to look at Mr. Earlforward than in order to give him an opportunity to calm himself, if that was possible. She knew that in certain moods solitude was best for him, ill or well. And she went down the dark stairs to the other bedroom, which was nearly as cold as the ice-cold stairs.

Mr. Earlforward also was worse. He seemed to be in a fever, yet looked like a corpse. Her arrival clearly gave him deep relief; he upbraided her for neglecting him; but somewhat timidly and cautiously, as one who feels himself liable to reprisals which could not be resisted. Elsie stayed with him and tended him for a quarter of an hour, and then went to the kitchen, which the extravagant gas-ring was gently keeping warm, while it warmed water and tried to dry Joe's miserable clothes.

Elsie had to think. Both men under her charge were seriously ill, and she knew not what was the matter with either of them. Supposing that one of them died on her hands before the morning, or that both of them died! All her bliss at the reappearance of Joe had vanished. She had horrible thoughts, thoughts of which she was ashamed but which she could not dismiss. If anyone was to die she wanted it to be Mr. Earlforward. More, she could not help wishing that Mr. Earlforward would in any case die. She had solemnly promised Mr. Earlforward never to desert him and a promise was a promise. If he lived, and "anything happened" to Mrs. Earlforward, she was a prisoner for life. And if Joe lived Mr. Earlforward would never agree to her marrying him and having him in the house with her, as would assuredly be necessary, having regard to Joe's health. Whereas with Mr. Earlforward out of the way she would be her own mistress and could easily assume full charge of Joe. Strange that so angelically kind and unselfish a creature could think so murderously; but think thus she did.

Further, the double responsibility which impulsively she had assumed weighed upon her with a crushing weight. Never had that always anxious brow been so puckered up with anxiety and hesitancy as now. Ought the doctor to be instantly summoned? But she could not fetch him herself; she dared not even leave her patients long enough to let her run over to the Square and rouse one of her friends there. And, moreover, she had a curious compunction about disturbing the doctor two nights in succession, and this compunction somehow counted in the balance against even men's lives! She simply did not know what to do. She desperately needed counsel, and could not get it. On the whole she considered that the doctor should be sent for. Many scores, perhaps hundreds, of people were sleeping within a hundred yards of her. Was there not one among them to whom she could appeal? She returned to Joe. He was talking in his sleep. She went to the window, opened it, and gazed out.

A lengthy perspective of the back-yards of the houses in King's Cross Road stretched out before her; a pattern of dark walls—wall, yard, wall, yard, wall, yard—and the joint masonries of every pair of dwellings jutting out at regular intervals in back-rooms additional to the oblongs of the houses. The sky was clear, a full moon had dimmed the stars; and fine weather, which would have been a boon to the day, was being wasted on the unconscious night. The moonlight glinted here and there on window-glass. Every upper window marked a bedroom. And in every bedroom were souls awake or asleep. Not a window lit, except one at the end of the vista. Perhaps behind that window somebody was suffering and somebody watching. Or it might be only that somebody was rising to an interminable, laborious day. The heavy night of the town oppressed Elsie dreadfully. She had noticed that a little dog kennelled in the yard of the very next house to T. T. Riceyman's was fitfully moaning and yapping. Then a light flickered into a steady gleam behind a window of this same house, less than a dozen feet away, with an uncanny effect upon Elsie. The light waned to nothing, and shortly afterwards the back-door opened, and the figure of a young woman in a loose gown, with unbound hair, was silhouetted against the radiance of a candle within the house. Across the tiny back-yard of T. T.'s Elsie could plainly see the woman, whose appearance was totally unfamiliar to her. A soul living close to her perhaps for months and years, and she did not know her from Eve! Elsie wanted to call out to her, but dared not. A pretty face, the woman had, only it was hard, exasperated, angry. The woman advanced menacingly upon the young, chained dog, and the next moment there was one sharp yell, followed by a diminuendo succession of yells. "That'll learn ye to keep people awake all night," Elsie heard a thin, inimical voice say. The woman returned to the house. The dog began again to yap and moan. The woman ran out in a fury, picked up the animal and flung it savagely into the kennel. Elsie could hear the thud of its soft body against the wood. She shrank back, feeling sick. The woman retired from her victory; the door was locked; the light showed once more at the bedroom window, and went out; the infant dog, as cold and solitary as ever, and not in the least comprehending the intention of the treatment which it had received, issued from the kennel and resumed its yapping and moaning.

"Poor little thing!" murmured the ingenuous Elsie, and shut the window.

No! She could not send anybody at all for the doctor. Common-sense came to her aid. She must wait till morning. A few hours, and it would be full day. And the risk of a disaster in those few hours was exceedingly small. She must not be a silly, frightened little fool. Joe was still talking in his restless sleep. She quickly made up the fire, and then revisited Mr. Earlforward, who also was asleep and talking. After a moment she fetched a comb and went to the kitchen, washed her face and hands in warm water, took down her blue-black hair, combed it and did it up. And she put on a clean apron. She had to look nice and fresh for her patients when the next day should start. For her night and day were now the same; her existence had become continuous—no break in consciousness—it ran on and on and on. She did not feel tired. On the contrary, she felt intensely alive and energetic and observant, and had no desire for sleep. And her greed seemed to have left her.

CHAPTER VI

The Second Refusal

SHE was running up the Steps (not as early as she hoped,
owing to a quick succession of requisitions from her two
patients at the last moment) to find a messenger in the Square
to dispatch for the doctor, when a sharp "Hai! Hai!" from
behind caused her to turn. The summons came from Dr.
Raste, who had appeared round the corner from King's Cross
Road. Elsie ran back and unlocked the shop-door. The ink
of her scrawled notice of closure to the public had been weeping freely in the weather of the last twenty-four hours.

"You were leaving your patient, Elsie," said the doctor, in
a prim, impartial voice, expressing neither disapproval nor
approval nor anything, but just holding up the mere fact for
her consideration.

She explained.

"He's worse, of course," the doctor remarked, his tone not
asking for confirmation—almost forbidding it.

He was impenetrable; or, as Elsie thought: "You couldn't
make anything out of him." He might be tired; he might
not be tired. He might have been roused from his bed at two
a.m.; he might have slept excellently in perfect tranquillity.
You didn't know; you never would know. The secrets of
the night were locked up in that trimly dressed bosom. He
was the doctor, exclusively. But one thing showed him
human; he had once again disturbed the sequence of his daily
programme in order to visit T. T. Riceyman's.

They passed through the shop, on whose floor more letters
were lying. At the door of Mr. Earlforward's bedroom, the
doctor paused and murmured:

"I'd better hear what you've got to say before I go in."

She took him to the dining-room, where he sat down on a

dusty chair. To Elsie's mind the dining-room was in a disgraceful state, and indeed, though the shop and office had not yet seriously deteriorated from last night's terrific cleansing, the only presentable rooms in the house were the two bedrooms. All the rest was as neglected and forlorn as a pet animal forgotten in the stress of a great and prolonged crisis. Elsie, standing, gave her report, which the doctor received like a magistrate. She wanted to ask about Mrs. Earlforward, but it was not proper for her to ask questions. Nor could she frame any formula of words in which to broach to the steely little doctor the immense fact of Joe's presence in the building.

"Been to bed?" he inquired coldly.

"Oh, no, sir!"

"Had any sleep?"

"Oh, no, sir!"

"Not for two nights, eh?"

"No, sir—well, nothing to mention."

When at length they passed into the bedroom, Elsie was shocked at the condition of the sick-bed. She had left it unimpeachably smooth, tidy and rectangular; it was now tossed and deranged into a horrible confusion, as though it had not been made for days, as though for days the patient had been carrying on in it a continuous battle with some powerful enemy. And in the midst of it lay Mr. Earlforward (whom also she had just "put to rights," and who after her tending had somehow not seemed to be very ill), unkempt, hot, wild-eyed, parchment-skinned, emaciated, desiccated, creased, anxious, at bay, nearly desperate, mumbling to himself. Yet the moment he caught sight of the doctor he altered his demeanour, becoming calm, still, and even a little sprightly. The change was pathetic in its failure to deceive; and it was also heroic.

"Well, my friend," the doctor greeted him, staccato, with his characteristic faint, nervous snigger at the end of a phrase.

"You're here very early, doctor," said Mr. Earlforward composedly. "At least it seems to me early." He did not know the time; nor Elsie either; not a timepiece in the house

was going, and the church-clock bell was too familiar to be
noticed unless listened for.

"Thought you might like to know something about your
wife," said Dr. Raste, raising his voice.   He made no reference
at all to Henry's exasperating refusal to go to the hospital on
the previous day.   "They tell me at the hospital that a fibroid
growth is her trouble.   I suspected it."

"Where?"

"Matrix."   The doctor glanced at Elsie as if to say: "You
don't know what the word means."   She didn't, but she
divined well enough Mrs. Earlforward's trouble.   "Change
of life.   No children," the doctor went on tersely, and nodded
several times.   Mr. Earlforward merely gazed at him with
his little burning eyes.   "There'll be an operation this morning.   Hope it'll be all right.   It ought to be.   An otherwise
healthy subject.   Yes.   Hold this in your mouth, will you?"

He inserted a clinical thermometer between Mr. Earlforward's white, crinkled lips, took hold of the patient's wrist and
pulled out his watch.

"Appears you can't retain your food," he said, after he had
put the watch back.   "Comes up exactly as it goes down.
Mechanical.   You're very strong."   He withdrew the
thermometer, held it up to the light, washed it, restored it to
its case.   "Well, we know what's the matter with your wife,
but *I* shouldn't like to say what's the matter with you—yet.
I'm not a specialist."   He uttered the phrase with a peculiar
intonation, not entirely condemning specialists, but putting
them in their place, regarding them very critically and rather
condescendingly, as befitting one whose field of work and
knowledge was the whole boundless realm of human path-
ology.   "You'll have to be put under observation, watched
for a bit, and X-rayed.   You can't possibly be nursed properly
here, though I'm sure Elsie's doing her best.   And there's
another great advantage of your being in hospital.   You'll
know how Mrs. Earlforward's going on.   You can't expect
'em to be sending up here every ten minutes to tell you.   Nor
telegraph either.   Something else to do, hospitals have!"
Another faint snigger.   "If you'll come now, I mean in half

an hour or so, I've arranged to get you there in comfort. It's all fixed." (He did not say how.) "I hear you can walk about, and you made your bed yesterday. Now, Elsie, you must——"

"I won't go to the hospital," Mr. Earlforward coldly interrupted him. "I don't mind having a private nurse here. But I won't go to the hospital."

The doctor laughed easily.

"Oh, but you must! And one nurse wouldn't be enough. You'll need two. And even then it would be absolutely no good. You can't be X-rayed here, for instance. It's no use me telling you how ill you are, because you know as well as I do how ill you are."

The battle was joined. Dr. Raste, in addition to being exasperated, had been piqued by the reports of his patient's singular obstinacy; he had now positively determined to get him into the hospital, and it was this resolve that had prompted him to give special attention to Mr. Earlforward's case, disorganizing all his general work in favour of it. He could not allow himself to be beaten by the inexplicable caprice of a patient who in all other respects had struck him as a man of more than ordinary sound sagacity, though of a somewhat miserly disposition; and the caprice was the more enigmatic in that to enter the hospital would be by far the cheapest way of treating the illness.

Mr. Earlforward's obstinacy, on the other hand, was exasperated and strengthened by the disdainful reception given to his marvellous, his perfectly reckless suggestion about having a private nurse. These people were ridiculously concerned about his health. They had their own ideas. He had his. He had offered an extremely generous compromise—a compromise which would cost him a pot of money—and it had not even been discussed; the wonder of it had in no way been recognized. Well, on the whole he was glad that the suggestion had not been approved. He withdrew it. He had only made it because he felt—doubtless in undue apprehension —that he was not yet beginning to progress towards recovery. He admitted to himself, for example, that whereas on the previous day he had been interested in his business, to-day his business was a matter of indifference to him. That, he knew, was not a good sign. But, then, to-morrow would certainly show some improvement. Indigestion—and he was suffering from nothing but acute indigestion—invariably did yield to a policy of starvation. As for hospitals, he had always had a horror of hospitals since once, in his insurance days, he had paid a visit to a fellow-clerk confined in a fever-ward. The vision of the huge, long, bare room, with its rows of beds and serried pain and distress, the draughts through the open windows, the rise and fall of the thunder of traffic outside, the semi-military bearing of the nurses, the wholesale-ness of the affair, the absence of privacy, the complete subjection of the helpless patients, the inelasticity of regulations, the crushing of individuality: this dreadful vision had ineffaceably impressed itself on his imagination—the imagination of an extreme individualist with a passion for living his own life free of the obligation to justify it or explain it. He had recalled the vision hundreds of times—and never mentioned it to a soul. He did not intend to die of his illness; he knew that he would not die of it, but he convinced himself that he would prefer anything, even death, to incarceration in a great hospital. Were he wrenched by force out of his bed, he would kick and struggle to the very last, and his captors should be stricken with the fear of killing him while trying in their misguided zeal to save him. He read correctly the pertinacity in the doctor's face. But he had never encountered a pertinacity stronger than his own, and illness had not weakened it, rather the reverse; his pertinacity had become morbid.

"I don't think I'll go into a hospital, doctor," he said quietly, turning his face away. The words were mild, the resolution invincible. The doctor crossed over to look him in the face. Their eyes met in fierce hostility. The doctor was beaten.

"Very well," said he, with bitter calm. "If you won't, you won't. There is nothing else for me to do here. I must ask you to be good enough to get another adviser. And"—he transfixed Elsie with a censorious gaze, as though Elsie was to blame—"and, please remember that if the worst comes to the worst, I shall certainly refuse to give a certificate."

"A certificate, sir?" Elsie faltered.

"Yes. A certificate of the cause of death. There would have to be an inquest," he explained, with implacable and calculated cruelty.

But Mr. Earlforward only laughed—a short, dry, sardonic laugh. The sun shone into the silent room and upon the tumbled bed and the sick, triumphant man, and made them more terrible than midnight could have made them. The doctor, with the pompous solemnity of a little man conscious of rectitude, slowly picked up his hat from the chest of drawers.

"But what am I to do?" Elsie appealed.

"My good woman, I don't know. I wish I did. All I know is, I've done what I could; and I can't take the private affairs of all Clerkenwell on my shoulders. I've other urgent cases to attend to." A faint snigger, which his will was too late to suppress!

"Elsie'll be all right," muttered Mr. Earlforward. "Elsie'll never desert me, Elsie won't. She promised me."

The doctor walked majestically out of the room, followed by Elsie.

CHAPTER VII

Malaria

"I SUPPOSE I must just do the best I can, sir," said Elsie on the landing outside the bedroom. She smiled timidly, cheerfully and benevolently.

The doctor looked at her, startled. It seemed to him that in some magic way she had vanquished the difficulties of a most formidable situation by merely facing and accepting them. She did not argue about them, complain about them, nor expatiate upon their enormity. She was ready to go on living and working without any fuss from one almost impossible moment to the next. During his career in Clerkenwell Dr. Raste had become a connoisseur of choice examples of practical philosophy, and none better than he could appreciate Elsie's attitude. That it should have startled him was a genuine tribute to her.

"Yes, that's about it," he said nonchalantly, with the cunning of an expert who has seen an undervalued unique piece in an antique shop. "Well, good morning, Elsie. Good morning."

He was in a hurry; he had half a hundred urgent matters on his professional conscience. What could he do but leave Elsie alone with her ordeal? He could not help her, and she did not need help in this particular work, which was, after all, part of her job at twenty pounds a year and food given and stolen. She was beginning to see the top of his hat as he descended the stairs. The stupid, plump, practical philosopher wanted to call him back for an affair of the very highest importance, and could not open her mouth, because Mr. Earlforward's desperate plight somehow inhibited her from doing so.

"Doctor!" she exclaimed with a strange shrillness as soon as he had passed from her sight into the shop.

"What now?" demanded Dr. Raste sharply, afraid that his connoisseurship should have been mistaken and she would stampede.

She ran down after him. His gaze indicated danger. He did not mean to have any nonsense.

"I suppose you couldn't just see Joe for a minute?" she stammered, with a blush. This now faltering creature had a moment earlier been calmly ready to do the best she could in circumstances which would scarcely bear looking at.

"Joe? What Joe?"

"Your old Joe. He's here, sir. Upstairs. Came last night, sir. He's very ill. I'm looking after him too. Master doesn't know."

"What in God's name are you talking about, my girl?" said the doctor, moved out of his impassibility.

She told him the facts, as though confessing a mortal sin for which she could not expect absolution.

"I really haven't a minute to spare," said he, and went upstairs with her to the second floor.

By the time they got there Elsie had resumed her self-possession.

The doctor, for all his detached and frigid poses, was on occasion capable, like nearly every man, of being as irrational as a woman. On this occasion he was guilty of a perfectly indefensible prejudice against both Elsie and Joe. He had a prejudice against Elsie because he was convinced that had it not been for her affair with Joe, Joe would still have been in his service. And he was prejudiced against Joe because he had suffered much from a whole series of Joe's successors. For the moment he was quite without a Joe. Also he resented Elsie having a secret sick man in the house—and that man Joe —and demanding so unexpectedly his attention when he was in a hurry and over-fatigued by the ills of the people of Clerkenwell. He would have justly condemned such prejudices in another, and especially in, for example, his wife; and it must be admitted he was not the god-like little being he thought he was. Fortunately Joe was in a state which made all equal before him.

"Oh dear! I do so ache, and I'm thirsty," the second patient groaned desperately, showing no emotion—surprise, awe or shame—at sight of the doctor and employer whom he had so cruelly wronged by leaving him in the lurch for inadequate reasons originating in mere sentiment. He had been solitary for half an hour and could not bear it. He wanted, and wanted ravenously, something from everybody he saw. The world existed solely to succour him. And certainly he looked very ill, forlorn, and wistfully savage in the miserable bed in the miserable bedroom of the ex-char-woman. He looked quite as ill as Mr. Earlforward, and to Elsie even worse.

"It's malaria," said the doctor in a casual tone, after he had gone through the routine of examination. "Temperature, of course. He'll be better in a few days. I've no doubt he had it in France first, but he never told me. When they brought back troops to France from the East, malaria came with them. All the north of France is covered with mos-quitoes, and they carry the disease. I'll send down some quinine. You must feed him on liquids—milk, barley-water, beef-tea, milk-and-soda. Hot water to drink, not cold. And you ought to sponge him down twice a day."

Elsie, listening intently to this mixture of advice and in-formation, could not believe that Joe's case was not more serious than the doctor's manner implied. Well implanted in her lay the not groundless conviction that doctors were apt to be much more summary with the sick poor than with the sick rich. And she was revisited by her old sense of this doctor's harsh indifference. He had not even greeted his former servant, had regarded him simply as he would regard any ordinary number in a panel.

"You won't have a great deal to do downstairs. In fact, scarcely anything," the doctor added, who apparently saw nothing excessive in leaving two patients in charge of one unaided woman, she being also housekeeper, shopkeeper, and domestic servant.

"Of course you can send him to the hospital if you care to," said the doctor lightly. "I dare say they'd take him in."

He, was, in fact, not anxious to insist on Joe's removal, thinking that he had already sufficiently worried the hospital authorities about the dwellers in Riceyman Steps.

To send Joe to the hospital would have relieved Elsie of the terrific responsibility which she had incurred by bringing him unpermitted into the house. But she did not want to surrender him. She hated to part with him. And privately, when it came to the point, she shared Mr. Earlforward's objection to hospitals. Joe might be neglected, she feared, in the hospital; he might be victimized by some rule. She had no confidence in the nursing of anybody except herself. She was persuaded that if she could watch him she might save him.

"I think I can manage him here, sir," she smiled. But it was a reserved smile, which said: "I have my own ideas about this matter and I don't swallow all I hear."

Dr. Raste began to put on his gloves; in the servant's room he had not taken off his hat, much less his overcoat. She escorted him downstairs. At the shop-door he suddenly said:

"If he *does* want another doctor there's Mr. Adhams— other side of Myddelton Square." His features relaxed. This remark was his repentance to Elsie, induced in him by her cheerful and unshrinking attitude towards destiny.

"You mean for master, sir?"

"Yes. *He* may be able to do something with him. You never know."

"I'm sure I'm very much obliged, sir," said Elsie eagerly, her kindliness springing up afresh and rushing out to meet the doctor's spark of feeling. He nodded. He had not said whether or not he would call again to see Joe, and she had not dared to suggest it. She shut the door and locked herself in the house with the two men.

CHAPTER VIII

A Climax

MR. EARLFORWARD woke up after what seemed to him a very long sleep, feeling appreciably better. He had less pain; at moments he had no pain. And his mind, he thought, was surprisingly clear and vigorous. He had ideas on all sorts of things. Most invalids got their perspective awry—he knew that—but his own perspective had remained absolutely true. Rising out of bed for a moment he found that he could stand without difficulty, which was yet another proof of his theory that people ate a vast deal too much. The doctor had been utterly wrong about him. The doctor had made a mystery about ordinary chronic indigestion. The present attack was passing, as the sufferer had always been convinced it would. A nice old mess of a complication they would have made of it at the hospital! Or more probably he would have been bundled out of the place with contumely as a malingering fraud! He straightened the bed a little, and then, slipping back into it with a certain eagerness, he began to concert plans, to reorganize and resume his existence.

The day was darkening. Four o'clock, perhaps. Elsie? Where was that girl? She ought to be coming. Had she got a bit above herself? Thought she was the boss of the whole place, no doubt, and could do as she chose! An excellent creature, trustworthy, devoted. . . . And yet—in some things they were all alike. Give them an inch and they'd take an ell. He must be after her. Now what was it he had noticed, or thought he had noticed, when he was last awake? Oh, yes! That was it. His keys. He had missed them from the top of the chest of drawers. He peered in the gloom. They were there right enough. Perhaps hidden before by something else. The room had been tidied, dusted, while he slept. He didn't quite care for that, but he supposed it couldn't be helped. Anyhow, it showed that she was not being utterly idle. Of course the girl was not going to bed properly, but she had ample opportunity to sleep. With the shop closed she had practically nothing to do. . . .

"Fibroid growth." Fibroid—like fibre, of course. He scarcely understood how a growth could be like fibre; but it was a name, a definition, and therefore reassuring. Much better than "cancerous," at the worst! An entirely different thing from cancer! But he was dreadfully concerned, frightened, for Violet. If she died—not that it was conceivable—but *if* she died, what a blank! Sickening! No! He could not contemplate it. Yet simultaneously in his mind was a little elusive thought: as a widower, freed from the necessity of adapting himself to another, and of revealing to another to some extent his ideas, intentions, schemes—what freedom! The old freedom! And he would plunge into it as into an exquisite, warm bath, voluptuously. He would be more secretive, more self-centred, more prudent, more fixed in habit than ever! A great practical philosopher, yes! In no matter what event he would discover compensations. And there were still deeper depths in the fathomless pit of his busy mind, depths into which he himself would do no more than glance—rather scared.

Elsie came in and saw a sinister sick man, pale as the dying, shrunk by starvation, with glittering, suspicious little eyes.

"Oh! So you've come, miss!" He wished that he had not said "miss." It was a tiny pleasantry of reproof, but too familiar. Another inch, another ell!

"Why! You've been making your bed again!" she exclaimed.

But she exclaimed so nicely, so benevolently, that he could not take offence. And yet—might she not be condescending to him? Withal, he enjoyed her presence in the bedroom. Her youth, her reliability, her prettiness (he thought she was growing prettier and prettier every day—such dark eyes, such dark hair, such a curve of the lips), and her physical power and health! Her mere health seemed miraculous to him. Oh!

She was a god-send. . . . She had said nothing about Violet. Well, if she had had news she would have told him. He hesitated to mention Violet. He could wait till she began.

"I'll run and make you some food," she said.

"Here! No so fast! Not so fast!" he stopped her.

He was about to give an order when, for the second time, he noticed that her apron was wet in several places.

"Why is your apron all wet?" he demanded sharply.

"Is it?" she faltered, looking down at it. "So it is! I've been doing things." (She appeared to have dropped the "sir" completely.)

The fact was that she had been sponging Joe.

Mr. Earlforward became suspicious. He suspected that she was wasting warm water.

"Why are you always running upstairs?" he asked in a curious tone.

"Running upstairs, sir?"

(Ha! "Sir." He was recovering his grip on her.)

She blushed red. She had something to hide. Hordes of suspicions thronged through his mind.

"Well, sir, I have to go to the kitchen."

"I don't hear you so often in the *kitchen*," said he dryly.

It was true. And all footsteps in the kitchen could be heard overhead in the bedroom. He suspected that she was carrying on conversations from her own bedroom window with new-made friends in the yard of the next house or the next house but one, and giving away the secrets of the house. But he did not utter the suspicion; he kept it to himself for the present. Yes, they were all alike.

"You haven't inquired, Elsie, but I'm much better," he said.

"Oh! I can *see* you are, sir!" she responded brightly.

But whether she really thought so, or whether she was just humouring him, he could not tell.

"Yes. And I'm going to get up."

"Not to-day you aren't, sir," she burst out.

He said placidly:

"No. To-morrow morning. And I think I shall put

on one of my new suits and a new shirt. I think it's about time. I don't want to get shabby. Just show them to me."

Elsie was evidently amazed at the suggestion. And he himself did not know why he had made it. But, at any rate, it was not a bad idea. He fancied that he might feel better in a brand new suit. He indicated the right drawers to her, and one by one she had to display on the bed the carefully preserved garments which he had bought for a song years ago and never persuaded himself into the extravagance of wearing. The bed was covered with new merchandise. He thought that he would have to wear the clothes some time, and might as well begin at once. It would be uneconomic to waste them, and worn or unworn they would go for far less than a song after his death. He must be sensible; he must keep his perspective in order. He regarded this decision to have out a new suit as a truly great feat of considered sagacity on the part of a sick man.

Elsie with extreme care restored all the virgin clothes to their drawers except one suit and one shirt, which for convenience she put separately into Mrs. Earlforward's wardrobe. As all the suits were the same and all the shirts were the same, it did not matter which suit and which shirt were selected. But this did not prevent him from choosing, and hesitating in his choice.

Elsie seemed to be alarmed by the scene—he could not understand why.

"Of course," he said, "being new they'll hang a bit looser on me than my old suit; that's all wrinkled up. I'm not quite so stout as I was, am I?"

Elsie turned round to him from the wardrobe with a nervous movement, and then quickly back again. The fading light glinted for a second on a tear-drop that ran down her cheek. This tear-drop annoyed Mr. Earlforward; he resented it, and was not in the least touched by it. He had not perceived the extraordinary pathos in the phrase "not quite so stout," coming from a man who had never been stout (or slim either), and who was now a stick, a skeleton; he thought she was merely crying because he had lost flesh. As if people weren't always either putting on flesh or losing it! As a fact, Elsie had not felt the pathos of the phrase either, and her tears had no connexion whatever with Mr. Earlforward's wasting away. Nor had they sprung from the still more tragic pathos of his caprice about a new suit. In depositing the chosen suit in Mrs. Earlforward's wardrobe Elsie had caught sight of the satin shoe which on the bridal night she had tied to the very bedstead whereon the husband was now lying alone. She thought of the husband lying alone and desperately ill and desperately determined not to be ill, and the wife far off in the hospital, and of her own helplessness, and she simply could not bear to look at the shabby old shoe—which some unknown girl had once worn in flashing pride. All the enigma of the universe was in that shoe, with its curved high heel perched lifeless on a mahogany tray of the everlasting wardrobe. Elsie had never heard of the enigma of the universe, but it was present with her in many hours of her existence.

Mr. Earlforward said suddenly:

"Was the operation going to be done this morning or this afternoon?" He knew that the operation had been fixed for the morning, but he had to account to Elsie for his apparent lack of curiosity.

"This morning, sir."

"We ought to be getting some news soon, then."

"Well, sir. That's just what I was wondering. I don't hardly think as they'll send up—not unless it was urgent. So I suppose it's gone off all right." A pause. "But we ought to know for certain, sir. I was thinking I could run out and get someone to go down and find out—I mean someone who *would* find out and tell us all about it—not a child. I dare say a shilling or two——"

With her experience Elsie ought not to have mentioned money, but she was rather distraught. The patient reacted instantly. It was evident to him that Elsie had old friends in the Square, or near by, upon whom she wanted to confer benefits through the medium of her employer's misfortunes. They were always bent on lining their pockets, those people were. He was not going to let them pick up shillings and

florins as easily as all that. His shop was perforce closed; his
business was decaying; his customers would transfer their
custom to other shops; not a penny was coming in; communism was rife; the political and trade outlook was menacing in
the extreme; there was no clear hope anywhere; he saw himself as an old man begging his bread. And the girl proposed
gaily to scatter shillings over Riceyman Square for a perfectly
unnecessary object! She had not reflected at all. They never
did. They were always eager to spend other people's money.
Not their own! Oh, no! He alone had kept a true perspective, and he would act according to his true perspective. He
was as anxious as anybody for news of the result of the operation and Violet's condition; but he did not see the need to
engage an army of special messengers for the collecting of
news. An hour sooner or an hour later—what difference
could it make? He would know soon enough, too soon if it
was to be bad news; and if it was to be good news a little delay
would only increase joy.... And, moreover, you would have
thought that even the poorest and most rapacious persons
would not expect money for services rendered in a great crisis
to the sick and the bedridden.

"I see no reason for doing that," he said placidly and firmly.
"Let me think now——"

"Shall I run down there myself? It won't take me
long."

She was ready in the emergency, and in deference to his
astounding whims, to take the fearful risks of leaving the two
men alone together in the house. Suppose Joe should rise up
violent? Suppose Mr. Earlforward should begin in his weakness to explore the house? He was already suspecting something; and she knew him for the most inquisitive being ever
born. She trembled. Still, she was ready to go, and to run
all the way there and all the way back.

"Oh, no!" he forbade positively. "That's won't do at
all." He was afraid to lose her. He, so seriously ill (he was
now seriously ill again!), to be left by himself in the house!
It was unthinkable. "Look here. Step across to Belrose's"
(Belrose—the man who had purchased Violet's confectionery

business). "I hear he's got the telephone now. Ask him to telephone for us to the hospital. Then we shall know at once."

"We don't do much with them," Elsie objected, diffident. The truth was that the Earlforward household bought practically nothing at Belrose's, Belrose's not being quite Violet's "sort of shop" under its new ownership.

Mr. Earlforward almost sat up in his protest against the horrible suggestion contained in Elsie's remark. What! Would Belrose say: "'No, you don't deal with me, and therefore I won't oblige you by telephoning to the hospital to find out whether Mrs. Earlforward is alive or dead'?" A monstrous notion!

"Don't be silly," he chid her gravely. "Do as I tell you and run down at once."

"And would you like me to ask them to telephone for another doctor for you while I'm about it? There's Dr. Adhams, he's in Myddelton Square too. They do say he's very good."

"When I want another doctor I'll let you know, Elsie," said Mr. Earlforward, with frigid calm. "There's a great deal too many doctors. What has Raste done for me, I should like to know?"

"You wouldn't *let* him do anything," said Elsie sharply.

He had never heard her speak with less benevolence. Of course he was entitled to give her a good dressing-down, and it might even be his duty to do so. But he lacked confidence in himself. Strange, but he was now in the last resort afraid of Elsie! She was like an amiable and tractable animal which astonishingly shows its teeth and growls.

"Leave the door open," he muttered.

As Elsie descended to the shop there was a peremptory and loud rat-tat, and then a tattoo on the glass of the shop-door. It frightened her. She thought naturally of the possibility of bad news by special messenger or telegraph from the hospital. But Mrs. Perkins's boy Jerry was at the door. He wore his uniform, of which the distinguishing characteristics were a cap with brass letters on the peak and a leathern apron initialled in black. In King's Cross Road an enormous motor-lorry throbbed impatiently in attendance upon the gnome.

"Here's yer umbrella, Elsie," said Jerry proudly. "I thought you might be wanting of it."

He made no inquiry as to sick persons. He was only interested in the romantic fact that he had used the vast resources of his company to restore the umbrella to his queen, carrying it all day through all manner of streets in his long round, and finally persuading that important personage the motor-driver to stop at Riceyman Steps on no business of the company's. Elsie took the umbrella from his dirty little hands, which were, however, no dirtier than his grinning face, and he ran off almost before she could thank him.

"Jerry!" she summoned him back, and he came, risking the wrath of the driver. "Come along to-night, will yer, after ye've done? Rap quiet on the door. I might want yer."

"Right O, Elsie!" He was gone. The lorry was gone.

Elsie went upstairs again with the umbrella, not because the umbrella would not have been safe in the shop, but because she felt that she must give another glance at Joe before she left the premises. It was an unconsidered movement. She had forgotten that Mr. Earlforward's bedroom door was open.

"Elsie," he called out, as she passed on the landing, "who was that?"

Her tired and exasperated brain worked with extraordinary swiftness. She decided that she could not enter into a long explanation concerning the umbrella and Jerry. Why should she? "He" was already suspicious.

"Postman," she answered, without the slightest hesitation, lying as glibly and lightly as a born, lifelong liar, and continued her way upstairs. She was somehow vaguely, indirectly, defending the secrecy of Joe.

In her room she put the umbrella in its paper again under her bed, gazing at Joe as she did so. Joe was very ill. She had given him two doses of quinine (which Dr. Raste, making Elsie ashamed of her uncharitable judgments on him, had had sent direct from a chemist's within an hour and a half of his departure), and she was disturbed that the medicine had not produced an immediate and marked effect on the patient.

Joe had got one arm through the ironwork at the head of the bed, and was tearing off little slips of the peeling wall-paper in the corner. She took hold of his hot hand, and silently guided it back through the ironwork on to the bed.

"Shall I give you another dose?" she suggested tentatively, with brow creased.

He nodded. He knew malaria and he knew quinine; and, fortified by his expert approval, she gave him another dose. Both of them had the belief that if five grains of a medicine did you ten per cent. of "good," ten grains would assuredly do you twenty per cent. of good, and so on in proportion.

"I'm coming in again in a minute or two. I've just got to go across the Steps on an errand," she said, and kissed him. Both of them had also the belief that her kisses did him good; and this conviction was better founded than the other one. She had said nothing to him about Mrs. Earlforward's opera-tion. He had learnt only that Elsie was mistress because Mrs. Earlforward was in hospital; the full story might have aggra-vated his mental distress.

"Elsie!" It was Mr. Earlforward's summons as she crossed the landing on her way down.

She put no more than her face—a rather mettlesome face—into the room.

"What do you keep on going upstairs for?"

Yes. He suspected. With strange presence of mind she replied promptly:

"I've just been up for the key of the shop, sir. I left it up in my room. I can't go out and leave the shop door on the latch, can I?"

"Well, bring me all the letters."

"Oh, very well. Very well!" She was hostile again.

This time she shut the bedroom door, ignoring his protest. Then she went upstairs once more and locked her own door on the outside and carried off the key. At any rate, if in some impossible caprice he should take it into his head to prowl about the house in her absence, he should not pry into her room. He had no right to do so. And she was absolutely determined to defend her possession of Joe. A moment later she bounced into Mr. Earlforward's bedroom, and carelessly dropped all the letters on to the bed—a regular shower of envelopes and packets.

"There!" she exclaimed, on a hard and inimical note, as if saying: "You asked for them. You've got them. And I wash my hands of it all."

Mr. Earlforward saw that he must walk warily. She was a changing Elsie, a disagreeably astonishing Elsie. He did not quite know where he was with her.

As she emerged from the shop into the Steps a young woman with a young dog, stopping suddenly, addressed her in soft, apprehensive, commiserating accents:

"How is Mr. Earlforward this evening?"

"He seems to think as he's a bit better, 'm, thank you, *in himself*," Elsie answered brightly. She was uplifted by the mere concern in the voice, and at once felt more kindly towards her master, was indeed rather ashamed of her recent harshness to him.

Dusk had now fallen, and she could not see very clearly, but the next instant she had recognized both the woman and the dog. Quite a lady! A sort of a sealskin coat! Gloves! Utterly different from the savage creature of the previous night. The dog, too, was different. A dog lacking yet in experience of the world, and apt to forget that a dog's business is to keep an eye on its guardian if it sets any store on a quiet and safe existence; but still well disposed towards its guardian, and apparently in no fear of her. More remorse for Elsie.

"Oh! I'm *so* glad! . . . And Mrs. Earlforward?"

"Oh, 'm! We haven't heard. We're expecting news."

"I do hope everything 'll be all right. Operation—internal trouble, isn't it?"

"Yes, 'm."

"Yes. So I heard. Well, thank you. Good night. Skip—Skip!"

Skip was the disturber of repose, and he responded, leaping. The two disappeared round the corner.

It was wonderful to Elsie how everybody knew, and how kind everybody was. She was touched. The woman had given her the illusion that the whole of Clerkenwell was filled with anxiety for the welfare of her master and her mistress. Her sense of responsibility was intensified. If the whole of Clerkenwell knew that she was secretly harbouring her young man in her bedroom! . . . She went hot. The complexity of her situation frightened her afresh.

Belrose's was at its old royal game of expending vast quantities of electric current. The place had just been lighted up, and had the air of a popular resort; it warmed and vitalized all the Steps by its radiance, which seemed to increase from month to month. What neither Mr. Earlforward nor anybody else of the old Clerkenwell tradition had ever been able to understand or approve was the continual illumination of the upper storeys. And yet the solution of the mystery was simple, and lay in a fact with which most of the district was familiar. Belrose had "gone in for wholesale." Elsie entered the shop very timidly, for she regarded her errand as "presuming," and in the midst of all her anxieties she had diffidence enough to be a little ashamed of it.

The shop was most pleasantly warm; its warmth was a greeting which would have overpowered some folk; and there was a fine rich odour of cheese and humanity. Also the shop was full. You could scarcely move in it. The stock was plenteous, and the character of the stock had changed. Advertised brands of comestibles of universal consumption were far less prominent than under previous régimes, and there was a great deal more individuality. The travellers and the collectors of advertised brands now called at the establishment with a demeanour different from of old; they had to leave their hard-faced, bullying manner on the doorstep. Two enormous and smiling young, mature women stood behind the counter. Their magnificently rounded façades were covered with something that was only white on Saturdays and Wednesdays, and certainly was not white to-night. Like the shop itself the servers were neither tidy nor clean; but they were hearty, gay and active, and they had authority, for one of them was

Mr. Belrose's sister, and the other Mrs. Belrose's sister; nevertheless, they looked like sisters; they both had golden, rough hair and ruddy complexions, and the same experienced, comprehending, jolly expression, and fat, greasy hands.

There were four customers in the shop, of course all women, and the six women seemed to be all chatting together. The interior was the interior of a shop in full swing, but it showed in addition the better qualities of a bar parlour whose landlord knows how to combine respectability with freedom of style. Miss Belrose, who was nearest the door, smiled benignantly at Elsie on her entrance, as if saying: "You are one of us, and we are yours."

When two outgoing customers squeezed themselves between Elsie and a pile of cheeses, and her turn came to be served, Elsie suddenly discovered that she could not straight away execute Mr. Earlforward's command. She had a feeling that shops did not exist in order to supply telephone accommodation gratis to non-customers, and she was simply unable to articulate the request; nor did the extreme seriousness of the case inspire her to boldness. She asked for a quarter of a pound of cheese, and was immediately requested to name any cheese that she might fancy, the implication being that no matter what her fancy it could and would be satisfied on the most advantageous terms.

Now Elsie did not want any cheese; she wanted nothing at all. Mrs. Earlforward, before vanishing into the hospital, had bought for the master a generous supply of invalid foods, which, for the most part refused by the obstinate master, would suffice Joe for several days, and of all such eatables as Belrose's sold Elsie had in hand enough also for several days.

She said "Cheddar," reacting quite mechanically to the question put; and then she was confronted with another problem. She had no money, not a penny. It would be necessary for her to say, "I must run back for some money," and having said that to return and somehow manœuvre Mr. Earlforward's keys off the chest of drawers and rifle the safe once more. And already he was suspicious! How could she do it! She could not do it. But she must do it. She

K

saw the cheese weighed and slipped into a piece of paper. The moment of trial was upon her.

Then the back door of the shop opened—she recognized the old peculiar, familiar sound of the latch—and a third enormous, white-clad, golden-haired, jolly, youngish woman appeared in the doorway. This was Mrs. Belrose herself, and you at once saw, and even felt, that her authority exceeded the authority of her sister and her sister-in-law. Mrs. Belrose was a ruler. As soon as she saw Elsie her gigantic face softened into a very gentle smile of compassion, a smile that conveyed nothing but compassion, excluding all jollity. She raised a stout finger and without a word beckoned Elsie into the back-room and shut the door. The ancient kitchen-parlour was greatly changed. It was less clean than Elsie had left it, but it glittered with light. More cheeses! And in the corner by the mantelpiece was the telephone. And through the window Elsie saw an oldish, thin little man moving about in the yard with a lantern against a newly erected shed. Still more cheeses —seemingly as many cheeses as Mr. Earlforward possessed books! The oldish man was Mr. Belrose, guardian and over-lord of the three women, and original instigator of this singu-lar wholesale trade in cheeses which he had caused to prosper despite the perfect unsuitability of his premises and other difficulties. Individuality and initiative had triumphed. People asked one another how the Belroses had contrived to build up such a strange success, but they had only to look at the mien and gestures of the Belroses to find the answer to the question.

"How are you getting on, my dear?" demanded Mrs. Belrose, who had scarcely spoken to Elsie in her life before.

"Master wished me to ask you if you'd mind telephoning to the hospital, 'm," said Elsie, after she had given some details.

"Of course I will. With the greatest pleasure."

Mrs. Belrose grabbed at the tattered telephone-book, and whetting her greasy thumb whipped over the pages rapidly.

"Where's them Saints now? Oh, 'Saintbury's.' 'Saint.' 'St. Bartholomew's Football and Cricket Ground.' I expect that's for the doctors and students. 'St. Bartholomew's Hospital.' This is it. Here we are. City 510. . . . Oh, dear! oh, dear! 'No telephone information given respecting patients.' Oh, dear, oh, dear!" She looked at Elsie. "Never mind," she went on brightly. "We can get over that, I should think."

She obtained the number and got into communication with the reception office of the hospital.

"I want you to be kind enough to give a message to Mrs. Violet Earlforward from her husband. She's in your hospital for an operation. . . . Oh, but you must, please. He's very ill. But he's a bit better, and it will do Mrs. Earlforward ever so much good to know. . . . Oh, *please*! Yes, I know, but they can't send anyone down. Oh, you don't count rules when it's urgent. It might be life and death. But you can telephone up to the ward. You're starred, so you must have a private exchange. Oh, yes. To *oblige*. Yes, Earlforward, Violet. And you might just ask how she is while you're about it. You *are* good."

She held the line and waited, sitting down on a chair to rest herself. And to Elsie:

"They're very nice, really, at those hospitals, once you get on the right side of them. I suppose *you*'ve got about all you can do?"

"Well, there isn't much nursing, and the shop's closed."

"Oh, yes, and the Steps do look so queer with it closed. Somehow it makes it look like Sunday. Doctor has been to-day, I suppose?"

"Yes, 'm. This morning," said Elsie, and stopped there, not caring to divulge the secret of Mr. Earlforward's insane obstinacy.

"Yes. I'm here. I'm listening. Oh, dear! Oh, dear! She's—— Oh, dear! Owing to what? 'Under—nourishment'? . . . He's rung off."

Mrs. Belrose sniffed as she hung up the receiver.

"Oh, Elsie! Your poor mistress has died under it. She died about half an hour ago. According to what *they* say, she might have pulled through, but she hadn't strength to rally

owing to—under-nourishment. . . . Well, I'm that cut up!"
Mrs. Belrose cried feebly.

Elsie stared at her and did not weep.

"Ought I to tell him, 'm?"

"Oh, yes, you must *tell* him. There's no sense in hiding
them things—especially as he's a little better. He's *got* to know.
And he'd be very angry, and quite rightly, if he wasn't told,
and at once."

"I'll go and tell him."

"Would you like me to come with you?"

"You're very kind, 'm," said Elsie, cunning even in disaster.
"I can manage. He's very peculiar, but I know how to
manage him. There won't be nothing to be done till to-
morrow, anyway."

She had another and a far more perilous secret to keep, that
of Joe. Therefore she dared not admit a stranger to the house.
Of course, soon she would have to admit strangers—but not
to-night, not to-night! She must postpone evil.

Mrs. Belrose lifted her immense bulk and kissed Elsie, and
then Elsie cried. Saying not a word more, she turned, opened
the door, and passed through the shop, rapt, totally ignoring
the servers and the quarter of a pound of cheese.

"To-morrow," she said to herself, "I shall tell her" (Mrs.
Belrose) "all about Joe. She'll understand." The mere
thought of Mrs. Belrose was a refuge for her. "But missis
can't be dead. It was only yesterday morning——"

"Leave me alone. Leave me!" breathed Henry Earlforward in a dismaying murmur when she gave him the news.
She obeyed.

CHAPTER IX

The Kiss

THAT night Elsie sat in the parlour (as she still to herself called the dining-room) by the gas-fire which she had lighted on her own responsibility. An act and a situation which a few days earlier, two days earlier, would have been inconceivable to her! But Joe's clothes had refused to dry in the kitchen; the gas-ring there was incapable of drawing the water out of them in the damp weather. Now they were dry; some of them were folded on a chair; upon these were laid the braces which she had given to him on his birthday, and which evidently he had worn ever since. To Elsie now these soiled and frayed braces had a magic vital quality. They seemed, far more than the clothes, to have derived from him some of his individuality, to be a detached part of him; she was sewing a button on the lifeless old trousers, and she had taken the button, and the thimble, needle, and thread from Mrs. Earlforward's cardboard sewing-box in the left-hand drawer of the sideboard. She was working with the tools of a dead lady. At moments this irked and frightened her; at other moments she thought that what must be must be, and that, anyhow, the clothes ought to be put in order; and she could not go upstairs and disturb Joe by searching for her own apparatus—which certainly did not comprise trouser buttons. She tried to be natural and not to look ahead. She would not, for instance, dwell upon the apparently insoluble problem of arranging a proper funeral for Mrs. Earlforward. How could she, the servant, do anything towards that? She dared not leave her patients. She knew nothing about the organization of funerals. She had never even been to a funeral. She had no knowledge of possible relatives of the Earlforwards.

"To-morrow! To-morrow! Not till to-morrow—all that!" she said doggedly.

But she failed to push away everything. In the midst of her great grief for the death of Mrs. Earlforward (a perfect woman and a martyr) the selfish thought of her own future haunted her and would not be dismissed. Would Joe ever again wear those clothes which she was mending? He had taken some Bovril (Mr. Earlforward also), but she could not persuade herself that he was really better. She was terror-struck by the varied possibilities attending his death. A dead man secretly in her bed! What a plight for her! She determined afresh to confide the secret of Joe to Mrs. Belrose to-morrow morning. Not that the mere inconveniences of death deeply troubled her. No! In truth they were naught. Or rather, if he died they would have absolutely no importance to her compared with the death itself. Having found Joe, was she to lose him again? She could not face such a prospect. . . .

And then Mr. Earlforward. She was beginning to be convinced that the master really was better. He had taken the Bovril. He had opened one or two of his letters. The shock of the news about Mrs. Earlforward, instead of shattering him to pieces, had strengthened him, morally if not physically. He might recover—he was an amazing man! And, of course, she desired him to recover. Could she wish anyone's death? She could not be so cruel, so wicked! And yet, and yet, if he lived, she was his slave for ever; she was a captive with no hope of escape. A slave, either bowed down by sorrow for the death of Joe, or fatally desolated by the eternal reflection that Joe was alive and she could not have him because of her promise to Mr. Earlforward! She saw no hope; she made no reserves in the interpretation of her vow to the master. She could not see that circumstances inevitably, if slowly, alter cases.

She yawned heavily in extreme exhaustion.

Then her ear caught a faint, cautious tapping below. All trembling she crept downstairs. Jerry was at the shop-door. In the turmoil of distress she had forgotten that she had commanded him to call for orders. She was glad to have someone to talk to for a little while, and she brought him into the office. She saw in front of her, on the opposite side of the desk, a young lad who had most surprisingly and touchingly put on his best clothes for important events. Also he had washed himself. Also he was smoking a cigarette.

Jerry, who was thin and pinched in the face, saw in front of him an ample and splendid young woman—not very young to him, for his notion of youthfulness was rather narrow, but much younger than his mother, though much older than Nell, his fancy of the Square, whose years did correspond with his notion of youthfulness. Elsie was slightly taller than himself. He thought she had the nicest, kindest face he had ever seen. He loved her brow when she frowned in doubt or anxiety; for him even her aprons were different from any other woman's aprons. He was precocious, in love as in other matters, but he did not love Elsie, did not aspire to love her. She was above him, out of his reach; he went in awe of her; he liked to feel that she was his tyrant. She was the most romantic, mysterious, and beautiful of all women and girls. Elsie very well understood his attitude towards her.

"I thought I might want yer to run down to the hospital for me, Jerry boy," she said. "But I shan't now. Mrs. Earlforward died this afternoon."

"It's all over the Square," said Jerry, spitting negligently into the dark fireplace, and pushing his cap further back on his head.

Elsie saw that he did not understand death.

"Yes," said she, "I suppose it is." She said no more, because of the uselessness of talking about death to a simple-minded youth like Jerry.

"It was very nice of you to bring me my umbrella like that," she said.

"Oh!" said he, falsely scornful of himself. "It was easiest for me to bring it along like that."

He had been standing with his legs apart; at this point he sat down familiarly and put his elbows on the desk and his jaw in his hands; the cigarette hung loosely in his very mobile lips. They were silent; Jerry was proud and happy, and had nothing in particular to say about it. Elsie had too much to say to be able to talk.

"Then ye haven't got anything for me to do?" he asked.

"No, I haven't."

"Oo!" He was disappointed.

"But I might have to-morrow. You'll be off at two o'clock to-morrow, won't yer?"

"That's me."

"Very well then." She rose.

Jerry was extraordinarily uplifted by this brief sojourn alone with Elsie in the private office of T. T. Riceyman's. He felt that he was more of a grown man than ten thousand cigarettes and oaths and back-chat with fragile virgins in the Square could make him. He sprang from the chair.

"Give me a kiss, Elsie," he blurted out audaciously. He was frightened by his own cheek.

"Jerry Perkins!" Elsie admonished him. "Aren't ye ashamed of yerself? Mrs. Earlforward dead! And them two so ill upstairs!"

"What two?" Jerry asked, rather to cover his confusion than from curiosity.

"I mean Mr. Earlforward," said Elsie. She was not abashed at her slip. With Jerry she had a grandiose rôle to play, and no contretemps could spoil her performance.

Jerry guessed instantly that she had got Joe hidden in the house, but he never breathed a word of it. He even tried to look stupid and uncomprehending, which was difficult for him.

"Aren't ye ashamed of yerself?" she solemnly repeated.

He moved towards the door. Elsie's glance followed him. She was sorry for him. She wanted to be good to somebody. She could not help Mr. Earlforward. She could do very little for Joe. Mrs. Earlforward was dead, and she could so easily give Jerry delight.

"Here!" she said.

He turned. She kissed him quietly but fully. There were no reservations in her kiss. Jerry, being too startled by unexpected joy, could not give the kiss back. He lost his nerve and went off so absorbed in his sensations that he forgot even to thank the sweet benefactress. In the Square his behaviour to the attendant Nell was witheringly curt. Nell did not know that she now had to cope with a genuine adult.

CHAPTER X

The Safe

NOT a sound in the house; nor outside the house. Not a clock nor a watch going in the house. Mr. Earlforward had listened interminably to get the time from the church, but without success. He knew only from the prolonged silence of the street that the hour must be very late. "Work!" he murmured to himself in the vast airless desert and void created by the death of Violet. "That's the one thing—the one thing." His faculty for compromising with destiny aroused itself for a supreme achievement. It was invincible. He would not think himself into hell or madness or inanition by yielding feebly to the frightened grief caused by the snatching away of that unique woman so solicitous about him, so sensible, so vivacious, so agreeable, so energetic, so enterprising, so ready to adopt his ideas—and yet so independent. Her little tantrums—how exquisite, girlish! There had always been a girl in her. The memory of her girlishness desolated him more than anything.

"Insufficient nourishment"? No! It could not have been that. Had he ever, on any occasion, in the faintest degree, discouraged her from satisfying her appetite? Or criticized her housekeeping accounts? No! Never had he interfered. Moreover she had plenty of money of her own and the absolutely unfettered use of it. He would give her such a funeral as had not been seen in Clerkenwell for many a year. The cost, of course, might be charged to her estate, but he would not allow that—though, of course, it would all be the same in the end.

He could not bear to lie in the bed which she had shared with him. The feel of the empty half of it, when he passed his hand slowly over the lower blanket in the dark, tortured him intolerably, and yet he must somehow keep on passing his hand over it. Futile and sick indulgence! He got out of bed, drew aside the curtains and drew up the blind. He could not see the moon, but it was lighting the roofs opposite, and its light and that of the gas-lamp lit the room sufficiently to reveal all the principal features of it. Animated by the mighty power of his resolution to withstand fate he felt strong—he *was* strong. His cold legs were quite steady. Yes, though he still had a dull pain, the attack of indigestion was declining. He had successfully taken Bovril. To work, seated at his desk, could not tire him, and ought to do him good.

A queer affair, that indigestion! He had never suffered from indigestion until the day after his wedding-night, when he had eaten so immoderately of Elsie's bride-cake. The bride-cake seemed to have been the determining cause, or perhaps it was merely the occasion, of some change in his system. (But naturally he had said nothing of it). However, he was now better. A little pain in the old spot—no more.

He opened the wardrobe to get his new shirt and new suit, and saw in the pale gloom Violet's garments arranged on their trays. The sight of them shook him terribly. He must assuredly save himself by the labour of reconstituting his existence. It was impossible for him to remain in the bedroom. He dressed himself in the new clothes, putting a muffler round his neck instead of a collar. Then he filled his pockets with his personal belongings from the top of the chest of drawers. None was missing. He picked up the pile of correspondence, which he had laid neatly on the pedestal. He could walk without discomfort. He must work. The grim intention to work was irresistibly monopolizing his mind, and driving all else out of it. He left the bedroom —a deed in itself.

On the landing, as he looked upwards, he could see light under Elsie's bedroom door. The candles that girl must be burning! He would correct her. Should he? Supposing she rebelled! Elsie had changed; he did not quite know where he was with her; and he did not want to lose her. She was his mainstay in the world. Still, it would never do to be afraid of correcting a servant. He would correct her. He would knock at her door and tell her—not for the first time. He mounted two steps, but his legs nearly failed him. He could walk downstairs but not up. Besides, if she knew that he was out of bed there might be trouble, and he wished to avoid trouble. Therefore, he turned and limped downstairs into the shop and lit it.

To see the shop was like revisiting after an immense period the land of his youth. He recognized one by one the land-marks. Here was the loaded bookstand, with its pair of castors, which *she* had devised. The shop was like a mauso-leum of trade. His trade had ceased. It had to be brought back to life, galvanized into activity. Could he do it? He must and he would do it. He was capable of the intensest effort. His very sorrow was inspiring him. On the floor at the entrance lay some neglected correspondence which bore footmarks. Servants were astounding. Elsie had been too negligent even to pick the letters up. She probably never would have picked them up. She would have trod and trod them into the dirty boards—demands for books, offers of books, possibly cheques—the stuff itself of trade. He picked them up with difficulty, and padded into the office, which also he lit. Cold! He shivered.

"I'm not entirely cured yet," he thought, and began to doubt himself. The fire was prepared—Violet's influence again. Fires had never been laid in advance till she came. He put a match to the fire and felt better. Undecided, he stroked his cheek. Stubble! How long was it since he had shaved? His face must look a pretty sight. Happily there was no mirror in either the office or the shop, so that he could not inspect himself. Work! Work! Memories were insinu-ating themselves anew in his mind. He must repulse them. Fancy her running off like that, without a word of good-bye, to the hospital, and now she was irrevocably gone! It was incredible, monstrous, the most sinister piece of devil's magic that ever happened. . . . Chloroform. The knife. Fibroid growth. . . . Dead. Vanished. She with her vivacity and her optimism. . . . He was fatigued. The pain had recurred. It was very bad. Perhaps he had been ill-advised to come downstairs, for he could not get upstairs again. He cautiously skirted the desk, holding on to it, and sat in his chair. Work! Work! The reconstruction of his life!

He fingered the letters. With one of them was a cheque, and it must go into the safe for the night. He would endorse it to-morrow. Never endorse a cheque till you paid it into the bank, for an endorsed cheque might be the prey of thieves. He bent down sideways to his safe with a certain pleasure. *Her* safe was upstairs in the bath-room. He would have to obtain her keys and open it and examine its contents. He took his own keys from his pocket, and, not very easily, unlocked his safe, and swung forward its door. The familiar act soothed him. The sublime spectacle of the safe, sole symbol of security in a world of perils, enheartened him. After all . . .

Then he noticed that the silver bag was not precisely in its customary spot on the ledge over the nest of drawers. He started in alarm and clutched at the bag. It was not tied with his knot. He unloosed it and felt crumpled paper within it. "6d"! Elsie's clumsy handwriting, which he knew so well from having seen it now and then on little lists of sales on the backs of envelopes! No! It was not the loss of sixpence that affected him. He could have borne that. What so profoundly, so formidably, shocked him was the fact that Elsie had surreptitiously taken his keys, rifled the safe, and returned the keys—and smiled on him and nursed him! There was no security at all in the world of perils. The foundations of faith had been destroyed. Elsie!

But in the agony of the crisis he did not forget his wife. He moaned aloud:

"What would Violet have thought? What would my poor Violet have thought of this?"

His splendid fortitude, his superhuman courage to recreate his existence over the ruins of it and to defy fate, were broken down. Life was bigger, more cruel, more awful than he had imagined.

CHAPTER XI

Prison

"JOE," inquired Elsie, "where's your papers?"

She had brought his clothes—dry, folded, and possibly wearable—back into her bedroom. She had found nothing in the pockets of the suit except some cigarette-card portraits of famous footballers, a charred pipe, three French sous, and a broken jack-knife. These articles, the raiment, and a pair of battered shoes which she had pushed under the bed and forgotten, seemed to be all that Joe had to show for more than twenty years of strenuous and dangerous life on earth—much less even than Elsie could show. The paucity of his possessions did not trouble her, and scarcely surprised her, for she knew that very many unmarried men, with no incentive to accumulate what they could immediately squander in personal use, had no more reserves than Joe; but the absence of the sacred "papers" disturbed her. Every man in her world could, when it came to the point, produce papers of some sort from somewhere—army-discharge, pension documents, testimonials, birth-certificate, etc., etc. Even the tramps who flitted in and out of Rowton House had their papers to which they rightly attached the greatest importance. No man in Elsie's world could get far along without papers, unless specially protected by heaven; and, sooner or later—generally sooner than later—heaven grew tired of protecting.

All day Elsie had been awaiting an opportunity to speak to Joe about his papers. The opportunity had now come. Mr. Earlforward could be left for an hour or so. Joe was apparently in less pain. The two bedrooms were tidied up. Both men had been fed. Joe had had more quinine. She could not sponge him again till the morrow. She herself had drunk two cups of tea, and eaten the last contents of the larder. She had lighted a new candle—the last candle—in the candle-stick. She had brought coal and mended the fire. The next morning she would have a great deal to do and to arrange—getting money, marketing, seeing the doctor and Mrs. Belrose, discussing the funeral with Mr. Earlforward—terrible anxieties—but for the present she was free.

Joe made no answer. He seemed to be trying to frame sentences. She encouraged him with a repetition:

"Where's your papers? I can't find 'em nowhere. You haven't lost them, have ye?" Her brow contracted in apprehension.

"I sold 'em," said Joe, in his deep, vibrating and yet feeble voice. He looked away.

"Sold 'em, Joe? Ye never sold 'em!"

"Yes I have, I tell ye. I sold 'em yesterday morning."

"But, Joey——"

"I sold 'em yesterday morning to a man as came to meet a man as came out of Pentonville same time as me."

"Pentonville! Joe, d'ye mean ye've been to prison?" He nodded. "What a shame!" she exclaimed in protest, not at his having done anything wicked enough to send him to prison, but at the police having been wicked enough to send him to prison. She assumed instinctively and positively that he was an innocent victim of the ruthless blue men whom some people know only as pilots of perambulators across busy streets.

"There was no option, ye know, so I had fourteen days."

She dropped on her knees at the bedside, and put her left arm under his neck and threw her right arm over his waist, and with it felt again the familiar shape of his waist through the bedclothes, and gazed into his homely, ugly face upon which soft, dark hair—a beard on the chin—was sprouting. This faith and tenderness made Joe cry.

"Tell me," she murmured, scarcely hoping that he would succeed in any narrative.

"Oh, it's nothin'," Joe replied gloomily. "Armistice Day, ye know. I had my afternoon, and I went out."

"Were ye in a place, Joe?"

"I had a part-time place in Oxford Street—carrying coal upstairs, and cleaning brasses and sweeping and errands. And a bed. Yes, in the basement. Sort of a watchman. Doctor he give me a testimonial. Least, he sent it me when I wrote and asked him." (No doubt whatever that she had been unjust to that doctor!) "I went down to Piccadilly to see the sights, and when it was about dark I see our old divisional general in a damn big car with two young ladies. There was a block, ye see, in Piccadilly Circus, and he was stopped by the kerb where them flower-girls are, ye know, by the fountain, and I was standing there as close as I am to you, Elsie. We used to call him the Slaughterer. That was how we called him. We never called him nothin' else. And there he was with his two rows o' ribbons and his flash women, perhaps they weren't flash, and I didn't like the look of his face—hard, ye know. Cruel. We knowed him, we did. And then I thought of the two minutes' silence, and hats off and stand at 'tention, and the Cenotaph, and it made me laugh. I laughed at him through the glass. And he didn't like it, he didn't. I was as close to him as I am to you, ye see. And he lets down the glass and says something about insultin' behaviour to these ladies, and I put my tongue out to him. That tore it, that did. That fair put the lid on. I felt something coming over me—ye know. Then there was a crowd, and I caught a policeman one on the shoulder. Oh, they marched me off, three of 'em! The doctor at the station said I was drunk, me as hadn't had a drop for three days! Next morning the beak he said he'd treat me lenient because it was Armistice Day, and I'd had some and I'd fought for the old country, but assaulting an officer of the law, he couldn't let that pass. No option for that, so he give me fourteen days."

"But yer master, Joe?"

"It was an old woman."

"Wouldn't she——?"

"No, she wouldn't," said Joe roughly. "And another thing, I didn't go back there either, afterwards."

"Did ye leave yer things there?"

"Yes. A bag and some things. And I shan't fetch it either."

"*I* shall!" said Elsie resolutely. "I won't let 'er have 'em.
I shall tell her you was taken ill, and I shall bring 'em away."

Joe offered no remark.

"But why did ye sell yer papers, Joe?"

"He give me four-and-six for 'em. I was on me uppers;
he give me four-and-six, and then we went and had a meal
after all that skilly and cocoa and dry bread. No good me
going back. I'd left without notice, I had."

"But why didn't ye come to me straight, Joey?"

Joe didn't answer. After all this inordinate loquacity of
his, he had resumed his great silence.

Elsie still gazed at him. The candle light went down and
up. A burst of heavy traffic shook the bed. And now Elsie
had a desire to tell Joe all about her own story, all about Mr.
Earlforward and the death of Mrs. Earlforward, and the
troubles awaiting her in the morning. She wanted to be
confidential, and she wanted to discuss with him a plan for
putting him on his feet again after he was better—for she was
sure she could restore his self-respect to him, and him to his
proper position in the world. But he did not seem interested
in anything, not even in herself. He was absorbed in his
aches and pains and fever. And she was very tired. So,
without moving her arms, she just laid her head on his breast,
and was indignant against the whole of mankind on his behalf,
and regarded her harsh, pitiless self as the author of all his
misfortunes and loved him.

CHAPTER XII

Asleep

MR. and Mrs. Belrose occupied a small bedroom at the top of their house. As for her sister and his sister, they fitted their amplitudes into some vague "somewhere else," and those of the curious who in the way of business or otherwise knew how nearly the entire house was devoted to "wholesale," wondered where the two sisters-in-law did in fact stow themselves. The servant slept out.

In the middle of the night Mrs. Belrose raised her magnificent form out of the overburdened bed and went to the window to look forth on the Steps.

"Charlie," said she, coming back to the bed and shaking her husband. He awoke unwillingly and grunted, and muttered that she was taking cold; an absurd suggestion, as he knew well, for she never took cold, and it was inconceivable that she should take cold.

"That light's still burning at T. T.'s—in the shop. I don't like the look of it."

She lit the room, and the fancies of night seemed to be dispelled by an onrush of realism, dailiness and sagacity. Mr. and Mrs. Belrose considered themselves to be two of the most sagacious and imperturbable persons that ever lived, and they probably were.

No circumstances were too much for their sagacity and their presence of mind. Each had complete confidence in the kindly but unsentimental horse-sense of the other. Mrs. Belrose, despite her youngishness, was the more impressive. She it was who usually said the final word in shaping a policy; yet in her utterances there was an implication that Charles had a super-wisdom which she alone could inspire, and also that he, being a man, could do certain things that she, being a woman, was ever so slightly incapable of.

"I don't like the look of it at all," she said.

"Well, I don't see we can do anything till morning," said Charles. Not that he was allowing his judgment to be warped by the desire to sleep. No; he was being quite impartial.

"That girl's got too much on her hands, looking after that funny old man all by herself, day and night. She isn't a fool, far from it; but it's too much for one girl."

"You'd better go over, perhaps, and have a look at things."

"I was thinking you'd go, Charlie."

"But I can't do anything if I do go. I can't help the girl."

"I'm afraid," said the authoritative and sagacious wife simply.

"What of?" asked the wizened slip of a husband.

"Well, I don't know; but I am. It'll be better for you to go—anyway first. I could come afterwards. We can't leave the girl in the lurch."

Nevertheless Mrs. Belrose did know what she was afraid of and so did Mr. Belrose. She helped him to put on some clothes; it was a gesture of sympathy rather than of aid. And she exhorted him not to waken "those girls," meaning her sister and his.

He went out, shivering. A fine night with a harsh wind moving dust from one part of the Steps to another. Nobody about. The church clock struck three. Mr. Belrose peered through the slit between the edge of the door-blind and the door-frame, but could see nothing except that a light was burning somewhere in the background. He rapped quietly and then loudly on the glass. No response. The explanation of the scene doubtless was that Elsie had come down into the shop on some errand and returned upstairs, having forgotten to extinguish the light. Mr. Belrose was very cold. He was about to leave the place and report to his wife when his hand discovered that the door was not fastened. (Elsie, in the perturbation caused by doing a kindness to the boy Jerry, had forgotten to secure it.) Mr. Belrose entered and saw Mr. Earlforward, wearing a smart new suit, moveless in a peculiar posture in his office-chair. He now knew more surely than before what his wife had been afraid of. But he had a very stout and stolid heart, and he advanced firmly into the office. A faint glow of red showed in the ash-strewn grate. The electric light descended in almost palpable rays on Mr. Earlforward's grizzled head. The safe was open and there was a bag of money on the floor. Mr. Earlforward's chair was tilted and had only been saved from toppling over, with Mr. Earlforward in it, by the fact that its left arm had caught under the ledge of the desk. The electric light was patient; so was Mr. Earlforward. He was leaning over the right arm of the chair, his body at half a right angle to the perpendicular, and his face towards the floor.

"I've never seen anything like this before," thought Mr. Belrose. "This will upset the Steps, this will."

He was afraid. He had what he would have called the "creeps." Gingerly he touched Mr. Earlforward's left hand which lay on the desk. It was cold and rather stiff. He bent down in order to look into Mr. Earlforward's averted face. What a dreadful face! White, blotched, hairy skin drawn tightly over bones and muscles—very tightly. An expression of torment in the tiny, unseeing eyes! None of the proverbial repose of death in that face!

"Mustn't touch it! Mustn't disturb anything!" thought Mr. Belrose, straightening his knees.

He left the office and peered up the dark stairs. No light. No sound. He felt for his matches, but he had come away without them, and he suspected that he was not sufficiently master of himself to look effectively for matches. Still, the house must be searched. Although much averse from returning into the office, he did return, on the chance of finding a box of matches, and the first thing he saw was a box on the mantelpiece. Striking matches, he stumbled up the stairs and came first to the bath-room. Empty. Nothing unusual therein except thick strings stretched across it and an orange box in the bath. A bedroom, well furnished, the bed unmade; a cup and saucer on the night-table; one door of the wardrobe ajar. Everything still, expectant. Then he found the living-room similarly still and expectant. He went back to the landing. No sound. The second flight of stairs dreadfully invited him to ascend. As he reached and pushed against the door at the head of those stairs another of his matches died. He struck a fresh one, and when it slowly flamed he stepped into the faintly fire-lit room and was amazed, astounded, thrilled, shocked, and very seriously shaken to descry a young man lying on the bed in the corner and a young woman, Elsie, lying in abandonment across him, her head sunk in his breast. And he heard a regular sound of breathing. There was something in the situation of the pair which penetrated right through Mr. Belrose's horse-sense and profoundly touched his heart. Never had he had such a sensation at once painful and ravishing (yes, ravishing to the awed cheese-monger) as he had then. The young man raised his head an inch from the pillow and dropped it again.

"She's asleep," said the young man in a low, deep, tired voice. "Don't wake her."

CHAPTER XIII

Disappearance of T. T.'s

THE transience of things human was wonderfully illustrated in the next fortnight. A short and drab account of the nocturnal discoveries of Mr. Belrose at T. T.'s appeared in one morning paper, and within six hours the evening papers, with their sure instinct for the important, had lifted Riceyman Steps to a height far above prize-fighting, national economics and the embroiled ruin of Europe. Such trivialities vanished from the contents-bills, which displayed nothing but "Mysterious Death of a Miser in Clerkenwell" (the home of Bolshevism), "Astounding Story of Love and Death," "Midnight Tragedy in King's Cross Road," and similar titles, legends and captions. Riceyman Steps was filled with ferreting special reporters and photographers. The morning papers next following elaborated the tale. The Steps became the cynosure of all England and the subject of cables to America, South Africa and the antipodes. The Steps rose dizzily to unique fame. The coroner's inquest on the body of Henry Earlforward was packed like a divorce court on an illustrious day and stenographed verbatim. Jurymen who were summoned to it esteemed themselves fortunate.

The Reverend Augustus Earlforward, a Wesleyan Methodist missionary, home for a holiday from his labours in the West Indies, and brother of the deceased, found himself in a moment extremely famous. He had nearly missed the boat at Kingston, Jamaica, and he saw the hand of Providence in the fact that he had not missed it. He had not met his younger brother for over thirty years, nor heard from him; did not even know his address; had scarcely thought of trying to hunt him up. And then at tea in the Thackeray Hotel, Bloomsbury, his stern eyes had seen the name of Earlforward written large in a newspaper. The affair was the most marvellous event, the most marvellous coincidence, of his long and honourable career. Wisely he flew to a solicitor. He caused himself to be represented at the inquest. He had reached England in a critical mood, for, like many colonials, he suspected that all was not well with the blundering and decadent old country. And the revelations of life in Clerkenwell richly confirmed his suspicions, which did not surprise him, because much commerce with negroes had firmly established in his mind the conviction that he could never be wrong. From the start he had his ideas about Elsie, the servant-girl asleep with a young man in her bedroom. They were not nice ideas, but it is to be remembered that he was taking a holiday from the preaching and practice of Christian charity. His legal representative put strange questions to Elsie at the inquest (during which it was testified, after post-mortem, that Henry had died of a cancer at the junction of the gullet and the cardiac end of the stomach), and these questions were reinforced by the natural cynicism and incredulity of the coroner. Elsie was saved from opprobrium by Dr. Raste's statement that she had called him in to the young man.

Elsie indeed was cheered by her inflamed friends as she left the court. She said never a word about the coroner or the missionary afterwards, and, inexcusably, she never forgave either of them. But the missionary forgave Elsie and permitted her and the sick young man to remain in the house.

Neither Mr. nor Mrs. Earlforward had made a will. Thus the whole of Violet's property, in addition to the whole of Henry's, went to Augustus.

Clerkenwell expected that the world-glory of the Steps would continue indefinitely; but it withered as quickly as it had flowered, and by the afternoon of the morrow of the inquest it had utterly died. The joint funeral of the Earlforwards did not receive a line in the daily press. Nevertheless it constituted a great spectacle in King's Cross Road—not by reason of its intrinsic grandeur (for it fell short of Henry's conception of the obsequies which he would bestow on his wife), but by reason of the vast multitude of sightseers and followers.

The Reverend Augustus, heir to a very comfortable competency unwittingly amassed for him by the devices of Mr. Arb, the clerk of works, the prudent policy of Mr. Earlforward and the imitativeness of Violet, found himself inconvenienced for ready cash, because before he could touch the heritage he had to fulfil various tedious formalities and tiresomely to wait upon authority.

He saw no end to the business, and he cabled to the Connexional authorities in Jamaica that he should take extra leave. He did not ask for extra leave; in his quality of a rich man he merely took it, and heavenly propaganda had to be postponed. The phrasing of that cable was one of his compensations in a trying ordeal.

He had various other compensations, of which the chief was undoubtedly the status of landlord with unoccupied property at his disposition. Not only all Clerkenwell, but apparently all London, learnt in a few hours that he had this status. Scores of people, rendered desperate by the house-famine, telegraphed to him; many scores of people wrote to him; and some dozens personally called upon him at his hotel, and they all supplicated him to do them the great favour of letting to them the T. T. Riceyman premises on lease at a high rent.

A few desired to buy the property. The demand was so intense and widespread as to induce in Augustus the belief that he was a potential benefactor of mankind. Preferring to enjoy the fruits of riches without being troubled by the more irksome responsibilities thereof, he decided to sell and not to let. And he entered into a contract for sale to Mr. Belrose. He chose Mr. Belrose because Mr. Belrose and all his women were Wesleyan Methodists, and also perhaps because Mr. Belrose did not haggle and was ready and anxious to complete the transaction, and, indeed, paid a substantial deposit before the legal formalities of Augustus' title to the property were finished.

Thenceforward event succeeded event with increasing

rapidity. The entire stock of books was sold by private treaty to a dealer in Charing Cross Road, who swallowed it up and digested it with gigantic ease. The books went away quietly enough in vans. Then the furniture and the clothes were sold (including Mr. Earlforward's virgin suits and shirts) to another sort of dealer in Islington. And a pantechnicon came for the furniture, etc., including the safe and the satin shoe, and it obtained permission from the highways authorities to pass over the pavement and stand on the flagstones of the Steps at the shop-door. And furniture was swept into it almost like leaves swept by the wind. And on that afternoon Mr. Belrose arrived from "across" with a group of shop-fitting and decorating contractors, and in the emptying interiors of the home and amid the flight of pieces of furniture, Mr. Belrose discussed with the experts what he should do, and at what cost, to annihilate the very memory of T. T. Riceyman's by means of improvements, fresh dispositions, and paint.

Idlers sauntered about watching the gorging of the pantechnicon and the erasing of T. T. Riceyman's from the Steps. And what occupied their minds was not the disappearance of every trace of the sojourn on earth of Henry and Violet Earlforward, but the conquering progress of that powerful and prosperous personage, Charles Belrose, who was going to have two shops, and who would without doubt make them both pay handsomely. Henry and Violet might never have lived. They were almost equally strangers to the Reverend Augustus, who, moreover, was lying somewhat ill at his hotel—result of the strain of inheriting. Violet had always been regarded as a foreigner by the district; she had had no roots there. And as for Henry, though he was not a foreigner, but of the true ancient blood of Clerkenwell, and though the tale of his riches commanded respect, he had never won affection, and was classed sardonically as an oddity, which designation would have puzzled and annoyed him considerably.

Violet and Henry did, however, survive in one place, Elsie's heart. She arrived now in the Steps, dressed in mourning—new black frock, new black hat, the old black coat, and black gloves. She had bought mourning from a sense of duty and propriety. She had not wished to incur the expense, but conscience forced her to incur the expense. She was carrying a shabby grip-bag, which seemed rather heavy for her, and she was rather flushed and breathless from exercise of an unaccustomed sort. A dowdy, over-plump figure, whom nobody would have looked twice at. A simple, heavy face, common except for the eyes and lips; with a harassed look; fatigued also. She had been out nearly all day. She pretended not to notice it, but the sight of the formidable pantechnicon, squatted in the Steps, brought moisture into her eyes.

She sturdily entered the shop, which, Charles Belrose and his company of renovators having left, was empty save for one or two pieces of furniture waiting their proper niches in the pantechnicon. A man was pulling down the shelves and thus destroying the bays. Dead planks which had once been living, burden-bearing shelves, were stacked in a pile along one wall. She had to wait at the foot of the stairs while a section of Violet's wardrobe awkwardly descended in the hairy arms of two Samsons. Then she went up, and on the first floor peeped into all the rooms one after another; they were scenes of confusion, dirt, dust, higgle-de-piggledyness; difficult to believe that they had ever made part of a home, been regularly cleaned, watched over like helpless children incapable of taking care of themselves. She lugged the grip-bag up the second flight, and went into the spare room, which was quite empty, stripped to the soiled and damaged walls— even the plant-pots were gone from the window-sills; and she went into the kitchen, where the tap kept guard with its eternal drip-drip over perfect desolation.

At last she went into her bedroom, which by a magic ukase from on high in the Thackeray Hotel had been preserved from the sack. A fire was cheerfully burning; all was as usual to the casual glance, but the shut drawers were empty, and Elsie's box and umbrella had gone back to Riceyman Square where she had been sleeping since the funeral. Joe was sufficiently recovered to sleep alone in the house, and had had no objection to doing so. Joe, fully dressed for the grand exodus, sat waiting on the sole chair. He smiled. Dropping the bag, she smiled. They kissed. With his limited but imaginative intelligence Joe did not see that Elsie was merely Elsie. He saw within the ill-fitting mourning a saviour, a powerful protectress, a bright angel, a being different from, and superior to, any other being. They were dumb and happy in the island of homeliness around which swirled the tide of dissolution and change. Elsie picked up a piece of bread-and-butter from a plate and began to eat it.

"Didn't yer get any dinner?" Joe asked anxiously. She nodded, and the nod was a lie.

"I got your bag and all your things in it," she said. "There's a clean collar. Ye'd better put it on."

Munching, she unfastened the bag.

"And I've got the licence from the Registry Office," she said. He scrutinized the licence, which by its complexity and incomprehensibility intimidated him. He was much relieved and very grateful that he had not had to go forth and get the licence himself. The clean collar, which Elsie affixed, made a wonderful improvement in Joe's frayed and dilapidated appearance.

"Has the doctor been to look at ye?" Elsie asked. Joe shook his head. "Well, ye can't go till he's been to look at ye."

The doctor had re-engaged Joe, who was to migrate direct to Myddelton Square that afternoon and would take up his duties gradually, as health permitted. He had already been tentatively out in the morning, but only to the other side of King's Cross Road to get a shave. Perhaps it was to be re-gretted that Joe was going off in one of Mr. Earlforward's grey flannel shirts. Elsie, had she been strictly honest, would have washed this shirt and returned it to the wardrobe, but she thought that Joe needed it, and her honesty fell short of the ideal.

There was a step on the stair. The doctor came into the island. And he himself was an island, detached, self-con-tained, impregnable as ever. He entered the room as though

it was a room and not the emptying theatre of heroic and un-
forgettable drama, and as though nothing worth mentioning
had happened of late in Riceyman Steps.

"Has my daughter called here for me?" he asked abruptly,
depositing his prim hat on the little yellow chest of drawers.

"No, sir."

"Ah! She was to meet me here," he said in a casual,
even tone. And yet there was something in his voice plainly
indicating to the observant that deep down in his recondite
mind burned a passionate pride in his daughter.

"I think you'll do, Joe," he decided, after some examination
of the malaria patient. "I see you've had a shave."

"Elsie said I'd better, sir."

"Yes. Makes you feel brighter, doesn't it? Well, you
can be getting along. By the way, Elsie"—he coughed.
"We've been wondering at home whether you'd care to go
and have a chat with Mrs. Raste?"

"Yes, sir. But what about, sir? Joe?"

"Well, the fact is, we thought perhaps you'd like"—he
gave a short, nervous laugh—"to join the staff. I don't know
what they call it. Cook-general. No. Not quite that,
because there'd be Joe. There'd be you and Joe, you see."

Elsie drew back, alarmed—so alarmed that she did not even
say "Thank you."

"Oh! I couldn't do that, sir! I couldn't cook—for you,
sir. I couldn't undertake it, sir. I'm really only a charwoman, sir. I couldn't face it, sir."

"But I thought you'd been learning some cookery from—
er—Mrs. Earlforward?"

"Oh, no, sir. Not as you might say. Only gas-ring,
sir."

This was the once ambitious girl who had dreamed of
acquiring the skill to wait at table in just such a grand house as
the doctor's. Extreme diffidence was not the only factor in
her decision, which she made instantly and positively as a
strong-minded, sensible, masterful woman without any
reference to the views of her protected, fragile idol, Joe—for a
quality of independence, hardness, had begun to appear in

Elsie Sprickett. The fact was that she wanted a separate home as a refuge for Joe in case of need, and she was arranging to rent a room in the basement of her old abode in Riceyman Square. Out of the measureless fortune of £32 which she had accumulated in the Post Office Savings Bank, she intended to furnish her home. It had been agreed with the doctor that after the marriage Joe should have one whole night off per week. She would resume charing, which was laborious but more "free" than a regular situation. If Joe should have a fit of violence it could spend itself on her in the home. She even desired to suffer at his hands as a penance for the harshness of her earlier treatment of him, of her well-meant banishing of the innocent victim deranged by his experiences in the war. With her earnings and his they would have an ample income. The fine sagacious scheme was complete in her brain. And the doctor's suggestion attacked it in its fundamentals. At Myddelton Square, worried by unaccustomed duties and the presence of others, she might have scenes with Joe and be unable to manage him. No! She must be independent; she must have liberty of action; and this could not be if she was a servant in a grand house.

"Oh! Very well, very well," said the doctor, frigid as usual, but not offended. Joe said no word, knowing that he must not meddle in such high matters of policy.

Scutterings, expostulations, reproofs on the stairs. Miss Raste entered, with the excited dog Jack. Her father had told her that if she saw no one familiar below she must mount two flights of stairs and knock at the door facing her at the top; but, in her eagerness, she had forgotten to knock. Miss Raste was growing in stature daily. Her legs were fabulously long, and it was said of her at home that in time she would be in a position to stoop and kiss the crown of her father's head. To everyone's surprise she impulsively rushed at Elsie with thin arms outstretched and kissed her. Elsie blushed, as well she might. Miss Raste had spoken to Elsie only once before, but out of the memory of Elsie's face and that brief meeting she had constructed a lovely fairy-tale, and a chance word of her mother's had set her turning it into reality. She had dreamed of having the adorable, fat, comfortable, kind Elsie for a servant in the house, and her parents were going to arrange the matter. For twenty-four hours she had been in a fever about it.

"Is she coming, papa?" the child demanded urgently.

"No, she can't. She says she can't cook, and so she won't come."

Miss Raste burst into tears. Her lank body shook with sobs. Everybody was grievously constrained. Nobody knew what to do, least of all the doctor. Jack stood still in front of the fire.

"Mummy would have taught you to cook," Miss Raste spluttered, almost inarticulately. "Mummy's awfully nice."

Elsie's sagacious scheme for her married life was dissipated in a moment. The scheme became absurd, impossible, inconceivable. Elsie was utterly defeated by the child's affection, ardour, and sorrow. She felt nearly the same responsibility towards the child as towards Joe. She was the child's for ever. And she had kissed the child. Having kissed the child, could she be a Judas?

"Oh, then I'll go and see Mrs. Raste," said Elsie, half smiling and half crying.

This was indeed a very strange episode, upsetting as it did all optimistic theories about the reasonableness of human nature and the influence of logic over the springs of conduct. No one quite knew where he was. Dr. Raste was intensely delighted and proud, and yet felt that he ought to have a grievance. Joe was delighted, but egotistically. Elsie was both happy and sad, but rather more happy than sad. Miss Raste laughed with glee, while the tears still ran down her delicate cheeks. Jack barked once.

Not that Jack had that very mysterious intuitive comprehension of the moods of others which in the popular mind is usually attributed to dogs, children, and women. No! Jack had heard footsteps on the stairs. A tousled, white-sleeved man in a green apron entered.

"We're ready for here now, miss," he announced to Elsie. And without waiting for permission he began rapidly to roll up the bed-clothes in one vast bundle. Next he collected the crockery. The bedroom had ceased to be immune from the general sack.

"They didn't have a lot of luck," said Mr. Belrose to Elsie and Joe that night in the Steps at the locked door of T. T.'s. It was the decent, wizened little old fellow's epitaph on Henry Earlforward and Violet. It was his apology for dropping the keys of T. T.'s into his pocket, and for the blaze of electricity from his old shop, and for the forlorn darkness of T. T.'s, and for the fact that he was prospering while others were dead. He did not attribute the fate of the Earlforwards to Henry's formidable character. He could not think scientifically, and even had he been able to do so good nature would have prevented him. And even if he had attempted to do so he might have thought wrong. The affair, like all affairs of destiny, was excessively complex.

Elsie, for her part, laid much less stress than Mr. Belrose on luck. "With a gentleman like he was," she thought, meaning Henry Earlforward, "something was bound to happen sooner or later." She held Mr. Earlforward responsible for her mistress's death, but her notions of the value of evidence were somewhat crude. And, similarly, she held herself responsible for her master's death. She had noticed that he had never been the same since the orgy of her wedding-cake, and she had a terrible suspicion that immoderate wedding-cake caused cancer. Thus she added one more to the uncounted theories of the origin of cancer, and nobody yet knows enough of the subject to be able to disprove Elsie's theory.

However, that night Elsie, with the sensations of a homicide, the ruin of a home and family behind her, a jailbird on her left arm and his heavy grip-bag on her right, could still be happy as she went up the Steps into Riceyman Square, and called at her old home to make certain dispositions, and passed on in the chill darkness to Myddelton Square. She was apprehensive about future dangers and her own ability to cope with them; but she was always apprehensive.

Joe, belonging to the contemplative and passionate variety of mankind, was not at all apprehensive. He knew his soul as intimately as a pretty woman knows the externals of her body. He was conscious of joy in retreading with Elsie the old familiar streets. He had a perfect, worshipping faith in Elsie's affection and in her powers. His one affliction was to see Elsie lugging the heavy grip-bag; but even this was absurd, for he had not yet the strength to carry it, and he well knew that she would never have permitted him to try.

People saw a young, humble, mutually-absorbed couple strolling along and looking at one another. More correctly, people did not see a humble couple, any more than people at a Court ball see a fashionably dressed and self-sure couple. Elsie and Joe were characteristic of the district. They would have had to look much worse than they did in order to be classed as humble in Clerkenwell. Nor were people shocked at the spectacle of the woman lugging a heavy grip-bag while the man carried naught. Such dreadful things were often witnessed in Clerkenwell.

THE END